WEIRDO

WEIRDO

CATHI UNSWORTH

SPIDERLINE

First published in Great Britain in 2012 under license from Serpent's Tail,
an imprint of Profile Books Limited

This edition published in 2013 by
House of Anansi Press Inc.
110 Spadina Avenue, Suite 801
Toronto, ON, M5V 2K4
Tel. 416-363-4343
Fax 416-363-1017
www.houseofanansi.com

Distributed in Canada by
HarperCollins Canada Ltd.
1995 Markham Road
Scarborough, ON, M1B 5M8
Toll free tel. 1-800-387-0117

Distributed in the United States by
Publishers Group West
1700 Fourth Street
Berkeley, CA 94710
Toll free tel. 1-800-788-3123

The characters and events in this book are fictitious. Any similarity to real persons,
dead or alive, is coincidental and not intended by the author.

House of Anansi Press is committed to protecting our natural environment.
As part of our efforts, the interior of this book is printed on paper that contains 100%
post-consumer recycled fibres, is acid-free, and is processed chlorine-free.

17 16 15 14 13   1 2 3 4 5

Library and Archives Canada Cataloguing in Publication

Unsworth, Cathi, author
Weirdo / Cathi Unsworth

Issued in print and electronic formats.
ISBN: 978-1-77089-387-0 (pbk.). ISBN: 978-1-77089-388-7 (html)

I. Title.

PR6121.N79W43 2013   823'.92   C2013-903735-7
                     C2013-903736-5

Library of Congress Control Number: 2013909843

Cover design: Alysia Shewchuk
Text design and typesetting: Crow Books

*We acknowledge for their financial support of our publishing program
the Canada Council for the Arts, the Ontario Arts Council, and the Government of
Canada through the Canada Book Fund.*

Printed and bound in Canada

MIX
Paper from
responsible sources
FSC® C004071

For Matthew, Yvette, Thomas, William and Sophie Rose

Death to come
to those we husband,
frightened crowds
running circles —
on the path and down the hill.
I'm not the man
here to murder
but in his time
he will come.
    Benedict Newbery,
    'Some Man's Business'

Normal is for shit
   Harry Crews

Part 1

* * *

SMALLTOWN ENGLAND

1
You're Already Dead

They had hidden her far from the rest of the world, deep within a forest. Nearly twenty years she'd been there now, still not long enough to stop the murmurs of hate, nor keep them from turning into a clamour each time her name was recalled. Whenever another case hit the headlines of teenagers killing each other.

Wicked Witch of the East, the tabloids called her. *Killer Corrine*, High Priestess of a Satanic cult that had gripped the teenage population of a Norfolk seaside town in the summer of 1984, bringing death in its claws. Social transgressor, female aggressor. Bloody weirdo, the locals said. They'd always known Corrine Woodrow was a wrong 'un. Never any doubt in their minds about her guilt and the need for her punishment to be both severe and eternal.

Keep her away.

Sean Ward had read all the files and all the news reports he could lay his hands on from the bloody summer of 1984. Had a teenage face in his mind, a girl with spiked and shaved black hair, thick lines of kohl around what were routinely described as 'the eyes of evil'. The picture of her at her arrest, rather than the smoothed-down, smartened-up teenager that had finally arrived at court, was the one they went on repeating. Usually next to the shot of a bleached-blonde Myra Hindley.

The forest was dense with pine, branches swaying under the force of the wind and slanting rain. The only other traffic Sean had seen on this B-road through the Cambridgeshire countryside was an ancient Massey Ferguson tractor, driven by a hunched figure in a woollen cap, that had lurched past at the last crossroads and disappeared down a cart track. Sean couldn't help thinking that he had taken a detour from the real world somewhere between here and the M11, got lost in a folk tale instead – travelling through the wild wood to the fortress where they kept the Witch bricked up.

The windscreen wipers swooshed as the rain pattered down on the roof of his dark blue Peugeot 207. He had long since turned off the radio, preferring the solitude and the drizzle to the darker clouds of war in Iraq that dominated today's headlines: George Bush and Tony Blair demanding Saddam stand down and knowing he wouldn't, pushing towards conflict at any cost.

Sean had had enough of conflict. He had been a detective sergeant in the Metropolitan police when his job had nearly killed him, in a spray of semi-automatic gunfire that the teenage drug dealer had fortunately not been capable of aiming with deadly accuracy. Had spent the best part of a year in hospitals and recuperation after that, his nights haunted by visions of the look in that young man's eyes.

He had a new line of work now, not so different from the old. Pensioned out of the Met, Sean had ended up doing the only thing ex-coppers really knew how to do – private detective work. He hadn't liked the idea of it, imagining a dull, endless line of cheating spouses and petty fraudsters. But it was preferable to life as a social worker or a prison guard, or worse still, slipping into the inertia of sofa and daytime TV, a life devoid of purpose.

To his surprise, he had found there was a new area of detection providing the sort of work that would allow his brain to go on doing what it had been designed for. A field opened up by the advancement of chemistry and physics, DNA technology; a boom area for lawyers with good money to pay.

Cold cases.

Which was why, having almost been felled by one child villain, Sean was now driving towards another – or whatever Corrine Woodrow had become in the years since her incarceration.

Janice Mathers, the QC who was behind this, the second attempt to appeal against indefinite sentence, was the type of lawyer that induced fury within his former profession – a trendy lefty who had made her name taking on unpopular cases in a quest to expose the miscarriages she felt were at the heart of the justice system. She'd had a fresh forensic test done on clothing recovered from the murder scene and, thanks to a new technique called Cluster DNA, had found evidence that cast doubt on Corrine's sole culpability.

Someone else's genetic imprint was smeared across it, a person unknown to the police, an anonymous entity who must have stayed clean ever since, never been caught for another offence or put on a file anywhere. She had engaged Sean to try and find this phantom accomplice who could be anywhere else on earth, including underneath, it by now.

He had taken Mathers' coin despite the disapproving faces of friends from his old squad, first amongst them Charlie Higgins, Sean's old chief super, the guiding light of his ten years on the Force. Not that he didn't have misgivings. Even if an injustice had occurred, what hope would the Wicked Witch of the East have for rehabilitation now? She would have to live the rest of her life under a false identity, permanently looking behind her back, never able to rest. Sean had seen what could happen at the first whisper of suspicion, seen the shit through the letterbox, the windows smashed, the graffiti scrawled and the fires lit. Seen it happen to innocent people, let alone those who really were tainted by past deeds.

But the real reason he had taken the case was becoming clearer to Sean with every mile he drove: after long months of inactivity, his brain was crawling. He needed a case, needed a purpose. He could do with a new identity himself – if this really was a folk tale, he would be the white knight on his charger – but he had never been comfortable with the 'hero cop' handle the press had bestowed on him while reporting his misfortune. Welcomed instead the anonymity of criminal archaeology.

Sean had been eleven years old when Corrine had committed her crime. He had no memory of it happening. Nor had he ever been to this part of the world before. After his stop here, he was headed further east, to the coastal resort of Ernemouth in Norfolk, where it had all begun, to meet with the man who had headed the original case, the now retired Detective Chief Inspector Leonard Rivett. But first, he wanted to meet Corrine. Wanted to look into her eyes and see what they revealed.

On the passenger seat beside him, the map showed that beyond the next bend would be the entrance to the perimeter fence of the high-security facility. It was a Victorian institution, as so many of them still were, forbidding brick pillars and arched iron gates guarding a grim stately home for the criminally insane.

The sentry waved him through with a bored expression and Sean found himself on a pale grey ribbon of road that stretched on through a clearing of heathland, the heather and gorse bushes dripping with rain. He saw no signs of life; not even the murder of crows you might expect to find circling such a desolate location. When the secure unit finally came into view, he understood why.

It really did look like a fortress with its turrets and towers, its slits of windows reflecting nothing but the iron hue of the sky. Sean felt a shudder of revulsion so deep that it was all he could do not to put on the brakes, swing round and head right back. Hospital had been bad enough, but this . . .

How long would it take in a place like this before you became infected too?

Taking a deep breath, he swallowed his fear and drove on.

2

In The Flat Field

August 1983

Edna Hoyle sat for a while at the kitchen table after her husband had gone. The skin on her cheek smarted from the hasty kiss he'd deposited there as he was leaving, one arm already in his jacket, cigarette still smouldering in the ashtray. It wasn't like Eric not to shave clean, nor to rush his tea as if he couldn't bear to linger in his own home one second longer. But then, these were not normal days.

Edna reached over and stubbed out the Silk Cut. The low-tar brand were Eric's most recent concession to doctor's orders to take better care of himself; they were supposed to be better for you than the Rothmans full-strength he'd been on since his teens. Trouble was, he seemed to smoke twice as many of these, smoked them with an ill-concealed rage that he was denying himself his pleasure. *God knows*, Edna thought, *how many he'll be on this time next week, when everything will change . . .*

She stopped that thought the only way she knew how, by applying herself to the chores at hand. She filled up the sink with hot water and Fairy Liquid, cleaned the glasses, the plates and the pans so that everything sparkled.

They were doing it for Samantha, she had to keep reminding him. *Their granddaughter. It wasn't her fault that her mother behaved the way she did . . .*

Edna winced, pulled the plug and dried her hands briskly. Ran a cloth over the surfaces, put the tea towel over the radiator, made sure everything in her domain was orderly.

From his basket in the corner, Edna's toy spitz, Noodles, lifted his head and yawned, revealing a pink mouth fringed with sharp white teeth. He got to his feet, shook himself and hopped out, tail curled over his hindquarters, tiny ears pricked.

"Tha's a good boy," Edna leant down to pet him, feeling a twinge of arthritis in her knee as she did. Noodles yelped, as if he was talking back to her, brushing his face against the side of her hand. With his shaggy gold coat and bustling walk, Noodles was an amusing canine mirror of Edna. But he was a sensitive one, too.

The pair of them climbed the thickly carpeted stairs up to the room Edna had spent the past few weeks renovating into a bedroom for Sammy.

Her eyes trailed over the wallpaper and matching bedspread she'd picked from Laura Ashley in Norwich. Edna had asked her best friend, Shirley Reece, who had granddaughters of a similar age to Sammy, for advice.

Shirl had been sure that the bright, simple, poppy pattern would go down well. Edna was no longer certain. The room was so small that the wickerwork dressing table and stool were blocking the view of the sea from the window. And the wardrobe that stood against the opposite wall really didn't look big enough to contain all of Sammy's clothes.

"Oh, Noodles," she whispered, "what if she don't like it?"

Noodles stared up at his mistress, his brown eyes offering sympathy.

Edna reached up to the shelves she'd had Eric put up. Here she had arranged the collection of knick-knacks won by her granddaughter at The Leisure Beach, along with the books Sammy left behind each time. A china Mickey Mouse and a series of Nancy Drew mysteries, the things she usually picked up first when she arrived for a summer stay. Edna was keenly aware that this time her granddaughter might not be so eager to go back to her childhood things, not now that she was coming here to live. She might take one look around her and throw all of Edna's carefully chosen home improvements in the bin.

But it wasn't Sammy's fault that her mother behaved the way she did.

As her fingers closed around the little figurine, the memories she had been trying to suppress all day, all month, all summer long, since her daughter Amanda had made the phone call that had turned their lives upside down, welled up in Edna's brain.

Amanda, the cause of Eric's first heart attack. Amanda with her too ripe figure and her platform boots, running off with an artist from London the moment she was eighteen – eighteen and eight weeks' pregnant. Edna's eyes closed as she tried to shut out the recollection of all that screaming, all that shouting, china hurled and furniture broken, fists raised and blood vessels bursting ... Eric lying in hospital attached to a ventilator, unable to speak but his eyes still raging while Edna wept by his side. Amanda not daring to contact them again until the baby had been born, using her from the very start as a weapon against their affections, against their better judgement.

No, it wasn't Sammy's fault, Edna repeated to herself, fingers tightening their grip ...

* * *

All along the seafront, the streetlights fizzled on. From the North Denes, where Edna stood in her architect-designed villa, Marine Parade stretched for another mile between the rolling humps of the sand dunes, until it reached the first of Ernemouth's piers.

The mid-Victorian Britannic was a testament to the town's dedication to commerce. Five fires and two schooners sailing off-course and into its 700ft-long rear end had done nothing to deter a succession of entrepreneurs rebuilding the pier and embellishing its theatre to accommodate still more patrons for the summer shows. Its current frontage looked out upon an amusement park, where giant snails trundled laughing children around. Above, this season's stars emblazoned in lights: *Cannon and Ball, The Grumbleweeds* and *Jim Davidson's Late Nite Nick-Nick*.

From here on, the second mile of Marine Parade was called "Golden", and not in reference to the sands that constituted this stretch of the beach, but to the entertainments across the promenade. Amusement arcades, every one named after a Las Vegas casino – The Mint, The Sands, The Flamingo, Caesar's Palace, The Golden Nugget and Circus Circus – all recreated in glittering lights on the façades of one-storey breezeblock caverns. Between the beachfront bars, Kiss-Me-Kwik sun hat vendors, candy floss and donut stands, they squatted like a blowzy row of ageing drag queens, demanding attention and making the most infernal noise about it.

Inside The Mint, Debbie Carver stood leaning against a pinball machine, trying to work out what was irritating her most – the shrieking, whistling cacophony of the machines, or the sound of Michael Jackson's "Thriller" blaring through the speakers above her head. Maybe it was the company she was keeping. The penultimate Friday night of the summer holidays and here she still was, stuck in the boring 'musies while her companion went on banging pennies into the slots, oblivious to her discomfort.

Not for the first time, Debbie wondered if she had been more foolish than kind to make friends with the girl who had moved into her road, in the terrace underneath the gasworks, nine months ago. Not that, when she looked back on it, she could even work out whether she'd had any choice about it.

Debbie had first encountered Corrine Woodrow in a nee-dlework class, halfway through last autumn term. She'd sat down beside her and started chattering away, like they had known each other all their lives. Debbie, who had been trying so hard to cultivate an aura of impenetrability, was completely taken aback.

Corrine didn't look friendly. She didn't wear a shirt or tie, just a tight, V-neck sweater with an equally skinny pencil skirt and a worn-down pair of stilettos. Long, dark brown hair fell into heavily kohled eyes. The smell of patchouli oil clung to her like a cloud.

She hadn't come from far away, Corrine told Debbie, just the other side of Norwich. But her mum had lived here before, her mum was Ernemouth born and bred, in fact. Corrine blushed when she said this, her fingers flying deftly across her sampler, working far faster and with more accuracy than Debbie could have managed while talking so much.

All the other girls in Debbie's class were soon talking about Corrine's mother too. Kelly Grimmer had it on good authority that Mrs Woodrow had a *reputation*. Debbie already knew where that had come from. There were motorbikes parked outside Corrine's house all day and all night.

But Debbie had never particularly liked Kelly Grimmer. She'd not been immune to the whispers herself when she had started to subtly alter her appearance, going a little bit further each time she got away without a bollocking from her dad. The black eyeliner, the pair of crimpers that had transformed her brown hair into a thatch of corrugated spikes. All the sanctimonious warning chunters only served to bring her closer to Corrine, and the more she had found out about her new friend's life, the more Debbie had wanted to protect her. She'd even got Corrine a job in the guesthouse where she worked the summer season – and had six long weeks to regret it.

Corrine worked away at the Pac-Man, chewing gum furiously as her fingers pushed the buttons. Unconsciously, her left foot moved to the rhythm, skinny ankle rising and falling out of her turquoise shoes. Corrine had been so proud of them, bought with her first pay packet. She'd not had a chance to spend any more on herself since; her mother snatched her wages off her as fast as she could earn them. Now those shoes, so pretty back at Easter, were scuffed and marked, the sides boated out and the heels in need of repair.

Debbie chewed at her black-painted nails, thinking about where she could have been tonight, if only she were a year older. How she could have been with Alex.

Alex Pendleton was the boy next door. Tall, black-haired, hauntingly handsome, he had taught Debbie all about music and style, implanting within her the desire to do anything he could. In the long term, that meant following him to Ernemouth Art College, where he was already in his second year. But right now, Alex was travelling around the country on Mars Bars National Express tokens and a hitcher's thumb, following bands with his friends, Bully and Kris. They wouldn't have minded Debbie coming. But her mum did. "Not until you've finished your O-levels," was what she had to say about it.

If she hadn't been lumbered with Corrine, Debbie could at least have tried to get through the doors of the pub they all drank in, Captain Swing's on the South Quay. There were a couple of boys in her class who had managed it, Darren Moorcock and Julian Dean, who had turned into goths over the summer and looked much older with the hair and make-up. But if she so much as mentioned the place to Corrine she would stick her bottom lip out like she was about to burst into tears.

Michael Jackson gave way to Wham!'s "Club Tropicana". Debbie shuddered inwardly.

* * *

Outside, the Golden Mile glittered and flashed, beckoning the punters with a neon wink. Horse-drawn carriages full of tourists clopped north from The Mint, past the new indoor leisure centre, the landscaped gardens and miniature village, all the way to the next pier.

Unlike The Britannic, The Trafalgar Pier had been commissioned with some civic pride in mind, to celebrate Nelson's famous victory. That it took another fifty years to erect suggested that the enthusiasm of the townsfolk had not been equal to that of the Aldermen who conceived it. Still, it was the grandest building on the seafront, twin towers surrounding a glass and steel pavilion. During the winter this became a roller-skating rink, but in its present summer incarnation as a beer garden it represented the ultimate triumph of the will of the people over any misplaced ideas for their betterment.

At the end of the Golden Mile, the horses would stop to deposit their excited cargo at the gates of the very pinnacle of Ernemouth's pleasure palaces, where the snow-capped tops of painted wooden mountains, spinning Ferris wheels and red-and-yellow-striped helter-skelter towers announced they had arrived at the Leisure Beach.

Its mile-long rollercoaster was the longest in all Europe. Its latest attraction, the Super Loop, spun revellers round in a gigantic circle at 100 mph. There was a queue beside it that had stretched the length of the park ever since the ride had been installed.

A queue that, from his office eyrie in the tower at the centre of the park, Eric Hoyle would, on any ordinary night, look down on with a smile, counting each head and the £5 entrance fee, £2.50 concessions, they represented. With the soft clack of an adding machine as a soothing soundtrack, he might pour out a finger of Scotch, light a cigarette and gaze out on his kingdom, eyes wandering across the cobweb of illuminations and out to sea, where the lights from the oil platforms would wink back at him.

But tonight was not an ordinary night. Tonight, Eric's eyes were fixed on only one thing, a photograph that he normally kept locked in his safe, a photograph Edna believed he had long ago thrown away in one of his fits of pique.

His daughter Amanda, wearing a psychedelic kaftan, her blonde hair tumbling out of a matching headscarf, holding in her arms the tiny bundle of his first and only grandchild.

The cigarette in his right hand was burning down to the filter, but Eric hadn't noticed. His shirt open at the collar, his tie thrown on top of a pile of paperwork next to the bottle of whisky and the tumbler that held more than three fingers tonight, he continued to stare, his eyes narrowed and his mouth set into a thin, grim line.

Beyond the Leisure Beach, Marine Parade carried on past the caravan parks and the windswept dunes of the South Denes to the very tip of Ernemouth, where the spit from which the town had first risen gave way to the North Sea. Here, atop a column that was a twin to the one in the London square, Admiral Nelson stood guard over the county of his birth, his eyes forever cast towards the horizon, warding enemy outsiders away.

3

Reality Asylum

March 2003

An hour later, Sean had found his way out of the forest and onto the A11 towards Norwich. The landscape began to alter, pine and scrub heath giving way to wide, brown, ploughed fields, fringed with coppices and long lines of poplars. He passed villages with duck ponds and flint-towered churches, gatekeeper's cottages and farmsteads, the sky getting bigger and the land lying lower as he went. Traffic kept up a steady flow around him and, though the clouds still lay sullen, he could turn off the windscreen wipers. But he kept the radio on.

He wasn't really listening to it now, just wanted the background hum of voices to distract him from what he had seen in the secure unit. What he had felt there. The appearance of Corrine Woodrow had come as a shock, nothing like what he expected. Stupid to think that she would be, but photographs had a way of doing that to you, of keeping a face suspended in time. Sean had been as much of a sucker for that as any other punter.

The doctor in charge of the institution had taken Sean into his study for some mild interrogation before allowing him to see her. Robert Radcliffe was an elegant man in his early sixties, his still-dark hair clipped neatly around his bald pate, a Jermyn Street shirt and Savile Row trousers visible beneath his white coat. For such a man to be in charge of a place like this, rather than coining it in Harley Street, suggested to Sean a dedication that ran deep and did not expect to be trifled with.

Dr Radcliffe had peered at Sean over half-moon spectacles, across the desk that, like everything else in the room, was bolted to the floor. "And what are you expecting to achieve by coming here today?" he enquired, in a rich baritone with a hint of Scots burr.

"I'm not entirely sure," Sean replied, opening his palms as if to assure the doctor of his honesty. "I've never worked a case like this before. I just wanted to meet Corrine before I hear what anyone involved in the original investigation has to say about her."

The doctor nodded, explained to him how Corrine was not regarded by anyone who worked here as a security risk, nor a potential danger to anyone other than herself. She was only on very mild medication now and had been responding well to courses of cognitive behavioural and art therapy. She had at last started to get something out of life again, discovering a talent she had abandoned long ago.

"Until the blessed Janice Mathers descended again." Dr Radcliffe fixed Sean with a granite stare. "I'm sure you are aware this is the second time Ms Mathers has made an attempt to have Corrine released, so I'll repeat to you what I said to her. This is a misguided cause and no good will come of it. Not for Corrine."

Sean kept his tone neutral. "Why do you say that?" he asked.

"It's all very well being liberal in theory," Dr Radcliffe closed the file that had been resting open on his desk. "But in practice, if these doors were to shut behind her, what do you think would become of Corrine? She has no friends, no family, no means of support. How long do you think she'd survive?"

"I was thinking just the same thing as I was driving here," Sean admitted.

"Well, then," the doctor raised his thick black eyebrows quizzically.

Sean offered him his blandest smile. "I'm sorry if by coming here I've caused you or Corrine any anguish. But I'm afraid I . . ."

"Have a job to do," Dr Radcliffe finished his sentence for him and stood up. "And there's nothing I can do about that. Very well, Mr Ward, if you would like to follow me."

Their footsteps echoed down grey-green corridors, past unadorned walls and the rows of windowless doors six inches thick. Sean's skin prickled as he followed the doctor, sensing myriad SOS signals emanating from inside the padded walls.

How long would it take before their madness infected you?

The wing where Corrine was kept was not as austere as the solitary blocks. Beyond the security checkpoint, inmates were allowed to move about unshackled; there were classrooms and common rooms where the art and craftwork they were encouraged to make was displayed on the walls, as if they were in a sixth-form college rather than a prison. Except for the omnipresent hum of CCTV cameras watching from every corner.

Dr Radcliffe stopped before one wall of paintings, pointed to a watercolour. A long blue wash of sky meeting sea, four figures in black with their backs turned, gazing out at the horizon where a flock of gulls took flight. Sean was no expert, but he could see how well the subdued palette had been employed to reflect the pale yellow of the sand and the gradually darkening blue of the sea. He rapidly assessed the other offerings on the wall, took in blacks and greys, violent splashes of red and green, cruder images that distinctly lacked the three dimensions of the maritime panorama.

"That's hers," the doctor said. "She probably doesn't realise, but this is in the best traditions of East Anglian watercolour painting. It takes real skill to get the light on the water like that."

There was pride in his voice as he said it, and if the comment had been designed to make Sean feel more uncomfortable, then it worked.

"Now then," Dr Radcliffe turned briskly, "this way, please. I've arranged for you to speak with Corrine in one of our quiet rooms."

Sean grimaced as he thought about it now, approaching the ring road around Norwich and spotting the first sign for Ernemouth.

That shy, shuffling figure, bloated from two decades on meds and little physical activity, hiding behind a long, dark brown fringe, threaded with grey. The pathologist's report from the autopsy running through his mind as she lowered herself into her seat.

Blunt force trauma to the rear of the cranium, blow forceful enough to leave a crater . . .

"Hello, Corrine."

Corrine sitting on a grey plastic chair, looking at the floor.

Multiple cigarette burns to the arms and face . . .

"I'm just here to ask you a few questions. I won't take long."

Corrine slowly shaking her head, her fingers twisting round each other in her lap.

Sixteen separate stab wounds to the chest and abdomen, patterns indicating wounds inflicted in a frenzy . . .

"Corrine, do you think you have been a victim of injustice?"

Corrine continuing to shake her head while rocking backwards and forwards in her seat. Sean facing her with his throat drying up, the words coming out all wrong.

The sign of a pentagram drawn in the victim's blood on the floor around the body...

"I mean, do you think it's fair that you should have been sent here? Or is there somebody else who should be here instead?"

Corrine finally speaking, wrenching out the words in a faint, childlike voice: "No... please... go..."

Sean leaning forwards in his seat, trying to make eye contact. "Corrine, was there somebody else there? Somebody else there with you?"

Looking up at him at last, repeating the words with rising hysteria. "Please... go... Please... go!"

And all he saw in her eyes was naked fear.

The rush-hour traffic was kicking in now and Sean was glad to shift his concentration to navigating his way through the system of flyovers and bypasses. The Ernemouth signs were getting bigger, adorned with jolly symbols of a racecourse, a funfair and caravan parks. One right turn and the road to his destination lay before him.

A long, straight ribbon cut through wide, flat marshland, dotted with white blobs of sheep, and the wingless remains of crumbling windmills. On the skyline, a row of wind turbines soared above these remnants of an earlier age, propellers cutting swathes through the darkening sky. But even they seemed like dwarves against the vastness above them.

The town crouched on the horizon, an illuminated clocktower staring out like one baleful eye. To his right, a vast expanse of water opened up a dramatic view of the estuary. Only the water could compete with the sky. Streetlights coming on as the road drew level with the train station and the sign that read *Welcome to Ernemouth.*

4

Fire Dances

September 1983

In the long hours since they'd had their lunch, Eric and Edna had been sitting in the lounge, straining to hear above the ticking of the clock, the rustling of Eric's papers and the clack of Edna's knitting needles, the sound of a car pulling into their drive. But when Noodles sprang from Edna's feet to stand on top of the sofa, yapping a staccato warning, they both looked up with a start, as if it was the last thing they had been expecting.

A Morris Minor, spray-painted purple, had stopped in the driveway. Edna tried to ignore the sinking feeling in her chest as she looked from the car to her husband, his expression propelling her towards the front door.

Amanda was the first to emerge from the ridiculous motor, in a cloud of honey-blonde hair and a pair of huge, brown, oval sunglasses. She hadn't lost her figure, Edna noted bitterly. Tight blue jeans and a denim jacket were worn casually over her slim hips and bulging chest, a pair of brown leather boots giving her height, gold glinting around her neck. The smile Amanda had plastered on with red lipstick was a mirror of her mother's and Edna could smell the Youth Dew from her doorstep.

"Mum," Amanda said, walking towards Edna with painted talons outstretched. The two women touched palms for the briefest of seconds as they strained to avoid closer contact, kissing the air around each other's faces. Edna's nose wrinkled as her daughter's perfume settled around them, a vaporous outrider encroaching on her territory.

"You're looking well," Amanda said as she stood back to take in the figure of her mother, regulation perm, pastel twin-set and theatrically pained facial expression all present and correct. Silly little dog standing at her feet with its top lip drawn back, body shaking indignantly as it growled at her.

For the past fifteen years, their contact had consisted mainly of phone calls arranging Samantha's summer visits and an exchange of gifts each Christmas that neither looked forward to unwrapping. Yet Edna seemed to Amanda to have been untouched by time. She stood on the doorstep exactly as she had left her.

"Thank you," Edna touched her hair self-consciously, wondering what had happened to her daughter's voice, why she sounded so different in the flesh to on the phone. There was not a trace of Ernemouth in it any more, Edna realised. You would have believed Amanda had been born within the sound of Bow Bells if you didn't know better.

Behind the brown lenses of her shades, Amanda's eyes flicked nervously to the space behind Edna's head that still hadn't been filled by her father and then back towards the Morris Minor. Slouching out of the passenger seat, as reluctantly as one would expect from someone his age, came the reason for all of this.

"This is Wayne," she said, the bonhomie in her voice as phoney as the accent.

He didn't look like much to Edna – a scrawny lad with a bumfluff moustache, a head of unkempt brown, curly hair, a bomber jacket and bovver boots. Nineteen years old, a painter and decorator: that was all he was.

But enough for Amanda to leave the artist husband she'd run off with all those years ago, Sammy's dad, Malcolm Lamb who, despite his unpromising beginnings, had ended up owning a large advertising agency in London. Employed to do up the family house in Chelsea, Wayne had ended up wrecking their marriage instead. Amanda had tried to convince Edna that some harebrained scheme about property development would keep them in riches once she got here. That a bit of sea air would be better for Sammy than any thoughts of staying with her dad, her public school and all her friends in London . . .

Edna thought that her face would crack with the effort of keeping her smile in place.

"Wayne," she nodded curtly.

Wayne dragged his gaze up from the crazy paving to grunt a greeting, then dropped it down again. No one made a move to shake hands. The three of them were trapped, suspended until the car's rear door slammed loudly behind them.

Sammy stood with her arms folded, head cocked to one side. Since the last time Edna had seen her, she'd had a fringe cut which sloped over her eyes, hiding their expression. The hair wasn't the only thing that had changed. Sammy's body had started to develop swells and curves, the way her mother's had at that age. And though she wasn't flaunting it – the pink-and-grey-striped T-shirt top, matching ra-ra skirt and pink plimsolls were exactly the sort of thing Shirl's girls wore – there was something about the sullen tilt of her posture that sent a tremor through Edna's heart. A voice whispering through her mind: *History is starting to repeat* . . .

Then Sammy raised her hand to push the thick wedge of

blonde hair out of her eyes, revealing fingernails with chipped pink polish that were bitten to the quick. With that one gesture, she suddenly became a child again, Edna's little Sammy.

"Nana," Sammy whispered.

"Come here, my darling," Edna opened her arms, "give Nana a hug."

With a sideways glance at Amanda that Edna didn't catch, Sammy ran to her grandma, burying her head on Edna's shoulder, her arms around her waist.

"Nana," she repeated. "Oh, Nana, I'm so pleased to see you."

Edna brushed the fringe out of Sammy's eyes as a fat teardrop fell from her lashes. A snakebite of love and rage bit deep within the grandmaternal gut. "There, there, Sammy," she whispered. "Nana's here now. Nana's here."

Amanda pushed her sunglasses up to the top of her head, eyeing the spectacle with pursed lips. Noodles, still growling and with every hair on his body standing on end, started to retreat backwards down the hallway, until his hind leg made contact with an advancing leather shoe. Noodles and Amanda looked up at the same time. The dog gave a yelp and ran to the sanctuary of his basket in the kitchen.

"What's all this then?" Eric's voice was gentle as he placed a hand on Edna's shoulder, but the eyes that stared over at Amanda were anything but. "How's my little girl?" he said.

For one second, Amanda thought he was talking to her.

"Granddad!" Sammy's head came up and her tear-streaked face broke into a tentative smile, exposing the wonky front tooth that she refused to have put in a brace.

"She's had a long journey, haven't you, love, feeling a bit tired out?" Edna suggested.

"Well, that's a shame," said Eric, "because I was just about to ask if she fancied coming in to work with me."

"I don't really think . . ." Amanda began. But the rest of the sentence stuck in her throat.

"Can I really, Granddad?" Sammy's face was radiant now, while the eyes of Eric and Edna had fallen upon their daughter like a Siberian wind coming up off the North Sea.

"Of course you can," Eric took hold of Sammy's hand, a smile twitching at his mouth.

"Dad," Amanda tried to start again. She waved her hand feebly towards Wayne, but his expression remained on the crack in the path it had been glued to since he'd got out of the car. "She's got to unpack and have her tea . . ." she tried to appeal to Edna instead.

"She can do all that later," said Eric, smiling broadly. "Now she's here, she'll want to enjoy herself, won't you, Sammy?"

Sammy nodded, flashing her mother a triumphant smirk.

"Don't worry," Eric went on. "I'll make sure she get her tea," the words dripped like acid from his lips. "That in't me who want to short-change her now, is it?"

* * *

"Debs!" Corrine's voice, more insistent now it had asked the same question three times, finally cut through her friend's reverie. The music that had been playing in Debbie's head, the record that Alex had brought home for her from his wanderings, a man with a low baritone intoning mysterious words about asking crystals, spreading tarots . . . "I said, what d'you reckon?" Corrine was holding up a folded page of *Smash Hits*, a photograph of a woman with mounds of eyeliner and a curly perm.

"She look ace, don't she?"

Debbie frowned. She thought the woman looked a mess, a beer girl trying to look weird but forgetting she still had a haircut like one of The Dooleys.

"I'm gonna get mine done like that," Corrine went on. "Soon as we get paid." Her hands reached for the packet of ten JPS on the tabletop between them and Debbie realised the magnitude of what her friend had just told her.

"What'll your mum say?" she asked.

Corrine scraped at a book of matches for a light.

"Don't care," she replied, fag in mouth. "I've been saving up for this all summer. It in't too much to ask, is it – one haircut and a pair of shoes what are already knackered?"

"Course not," Debbie felt guilty now. Thanked God she hadn't spoken aloud about The Dooleys. She took another look at the woman in the magazine.

"NYC's latest disco darling Madonna . . ." was as far as she read before there was a tapping on the window. Outside in the Victoria Arcade, Darren Moorcock and Julian Dean were waving at her.

"Cor," Corrine noted. "They look different."

Darren had grown his hair down to his shoulders and dyed it jet-black. Julian, whose skin as well as hair had been black to begin with, sported a tightly curled pompadour, fixed with glistening wet-look gel. Both of them were wearing black shirts, waistcoats, skin-tight jeans and pointed shoes with rows of silver buckles on them.

Debbie's face cracked into a grin, and she motioned for them to come in.

"They look great," she said as the bell jangled above the door. "Budge over, Reenie."

"Are you all right?" Darren sat straight down next to

Debbie. It wasn't that long since he was the same size as her, but now he seemed to have shot to nearly Alex's height. He had black eyeliner on too. It really suited him.

Darren glanced with approval at Debbie. "I see Alex in the pub last night. In Swing's," he added, with a certain measure of pride.

Debbie's eyes widened. She and Darren had always got on all right, thanks to their mutual propensity for spending lunchtimes in the art room. But last term, he had been just a short, squeaky-voiced kid with freckles. Now he seemed to have bloomed into something vastly more interesting.

"Can you get served in there then?" she asked.

"Yeah," Darren nodded. Even his voice had changed, dropped into a lower register. "You should come down with us sometime." He tried not to blush as she looked through the corrugated strands of her fringe at him.

"When you next going?" she asked, trying not to sound too eager. Tonight was the last Friday before they started school again and she really didn't want to spend it trailing up and down the Front.

"Tonight, I reckon," said Darren, looking over at Julian. "In't we, Jules?"

"What you say?" Julian put down the magazine Corrine had thrust at him.

"I say we're gonna go up Swing's tonight, in't we?"

Julian nodded his head. "I reckon," he said.

"What time?" asked Debbie, noting the way Corrine was gazing at Julian and feeling that, for once, things were going to go her way.

"About seven," Darren said. "D'you want us to meet you somewhere?"

"Well, we get off about six from work," Debbie spoke quickly, "so we'd have to get changed and walk down from there ..." She rapidly calculated how long this might take. "What about we meet you at the bus stop outside the town hall, about ten to seven?"

Darren was nodding, but Corrine had started to frown. "What's that, Debs?" she asked.

"Tonight," it suddenly came to Debbie how to play this, "I'm just saying we could go out with these two in town," she was careful not to say anywhere specific, "after work."

"Oh," Corrine's frown deepened as she tried to process this unfamiliar idea.

But Julian came to the rescue. "I can do you a tape," he said, "of that Madonna 12-inch. I've got it at home. Well, it's my sister's really, but she won't mind."

"Really?" Corrine's head snapped round. "You sure?"

"Ten to seven at the bus stop, then," said Darren.

"You're on," said Debbie, light shining in her eyes.

✳ ✳ ✳

Once the gaffer had seen Eric arrive, word got around the stallholders fast: the Princess was coming. This meant there would have to be some slight readjustments to the darts that could win you a cuddly toy, the hoops that went over the goldfish bowls and the wooden targets that you shot with a pellet gun. Normally, the odds in all these games were just slightly tilted, so that it was a fortunate punter indeed who could win a prize through skill or strength alone.

But the shelves above the bed she still hadn't seen were testament to how lucky the Princess had been at securing the trophies of the Leisure Beach.

"Hold you hard," Ted Smollet nudged his young nephew Dale in the ribs, "here she come." The fag that perpetually hung from the corner of his lips seemed to tremble, along with the salt-and-pepper eyebrows that grew in clumps above his beady, brown eyes. He grunted and said to himself: "She's filled out a bit."

Dale, who had been forced by his mother to work the summer if he wanted a new Norwich City FC season ticket this year, reluctantly followed his gaze. Dale didn't much like Uncle Ted, a wiry, skinny old man, whose inkily tattooed arms were a testament to a life working the fairgrounds. But he had to admit, working on the Leisure Beach had its compensations. Ten different holidaymakers he'd managed to lure into moonlight trysts in the sand dunes so far this year, none of them all that bad looking neither. Even his best mate, Shane Rowlands, who worked in the holiday camp up North Denes, had not had near that level of success. There was something special in the air here.

Like what was walking towards him now.

Her clothes were more suited to a kid, really, but what they were hiding wasn't. Shapely calves, tanned like honey, narrow hips and above that, bulges that the loose T-shirt wasn't doing anything to hide. A blonde head with a sloping fringe that covered half her face, a tilt to her neck, a little air of mystery about her.

Ted dug him in the ribs again. "Put your tongue away, boy," he said. Then began his customary chant: "Magic darts, let's play magic darts! Bullseye bags the Teddy, double tops will get you Nelly, lions and tigers by the score, you only got to hit the board!"

Dale could feel his cheeks flush as she stopped in front of the stall, not even looking at him, just running her gaze over the racks of bears, elephants, lions, tigers and the rest of the glass-eyed menagerie, with a bored expression, the twitch of a sneer on her upper lip.

Dale's palms went sweaty around the clean pair of arrows in his right hand.

"Yes please, young lady?" Uncle Ted squawked, flipping a toy parrot round in his hand, making out that it was doing the speaking. "See something you like?"

Dale could have killed him. The Princess's visible eye fluttered down and her top lip arched even higher, revealing a wonky tooth that only seemed to make her sexier, only made Dale shift his weight from foot to foot more uncomfortably.

"Nah," she said. "It's all kids' stuff, ain't it?" She tossed her head, ducking under her fringe again and moved off, not having given Dale a first glance, let alone a second.

"Sweatin'?" asked Uncle Ted.

* * *

Due west as the seagull flies, on the opposite side of town, was an Ernemouth built on a different kind of commerce, the docks of the River Erne. Though the heyday of the herring fleet was long gone, the stock fished out some thirty years since, the port was still full of ships; container boats, tankers and ferries replaced the old smacks and wherries.

It was less likely to find a tourist around here, but along the South Quay were the remains of the Town Wall built on the orders of Henry III, elegant eighteenth-century merchants' houses and the ruins of a Franciscan monastery. South Quay turned into Hall Quay as it passed the ornate Victorian town hall.

Making for the bus stop next to it, Debbie could hardly believe her luck. She hadn't even minded that Corrine had borrowed her crimpers and half her make-up either – it had got her this far.

She didn't have to hold her breath for the boys to turn up either. As they rounded the corner she could see that they were already waiting, sitting on the bench sharing a wrapper of chips, swinging their long, skinny legs.

"Cor, let's have some!" Corrine dived into their meal before they could even say hello.

"All right?" Darren looked amused. He also looked as if he had gone home and done his hair again since they'd met at the café. Debbie had attempted a little backcombing of her own and was pleased with the results – it added a couple of inches to her height, at least.

Debbie nodded, noticing how blue his eyes looked in the golden glow of the last daylight hour. For a moment they stared at each other.

Then Corrine's squeals filled the air. "Oh my God!" She was clutching a cassette in fingers sticky with salt and vinegar. "He give me the tape, Debs, he did! I've got Madonna, I don't believe it."

Julian winced as she slapped him heartily across the shoulders.

"So where we now going?" she asked.

"You'll see," said Darren, inclining his head to the right.

He made sure he was walking next to Debbie as they crossed the road in front of The Ship Hotel, made their way down the narrow passage beside the Midland Bank. He knew Julian wasn't really interested in Corrine, but he was too good a mate not to play along.

"What, we goin' back up town?" Corrine's bewildered voice came from behind them.

"No," said Darren, smiling at Debbie as they reached the side of an old, white-painted pub, where a sign hung over the alleyway above the door – a man in a tricorn hat and a velvet cloak, hanging from the scaffold, flames rising up around him, the silhouettes of people holding pitchforks aloft. In medieval-style lettering, the words *Captain Swing's*.

Darren pushed the door open and they followed him in.

5

Eastworld

March 2003

By the time he had pulled into the parking bay in front of The Ship Hotel, Sean had almost lost the feeling in his legs. The insulation of his flesh and the car heater combined didn't make any difference; the metal plates and pins that held him together now reacted directly to the elements, so that on a dank evening like this, he knew the true meaning of being chilled to the bone.

He got stiffly out of his seat, leaning for a moment against the car roof as he took in his surroundings. The smell of the river filled his nostrils. Traffic streamed past the dockside and over the bridge opposite the hotel, the dark bulk of container ships lined the sides of the quay. To his right rose the clock tower he had seen from five miles away, from the front of the gothic town hall.

The hotel had a black-and-white mock Tudor façade and red-tiled roof. Sean locked the car, gathered up his bags and went up the steps to check in. The front door opened into a red-carpeted corridor with a lounge bar to the left and the frosted door of the dining room on the right. The smell of meat and gravy hung more heavily on the air than the piped muzak coming from the bar.

Sean glanced in, saw a copper range over a gas-powered log fire, horse-brasses dripping from the beams around it and pots of aspidistras each side of the hearth. A sparse collection of middle-aged drinkers sat nursing half-pints over the cross-word pages of newspapers with all the seriousness of those who had nothing more to fill their days with. One stout woman with a wiry, salt-and-pepper bob and a tweedy coat, looked up and gave him a lingering assessment.

"Reception's that way," she said in a loud, plummy voice, pointing down the hallway and causing a few of her companions to raise their grizzled heads.

"Thanks," said Sean, feeling strangely embarrassed as he moved along the red carpet.

The receptionist greeted him with a cheery hello, in a voice that twanged hay bales and tractors. A nose with a diamante stud in it and hair streaked black, white and red, she wore a smart black skirt suit and crisp white blouse. A badge with the hotel's logo of an old fishing boat was pinned to her lapel, above an enamel plate that told him her name was *Julie Boone, Hotel Manager*.

She didn't look much older than twenty. Funny how the fashions that had seemed so threatening when she was a baby were now so commonplace as to not even elicit comment. Unless Julie was part of a satanic cult too.

"Thank you, sir," she took his form and credit card. "Oh, I see you're up from London, Mr Ward. Can I ask how you found out about us? We like to know how word get about."

"You came recommended," said Sean, "from the Ernemouth tourist board."

Julie looked delighted. "We've put you in room 4, that's on the second floor with a nice view over the harbour for you.

Lift's just to the right here," she waved her hand and then caught herself, "or do you want a hand with your bags?"

All he had was a hold-all, a briefcase and his laptop, but of course, she would have noticed his slow-shuffling gait as he approached the desk. Again, he felt a twinge of embarrassment, the way that his body had changed so that he no longer passed as normal.

"No," he told her, "I'm fine."

The room looked like it had been freshly plastered, repainted in the obligatory magnolia and then decorated by someone determined to make up for all that lack of colour. Sean took in the bright counterpane and curtains, all geometric turquoise, coral and yellow. A brief flash of memory: his mother doing the house up with fabrics like this when he was a child, a big squashy sofa with buttons on it. He moved towards the window, dropping his cases beside the bed. Julie was right, the view was pretty, the harbour and bridge lit up with mock gas-lamps, the pilot lights of the ships reflected in glittering streaks on the dark water of the Erne.

The bathroom was more to his liking: a large tub with a chrome power shower. He peeled off his clothes and stepped under the water, turning up the heat. Rivulets ran across a patchwork of scars down his right arm, where a spray of bullets had landed as he raised the limb instinctively to protect himself. Down his legs, hit when the gunman stumbled and fell, and where the worst of the damage had been done. Lumps in his kneecaps with metal screws underneath. Rods down his thighs. He hadn't been expected to walk again.

It was 6.15 by the time he stepped back out onto the pavement. He was running a little bit later than planned, but not too late. The place wasn't far. From the tourist map he'd picked up in reception, he navigated the few short turns to get him there.

The buzzer was on a thick metal door between a cut-price shoe shop and a Marie Curie's. A small, laminated strip reading EANG in a metal slot beside it. No plaque or anything, not even the newspaper's actual title on display, just the initials of its parent company, East Anglia News Group.

He pressed the buzzer and waited. All the shops on the strip seemed to have closed for the night, but a steady flow of people drifted past. Overweight women pushing prams, trailing overweight children with cartons of fries in their hands. Teenage boys in slouchy jeans and hooded tops, hawking gobs of spit onto the ground. Teenage girls in short skirts and bare legs, shouting to each other and laughing. Most of the women, young and older, had multicoloured haircuts like Julie Boone's and a similar array of facial silverware. Not so different from the inhabitants of any high street in London, but for their voices. And the fact that, despite the chill of the early evening, nobody was wearing a coat.

A woman's voice came through the intercom: "*Ernemouth Mercury.*"

"Sean Ward to see Francesca Ryman, please," he spoke into the grill.

"Do you have an appointment?" the tone was vaguely challenging.

"She is expecting me, yes."

"Oh." A pause, a crackle of static. "All right then, sir, come straight up the stairs, and take the first on the left." The buzz of an electronic lock being withdrawn.

Sean pushed the door open, went up one flight of stairs to the reception where the owner of the voice sat behind a modern black desk, a banner with the newspaper's masthead above her on a perspex screen. A small, open-plan office spread out behind her.

A middle-aged woman in a cream blouse and blue cardigan, thick chestnut hair cut into a wavy wedge, and grey-green eyes that ran over him speculatively. Sean gave her his warmest smile but her expression remained cool. "You need to sign here," she pushed across a book and a pen. "If you'll just hold on." Raising the receiver of her telephone, she tapped out three digits.

"A Mr Ward to see you, Fran, says he's expected, only I don't have anything written down for you in my book. Oh, OK. That's right. I'll tell him."

She put the phone down and pointed in the direction of the office. "Go straight through, she's right at the end there," she said.

The *Ernemouth Mercury* was a small operation. To his left, with their desks arranged around a whiteboard, was the advertising department: two young men with jackets draped over the back of their swivel chairs and hair gelled up, yakking away on the phones; an older guy with the thickened red face of an experienced drinker, hair tinted several shades of blond, sharing a joke with someone on the other end of the line while rearranging his bollocks in his navy-blue trousers.

To his right, four women at desks that faced each other, their screens covered with Post-it notes, all of them tapping away furiously. Two of them were about the same age as the ad boys, dressed in prim black skirt suits with their hair pinned up. The third had bottle-thick glasses and wavy brown hair, dressed more casually in grey sweater, jeans and trainers. The fourth was an older woman with hair dyed a violent shade of orange, a pea-green blouse and matching eyes that locked on to her screen in deadly seriousness.

Francesca Ryman's desk was placed before a wall of front covers. *Holidaymaker Special*, Sean read, *Wartime Memories Souvenir Issue*. She had already got to her feet, the smile on her face a contrast to the greeting he'd just been given.

In fact, the editor was distinctly different from everyone else in the room. She looked to be in her early thirties, tall, thin and angular, with a thick head of black hair swept up into the hairstyle her juniors were obviously emulating, only it looked more rakish on her, like she was deliberately subverting office style. She had on a grey, tailored trouser suit, an open-necked turquoise shirt. Her eyes were the same colour as the shirt, large and direct, set above high cheekbones and dark red lips.

"Hello," she said, even white teeth glinting. None of that local dialect for her either.

"Ms Ryman," Sean shook her hand. It was smooth and cool, a solid silver bracelet encircling it. He was aware of every head turning, the murmur of conversation and keyboard rattle dropping in volume. "Thanks for seeing me."

"A pleasure," she said. "I expect you're hungry? There's a place nearby I can recommend that's discreet," she looked around the room meaningfully. "Decent enough food too."

"Sounds good to me," said Sean. Francesca Ryman was behaving exactly as he had anticipated when he'd spoken to her on the phone before he left London – a bored provincial editor getting a whiff of something big and not even wanting her staff in on it until she thought she had it in the bag. Sean didn't like the thought of having to place his trust in anyone who made a living from this game. But, when you were a stranger in a strange town, an ally on the local newspaper was a necessary evil. Besides, Mathers had insisted on him making this contact, had said she would be useful.

The editor put her laptop into her briefcase, shrugged into a black wool overcoat and wound a pale yellow scarf round her neck. As they exited the office, Ward watched the eyes of her staff follow, locked on Francesca with something like awe.

"Night, Pat," she said to the receptionist, who was belting a tan mac around her waist.

The woman glowered at Sean. "Mind how you go," she said.

6

Hex

September 1983

"Now, class, I'd like to introduce you to a new pupil who's joining us. This is Samantha Lamb, she's from London originally but she's got grandparents here, so she's no stranger to Ernemouth. I hope you'll all do your best to make her feel welcome."

Even as Mr Pearson spoke, the look in his narrowed, ice-blue eyes suggested to the class in front of him that should he find out that welcome had been unforthcoming, there would be a price to pay. A tall, thin man in a brown suit, wavy, collar-length brown hair and a pencil moustache, Mr Pearson had a slightly chilling, cadaverous look about him that was enough to intimidate most of his teenage charges, including an inseparable trio of troublemakers – Neal Reeder, Shane Rowlands and Dale Smollet – whom cruel fate had even managed to arrange alphabetically.

Since Miss Lamb had joined the class a week into the new term, it was no longer possible to place her by order of surname. There was only one spare desk left now, next to Corrine Woodrow, who came at the end of the class both by dint of her surname and her results.

"Samantha, would you like to go and take a seat, next to Corrine there?"

Not that there was anything malicious about the girl. In fact, it was a minor miracle she made it into class at all, considering her background. Which was why Mr Pearson was prepared to let her new hairdo slip under his radar. Even if she did spend every lesson doing what she was doing now – staring out of the window, mouth open, swinging one leg back and forth to whatever music was playing in her head. As the nervous-looking new girl approached her, Corrine slowly turned her head and gave a puzzled smile.

"Stuck-up cow," remarked Rowlands to Reeder, in a low murmur.

Loud enough for Dale Smollet to catch. He was glad that, sitting in front of his two best friends, neither of them could have seen his face as Samantha Lamb walked into the room and stood in front of them, biting her lip with that crooked front tooth, head tilted to hide one eye behind a golden curtain of hair, while the other one flicked despondently round the room and then came to rest back on the floor. Followed her gaze down her honey-coloured legs to her long white socks, noted the curve of her ankles and bit his own lip.

The blonde girl looked scared, which didn't surprise Corrine. Meeting Pinhead Pearson for the first time did give you the creeps. But Corrine knew he was all right really, so she smiled encouragingly. "All right?" she said.

"Hello," the other girl replied, still looking worried, putting a blue-and-pink-striped canvas bag down on the top of her new desk. Corrine liked the look of that bag. She lifted the lid off her own desk and pointed to where she had all her books, pens and pencils neatly arranged inside. A page cut out from

Smash Hits taped under the lid, Madonna with a big black crucifix earring and bright yellow and mauve eye-shadow.

"Put the stuff what you don't need in your desk, like this," she said.

The new girl just stared at her.

"And when you've done that," Mr Pearson loomed into view, "here is your curriculum."

He handed Samantha a piece of paper with her timetable. Her results from the public school she had previously been attending in London put her in the top stream, so Corrine wouldn't be much help showing her around.

"Deborah Carver," Mr Pearson looked across to the other side of the classroom. "You have the same lessons as Samantha here, can I trust you to show her how to get about?"

Debbie opened her mouth but it took a while for the words to come out. She had been staring at the new girl with a strange feeling of dread coiling inside her. She didn't know why, or what it was about her. Later she would imagine that she had been struck by a premonition, that this girl who looked so shining and pretty actually had a black cloud hanging over her head that was about to open up on her world.

On all of their worlds.

* * *

Three hours later they were back clustered around their desks, Corrine and Debbie sharing their packed lunches with the new girl the way they always did with each other.

"So where d'you live then, Sam?" Corrine enquired.

"Marine Parade," the new girl replied, "North Denes end."

Debbie managed to swallow the mouthful of sandwich she had been chewing with a gulp of relief. North Denes was the other side of town from them. At least they wouldn't have to walk home with her and all.

"That's where my nana and granddad live," Samantha went on. "But I'm moving soon." She looked down into her Tupperware lunchbox, at the remains of her sandwich.

"My mum's bought a house on Tollgate Street. I've got to go there in a couple of weeks. I wish I didn't have to." Samantha sighed, passing the final quarter over to Corrine, whose contribution to the meal had been only a packet of cheese and onion crisps.

"You sure?" even Corrine thought this was going a bit far.

Debbie's throat contracted again as the words sank in.

Samantha nodded. "Not hungry," she explained. Her eyes rose to meet Debbie's.

"But Tollgate Street's really nice," said Debbie, her face flushing as she thought: *And it's right near Swing's.* That pub and the art room were the only places she wanted to spend her life right now. She had deliberately avoided showing the new girl her usual lunchtime hangout. But how long would Corrine be able to keep anything secret?

"It's not that," Samantha said, flicking a strand of hair out of her eyes, "it's Mum. I don't want to live with her, I want to stay with my nana and granddad."

"She an old cow then, your mum?" asked Corrine, her mouth still full of sandwich. "Mine fuckin' is." Her face curdled into a grimace before she went back to her chewing.

Samantha gave the first genuine laugh she had uttered all day. "She's a bitch, all right," she agreed, then paused. "And a whore," she added, staring at Corrine with a smile.

Debbie gave up on her half-eaten sandwich. Her fingers crumpled it into the foil.

"So's mine," Corrine said matter-of-factly. "She nicked all the cash I earned at the guesthouse this summer and it still weren't enough for her, fuckin' old slag. Still, I showed her, din't I, Debs?" She twirled a finger through the permed and highlighted hair that had been worth the black eye she'd managed to disguise by copying the colours of Madonna's make-up.

Debbie tried to give her friend a look that would tell her to shut up, but Corrine was well away. "So what did your mum do?" she asked.

"Got herself a boyfriend," Samantha offered her lunchbox again, the mint Club biscuit she had intended on keeping for herself the only thing left in it.

"Really?" said Corrine, accepting the bait, remembering the motley collection of boyfriends she'd put up with in her time. "What is he, a druggie? A biker?"

"He's a brickie," Samantha scowled, "and he's only four years older than we are."

"Yep," Corrine nodded her head, "she's a slag all right, your mum."

The pair of them dissolved into laughter.

Debbie felt something crawl inside her stomach. This was worse than she'd anticipated.

"Right!" she said, snapping shut the lid on her lunchbox. "Who's coming outside? I in't sitting here all lunchtime, this weather."

"OK." Samantha shrugged and turned her head slowly towards Debbie, her eyes running up and down her. "We'll catch you up, then."

Corrine, who had been poised to jump down from her desk, checked herself just in time.

"I don't feel like going out," Samantha explained to her. "Do you?" She smiled at Corrine, saying something with her eyes that Corrine thought she understood.

"Uh, no," Corrine sat back down. "I'll stay here with you." She flicked a glance round to the back of the class, to where Reeder, Rowlands and Smollet were sat in their usual huddle, talking bollocks and throwing paper pellets around the room. Smollet averted his gaze quickly and Corrine saw a flush of red travel up his neck.

She turned back and winked conspiratorially. "I'll protect you."

*　*　*

Debbie fixed her eyes on the poster on Alex's wall. With her donkey jacket spread face down on the floor in front of her, she began to sketch an outline in tailor's chalk. A dark pulse of music filled the room.

Lounging on his single bed with his back to the wall, sketch-pad balanced on his knee, Alex watched her work, peering up at the icon she was copying. A new poster from his summer travels, the concert promotions that mapped the trails he had taken around the country. Not an inch of his bedroom wasn't decorated. Magazine photos peered out around The Damned at the Electric Ballroom, UK Decay at the Lyceum and his oldest, most treasured remnant, The Sex Pistols at West Runton Pavilion. The black sunglasses of The Ramones, the quiffs and curls of The Cramps, The Clash standing down an alleyway. Arranged around them were his own sketches, friends captured in moments when their minds were elsewhere. Alex was always trying to nail the essence of a character with his pencil. Like the earnest frown on Debbie's forehead just now.

"How's school today?" he asked her. "D'you go in the art room?"

Debbie paused, the chalk hovering over the fabric. "Yeah," she said, "at lunchtime."

She had fled there when Corrine had stayed behind with the new girl, found Darren and Julian and distracted herself with their company until the dreaded bell had summoned her back to the afternoon's chores of showing Samantha Lamb to her classes.

"Only," she put the chalk down and sat back on her heels, lifting up her mug of tea, "there was a new girl." She took a slow sip, looking down at the beginnings of her new creation. "I got lumbered with showing her around, so I din't do as much as normal."

Alex raised his eyebrows. "You din't like her, then?"

Debbie cut him a sideways glance. "No," she said. "Corrine did though."

She put the cup down and picked up the chalk, bent back over her drawing, trying not to think of the argument they'd had on the way home, Corrine trying to assure her that she was only being nice to the new girl and that Sam was lovely really, showing her the little pencils she'd given her, white with pink love hearts down the side. Sickly childish things.

"How come?" Alex watched Debbie's face change, the colour rising in her cheeks.

"Well," said Debbie, not looking up, "Pinhead made them sit together and she started sucking up to Reenie straight away. Told her that her granddad own the Leisure Beach and she can take her there any old time she like, get free rides and everything."

"Oh yeah?" said Alex. "Well, maybe that in't such a bad

thing, Debs. Look, I know you done your best for her, but you and Reenie in't really got a lot in common, have you?"

"No," Debbie said, trying to keep the wobble out of her voice.

"I mean," Alex went on, "she don't like the same things you do, do she? You said yourself you only got her to go down Swing's the other week 'cos she thought she was in with that, what's his name, Julian?"

Debbie nodded, swallowing hard. "Yeah," she said.

"He was a good bloke," Alex considered, and then said more gently, "and so was that Darren. You like him, don't you?"

Debbie nodded her head. But it wasn't his face that danced before her eyes. It was Corrine, standing in the middle of the alleyway on their shortcut home, raging at her: "Now you've got that Darren to play with, that in't even like you want me no more, is it?" Poking Debbie in the breastbone with a hard little finger. "See! You don't even try and deny it. What do you even care about Sam for?"

Alex put his sketchpad down, slid off the bed and down next to her. The youngest of three boys by ten years, Alex's own brothers had always been remote, leaving home while he was still a child. Debbie had always seemed more like his real sibling.

"That's really good," he said, putting an arm around her, looking down at the drawing.

"D'you think?" Debbie sniffed, glad for a change of subject.

"Yeah," said Alex. "Let me get some paint. I'll help you with it."

7

Silver

March 2003

On the pavement outside, Francesca laughed. "Oh dear," she said, placing her hand on Sean's arm for a moment. "Sorry about that. That's what you call an Ernemouth welcome. I had it all myself when I started here, especially from Pat. She's been here the longest, had that job since she was sixteen. Likes everyone to know who runs the place."

"Well, you must have made a better impression than I did," said Sean. "She's like your guard dog now."

"I have my ways. Now then, we go down here," she led him down a Victorian arcade, past shops selling jewellery, souvenirs and women's clothing.

"There's not much in the way of sophistication here," said Francesca, eyes flicking towards a display of mannequins in florals that had probably been there half a century. "But what you can find is always in the oldest part of town."

When they came out at the bottom, Sean thought for one horrible moment that she was about to lead him back to his hotel and that institutional smell of meat and gravy. But instead she stepped to the left, went through a cutting into a square of Georgian houses.

"See there, at the bottom," she pointed to some much older buildings, remnants of the old Town Wall and a preserved peel tower. "That's the Tollhouse. The old jail. Where Matthew Hopkins, the Witchfinder General, used to take the local girls to make them confess." She raised one eyebrow suggestively.

Sean laughed politely, wondering if this was a demonstration of how she got her staff onside or whether the vaguely flirtatious, familiar manner was just for him.

"Here we are." She stopped outside one of the townhouses, and Sean saw that it had been converted into a restaurant. A cream sign hung over the door, black letters spelling out the name: *Paphos*.

"A Greek," noted Sean.

"The best in town," Francesca replied. "There's quite a lot of Cypriots in Ernemouth."

Before they had got to the top of the steps to the door, a man had opened it for them. Tall and muscular, with thick, jet-black hair and a wide smile that revealed perfectly straight white teeth, he was almost film-star handsome.

"*Kalespera*, Francesca," he said, taking her hand and making a little bow. "A pleasure as always. And you, sir," he added, "of course."

"Did you . . . ?" she began.

"Yes, Achillias said. This way, please." He swept them past the reception desk and up a staircase, into an empty dining room that had been redecorated in keeping with its original design: mahogany floorboards, duck-egg blue walls, heavy drapes at the window and tables set with crisp linen and silver candelabras. "I put you here," he pulled out a chair from the table set in the bay window, overlooking the square. "We've kept the bookings downstairs until nine."

"Thanks, Keri," she said, touching his arm the way she had done with Sean earlier. "I appreciate it."

Keri looked at her with the same level of admiration Sean had observed in her staff. He took their coats, leaving them with the menus and wine list. Sean felt a stab of hunger.

"Do you want some wine?" Francesca asked him over the top of her menu.

"Sure," said Sean. "I'll go a glass of red."

"Might as well make it a bottle," Francesca spoke like a true veteran. "Don't worry, this is on my expenses. Keri, can you get us a bottle of red and some mezze?"

She paused as the waiter departed, then turned back to Sean. "So what was it that you wanted to discuss with me?"

Her turquoise eyes were sharp. Sean leaned back in his seat, tried to appear relaxed. "I've never worked a case like this before," he told her. "Never been to this part of the world either. You can read old reports as much as you like, but it doesn't give you a feel for the place. That's what I'm hoping for. A little local insight."

"I see," she said.

"Like," he went on, "can I expect the same kind of welcome that I got from your secretary from everyone in Ernemouth?"

"Probably," she nodded. "Pat's a very good introduction to this town, as it goes. You won't get a squeak out of her yourself, but once she gets home, the phonelines will be burning about the strange man who came into the office today. That's why I didn't want them to know what your business is. I mean, she *will* find out. First rule of Ernemouth – walls have eyes and ears around here. I just wanted to give you a head start."

Sean nodded. "Makes sense," he allowed. "So what are you going to tell them?"

"That you're an old friend down from London. Let them make of that what they will. Hopefully they'll get distracted by their own idle gossip into thinking you're something you're not." She raised her eyebrows, looked over his shoulder.

"Ah," she said. "Good. Here come our starters."

Sean studied her as Keri arranged the bowls of dips, olives, pastries and pitta on the table, poured their drinks and then smilingly departed. He realised that she had chosen the seat that had the only clear view of the whole room. Walls have eyes, indeed.

"So," he prompted, reaching for the bread. "How long have you been here?"

"I've worked for the *Mercury* just over three years," she said, spooning hummus onto the plate. "When I got the job it was just me, Pat and Paul Bowman, the Peter Stringfellow lookalike in charge of advertising. The old editor had been doing everything else himself for years, until he dropped dead at his desk from a heart attack. I had to work my arse off to turn the thing around. But it was good to do it, you know," she picked up her glass, took a contemplative sip. "We've come a long way."

"And before then?" Sean asked.

"I worked on a national for five years," she said. "From news reporter to section editor. But, you know – not much chance of ever becoming an editor there."

"Still," said Sean, wondering why she would have made a move to a dismal backwater like this. "Must have been a bit of a culture shock coming here."

"Not entirely," she smiled.

Sean lifted a triangle of pastry to his mouth, tasted warm, crumbling feta and spinach inside. It didn't take long for them to clear their plates.

"But what about you? I mean, I've done my research about why you're here," Francesca said. "I understand why you want your insight. But," she looked up again without missing a beat, "shall we order our main course first?"

"I know what I want," said Sean, as Keri appeared soundlessly by his side. "A big plate of moussaka," he said, looking up at the waiter.

"I'll have the same," said Francesca. "You won't be disappointed."

Once Keri had gone, she leant forward in her seat, long fingers curling around the stem of her glass. "So what have you got that's new?" she asked. "Forensics, I presume, DNA? Nothing that anyone's actually come forward and said?"

"Correct," he nodded. "You didn't imagine there was any chance of that happening?"

She shook her head. "Too many people's lives were ruined," she said. "When you're in a small town like this and the spotlight falls on you for such a terrible reason, the collective shame is unbearable. They offered up their sacrifice twenty years ago and expected to get left alone in return. You won't find many who'll want to go raking it over."

"Not even the editor of the local paper?"

The question hung on the air as Keri placed plates of moussaka down, topped up their glasses and left them to their meal. Sean took a few forkfuls. Francesca was right; he wasn't disappointed. For a while, they ate in silence, and he savoured every mouthful.

"Is it good then," she eventually said, "what you've got? Do you think it's enough to change the story? To risk stirring up the hornets' nest and everything that'll go with it?"

Sean blinked away the memory of Corrine Woodrow's

eyes, the sudden wave of fatigue that ran through him at the memory, triggering the ache in his legs that the food had been helping him ignore. *The shadow of a young man stepping out from under the trees . . .*

"The evidence suggests I can," he said.

They stared at each other across the table. Then Francesca turned her head, gazed out of the window, into the night. *"Ta en oiko me en demo,"* she murmured.

"What was that?" Sean asked.

She turned back to face him. "Then you're going to need help, aren't you?" she said.

8

Because the Night

September 1983

"If you could have anything," said Samantha, "anything in the world, what would you most want?"

Corrine's eyes opened and she squinted against the sun that was warming her as she lay on the soft slope of a dune. Still slightly queasy from the combination of the rides and all the ice cream they had put away afterwards, she had almost drifted off in this sheltered hollow they had found among the North Denes.

"Dunno," she said, drawing in her bottom lip. "I s'pose . . . I'd like today to go on forever."

"Oh, come on," Samantha shifted herself from her back to her elbow, turning to face her new friend. "That can't be it – you must want something more, surely?"

Corrine's mind struggled against the torpor of the Sunday afternoon heat. Three times they'd ridden the rollercoaster today, twice on the Rota, then the Ghost Train, the Superloop and finally the Waltzers, the boy swinging their carriage around as he joked with them, making her dizzy with laughter at the thrill of it all. A walk down the Front after and sweet treats at Mario's at the top of Regent's Road, bought with the five-pound note Sam's granddad slipped into her hand as they'd left the Leisure Beach.

She didn't think life could get much better.

Sam's eyes gazed down at her intensely, somewhere between green and blue they were, the same colour as the North Sea. There was a vague smile on her lips, a piece of marram grass in her hand that she had been chewing, now waving just above Corrine's nose.

"Go on," Samantha said, "tell me." She lowered the grass so that it started to tickle.

Corrine flinched. "Pfffff!" she tried to blow the stem away, inching sideways as she did. "Don't, Sam," she pleaded.

But Samantha moved in closer, her head blocking the sun. Her smile deepened, her crooked tooth glinting. "Tell me," she said, "or I'll tickle it out of you."

"No!" Corrine tried to sit up but Sam was faster, pinning her arms down to her sides and sliding her leg over Corrine's torso, so she finished up sitting on her chest.

"Tell me!" Sam goaded, flicking the stem over the top of Corrine's nose.

"Get off!" Corrine could hardly breathe. She screeched and kicked her legs up, pitching herself sideways and sending the pair of them rolling down the side of the dune. A wave of hysterical laughter engulfed the pair as they went, landing up in a heap of tangled limbs, sand in their mouths and their hair.

"Look what you've now done!" Corrine extricated herself quickly, jumping to her feet, her face a vivid red. "You've ruined me hairdo!" She put her head upside down and tried to shake the sand out, staggering on her feet as stars danced before her eyes.

"No I haven't," said Samantha, still sitting, still with the piece of grass in her hand, looking up at her through the curtain of her fringe. "Don't be such a baby. Sit down, there's something I want to tell you."

There was an edge to her voice that made Corrine stop immediately and do as she was told. Despite having almost succumbed to a full-blown panic attack only moments before, the fear of losing out on days like this was greater than any physical discomfort.

"What?" she said, gingerly hunkering down.

Samantha's expression changed as rapidly as a cloud flitting across the sun. Her smile dissolved, her face became solemn, her eyes now more green than blue. "I've never had a real friend," she said, "not someone I could tell all my secrets to. You want to be my friend, don't you?" Her voice was pleading, a mirror of her eyes. "Or are you just like everyone else – you only want to know me 'cos of who Granddad is and what you think you can get out of it?"

Corrine felt a rush of shame that was reflected in the colour of her cheeks. "Course not," she said, trying to look Sam in the eye without blinking. "Please don't think that, Sam."

"I mean," Samantha turned her head away, stared towards the sea, "it's all right for you. You've got Debbie, she's a real friend, isn't she? Whereas I . . ." she bit her bottom lip. "I've got a mum who's just run off with an embarrassing bloody kid and a dad who hasn't got the guts to stand up to her. Neither of them cares about me. They've just dumped me here, where everyone just thinks I'm some spoilt little posh bitch."

"No they don't . . ." A second front of panic assailed Corrine now, she couldn't think of the right words to say. "They don't, honest."

"Ha!" Samantha's head snapped round. "I heard what that

boy said the minute I stepped into the classroom. That Shane Rowlands and his scabby mates. They were laughing at me, all of them. And your precious Debbie," her eyes narrowed as she said it, boring into Corrine's, "doesn't like me either. She makes that quite obvious."

"Look," said Corrine, reaching out her hand, "you don't want to listen to Rowlands, he's a knob end, everyone know that. No one care what he think. Everyone like you, Sam."

The look in Sam's eyes said she didn't believe her. Corrine thought she had better go further. "And if they don't, well . . . then I don't like them either."

"Really?" Samantha's eyes softened, blue flooding into the green.

"I'll always stick up for you, you know I will," Corrine said fiercely. "I don't take no shit off no one."

Samantha nodded solemnly. "All right," she said. "Give me your little finger."

Corrine did as she was told.

Samantha ran the side of the marram grass across the top joint of Corrine's finger, fast and deep, drawing blood. Kept hold of her hand as Corrine recoiled.

"No," she said, digging her nails into the other girl's hand, "wait. Now I have to do it."

The sudden pain bringing tears to her eyes, Corrine watched as Sam repeated the manoeuvre on her own little finger, making the cut without even flinching. Then she pressed their fingers together, holding them fast with her other hand.

"Now our blood has mingled," she said, that intense expression back in her eyes, "we're sisters. No one knows but us. But we share all our secrets from now on. Right?"

Corrine nodded, locked in the thrall of that stare.

"Good!" said Sam, letting go of her hand and jumping to her feet. "Now let's go and see Nana. She's made some cakes for our tea. Come on, I'll race you."

And she sprinted away over the dunes, faster than a bewildered Corrine could catch up with.

* * *

Edna's insides churned as she sat at the kitchen table. Her eyes kept darting from the clock, where the minutes dragged towards seven o'clock, and the ceiling. Sitting on her rigid lap, Noodles was being stroked to within an inch of his life.

Edna was wishing she had X-ray vision, wishing she could see what was going on up there in Sammy's room, between her granddaughter and that ... creature she had brought home with her. Wished that Eric would hurry up and get home. Wondered if she dared go up and suggest, since it was a school night, that it was time Sammy's guest was leaving ...

She and Eric had been so delighted at the prospect of meeting their granddaughter's new school friend. Until she had opened the front door on Corrine Woodrow and gazed upon the rigid waves of garishly highlighted hair, violet eyeshadow and lipstick. Edna winced at the memory of a hand closing in on her fairy cakes, black-painted fingernails encased in a lace mitten. A thieving hand, if ever she had seen one.

Noodles, fed up now with being ground into his mistress's thighs, looked up and yapped, jumped off Edna's lap and shook himself furiously, sweaty-palm-dampened fur springing back to attention. Then, casting a look over his shoulder as if to say, *If you won't sort it out then I will*, he trotted briskly up the stairs.

* * *

"There," said Corrine, stepping back from the stool so that Sam could see herself in the mirror. "What d'you reckon?"

Samantha's cool gaze took in the transformation. Her hair had been backcombed so that it stuck up and out, her eyebrows plucked and pencilled in. Black eyeliner and thick mascara against shocking pink and yellow eyeshadow, vivid, angular streaks of blusher down each cheek and Clara Bow lips outlined in black and filled in with purple gloss.

Corrine looked from the reflection to the palette she held in her hands, a row of pouting lips in every colour from sugar pink to deep mauve, a sweet little brush to paint them on with. "This is ace," she said. "You must have got it up London, I in't seen anything like this round here, or I'd have . . ." she stopped herself just in time from saying, "nicked it".

"Keep it," said Samantha airily, moving her head to a different angle. A picture of Siouxsie Sioux cut out of *Record Mirror* had been taped to the dressing-table mirror. Corrine had done her best to replicate the look over the past hour, while Tommy Vance counted down the Top 40 from the transistor radio on the windowsill.

"You're pretty good at this, aren't you?" Samantha allowed.

"Well, I'm hopin' to become a beautician," Corrine said, blushing. She'd never revealed this secret hope to anyone, not even Debbie. It had just sort of blurted out without her thinking. But, she supposed, now that she and Sam were sisters . . .

"I expect you're good at art as well?" Samantha continued.

"Well, I in't bad," said Corrine modestly. "I just . . . Oh, hold up, what's that?" She heard a scratching at the door and went towards it, opening it up a crack. "Ahh," she said, regarding the furry nose that poked through it and crouching down to stroke it. "What a sweet little dog."

"No he isn't." Behind her, Samantha's voice turned icy. "He's a nosy little sneak."

Noodles gave a sudden yelp and shot backwards, seconds before the shoe that was hurled in his direction pinged off the doorframe.

"What the . . . ?" the missile deflected off Corrine's shoulder and she slammed the door in shock.

"Ha! That told the little rat!" Samantha started to laugh.

"What's going on?" Having reached the top of the stairs, Edna was just in time to see a lace-mittened hand reaching towards her pet and his violent retreat from it, Noodles shooting across the landing and disappearing under her bed. When she heard Sammy shriek, she raced towards the door, her own voice shrill in her ears, and pulled it open.

Corrine stared back at her with round, startled – and to Edna's mind, guilty – eyes.

"What you now do to my dog?" Edna demanded.

"Nothing," Corrine protested.

"Don't you nothing me," pent-up rage now coursed freely through Edna's veins, "He just come running out of here like a bat out of hell! Now what have you—"

"Nana!" Samantha jumped to her feet. Edna's eyes locked onto the sluttish apparition that appeared to be speaking with her granddaughter's voice.

"—done?" she finished, the word choking in her throat.

Corrine didn't wait to hear the rest of it. "I'd better go," she said, bending down to snatch her bag off the floor.

"No, wait!" Sam called after her.

Corrine glanced backwards. "See you at school," she said, dodging past the old woman and clattering down the stairs, out the front door, before anyone could catch her.

"What did you do that for?" Samantha snarled into her grandmother's face.

* * *

Corrine ran halfway down Marine Parade before she got the stitch and had to slow down, still looking nervously over her shoulder every ten seconds or so. *Well, that's that ruined, in't it?* she thought. *I'll never get invited back there again.* She kept jogging until she reached the safety of the Front, the panic of being shouted at propelling her to get as far away from Sam's house as fast as possible. Corrine never stopped to think when people started getting angry. Experience had taught her that flight was safer than fight.

By the time she was at the 'musies, sadness had replaced fear. The thought of all those treats slipping from her grasp. Still, thank God she had put the lip palette in her pocket before it had all gone off.

She caught sight of a clock as she slipped into The Mint, wondering if anyone was about. Seven-thirty, it said. She scanned the room rapidly. No one here she knew. She fished in her jeans pocket for change. There weren't much there.

Corrine thumbed some coppers into one of the slots. The machine ate the lot, laughing back at her with an electronic whoop and whistle.

Worry started to replace sadness. The season might be over, but Corrine's mum still didn't expect her to come home empty-handed of a night. Corrine thought of that fiver, so easily given to Sam, so easily spent by her. Grimaced at her own stupidity, thinking she could win that much on the one-armed-bandits.

She leaned back on the machine, slowly counting out what

little she had left. Gradually noticed the man looking at her. A lead weight came down on her stomach, her heart.

* * *

Corrine came out from under Trafalgar Pier and went straight across the Front to the public toilets on the other side of Marine Parade. In a piss-stinking cubicle covered in graffiti, she leant over the bowl and was sick, fairy cakes and ice cream curdling with a more recent addition to the contents of her stomach. Kept spitting in the bowl, trying to get the taste out of her mouth. But before she went back to the sinks and the drinking fountain, she made sure the green note was still in her pocket.

Outside, she leant against the wall for a moment, lighting up a JPS. Noticed a man hurrying out of the Gents, his head down, hands inside the pockets of his Macintosh. A few moments later, another figure appeared at the doorway and stopped there, leaning against the doorframe, one ankle crossed over the other. Smoke wreathed his head like the tendrils of a sea mist. He raised the cigarette to his lips, the light briefly illuminating a pair of green eyes behind a thick, black thatch of hair.

"Reenie," he said, his voice soft, his accent not quite the Ernemouth norm. "And how's the night treating you?"

"Bollocks," said Corrine and spat on the pavement. "As usual."

"Hmmm." His eyes ran her up and down slowly as he took another drag on his cigarette. "Well, I could say the same myself. You got enough now, or you hanging round?"

Corrine shrugged. "Reckon I have," she said, rubbing her hands together. "Don't feel like goin' home much, though."

"Come to mine, if you want," he offered. "It's safe. And I can show you something that makes all this a bit more . . ." his eyes flicked up and down the seafront, " . . . bearable. Something I've been learning."

"I don't know," Corrine frowned. She'd heard talk like this before. Normally from the stoned mouths of the druggie losers her mother entertained.

The boy laughed. "God, Reenie. You should know you're safe with me by now."

"I don't mean that," Corrine felt herself blush. "I in't doin' no drugs is what I mean."

"Not drugs," he said, shaking his head. "Magick . . ."

9

Nocturnal Me

March 2003

Sean stood on the front steps of The Ship Hotel. The music had changed in his absence, blaring loud enough to spill out onto the street, along with a babble of voices. The bar was full of people, competing to be heard over Michael Jackson's histrionic appeal on behalf of planet Earth.

He and Francesca had lingered another half an hour over the balloon glasses of twelve-star Metaxa, coffee and Cyprus Delight that Keri had provided gratis with another one of his film-star smiles. As he had promised, the upstairs remained empty until nine, and they had been able to talk further about the case. Francesca seemed to know the background. Suggested that some remnants of the scene that produced Corrine's gang still lingered around the place that had nurtured successive generations of Ernemouth weirdos and was undergoing something of a renaissance these days: Captain Swing's pub. That if he wanted to find anyone with a long enough memory who might be persuaded into giving him some local insight, then that would be where to look.

She had left him with a brown envelope stuffed with cuttings as she got into her cab outside the restaurant. He might have seen them already, but this was the most interesting stuff the *Mercury* had printed. How she had ascertained that, she didn't say.

Sean felt for the room key in his jacket pocket, pushed the front door open. Two women standing chattering in the hall-way snapped their heads round as he crossed the threshold, running him up and down with glittering eyes. A thin, mousey blonde with a servile expression and a short, thickset brunette, whose pugnacious countenance was in no way softened by a liberal slathering of make-up.

Sean felt their eyes on his back the whole way down the hallway. Back upstairs, he put Francesca's envelope on the bed. Music pulsated through the floorboards, bass-heavy, tune-light, with an over-emotional diva Whitneying away over the top. It was meant to be good-time, party music. But it had the same edge to it as the tunes of the high-rise pirates booming out of the estates on Sean's former beat: narcotic emptiness underpinning vocal hysteria. Like an itch that you could never scratch.

It made his instincts prickle. He moved into the bathroom, picked up some hair wax and rubbed it on his fingers, teasing his hair upwards.

Goths, weirdos, emos, whatever they called themselves ... He'd come across a few in his time; they were usually the ones on the receiving end of the violence in London, not the instigators. Interesting cross-pollination of imagery between their music and the gangsta gangs' though: horror elements binding them both, skulls and Mexican wrestling masks, Gothic script tags. The juvenile delinquent way of time immemorial, Sean supposed.

He went back into the bedroom, took off his shirt and hung

it in the wardrobe, replacing it with a plain black T-shirt. Put his leather coat back on and checked his reflection.

Satisfied, he stepped back through the front door of The Ship, turned right past the bank and then up the alleyway beside it, as Francesca had instructed, the discomfort of his legs easier to ignore now that adrenalin was pumping and, in a perverse way, now he could be glad if he no longer passed as normal. He was going to a place where that would be a distinct advantage.

Halfway down the cutting, a pub sign hung over a side door. Black background, white face. A man with a wide-brimmed hat pulled over one eye, twirly moustache and pointed beard. Flames dancing yellow around his visage and above, medieval script spelling out: *Captain Swing's*.

Sean didn't go straight in. He walked to the top of the alley. On his right was the white-painted pub, on his left a second-hand bookshop. A narrow road and beyond it a car park, the back of a department store.

He turned back towards the pub. The face on the pub sign looked familiar. Sean had first seen it on May Day 2000, in the thick of the riot at Trafalgar Square, an eerie glimpse of a stark white face through flailing arms, shields and batons: took him a couple of seconds to realise it was a mask. He noticed it again some months later on a T-shirt worn by one of the scrotes at Meanwhile Gardens Skatepark. A colleague with teenage kids explained where it had come from – a comic strip about a futuristic anarchist who modelled himself on Guy Fawkes. Now here he was again.

Sean pushed open the heavy oak door and walked into a waft of warm air, Bob Marley's "Buffalo Soldier" riding on top of it. An improvement on The Ship, at least. He took in a walnut, horseshoe-shaped bar with a brass top. To his right, a row of tables and chairs beside the window were taken by a smattering of teenagers, multi-coloured hair worn in long fringes or razored spikes, pierced eyebrows and lips. Resting against the bar opposite them, a much older guy in biker's denim and leather, snake of a plait running down his back and a salt-and-pepper goatee beard on his chin.

Nearer to where Sean stood, where the bar curved to the right, sat a couple of men who could have been the fathers of the emo kids. A big bloke in a green army fatigue jacket sitting on a bar stool, a wide face with not dissimilar features to the fearful Pat, although lit with a more approachable smile. Next to him, standing, a shorter man in a battered black leather jacket, KILLING JOKE painted onto the back of it. His short, spiky hair was defiantly dyed black, despite having receded to the middle of his crown.

They looked about the right age. Sean moved in their direction, passing them to hone in on a spot where he could subtly examine the opposite side of the pub too, noticing the sort of crutch he was all too familiar with, propped up beside the larger man's bar stool.

Sean leant against the counter. He hadn't seen any sign of a landlord, so far, but three men were talking by the side of the pool table that dominated this side of the pub, along with an old-fashioned jukebox, the sort that still played 7-inch singles. Sean turned his head and saw one of them break off his conversation, walk over and lift up the hatch, coming around the bar to greet him.

"Good evening, sir," he said. "What can I get you?"

The man looked to be in his early forties, a round, smiling face with brown eyes, crinkly ginger hair and sideburns, an old beige cardigan with leather buttons over a striped shirt. He spoke with a London accent.

"Pint of the Foster's, please," said Sean. He had already overdone it with the booze tonight but he could scarcely come into a place like this and ask for a mineral water.

"Right you are," the landlord's smile was as crinkly as his hair.

"That's an interesting jukebox you've got there," said Sean, taking his wallet out of his jacket pocket. As he spoke, Martha and the Vandellas replaced Bob Marley. "Jimmy Mack", one of his all-time favourites. "Good music and all," he added, as the landlord placed the pint down on the mat.

The man beamed. "Glad you think so. You could say it's a pub heirloom. Most of the stuff on that jukebox has been there twenty years. You a bit of a connoisseur then?"

"I was brought up on it," said Sean, handing over a fiver, antennae prickling. "You've not been here twenty years yourself, though?"

"On and off." He took the note. "Come here, went away, come back again. Ilford, Israel, Arizona, Ernemouth – maybe I should have that written over the door. You're from London, ain't you?"

"Ladbroke Grove, born and bred," said Sean, feeling prickles running up and down his legs, feeling eyes on him now.

The landlord handed Sean his change.

"Thanks," said Sean, "Mr ... ?" he realised he'd forgotten the name Francesca had told him, hadn't taken notice of the publican's sign above the door when he came in either. Not like him. He'd been too busy thinking about Captain Swing.

"Farman," said the landlord, offering his hand. "Marc Farman."

"Pleased to meet you," Sean shook.

"And you are?" the landlord asked.

"Sean Ward," he said, thinking: *Farman was here twenty years ago, how many of the rest of them were?* His eyes made a quick swoop around the pool table.

The two guys playing were old punks, the taller one still with a black Mohican that flopped sideways on his head, his shorter friend with a shaved head, a row of sleepers up one ear lobe. A couple of girls watched them, one small and dark, the other, much younger, with a bright pink barnet. To their right, on a different table, another biker type with a beard and granny glasses sat with a girl with long black hair, wearing a leopardskin coat.

Was Farman part of Corrine's gang, come back to reclaim his old roost? He picked up his pint, took a contemplative sip, as the landlord leant across the bar towards the guys who had originally caught his eye.

"Mr Ward here's interested in our jukebox," Farman said. "He's a man of taste. Mr Ward, these are some regulars of mine, Shaun and Bugs. They can remember when the thing was installed."

Shaun, the one with the crutch, offered his hand. It was big, thick and calloused, the hand of a manual labourer. "Had me first drink in here the summer of '81," he nodded confirmation. "What bring you round here then?"

"I work for the government," Sean improvised a line from a discussion he'd been half-listening to on the radio earlier. "Green industries. You know, wind farms, bio-fuels. I'm doing a sort of recce, seeing what's feasible."

"Oh," Shaun's thick black eyebrows shot up. "Green industries, we could do with a few more of them around here.

See this?" he motioned to the crutch. "Industrial accident. Local poultry producer," he tapped the side of his nose, "in the days before Health and Safety."

"You something to do with that wind farm," asked the one called Bugs, a more nasal voice, a more suspicious look on his face, "what they now put up over Scratby?"

"That's partly it," said Sean, "wind power, sea power, new crops that can be farmed for bio-fuels ... Area's ripe for redevelopment, isn't it?"

"Could say that," Bugs said into his pint. "Now all the oil's run out, people don't care too much about us no more."

"I just have to put in the research first, the geography, the chemistry of the soil," Sean warmed to his theme. "Then there's the planning for expansion, how much land would be available, how much work it could generate. Get a study written up for the department ..." He could see Bugs's face start to glaze over. "So really," he said, not untruthfully, "I'm just nosing around."

"Right," Shaun said, his smile deepening, "but what I meant was, what brought you here? To this pub? That in't the first one visitors normally come to ..."

"Oh," said Sean, "I just found it. They put me in The Ship Hotel, and I didn't care much for the music there."

"That's right," Bugs nodded.

"So I just took a walk, saw the sign for this pub and it lured me in. You got to admit, it's unusual. Who's Captain Swing?"

Farman leaned over his taps. "An old legend," he said. "'Bout two hundred years ago there was an uprising round here and he was the leader. The oiks against the toffs, you know." He chuckled. "That's why the pub's named after him, 'cos most people round here think that's what we are."

"He looks like Guy Fawkes," said Sean.

"Well," said Farman, "no one knows what he really looked like. I had a new sign painted when I come here, Bully done it," he nodded towards the punks at the pool table. "Owner before me changed the name to The Royal Oak and took the old sign away, put in big screen sport like every other half-arsed boozer round here, run it into the ground. We just wanted to make it like it was, didn't we? Only that old sign was a bit corny, so Bully done a better one."

"You see that little old bookshop next door when you come in?" asked Shaun. "Old Mr Farrer who run it, he could tell you more. Know all the local history, he do."

"Thanks," said Sean, "I might pay him a visit, then. Now, can I get you gents a drink?"

He passed another half an hour with them, letting them tell him about themselves. Shaun had retrained on the pay-off he got from his former employer, now made a living in IT. Bugs had been unemployed since the last oil rig was dismantled.

As he left by the side door, he nearly walked straight into the girl in the leopardskin coat who was talking on a mobile phone out there.

"Sorry," he said, putting out an arm to catch his balance on the wall. An almighty pain shot up his left leg, like an intravenous injection of molten lead.

"I better go," she said into her phone. "Yeah, see you tomorrow." Then she turned to him. "Are you all right?" *Something about her voice.* Sean tried to bite down on the agony, as he looked at her. Thick black hair cloaked her features and the street lighting was too dim to make out very much more.

"Yeah," he said, dredging up the ghost of a smile. "Old war wound. Plays me up in cold weather something chronic."

"Right," she said, putting her hand on his arm for the briefest of seconds. "Well, mind how you go." She moved past him and back through the door of the pub, but not before he had registered the strange tattoo on her hand, an eye staring out between her thumb and forefinger, like the ones Greek fishermen painted on their boats to ward off the evil eye. Only bright green instead of blue.

Another nutter down a dark alley, Sean thought, as he walked down to the quay.

10

This is Not a Love Song

"What does that thing mean," asked Samantha, "on Debbie's jacket?"

Corrine looked across the room, to where her neighbour was sitting in a huddle with Darren and Julian, the garment in question hung on the chair beside her, painted with a head and a star, the letters *M* and *R* on each side of it.

"I don't know," said Corrine, annoyed that Sam was still taking such an interest in Debbie. "Some band she like, I reckon."

"Must be a funny kind of band," considered Samantha.

"I know," said Corrine, "she get it all from Alex, the boy what live next door to her. He go to the art college and whatever he do, she have to copy."

Corrine blushed as the words left her tongue. She didn't know why she was being so nasty, or why she felt so jealous. How things had changed so much in the space of what was really only a few weeks.

After Sam's nan had shouted at her, she never expected to be allowed into the enchanted kingdom again. But the next day at school, Sam had brushed the entire incident off, told her she'd put the old girl straight. Corrine didn't have to worry, they could go back up the Leisure Beach again next weekend, bring Debbie along as well, if she liked. Granddad had *said*.

Feelings stirred in Corrine that she had never known before. Even the crush she had been nurturing on Julian was long since forgotten.

"What makes him so special?" Samantha asked.

Corrine snorted. "He's one of them weirdos," she said. "Like them pair," she glared at Darren and Julian, telling herself she was angry with Debbie for going off with them, convincing herself that it had been that way around. "Hanging round Swing's the whole while. Like that make them hard."

Julian stared back at her, a faint smile playing on his lips.

"Right," said Samantha, nodding thoughtfully.

Debbie looked up and her stomach lurched. Samantha Lamb was staring right at her, Corrine beside her, scowling. She hadn't realised that they had come in to the art room at last, but she might have expected it. It obviously wasn't enough for Lady Muck to walk off with her best friend; she must want something more, something that was hinted at by her attempts to mess up her posh hair, how she now wore her tie skinny with the top button undone like Debbie did. The way she kept on looking at her with those X-ray eyes, scanning every inch of her clothes, her hair, her bag . . .

Samantha tried to smile at her, so she quickly looked back down at the picture she and Darren had been working on. Tried to lose herself once more in the design for a fictional record cover for her favourite band that she had been so enjoying only moments before.

"I want to go there," said Samantha.

"You what?" said Corrine.

"To Swing's." Still looking at Debbie, Samantha smiled.

* * *

"You're the one who wants to be a beautician," said Samantha. "Go on, put it on."

Saturday afternoon in Sam's grandparents' bathroom. Corrine still didn't feel comfortable being there, even though the old girl was out with the rest of the blue rinses and Granddad was at work. She didn't trust that either of them wouldn't walk in at any moment and find out what they were up to.

Music blared across the landing from Sam's bedroom, one of the pile of records she had bought in Wolsey & Wolsey's that afternoon. It sounded like a racket to Corrine, but Sam had been delighted with it – it was by that band that Debbie liked. All Corrine could think was that they would never be able to hear the front door going over that dirge.

She opened the packet of hair dye with nervous fingers. Sam had been more than generous today, so she'd better do like she said. After the record shop, where she had bought Corrine the new Madonna 12-inch, they had been into Chelsea Girl. Sam had got herself an entire new outfit and treated Corrine to a pair of fishnet tights and some day-glo yellow socks. Then it had been off to Woolies for the hair dye and a pair of crimpers, just like the ones Debbie had.

"Where d'you get all the money from, Sam?" Corrine couldn't help but ask. By her estimation, her friend had got through thirty quid, at least, without breaking a sweat.

"Dad sent me a cheque," came the reply. "Must be feeling guilty."

The hair dye was permanent, labelled Raven Black. She'd better not fuck this up.

Corrine had just got the last of it on, making sure she had

the whole lot piled carefully on top of Sam's head, catching any last dribbles as they slid off the layer of Vaseline she had put around the hairline, when she had the sensation she was being watched.

She turned round slowly.

Two brown eyes stared back at her, Noodles' head cocked to one side as he studied what she was doing.

"Oh, my good God," Corrine breathed a sigh of relief, "you din't half give me a fright."

"Not again," Sam's eyes narrowed. "I told you he was a sneak. Trying to get us into trouble again are you, you dumb little mutt?" She rose to her feet.

"No!" said Corrine, suddenly scared. "Don't move, your hair . . ."

But Noodles had already bolted.

Sam sat back down, a weird smile playing on her lips.

* * *

Edna didn't get back until gone six. She had tried to enjoy herself with Shirl and the girls, doing their usual rounds in Norwich. But when it came to the part that she normally relished, the cream tea on Elm Hill, Edna found she had lost her appetite.

"What is it?" Shirl had asked, frowning at the barely touched scone on Edna's plate.

Edna had looked back with watery eyes. "It's Sammy," she confessed. "We had a row . . ."

It had been a relief to finally say it, to hear the clucking of sympathy from the others as she dabbed at her eyes with a hanky. How she mustn't blame herself — teenagers were always difficult and the upheaval Sammy had been through was bound to affect her. How their granddaughters often came home with unsuitable friends, but it was better to let them get it out of their system and find out for themselves. If Edna tried to ban Sammy from seeing this Corrine it would only make them stick together more. Anyway, this punk thing was a phase a lot of them went through, they'd all seen it.

"Think of it this way," Shirl had said. "At least she's not having to grow up in the middle of a war like we did. The worst thing what can happen is her having a silly haircut. It's not like a doodlebug's going to drop on her head."

Reflecting on the terrors of her own teenage years had at least put Edna's worries into some kind of perspective. But returning to a house shrouded in darkness, a thin claw of fear started to stroke her insides the moment she turned the key in the lock.

"Hello?" she called into the hallway, turning the light on.

There was something wrong. The house was never this silent, this still. Normally Noodles came bounding out of his basket to meet her the second her feet were over the threshold.

"Noodles?" she called. The hall started back at her, the pendulum of the grandmother clock slowly swinging on the wall the only sound.

Edna went into the kitchen, turned on the lights and deposited her day's purchases on the table. He wasn't in his basket. The claw snagged deeper into Edna's gut.

"Noodles?" She went back into the hallway, into the lounge and the dining room, turning on all the lights, looking underneath the sofa and the chairs. It took her a while to register the alien smell in the air. Back in the hall, the source of the acrid aroma finally sunk in. "Hair dye," she said aloud, stomping up the stairs.

The harsh glare of the bathroom light threw into stark relief a sight that made Edna almost sink to her knees. Across the black and white lino of the floor, dribbled onto the avocado bath and toilet mats and over a pile of once-fluffy white towels, now scrunched up and thrown hastily into the bath, were broad smears of black and purple. Flecks of it sprayed over the white enamel of the sink, splashed across the mirrors, the shower handle turned the colour of a freshly minted bruise and as for the bath itself . . .

"Sammy!" shrieked Edna. She tried to summon a mental picture of her granddaughter, but all she could see was Amanda's face, her eighteen-year-old face, laughing at her.

"Sammy!" she staggered onto the landing, throwing open the miscreant's door, finding nothing but a pile of discarded clothes and magazines, the low hum of a record player that had been left on.

As she bent down to turn it off, she heard a plaintive whimper.

"Noodles?" The red fog dispersed as the sound pierced Edna's heart.

He came crawling towards her from where he had been cowering under the bed, crawling on his belly.

"Oh, my God," Edna whispered, taking him into her arms. "Oh, my baby . . ." her eyes widening in shock.

Noodles, shorn of his beautiful blond locks, the fur hacked away, only a skinny, shivering, shaking rat where a luxuriant dog had once been. Just one tiny tuft of fur left between his ears, a splodge of black dye around it. One of his eyes turned purple.

Edna rocked him in her arms as the tears poured down her face.

* * *

Market Row was all that was left of the narrow passageways that once encircled Ernemouth market square like strands of a cobweb, houses built so close that their half-timbered upper stories almost touched. Debbie's grandma had often told her about when she was courting her granddad, they used to sit on the windowsills of their opposing houses and hold hands across the street. Grandma's Row had been levelled by the Lüftwaffe forty years ago, as they dropped surplus bombs on the last town on the radar before roaring back over the North Sea to Germany. But Debbie thought of it now, as Darren slipped his fingers between hers and she smiled up at him.

They'd had a good day today. Been up Norwich, bought a load of records in Backs and seen a really cool pair of Robot boots in the shop at the bottom of Elm Hill that Debbie was determined to save up for. Had chips on the Haymarket and half a cider in The Murderers before they caught the train home.

Back at Darren's, his parents were out so they could play their new records as loud as they wanted while Darren heated frozen pizzas for their tea. A song about lullabies from heaven rolling through Debbie's mind now, like a big wheel spinning in the night sky.

They hadn't intended to stop by Swing's that evening. Darren was just going to walk her home, maybe come in for a coffee and listen to records some more. But as they approached the big, white building along the back of Palmers' car park, the orange glow of the windows seemed to exert a siren-like pull on both of them. Darren fished into his pocket. "Hmmm," he said, extracting some silver. "I've got about a quid left here. D'you want to go in just for one?"

Debbie knew she had only coppers left in her own purse, but

the call was strong in her too. Besides, if they spent an hour in Swing's, she could still get home at a reasonable enough hour and it would prolong the time they had together.

"Yeah," she said, "why not? If Al's about, he might get us another."

"Great." Darren beamed and lent down to peck her cheek.

The front door of Swing's opened to the sound of Bob & Marcia's "Young, Gifted and Black", a favourite of the landlady, Jane. The place was packed. The first person Debbie recognised was Bully, leaning at the bar, his Mohican coloured black down one side and pink down the other. He had on ripped jeans and baseball boots, a Clash T-shirt under a black shirt with zips down the side of it. Rows of silver rings down his earlobes and one in his hooked nose, giving off a fearsome front that was far removed from his real personality. Bully was laughing with Jane as he grappled his fingers around three pints.

"Debs!" He put them back down when he saw her, clocking her Backs bag. "Been up Norwich, have ya? All right, mate?" he nodded at Darren, not knowing his name.

"Yeah, we have," said Debbie. "This is Darren."

Darren swelled with pride as Ernemouth's hardest punk offered his hand and bought them both a drink. Looking over Bully's shoulder he could see Alex and Kris at the far corner table, with Kris's girlfriend Lynn, Shaun and Bugs and a couple of others.

"Come on then," Bully gathered his round and led the way.

They were virtually on top of them before Debbie realised who it was sitting with Alex. First, she noticed Corrine, sitting slightly apart with her arms folded, looking at the floor, not joining in. Only it took her a moment to recognise her. She'd gone and dyed her hair a strange burgundy colour, steamed all the perm out with a pair of crimpers and made a half-hearted attempt at backcombing it, so that half of it stood up at the back of her head and the rest flopped down over her eyes.

"Reenie?" Debbie enquired. Corrine looked up, startled. For a second they stared at each other, both experiencing a rush of guilt that came from neither expecting nor wanting the other to be there.

"Debs," Corrine spoke in a whisper, a spark of fear dancing in her eyes.

Debbie frowned. "What . . ." she began. Then she followed Corrine's gaze across the table.

There was a girl sitting next to Alex, his left arm casually draped around her shoulder. A girl with crimped black hair falling over her face, wearing the exact outfit that Debbie had bought the last time she and Corrine had been in Chelsea Girl – a black mohair jumper and a red tartan miniskirt, thick black tights and a pair of buckled winklepicker shoes. They were locked in conversation, their bodies leant into each other.

"Who . . . ?" Debbie felt Darren nudge her in the ribs.

"I don't believe it," he whispered.

The girl's head slowly turned and she brushed her fringe out of her eyes so that Debbie could clearly see the arched eyebrow, the crooked smile, the eyes that danced with triumph in their unfamiliar new setting.

"Neither do I," Debbie put her drink down on the table before it slid out of her hand.

"Oh, hello, Debs," said Samantha.

Part Two

* * *

SOME GIRLS WANDER BY MISTAKE

11

Stations of the Crass

May Day 2000: ducking through the blue line that circled the stone lions in Trafalgar Square with a camera in his hand. Trying to focus on a single face through the smoke and screaming, the writhing mass of bodies, the clash of horseshoes on concrete and the tattoo of truncheons on riot shields. Zooming in on something bright white in the thick of the crowd, a plastic mask with a twirly moustache above the deep slash of a grin. A face that changed before his eyes into that of a teenage girl, with her head shaved and her face all covered in soot. Pleading with him through her eyes as the shapes changed around her, became a hand holding a bottle with a rag stuffed down the neck, the flame from a Zippo igniting it in a tremendous *whoosh* ... and suddenly he was standing in the middle of cornfields that stretched as far as the eye could see. The flat fields under a blue sky and the crops burning out of control, thick black smoke pluming out of them, a wall of flame roaring towards him. A figure rising up out of the smoke, taking on human form ...

Sean awoke sweating, the dream still vivid in his head and ringing in his ears as his eyes opened on brightly patterned curtains in an unfamiliar room.

* * *

Francesca let the dogs out of the back door, watched them streak ahead up the garden to the gate. In the last minutes before dawn, the world looked as if it had been painted deep blue. The air was still and cold, the only sound the distant rumble of a lorry going across Brydon Bridge, the structure she still thought of as 'new' nearly two decades since she'd watched it go up.

But as last night had proved to her, the past is only ever a breath away.

The dogs jumped around her as she opened the gate with gloved hands, whining to be loose in the marshes, their favourite place. Francesca's too. This ritual she had made for herself, greeting the dawn from up on the old marsh wall each day, had helped to keep her sane these past three years.

Francesca had never dreamt she would ever come back to Ernemouth. But by the time the vacancy on the *Mercury* had made up her mind for her, her mother had only six months left – and she could never have left her dad to face the enormity of that alone. Instead, she did as her mum would have, put her back into the task ahead, shutting off her own petty wants and needs in the process. Never giving into them since.

Until last night.

The dogs stopped on the top of the bank and wheeled around to wait for her, lean black bodies silhouetted against the first pale fingers of pink in the sky. Every morning when she reached this place, Francesca saw the landscape anew. To the east, the sun rising above the town, waking the stones, painting the bricks from grey to red and then spreading its colours into the west, where the convergence of three rivers filled the horizon with water as far as the eye could see. Every day it was different, as the seasons slowly turned, connecting her to this earth, these low wetlands she had so despised as a child, now a place of succour and solace.

A skein of pink-legged geese flew overhead, filling the air with their honking.

Until she had taken that first telephone call from Sean Ward, Francesca had wondered if her ambition had died here, on the edge of the Broads, at the end of the world. Now she felt like she had woken from a long, dreamless slumber with the answer to why she had stayed. That somehow, somewhere deep inside, she must have known that all those things left so long undone couldn't lie still in the ground forever.

Now, with sad eyes and a shuffling gait, a man had come to kick over the headstones, raise the dead to tell their tales.

And she was here to make sure he did it right.

*　*　*

Dale Smollet stole out of the bedroom on tiptoe, holding his breath. In the guest bathroom he took a long look at himself in the mirror while he cleaned his teeth and wet shaved, examining the set of his jaw and the fine lines around his eyes, fussing his neatly cut and highlighted hair into shape with some wax and daubing himself with cologne.

Dale liked to think he still looked pretty sharp for thirty-six. He slapped his hand against a stomach kept rock hard by regular trips to the gym and an iron self-control that kept him from giving into canteen food or late-night indulgence in takeaways, unlike so many of his colleagues. Satisfied with his appearance, he crept into the guest room, where he always kept plenty of spare clothes for the times he was working anti-social hours and didn't want to disturb his wife.

Dale dressed rapidly, putting his mobile on top of the bed so that if it vibrated it would do so without making a noise. Crisp, pressed yellow shirt and grey, narrow leg trousers. A pale grey cashmere V-neck over the top. Not so very different from how he dressed as a teenager – or how he aspired to back then. Just better materials, a more expensive cut. Dale could afford to maintain his lifetime love affair with Italian clothes. Despite his long and devoted marriage, there had been no children.

He trod lightly down the stairs to the kitchen, his ears straining for the slightest sound, his palm moist against the metal of his phone.

Dale had been a policeman for the past fifteen years, had risen up through the ranks from constable to detective chief inspector. Not many things scared him. One of the few that did was already waiting outside his back door, a big, brown shape outlined against the frosted glass as he turned on the light, like a grizzly bear was leaning there. What it really was, was a sheepskin coat and a head of thick, slicked-back hair under a black felt trilby hat with a feather in the side of it. Smoke rising up from a panatella cigar, held in a paw-sized hand. Turning slowly as he heard the key unlocking the door.

"Len," said Dale.

The former boss of Ernemouth CID looked back through heavily lidded eyes and said nothing, just motioned his head to indicate that Dale should step outside. It wasn't until they had walked through the inky darkness of the garden, clicked the gate behind them and stepped out onto the lamp-lit pavement that the older man finally spoke.

"We got a spot of bother," he said.

* * *

The flame from the final candle lit the parchment at 6.36 a.m., filling the already heady air with the smells of musk, lilac, lavender and cloves. For a few seconds the flames leapt as the oils around the parchment ignited, then the paper rapidly crumbled as it was consumed, the light guttering out four hours precisely since the new moon had begun to wax.

A hand reached down to lift the dish that contained the ashes of the spell. Tattooed between the thumb and forefinger was a bright green eye.

Four minutes later, as the golden rim of the sun appeared above the blue horizon, the hand threw the ashes up into the sky, while the waves whooshed and hissed against the shore. Black paper petals falling slowly, like rain.

* * *

The sign on the front door said OPEN, so Sean pushed and stepped inside, a tinkling bell above his head announcing his arrival. Farrer's Book Shop was one of a kind you rarely saw any more in London. A big old emporium, lined from wall to wall and from floor to ceiling with solid oak bookcases, several more running across the width of the room. Each one was crammed full of titles old and new, paperback and hardback, spines made of leather with their titles tooled in gold leaf, brand new spines of shiny card and battered, broken old ones held together by sellotape, the collective whole giving off the slightly dusty, musky aroma that surrounds the printed word.

The shelf directly in front of Sean was labelled: LOCAL INTEREST. A couple of books had been placed face outwards to attract the eye. *Ghosts of the Broads* – a cowl-wearing skull transposed over a twilit stretch of water. *Unquiet Country* – the grimy face of a farm worker staring accusingly at the camera from another century, a face that flashbacked the nightmare that had curtailed Sean's attempts at sleep four hours earlier.

"Good morning, sir."

The voice was quiet, slightly sibilant and came up beside Sean's right-hand side on feet that trod so softly that he nearly jumped upon hearing it.

A little old man was standing there, looking up at him with bright blue eyes, a fragile wisp of white hair atop an egg-shaped head, a pair of half-rim spectacles on a cord around his neck and a smile that seemed almost beatific in its benevolence.

"Is there anything I can help you with?"

"Hello," said Sean, smiling back at him. "I hope so. Local interest is what I'm after and I hear you're a bit of an expert, Mr Farrer."

The old man laced his fingers across his chest. "Well, I wouldn't go that far," he said. "An amateur historian at best. But I do have the advantage of having been around an awful lot longer than most people, I suppose." He chuckled. "And I remain curious. Is there any specific area towards which your interest leans? History? Geography? Folklore, perhaps?" He nodded at *Ghosts of the Broads*. "I've always been rather fond of that one."

"Well, what I'd like to know," Sean said, "is more about Captain Swing. I saw the sign over the pub next door yesterday and it's not a name I've ever come across before, so I went in and had a word with the landlord. He didn't know all that much, but there was a fella in there tipped me off to come and see you."

"Ah," the old man's face radiated pleasure. He had very smooth, very pink skin for a man of advanced years. "The good Captain. That pub has borne the name for at least a century, you know." Farrer's fingers rippled across his chest. "He led an uprising here, a rural equivalent of the Luddites, if you like. In the 1820s, when the threshing machine was first invented and threatened to do all the labourers out of a job. When Swing first rose in 1830, there'd been two bad summers already, crops had failed from too much rain and people were fairly destitute."

Farrer's blue eyes stared past Sean's, as if he was seeing back through time. "But the Captain took their despair and turned it into anger," he continued. "He banded them together against their oppressors, organised guerrilla attacks, smashing the new machinery and burning the fields, then dissolving away before anyone could catch them."

Sean felt himself start to sweat under the collar as Farrer's voice became louder. "The name of Swing spread like wild-fire across sixteen counties, as far away as Kent and Dorset, Huntingdonshire and Gloucestershire. Coming so close to the French Revolution, it put fear of God through the gentry."

"You almost sound like you were there," said Sean.

Farrer's eyes came back to Sean's with a twinkle. "Thank you," he said. "But let me tell you the most remarkable thing of all about Captain Swing. He never actually existed."

His right hand fluttered down to the shelf, picked up the book called *Unquiet Country*. "Here," he said. "This will tell you all about it."

"Thanks," said Sean. "I'll take it."

"Good, good," the shopkeeper looked delighted. "Now, is there anything else?"

"This'll do for now," said Sean. "Thank you."

The old man nodded, and putting on a deft show of speed, led the way to his till. Sean waited until he was handing the money over to attempt to claw back an advantage.

"You said that pub had been called Swing's for over a hundred years," he said.

"Indeed," Farrer took the ten-pound note from him, put it in his till.

"But the landlord told me it was renamed The Royal Oak for a while. Back in the '80s, I think. Now, why would that have been?"

Farrer's nose twitched as he handed Sean back a penny change. "Well now," he said, voice descending back to a whisper. "I don't know how much you do know about our local history, but I'm guessing this is your first visit to Ernemouth?"

"That's right." Sean pocketed the penny.

"There was some trouble here, back then. Specifically relating to that pub and the people who drank there. There was a very grisly murder, and then . . ." Farrer looked across to the door, "a witch-hunt."

Sean pretended to look puzzled. "Are you talking about the 1980s?" he said, "or the 1880s?"

But the bell tinkled and the door opened before the old man could reply; another customer sweeping into the shop appeared to distract him.

"Oh, hello, my dear," Farrer said, the beatific smile returning to illuminate his unlined countenance. Then he looked back at Sean. "I'm sorry, sir, would you excuse me? I have a customer just arriving who needs to take possession of a specific delivery."

"Not at all," said Sean, trying not to grind his teeth. He turned to see the object of Farrer's attention.

There she stood, in her leopardskin coat, long black fringe still obscuring half her face, even in broad daylight.

"But do come back," he heard Farrer say, "any time."

Again, Sean found himself having to fight his own imagination, having to strain not to give in to the notion that here was Corrine Woodrow, in her 1980s incarnation, standing right in front of him. But as he got closer, he could see that the eyes peering out from under the fringe were green. Corrine's, he assured himself, were brown.

The girl said something to him, but he couldn't make out the words.

Sean blinked. "What's that?" he said. *Something about her voice . . .*

"I said, are you feeling better now? The old war wound, remember?"

Sean forced himself to smile, his stomach starting to churn. Pinpricks going up his legs. "Of course," he said. "I'm fine, thank you. I'll, er . . ." he reached for the doorhandle and she stepped to the side of him. "I'll be on my way."

"Be seeing you," she said, as he closed the door behind him.

Sean hurried away, back down the cut to the quay. Yesterday's clouds had parted on a pale blue sky, the sun glittering off windowpanes but not offering much in the way of heat. Seagulls whirled overhead, screeching to each other and the smell of the river filled his nostrils. It was just a normal new day in a normal old town. The pain in his legs subsided as he felt his heartbeat returning to a normal rate.

"Get a grip," he said to himself. He thought of Francesca's cuttings lying on his bed. "And get back to the paperwork."

He had two more hours to kill before his meet with Rivett.

12

Notice Me

October 1983

"This is your room," said Amanda, pushing open the door. "What do you think?"

It was right at the top of the house, looking out over rooftops, chimneys and the iron and glass ceiling of the Victoria arcade. Amanda had decorated it in grey, black and red striped wallpaper, matching duvet set, black lacquer furniture and red vinyl cushions. Not that she expected to see any gratitude in her daughter's sullen countenance.

"Oh," said Samantha, top lip curling. She did her best to maintain the bored expression, but Amanda detected a rapid widening of the pupils indicating disbelief that her terrible mother could have fashioned a room for her so well.

A smile twitched on Amanda's lips but she suppressed it. She supposed Sam thought she was the original rebellious teenager and she had certainly succeeded in shocking her grandparents. Although, of course, Edna had refused to believe Sam could have been capable of instigating any of it herself, had placed the blame squarely on the influence of her dim little school friend – and, by implication, on Amanda herself, for sending her daughter to such a low place of learning as Ernemouth High.

Amanda had known her parents would be angry when she didn't send Sammy to the local public school and Eric had been straight on the phone to Malcolm, expecting him to intervene. But Malcolm was drunk and started crying, admitting that he didn't have the money, he'd just put the house in Chelsea on the market in a last-ditch attempt to keep his business afloat. Things were much worse than Eric and Edna had dared to imagine.

Amanda stuck to her guns when Eric offered to pay the school fees, said that it would be better for her daughter to mix with the local kids, reminded her parents that it had never done her any harm. She knew Sam better than they did, knew that there were worse influences her daughter could come under in that seafront villa. It was time she had the spoilt little madam back under her watchful eye.

Samantha's gaze travelled across the floor to a new stack hi-fi system. She flicked a glance up at her mother as she moved towards it, as if weighing up the wisdom of what to say next. "Thanks," eventually emerged.

Amanda raised one eyebrow. "You should find you get plenty of light in here as well," she said, "if you want to take up painting something other than Nana's dog."

Samantha looked up sharply and Amanda caught it again, the widening of the pupils, along with a flash of colour rising to her daughter's pancaked cheeks. She held her gaze, daring Sam to deny it as she had done so vehemently when they were in front of the others. It was rarely so easy for her once they were alone.

Samantha blinked, then turned back to the hi-fi. She lifted the lid on the record player, pretended to study the turntable, running her fingers across the dials.

The silence that stretched between them was broken by the sounds of feet on stairs. With a grunt, Wayne appeared at the doorway, hefting a box of Samantha's belongings. "Where should I put this?" he said.

"Samantha?" Amanda continued to bore into her daughter with her eyes.

"Just down there," Samantha nodded towards the side of the bed without looking up, her face now a darker shade of red than her foundation could conceal.

"Thank you," Amanda added in her most caustic tone.

"Thanks," Samantha uttered, barely audibly.

"Right, well, we'll leave you to sort it out yourself, get it how you want it," Amanda's gaze caught Wayne's eye as he carefully deposited the box down, and gave him a wink. "We'll give you a shout when dinner's ready."

"What about the rest?" asked Wayne. There were six more boxes in the hall.

"Sam can fetch them," said Amanda, "when she's ready. I'm sure she'll manage." She started off back down the stairs and Wayne made to join her.

"Oh, Way-e-ane," Samantha said softly, mocking her mother's voice the moment she was out of earshot. He jerked his head round. The girl was coiling a strand of hair around her finger, sticking her rapidly developing chest out as far as it would go. Not for the first time, he felt profoundly uncomfortable in her presence.

"Thanks, Way-e-ane," she continued, top lip rising up into a sneer. "Now go on, boy, follow your mistress. Heel!"

A vision of the scalped pooch danced before Wayne's eyes as he hurried after Amanda.

In the kitchen, Amanda was opening the fridge. She put a

bottle of Riesling and a can of Foster's down on the counter, reached into the cupboard above for some glasses.

"I think we've earned this," she said, handing Wayne his beer and sloshing out a good slug of wine for herself. "Cheers."

Wayne didn't bother to pour his out. He clinked her green glass goblet with his tin and took a long, grateful guzzle. "Thanks, darling," Amanda put her hand on his shoulder and gave him a squeeze, remembering her mother's face after Wayne had redecorated her bathroom for her, the twitching cheek and the blinking eyes when she had been forced to thank him. "You've done a lot for me and I'm really grateful."

Wayne put his arm around her waist. "I told you, babe. Anything for you."

"Ahhh," she reached up to kiss him. At the same moment, a muffled, thudding bass sound announced that Samantha had worked out how to use her new record player. Amanda rolled her eyes. "Well," she said, "I did warn you it wouldn't be easy."

Wayne stared into his lover's eyes. "She did it, didn't she? The dog . . ."

Amanda swallowed a mouthful of wine. "Yeah," she said, nodding. "I reckon she did."

A succession of images flashed through her mind. The shiny, rigid bodies of four little goldfish, lying on the carpet. A canary, feet in the air at the bottom of his cage, neck broken. A pair of terrapins with their heads wedged upside down between two rocks in their tank. Despite Samantha's wide-eyed denials that she had anything to do with it, her attempts to shift the blame onto the cleaning lady each time, Amanda had never dared buy her daughter any animals again.

The High Mistress of St Paul's calling her and Malcolm into her study, telling them about the girl found tied up with a skipping rope and locked in a broom cupboard. Explaining how, though she had no concrete proof, she knew who the ringleader was and if such incidents continued, she would be forced to take drastic measures. Well, that had been one embarrassment spared by their move back here. Amanda had been certain that the shock of going to Ernemouth High – where, if her own experiences were anything to go by, the kids were much more able to take care of themselves than those doe-eyed princesses in public school – might have knocked some sense into her daughter. That she would blanch at the prospect of picking on anyone her own size. But, it seemed Sam had found someone smaller almost immediately.

"Not that Mum will ever believe it," she said. "She couldn't let herself. It would send her mad if she did." Malcolm had never wanted to hear it either, had gone on firing cleaners until Amanda had put her foot down, pointed out the unlikely odds that they had hired three pet murderers in a row. And the hell he had given her for daring to think such things . . .

"What about your dad?" Wayne said.

"He recognises his own kind," a sliver of ice came into her voice. "He'd let her get away with murder, he would. No," she squeezed Wayne's shoulder again, forced a smile back onto her face. "The best thing you can do with her moods and her constant provocation is to ignore it. Don't give her the attention. She's not so bloody special as she thinks she is."

"She's not anything like you," said Wayne, and the look in his eyes brought a lump to Amanda's throat.

"Well," she said, "in one respect, I hope she is."

Wayne frowned. "And what's that?"

"That in two years' time – or maybe even less, if we're lucky – she'll be out that door and never come back."

Before Wayne could reply, the telephone in the hall started ringing. Almost simultaneously, footsteps clattered down the stairs.

"I'll get it!" yelled Samantha.

"She's expecting someone," Amanda's voice dropped to a whisper. "Let her."

She waited until she heard her daughter answer. Then she went to the kitchen door and pretended to close it, just leaving it a fraction ajar so she could listen in.

Wayne crumpled the empty can in his hand and tossed it into the bin. Shaking his head, he went to the fridge and found another.

* * *

"I've come to say," Corrine stood on Debbie's doorstep, barely able to look her friend in the eye, lips twisting the way they always did before she started crying, "I'm sorry."

Debbie hadn't seen Corrine for a week, not since she had bolted out of Swing's moments after she and Darren arrived. She hadn't been to school and it didn't look like she had been home either. She still appeared to be wearing the same outfit, although someone had obviously tried to help her with the mess she'd made of her hair.

Unlike her clothes, it was freshly washed, hanging around her ears in a dull shade of burgundy, ragged around the edges. She was twisting the handles of a plastic shopping bag in one hand, the end of a cigarette almost burning the fingers of the other.

"Please say you forgive me," she whimpered, as the first tears started to make black kohl tracks down her cheeks.

"Forgive you for what?" said Debbie. So shocked was she

by the pitiful state of her friend that the injustices of the last few weeks were almost blotted from her mind. Almost, but not quite. She wanted to hear Corrine say it.

"For going off with Sam," Corrine choked out, "and for taking her in Swing's."

"I see," said Debbie, leaning against the doorframe but still not opening up completely.

"I din't want to," Corrine's eyes were pleading and her nose had started to run, "but she made me. You gotta believe me, Debs, I din't realise what she was like, until . . ."

But she couldn't get the words out. Instead, she convulsed with tears, throwing her cigarette to the ground and stamping on it, wishing she could crush out the memory of that poor little dog.

"All right," said Debbie, "you better come in."

"Who is it, love?" called her mum from the kitchen.

"All right, Mum, s'only Reenie," Debbie replied. "Go on up," she told Corrine, "and I'll make us a cup of tea. Won't be a sec."

Corrine did as she was told. Debbie needed to head her mother off before she could say anything. Thankfully, her dad had already started his evening shift cabbing.

In the kitchen, Maureen Carver wiped her hands on a towel. She'd been baking and her pinny was covered in flour, her face flushed and hair frizzy from the heat. The concern on her face was down to the fact that her daughter had already told her that Corrine had skipped school all week. That's all Debbie had said, but it was obvious there must have been a bust up between them. She had never seen her daughter so moody.

Not that Maureen had ever been comfortable with this friendship. Of course she felt sorry for Corrine – what decent person wouldn't, the kid hardly had a chance in life with a mother like that. She had let her daughter bring her new friend over and never begrudged feeding her – so long as, in return, Debbie swore she would never even think of setting foot through Corrine's front door.

Maureen was afraid that Corrine would end up following her mother's way of life – and what if Debbie somehow got herself embroiled in any of that? She had been so relieved that the girls seemed to have been drifting apart of late and that Debbie had found herself such a nice young man as Darren Moorcock.

"Mum," said Debbie softly, closing the door behind her. "I don't know what's happened but she's in a right state. Please don't say anything about school until I know what it is."

"All right," Maureen conceded. "Do you think she'll be staying for tea, then?"

"Probably," nodded Debbie, and her heart felt heavy as she said it. Maureen wasn't the only one who'd felt Corrine's absence as a burden being lifted. Only Debbie felt guilty for thinking that way. "Is it OK if I take some tea and biscuits, try and calm her down?"

"Course it is, love," Maureen nodded to her freshly baked ginger snaps cooling on the rack. "Help yourself."

Corrine was sitting on Debbie's bed, staring out the window. A teardrop had run to the bottom of her nose and was hanging there, over her lips. She had a book on her lap but as soon as Debbie came in, she snapped out of her reverie and thrust it back into the shopping bag that sat beside her.

"Here," said Debbie, putting the tray down and passing Corrine a cup of tea and a plate piled high with biscuits. She took her own drink and sat on the other end of the bed, waiting for

Corrine to work her way through the food, which she did with the speed of a velociraptor. Only when she realised she had an empty plate in front of her did she stop to say: "Ooh, my God, I'm sorry – did you want one? I was so starvin' I din't think."

Debbie shook her head. "What's happened, Reenie?" she asked instead. "Why in't you been in school all week?"

"I was scared," said Corrine, and that same look came back in her eye that Debbie had seen in Swing's. "It's Sam, she in't normal. That weren't me she wanted, I see that now. She just used me so she could be more like you."

Debbie's heart beat faster. "What do you mean? The hair and that?"

Corrine nodded miserably. "She made me do it for her. And then she . . ." Her face scrunched up again, her shoulders started to shake.

"What happened, Reenie?" said Debbie. "What did she do?"

But Corrine waved her hand. "I can't . . ."

"It's OK," Debbie dared to lean across and put her hand on Corrine's arm. For once, her friend didn't flinch from human contact. Debbie tried another tack.

"Where you been, anyway?" she said. "You in't been home, have you?"

"No," said Corrine, wiping her nose on her sleeve. Debbie reached for the box of tissues on her dressing table and handed them over. Corrine blew her nose loudly. "I've been at Noj's."

Debbie frowned. "Who?"

"Noj," her friend replied. "You don't know him. I met him up the Front."

Debbie had never even heard this strange name before and it worried her almost as much as whatever it was Samantha Lamb had done to Corrine.

"It's all right," Corrine looked at her earnestly. "It's safe. His old man's gone on the rigs and when he do, his mum go off round her fancy man's, leave him on his own. He look after me all right. Better'n round my house, any road." Corrine shivered.

"Did she do this?" Debbie lifted a strand of Corrine's hair. It looked as though all the bits that had bleach on them had snapped in half. Corrine nodded.

"She said she knew what she was doin'. Maybe she did," her eyes flashed with sudden anger, "if she wanted to make me look like a twat."

"What are you going to do?" said Debbie, almost as much to herself as to Corrine.

"Go to the hairdresser's, I s'pose." Corrine shrugged. "Get it all cut off and start again."

"No, I mean . . ." Debbie began, but then thought better. "Have you got any money?" she said instead, feeling that weight coming down again as she did so, that pair of Robot boots staying in the shop in Norwich for another month.

"No," said Corrine, and her face hardened, her eyes lost their focus on Debbie's, stared past her instead out the window, at the streetlights blinking on.

"I could help you," she heard Debbie say. "I've got a few quid saved up . . ."

Corrine shook her head. "No, Debs," she said. "You done enough for me letting me in just now. I don't want no more from you. Anyway, I reckon I should be goin' . . ."

"No, don't," said Debbie, "Mum said you could stay for tea . . ."

But Corrine had got to her feet, her bag in her hand. "I can't. There's something I now gotta do. I just wanted to make sure we're still friends. We are, in't we?"

Debbie nodded. For a brief second, Corrine took her hand and squeezed it. "Don't worry about me, though, honest," she said. "Noj's old man's away for another week, at least."

"In't you coming back to school?" was all Debbie could find to say.

"Not," Corrine pushed her hair back off her face, "'til I've sorted this shit out." She forced a laugh. "Tell you what, though, one thing you could do," she said, her face becoming serious again. "Don't tell no one. Especially," she scowled, "not *her*."

✳ ✳ ✳

Debbie sat on her bed in a daze after Corrine had left. She didn't want to think what else that girl could have done to Corrine that was worse than the mess she'd made of her hair. What was so bad that Corrine couldn't even speak of it?

As she stared through the window to the house next door, she saw the light go off in Alex's room. A few seconds later he came out of the door, smiling to himself, fussing with the front of his hair. He strode swiftly up the road, heading north, up town.

✳ ✳ ✳

Corrine's spirits lifted as she left Debbie's house. She was so pleased that things were all right between them again that it had suddenly given her a whole new sense of purpose. She had worked it all out as she was saying it – but it was so obvious. The only bad part would be getting the money. But she had learned the ways to deal with that now.

She kept to the back streets until she got to St Peter's Road, where she turned right towards the seafront and Trafalgar Pier.

The beer garden had reverted to its winter life as the roller-skating rink, but Corrine didn't join the line of teenagers queuing up to get in. Instead she ducked into the shadows along the side of the pavilion, the distorted sound of "Thriller" pumping through the walls, and along to the end of the pier, where all the sounds dissolved into a background thrum and the sea made its own music as the waves hissed over the stones.

Corrine stared out at the lights of the distant oil rigs. There were so many of them now, all across the horizon. She had counted twelve before she sensed the man standing beside her, the familiar musk of cheap aftershave announcing his presence. It was exactly as she had anticipated and it meant she would soon have the money to sort out her hair.

Only what came next was not part of her plans.

She hunkered down on the cold, soft sand, under the dark criss-crosses of the beams that held up the pier. The man grunted, his hands on his zip, shuffled towards her.

"Excuse me, sir," came a voice from beside her. "But would you mind explaining exactly what it is that you're doing?"

Corrine realised what it was before the john did. But even as she made to scramble to her feet and take flight, a flashlight dazzled her eyes and a hand came down on her shoulder.

"You as well, miss," said the policeman.

13

Persons Unknown

March 2003

Sean drove down a seafront lined by pensioners defying the chill of a March morning, huddled onto every bench like a flock of weather-beaten grey birds. To his left, white peaks of choppy waves hurried along the sullen strip of dark blue sea and a lone dog chased a scent along the shoreline. To his right, a succession of amusement arcades flashed their lights and shrilled their wares. A grand old Victorian hotel sat at the end of the Golden Mile, painted puritan white against the lurid glare of its companions, shielded by a landscaped front garden, a pomander to the pestilence of the tourist tat. Sean slowed down as it came into view. His destination lay on the next corner, another impressive piece of nineteenth-century architecture, a grey flint and cream-stuccoed mansion with a portico entrance. Len Rivett's "office": the Masonic Lodge.

As he pulled into the car park, he saw a man standing in front of the door in a sheepskin coat and a black trilby with a feather in the side of it, smoking a thin cigar. He recognised the face at once from Francesca's clippings. It hadn't changed much.

As Sean got out of the car, Rivett smiled and raised a hand in greeting, his eyes hidden beneath the brim of his hat.

"Mr Ward," he said, dropping the butt of his cigar onto the gravel and putting a grey slip-on shoe down on top of it. "Welcome to sunny Ernemouth. Len Rivett at your service."

Sean took Rivett's outstretched hand, big, blunt fingers adorned with gold rings, wondering if he was about to test his nerve with a bone-crushing shake. But the former DCI's grip was as friendly as his smile.

"Hello, sir," Sean said. "Thanks for taking the time to see me."

"Not at all," said Rivett. "You got here all right, then. Take my tip about the hotel and all?"

"I did, thanks," said Sean. "It's very nice."

Rivett nodded. "Better than the ones along here," he said, indicating the towering confection Sean had just driven past. "They all look nice out the front," he winked, "but inside, they're crawling with cockroaches. Anyway," he put his hand down on Sean's shoulder and ushered him through the front door, "allow me to give you the tour."

* * *

"I heard a lot about you," Rivett spoke over the top of his menu. "You're a brave man."

Sean looked up from a carvery list that was as frozen in time as his companion and met his dark brown eyes. Rivett had shown him the Main Lodge Room with its chandeliers, chequerboard floor and heraldic plaques, where Prince Albert dined when he was Honorary Colonel of the Norfolk Artillery Militia, a hundred years ago. Now they were in the rear bar, a long, elegant room with claret leather chairs.

"No," Sean shook his head. "I forgot my training, went with my gut and didn't ascertain the risks properly. At best, I'm a lucky man."

Rivett grimaced. "Where'd they put him anyway, the little scrote?"

"Durham," said Sean. "As far away from me as possible."

"Yeah," Rivett nodded. "But still not far enough. Which is kind of how I feel about Miss Corrine Woodrow."

Streaks of silver ran through his thick, dark hair. Thin lattices of veins down his nose and across his cheekbones attested to the leisure activities of a retired DCI. But the eyes beneath his bushy brows were still as hard and sharp as flints.

"Yeah," Sean nodded, "I can understand that." He spread his hands out in front of him, the same gesture he had used with Dr Radcliffe. "Only I can't afford to be too picky with what comes my way these days."

"Or whose coin you take, I suppose?" Rivett spoke lightly, a smile playing on his lips.

"No." Sean shrugged. "But it's not the money, to be honest. This is the first thing that's come my way in a long time that feels like real work. It's not easy, being pensioned out of the job you love."

Rivett nodded, his eyes softening. "I do know what you mean, boy, I do know what you mean. Must be especially hard at your age."

He raised a finger, attracting the attention of a hovering waiter.

"What d'you fancy? I can most heartily recommend the T-bone steak."

"Then I'll have that," said Sean, closing his menu. "Rare."

"Good boy," said Rivett. "Two of the usual, Terry," he said

to the waiter. "And keep the mineral water coming." He winked at Sean. "We need clear heads to go over ground as old and hard as this."

"Right," said Sean, and reached into his briefcase for the folder that contained all the paperwork he'd been given. "This is the legals, if you want to take a look . . ."

Rivett took the file with an expression of disdain and tossed it down on the seat beside him. "Let's not ruin our appetites before it come, eh?" he said. "But seriously," he leant forward to lift the bottle of water and fill both their glasses. "What do you make of it? What she got you runnin' after that old mawther for?"

"Mathers?" said Sean, thinking that was what Rivett had said. "Well, I tend to agree with what the doctor said at the secure unit. Corrine Woodrow's better off staying where she is. Problem is, Mathers got a new forensics test that showed someone else's DNA all over the shop. Which ain't saying Woodrow is innocent, just that someone else was in there with her, giving her a hand. It's all in there," Sean nodded towards the file.

"Is that right?" Rivett raised one eyebrow but looked otherwise unsurprised.

"Yeah, it is," said Sean. "Only science can't tell us who it is. There's no record of them on the Police National Database, so either they've managed to keep their nose clean ever since or maybe they just ain't with us no more."

Rivett scratched his chin. "Interesting," he said.

"So," Sean pressed on, "I'm here to try and find out who this person's most likely to be. Which is why I wanted to call upon your powers of recall and see if you can't lead me in the right direction. You were in charge of the original case and you saw it all the way through to conviction. You know who her friends and associates were. Mathers managed to track down some of the surviving members of her little gang, ones she went to school with, who volunteered swab tests that put them in the clear – the names are on a list in there," he nodded to the folder. "But that's only a handful of people. I need to find out who we've missed. Could we be looking at someone older than her, someone connected with her mother, maybe? I know it was a long time ago, I'm not expecting any answers to magically appear, but if you could just think on . . ."

"Terry," Rivett looked up as the waiter appeared with a trolley and placed white china plates bearing thick T-bones in front of them. As Terry spooned fries, mushrooms and tomatoes alongside the meat, an expression of carnivorous satisfaction settled across the former DCI's features. "Proper job," he said. The waiter put down a cruet set and bottles of sauce before he wheeled respectfully away.

Sean watched Rivett reach for the HP and slather it liberally over his meal.

"Looks good," he said.

"You won't get no better in this town," said Rivett. "Look at that," he cut his steak and watched the blood flow out. "They say rare and that is rare. How often do you get that?"

"Well," said Sean, taking the tomato ketchup for himself, "it's pretty rare."

"Ha!" Rivett looked delighted. "You're like me, in't you, boy? Always think with our guts first. We're gonna be all right, I reckon." He nodded, chewing with relish.

It seemed obvious to Sean that here was a man delighted to be sprung out of the indolence of retirement, who needed a purpose as much as he did.

"What else is in that file of yours, then?" Rivett waved a forkful of chips in its direction.

"I've drawn up a list of witnesses to the original case I'd like to try and speak to," said Sean, as he cut into his steak. "Or if you could help me track them down, I'd be grateful. If you've an opinion on anyone else you think looks likely, I'd like to hear that too."

"Right," Rivett speared a mushroom and held it up as if assessing it as a potential fit. "Well, don't you go worrying about my memory, I don't need no microchips to keep that in order. Certain faces are already rising to the surface. Not very pleasant ones, mind, but then Miss Woodrow din't exactly keep polite company."

Sean worked on his steak. Despite its generous size, it seemed oddly tasteless. He should have been starving by now, since he'd only had black coffee and a round of toast for his breakfast. But somehow his appetite was evading him.

"What did happen to the mother?" he asked.

"What you'd expect, really," said Rivett, who had just about cleared his own plate. "She couldn't stay round here no more, which come as a bit of a blow to her, seeing as she was a junkie with connections to all the local drug scum. After her house got firebombed she upped and went to Norwich, where she continued to ply her trade." He looked down at Sean's plate. "'Til she come across one punter who din't take too kindly to her sideline in petty larceny and beat her to death with a tyre iron one night. Not that I would have made her for this, anyhow. She were one of them types always getting some other mug to do her dirty work, usually a member of our local motorcycle community. But, at the death, she din't even have them left as friends. What's the matter, boy, in't you hungry?"

"I don't know why," said Sean. "It's delicious, but . . ."

"Let me give you a hand." Rivett's fork bore down on his chips. "Waste not, want not."

Sean managed a few more mouthfuls of steak and a couple of mushrooms while his companion demolished the rest of his lunch around him.

"Right, well," Rivett wiped his mouth with his napkin. "I've had a word with the new gaffer and he's made the old files available for us to look at. What I suggest we do now is go down the station with your list, introduce you to him and see what we can't dig up." He raised his hand to the waiter again. "Put that on my tab, will you, Terry?" He reached out his wallet for a fiver tip. "And that's for yourself. That's if," he looked back at Sean, "you sure you don't want no more?"

"No," said Sean, "I'm fine."

His stomach said the opposite.

* * *

Ernemouth police station sat behind the northwest end of the market square, a navy-blue hoarding over the first floor proclaiming that the Norfolk Constabulary were *Working for you*. Electronic doors opened in a whoosh to let them through and Rivett led the way to an open reception where a young man who scarcely looked old enough to shave wrote down Sean's name in the log book and issued him a pass. Then they took a lift up to the first floor to Detective Chief Inspector Smollet's office.

"He's our youngest ever DCI," Rivett told Sean. "Was only in his short trousers when this case happened. But they rise up the ranks so fast these days, what with all them computers to help them."

He rapped on the door, scarcely waiting for an answer before he pushed it open.

One look at Smollet and Sean divined the reason for the undercurrent of scorn in Rivett's last comment. His successor had the appearance of everything that would be anathema to the old order. A neat, groomed, smoke-free appearance. An office decked out in Ikea minimalism. Flow charts on the wall behind him, a laptop in front of him and a PC to his right. A framed picture of the wife on his desk and an overpowering smell of cologne as he rose and stretched out a manicured hand to shake.

Smollet's tanned and blandly handsome face smiled a welcome as his eyes flicked appraisingly over Sean's leather coat and cashmere V-neck.

"Mr Ward," he said. "Used to be with the Met, right?"

Sean nodded. "Yes, sir."

"Right," Smollet sat back down, indicating that they should take a seat. Sean took the chair nearest to him, but Rivett remained standing. "Len told me all about you. Has he been taking care of you?"

"Very much so," said Sean. "It's good of you both to be so helpful."

"Not at all." Smollet leaned forwards across his desk, steepling his fingers, glancing just above Sean's eyeline at Rivett. "Anything you need that we can provide, we'll do our best to accommodate. We in't got nothing to hide here."

"He's given us a list," said Rivett, waving the folder. "I'd like to take it down to records, if that's all right with you."

"I have a duplicate for you here, sir," Sean reached into his briefcase and offered an identical file. "Just so as you know all the facts as I do. If there are any points you'd like to raise . . ."

"Thank you," Smollet took the folder and placed it to the side of his laptop. "I'll go through it this afternoon and come back to you if I need any clarification. Len and I thought it would be best if he took you through the old case files first, seeing as he is considerably more familiar with them than I am. At this point, I'd just like to welcome you here. If you're not happy with anything," his eyes flicked up again for a second, "anything at all, you just let me know. My numbers," he plucked a card from a stack by the side of his in-tray, "in case you don't already have them."

"Thank you, sir," said Sean, reaching into his wallet to exchange one of his own.

"And now," Smollet got to his feet again, "I'll leave you in Len's capable hands."

He looked as if there was an unpleasant smell lingering under his nostrils that would disperse the minute the two of them left. Rivett seemed to concur, making for the door.

"Can I just ask," Sean said, remaining seated, "about the detective who made the original arrest. Paul Gray, I believe his name was. He still around?"

Smollet looked towards Rivett, frown lines creasing his forehead.

Rivett's expression mirrored the one he had used on the steak. "Should be able to dig him up for you," he said. "That's one I know who in't gone far. If you'd care to follow me?"

Sean looked back at Smollet, whose eyes rested one more beat on Rivett before returning to Sean with a brief smile, nodding his assent. Sean got to his feet, feeling the tension between the two men, wondering which one of them was really in charge.

14

The Latest Craze

Detective Sergeant Paul Gray looked through the hatch at the girl he'd apprehended under the pier. She was sitting on the iron bed with a book in her lap, flicking through the pages without giving the appearance of taking anything in. Her left foot bobbed up and down frantically and she was chewing hard at her gum, constantly pushing her ragged hair out of her eyes. Trying to look tough, he supposed.

She hadn't come in quietly, unlike the old pervert he'd been trailing. Like so many of his kind, he'd started snivelling the moment he was cuffed, and throughout his interview remained meekly acquiescent. Now he sat blowing into his hanky at the end of the cellblock, awaiting a lift to the magistrates in the morning.

This one had given no ground, except for her correct age, fifteen. She hadn't been doing anything, she maintained, just going for a walk on the beach and what was the law against that? Unfortunately for her, rules stipulated that school children had to be kept at the station until a parent, social worker or head teacher could be informed. Once she realised she couldn't just walk out again, she had exploded.

It had taken all of Gray's patience to wheedle out her name and address; that and the duty sergeant's suggestion that she be allowed to keep her precious book with her while she waited in the cells.

Roy Mobbs had close to twenty years' experience on Gray. Said the surname Woodrow rang a bell with him somewhere. When Gray came back with the mother's name, it triggered his powers of recall: he slapped a palm across his forehead and picked up the phone, got the name of her social worker from the girl's headmaster instead. They were now waiting for a Mrs Sheila Alcott to arrive.

Corrine looked up from her book, realising she was being watched.

"D'you want anything?" Gray asked, trying to sound friendly. "Cup of tea? Coffee?"

She stared at him, surprise passing across her face. "Cup of tea would be nice," she concluded.

She was seven years older than Gray's own daughter.

"How d'you like it? Milk and sugar?"

Corrine nodded. "Two sugars, please," she said. "You got any biscuits?"

Gray brought it into the cell himself. He was concerned, in the way of a father rather than a policeman, as to how she had ended up like this.

"Thanks," she said, taking the mug from him and clutching it in both hands. Close up, her eyes looked like a panda's, surrounded by smudged make-up.

"I found you these, and all," Gray had filched a couple of custard creams, put them on a saucer. The girl demolished them in seconds, then slurped noisily at her tea. Skinny little thing, she was. Gray wondered when was the last time she'd been fed.

He glanced at the book she'd left face down on the bed. It was an old volume, bound in black leather, and adorned with gold-leaf etchings – a queen with a crown, a man on a camel, a dragon with outstretched wings – that resembled a medieval bestiary.

The Goetia, he read, *The Lesser Key of Solomon the King, Clavicula Salomonis Regis*.

Was it some kind of history book? It hardly seemed likely.

Translated by Samuel Liddell MacGregor Mathers, he read on. *Edited with an introduction by Aleister Crowley*.

"What you now reading?" he asked, trying to think where he had heard the name Crowley before.

Black-painted fingernails immediately snatched the book away. "Why d'you care?" the mask of hostility came up over her features as swiftly as it had been dropped. "You in't takin' it. It's a rare book, what was en-trust-ed to me," she stumbled over the last sentence, like it was a line she'd had to practise. "I gotta keep it safe." The biscuit saucer and tea mug now discarded, she clutched the tome across her chest with both arms.

"Hey, now," Gray fought the urge to laugh, not wanting to seem to mock the girl. She had shown a certain cunning earlier this evening, but it was clear she had the emotional volatility of a much younger child. "I got no intention of taking it from you, I just in't seen nothing like it before. Is it part of your school work, or something?"

Corrine's expression shifted from aggression to puzzlement. "Noooo," she said, shaking her head slowly. "But, I s'pose you could say I am learnin' from it."

"That's good then," said Gray. "What kind of thing?"

The girl tilted her head sideways and stared at him through narrowed eyes. "How to protect myself," she eventually said.

All Gray's feelings of amusement drained away. "Right," he said. "Well, I can see . . ."

A rap on the door cut his sentence short. "Paul, you in there?" Roy Mobbs' voice came through the hatch. "Social worker's now here."

"Right," he said. "Better show her in, then."

"Oh, fuckin' hell!" were Corrine's words of greeting to this news. She scrabbled up the bed until her back was against the wall, drawing her feet up beneath her. As Gray turned to open the door, he saw her shove her book underneath her grubby top and bring her arms down defiantly on top of it.

On the other side of the cell door stood a short woman with frizzy salt-and-pepper hair, wearing a brown anorak. She looked like she had just been disturbed from her gardening.

"Sheila Alcott," she said, offering a red hand. "In there, is she?"

"That's right," said Gray. Sheila might have had the look of a rural hippy, but there was an edge to her voice that suggested the schoolmarm.

"DS Paul Gray," he said, "pleased to meet you, Mrs Alcott."

"I came as quick as I could," Sheila said, concern in her watery blue eyes. "I'm afraid I live at the other end of the Acle Straight and I was up to my ears in compost when you called. I hope I haven't kept you unduly."

She took a spotted handkerchief from her pocket and blew her nose. There was a piece of straw sticking out from the tangled depths of her hair.

"I've been afraid this sort of thing would happen to Corrine before too long," she went on. "Might I be allowed a few words with her, then?"

Gray was just opening his mouth to reply when a loud

female voice resounded down the corridor.

"Where is she, then? What you now done with my daughter, you bunch of old bastards?"

Gray looked up at the woman who stomped towards them, a blazing fury flashing in her coal dark eyes.

"Oh dear," said the social worker. "You've found Mrs Woodrow, then."

No one had summoned her, except, Gray thought, for the jungle drums that beat beneath the pavements of Ernemouth, the grapevine that seemed to exist between the walls and the stones in the places Mrs Woodrow's sort hung out.

Though, she didn't look how he would have expected. She wasn't ravaged by the sins of her lifestyle with an emaciated figure, bad skin and lank, greasy hair. Instead, she resembled the young Elizabeth Taylor in black biker's leathers, clouds of raven hair falling down around her shoulders.

"Where is the little bitch?" she demanded, pulling up on six-inch platform heels.

* * *

Corrine's blood turned to ice as the screaming match began outside. She tried desperately to recall the things that Noj had started to teach her, the incantations she was supposed to say against her mother's power. But the terror of hearing the old bitch's voice and the thought of her getting her hands on the sacred book had turned her mind into a raging blank, like a television set left on after the last programme had gone off the air.

She hadn't been supposed to take any of Noj's books when she left his house this afternoon. But she had wanted to learn more quickly. Desperately, she pushed it further down her waistband, hoping against hope that it would somehow go unnoticed.

Then something peculiar happened.

Noj's eyes appeared in her mind, clear, green and focused. The static in her head dissipated as his voice poured into her ears, telling her what she should do. "Close your eyes, Corrine. A sphere of white light is around you. Can you see it?" Corrine nodded. Behind her eyelids, she conjured forth a shimmering ball of white light.

"Now watch as the light starts to blur, and takes on the colours and shapes of the room around you." Corrine had the strangest sensation, as if she had started floating through the air. She could see the mousey-beige blanket, the green-grey paint of the cell walls and the mud-brown of the floor passing through her arms and down her body. All the sounds in the corridor outside disappeared as she felt the circle of light enfold her.

"Fade into the light," she heard Noj say. "Fade into the light and disappear."

She didn't hear the door open, nor see the shapes of several people standing over her.

"She's passed clean out," said Sheila Alcott, gently lifting Corrine's right eyelid.

"In that position?" Gray said. Corrine was sitting bolt upright.

"She's catatonic," Sheila spoke as one who had seen this sort of thing many times before. "We need to call an ambulance."

* * *

Corrine woke up with a strange smell in her nose. Blinking rapidly, she tried to take in her surroundings. It took her a few moments to grasp that she was in a hospital bed, and another few more to realise how she must have got here.

There was a brief moment of panic when she thought she had lost Noj's precious book. But when she turned her head she could see it, sitting safely on top of the table by her bed. Her mother, the police and the social worker were all gone and everything was quiet – she wasn't in a general ward but in a little room of her own. Sunlight slanted across the sheets from the blinds on the window.

That was when Corrine knew that magick really worked.

15

I Blood Brother Be

March 2003

Sean arranged the mugshots on the table in front of him. Corrine's known associates, arrested after Gray had caught her at the murder site, all subsequently released without charge. Their statements, paper-clipped to the back of the photos, attesting to the fact that one raid on Captain Swing's public house had netted virtually the lot of them.

Familiar faces jumped out at him.

Marc Anthony Farman, 14, of 52 Regent's Road, Ernemouth. Pupil of Ernemouth High School. Cautioned for truancy and underage drinking.

The pub's current landlord, starting out as he meant to go on.

Shaun Terence McDonald, 18, of 23 Havelock Road, Ernemouth. Employee of Maples Poultry.

The man with the crutch and the friendly face. Then there was his mate Bugs, or to give him a formal introduction, *Harvey Matthew Bunton, 20, of 74 Scratby Road, South Town, Ernemouth. Employee of Locke & Co Transit.*

The skinhead and the punk who had been playing pool the night earlier were, respectively, Kristian Kemper and Damon Patrick Bull, then both eighteen, of a shared address at 21A

St Peter's Road and employed by the council as landscape gardeners. Which maybe explained the attention they paid to the foliage on their heads.

So, thought Sean, keying their details into his laptop, you are the old tribe.

Three hours into his excavation of Ernemouth's records, he felt the first prickling of the old excitement, like a hound picking up a scent off the breeze. These faces in front of him were his first tangible leads back in time. He picked up the punk's mugshot, heard Farman saying: *"That old sign was a bit corny, so Bully done a better one . . ."*

The youthful Bully bore a striking resemblance to Travis Bickle that he'd done little to tone down since.

Rivett had found all the files that matched with Sean's list. But as hard as he stared at them, he couldn't make out in any of their faces a suggestion of the one he had been most certain he would find – the girl with the tattooed hand. *Where are you?* thought Sean. *Who are you?*

He drummed his fingers on the tabletop, opened up his email. One from Francesca, using a private Hotmail, rather than her work account, telling him that she had found a retired social worker who had once been Corrine's caseworker and was about to pay her a visit.

Sean closed the message and swivelled in his chair. Down in the basement was a different world from Smollet's streamlined station above. Alf Brown, who looked after the records from within a steel and Plexiglass podule, was another old-timer who must have been teetering on the brink of retirement, with a balding dome and drooping moustache, the stub of a pencil stuck behind his left ear.

The rest of the floor space was divided into cubicles with

corkboards, many of them sporting vintage crime prevention posters, curled and yellowing with age. The remains of the old incident room, Sean couldn't help but think. Boxes of unfiled paperwork crowded the desktops, but only one young PC was inputting any of it, keeping his head down, fingers tapping steadily away.

Across from Sean, sitting at a vintage Apple Mac almost bigger than the desk it had been placed on, Rivett was clicking a keyboard, eyes running up and down his monitor. An old transistor, hidden somewhere within Alf's chamber of filing cabinets, was tuned into Radio 3, the distant chimes of classical music adding a funereal air to the proceedings.

Sean wondered if it was always this quiet or if an exception had been made for his visit.

"Len," he said.

Rivett turned his head. "Yes, detective?"

"You said you might be able to find me a number for Paul Gray?"

Rivett raised an eyebrow. "That's right, I did," he said. "Two ticks."

He lifted the receiver, pressed a digit and said: "Oh, hello, Jan, it's Len. Reckon you could find me a number for Paul Gray? That's right. That's the one. Thank you." He scribbled something down on a Post-it note.

"There you go," Rivett offered the number without rising, so that Sean had to get to his feet and walk across to him.

"That's local," said Rivett, "Sandringham Avenue. Over North Denes way."

"Thanks," said Sean, sitting down to dial. He was in luck. A man answered after the third ring, sounded cheerful as he repeated the number and then said: "Hello."

"Hello, am I speaking to Paul Gray?" Sean kept his eyes on Rivett as he spoke. The old sweat swivelled nonchalantly in his chair.

"Who's calling, please?" the tone was still friendly, just a note of wariness creeping in.

"My name's Sean Ward, I'm a private detective looking into a case you once worked on, wondered if I might pick your brains about it."

"Oh?" the voice sounded surprised. "What would that be, then?"

"I'm sure you won't have forgotten it," said Sean, watching Rivett turn back to his screen and give the impression of resuming his searches. "Corrine Woodrow, summer of 1984."

There was a moment's silence at the end of the phone. Rivett narrowed his eyes like he was reading something interesting.

"Cor, dear," Paul Gray finally said. "What you diggin' round that for?"

Sean explained, as he had to Rivett, about Janice Mathers and the new DNA test.

"I see," Gray said. There was another lengthy pause. "Len Rivett know, do he?"

He spoke as if Rivett was still in charge of the station.

"He gave me your number," said Sean.

Gray made a sound like a sigh. "Right," he said. "I see." All the traces of humour had faded from his voice.

"Well, like I say, I wouldn't mind a chat with you about it," said Sean. "I'm in town for a while, wondered if you might be able to spare me an hour or so, tomorrow morning?"

"Don't suppose I can refuse, can I?" said Gray.

Sean ignored the weary note of sarcasm. "What would suit you?" he asked.

Gray sighed again. "You can come here, I suppose. Number 48, Sandringham Avenue. Make it ten o'clock, if you don't mind. The missus'll be at work by then. I don't want to bother her with this."

"Right you are," Sean tapped the details into his mobile, along with Gray's number. "I appreciate it, Mr Gray. I'll try not to take up too much of your time."

"Right," said Gray, "see you then."

Rivett had moved off to stand over the printer while it disgorged the information he had been downloading from the computer. He strolled back with a sheaf of paper in his hand. "Here's what's left of the biker gang Old Ma Woodrow used to knock about with. The ones that didn't end up under a lorry down the Acle Straight, although they might be a few limbs short of what they were. They do tend to get that way."

He placed the print-outs down beside Sean's laptop. "Anything else you require?"

"Well," Sean looked at the clock on his computer that was inching towards 6 p.m., "I think I've probably kept you long enough for one day, Len."

Rivett wrinkled his nose. Sean had an inkling he had wanted to spin this one out into the night, make it feel like the old days, polish off the session with a few more jars at his office. The former DCI's company was the last thing Sean needed where he was heading, but he didn't want to put Rivett's nose out of joint needlessly either.

"Tell you the truth," he said, "my bloody legs are killing me. If I don't get to lie down for half an hour, a couple of times a day, I stop being able to function properly. It's embarrassing to admit it. But I've just about reached that point now."

Rivett's expression changed. "Course," he said. "I never

even thought. You go on, I'll let Alf lock this little lot up for the night and we can start again tomorrow."

"Thanks," said Sean. "You're a good man."

"That has been rumoured," said Rivett, winking.

* * *

Rivett watched Sean limp through the door of The Ship Hotel, thinking of bullet holes in flesh. The man carried himself with dignity, didn't let the pain show on his face. Rivett admired that about him. He weren't like most of the flash bastards he had encountered from Met Lands in his time. Ward was a thinker, not a blagger, Rivett could tell.

He had got to the hotel before Ward did, thanks to his knowledge of the notoriously tricky Ernemouth one-way system, parked up his own car well out of sight. Rivett just wanted to be certain that Ward wasn't spinning him a line about this leg of his, wanting to be rid of him so early of an evening.

He lingered on the corner a while, took his mobile out of his pocket while he watched, glancing down every few seconds to check his messages. When Sean didn't re-emerge after fifteen minutes, Rivett put his phone away, went back to the Rover and headed out to the seafront. Past the flashing lights, the scaffold-covered remains of the Trafalgar Pier and the beckoning windows of the Lodge, on to the Leisure Beach.

It was an eerie sight, off-season. The street lights casting shadows against the dark hump of the rollercoaster and the skeletal frames of the wheels and loops, the silent turrets and towers. Rivett showed his pass to the security guard who manned the gate to the staff car park and the man nodded him through.

Tasting salt on his tongue, Rivett walked through the

deserted kingdom towards the tower in the middle where one lonely light, right at the top, cast a pale yellow glow against the blackness of the sky. Took the lift up and knocked at the office door.

* * *

Sean walked a circuit down the quay and then back towards the town centre, getting a feel for the layout. He wanted to try and see it through the eyes of the locals and he'd always found it was easier to work out how everything fitted together by walking.

He hadn't been that economical with the truth when he told Rivett his legs had been playing him up. But after half an hour's kip to chase his medication down and a read of Mr Farrer's book, he felt better than he had done since he'd got here. He knew it was partly psychological – he had something to get to grips with now, an adrenalin rush that buoyed him down King Street.

Coming up it the other way from the night before, he took in a nightclub and three pubs clustered together, special promotions posters in every window, bouncers on the door of each. These shaven-headed guardians looked bored, blinking ahead into the street as vocodered chart music blared through their half-empty premises. Through the door of one, Sean caught sight of Francesca's ad manager with his two protégées standing up at a tall table in the middle of the floor, drinking pints of lager. Modern drink-up fittings only served to emphasise the paucity of trade.

He looked up as he passed the *Mercury* office. The lights were still on up there. He wondered if it was Francesca, back from her meet with the social worker. Wondered again what it was she was trying to prove in a place like this. Or what she had been running away from. Half of him was tempted to press the buzzer and ask her.

But he ambled on, taking a different route, past the market place. Apart from the grand, '30s-built department store, which the car park in front of Swing's belonged to, every shop appeared to be either a charity or cut-price outlet. He thought back to what Bugs had said about North Sea oil. All that money gone and nothing to show for it.

Sean turned left into Market Row. Down here was the pub where, Rivett had informed him, the bikers liked to hang out. The Back Room it was called, a red sign over a slim passageway between two half-timbered buildings. The music that pulsed from these walls marked its difference from the King Street boozers: Deep Purple's "Smoke on the Water". He should pay it a visit too, he thought as he passed, maybe tomorrow night. But he hadn't finished with the drinkers in Swing's yet.

Sean saw in his head the green eye tattooed on the goth girl's hand. She had been playing on his mind all day. It was her, he realised, as he turned left at the bottom of the row and on to his destination, that he most wanted to bump into tonight.

As he walked through the door, Shaun and Bugs were sat exactly where they had been the night before, a paper spread before them on the bar.

A song was playing that he had never heard before. Dramatic, slightly operatic: strings and crashing piano, a man singing in a baritone about skies, stars and moons.

"I said he'd be back," Shaun, whose barstool faced the door, nudged Bugs, whose back was towards him. "All right, mate?"

"Evening, Mr Ward," Bugs greeted him, putting down an empty pint on the bar and wiping his mouth with the back of his hand.

"Sean, please," he replied. "I owe you guys a drink," he said. "Farrer's bookshop did have something on Captain Swing. Interesting old fella, ain't he, Mr Farrer?"

"You could say that," a sliver of a smile played across Bugs's mouth.

"Sorted you out, did he?" Shaun grinned.

"He certainly did," Sean nodded, watching out of the corner of his eye the landlord further down the bar talking to the biker he'd seen talking to the tattooed girl the night before. He did a quick strafe of the pool table area. She wasn't there. No Bully or Kris either. Instead, the younger emos clustered around that end of the bar. Business was definitely better in here than any of the other pubs he had passed.

"So, what you having?" he asked.

"Pint of Adnams, please," said Shaun.

"I'll have the same," Bugs nodded at the pump. Farman caught his eye and broke off his conversation with the biker, walked towards them, rubbing his fists against his chest.

"Couldn't keep away?" he said to Sean. "Nice to see you again, Mr Ward. What'll it be?"

"Two pints of Adnams and one of the Foster's," Sean replied.

"You got a book then," said Shaun. "Any pictures of the Captain in it?"

"No," Sean smiled, "and there ain't likely to be. That was the genius of it. The Captain was everyone and no one. A phantom. He didn't really exist, so he couldn't be caught. Whoever in the community could read and write would pretend to be him, and those people were usually involved in the printing game, so they could make pamphlets and spread the word. That picture you have on the sign is as good as any."

"Cor," said Bugs, raising the pint Farman had passed across to him. "Make you feel proud, don't it?"

"Don't it just," said Farman, pulling the final pint.

"That's why he was such a threat," Sean recalled more details from the book. "And you know how he got his name? People would make effigies of the landowners, then hang them from the scaffold outside their front doors."

Bugs gave a great guffaw of approval.

"I should put up some information about that," said Farman. "People like to know these things. Especially our customers."

"I saw one of yours in there, actually," Sean glanced across at the biker, who had remained at the bar but moved closer towards Shaun. "The girl with a tattoo on her hand, she was in here last night."

Farman's brow furrowed. "A girl?" he said.

"With black hair and a fur coat," said Sean.

The biker was staring at him now, slate-grey eyes behind wire-rimmed granny glasses. Not a very welcoming expression. He had a gold stud beneath his bottom lip, glinting in the brown curls of his beard. Sean knew he hadn't seen that face amongst the mugshots they'd gone through today. He looked about ten years younger than the others so he couldn't have been part of the original crew. Those that were continued to look bemused.

"You got me," said Farman, handing Sean's pint across. "That'll be £8.25, please."

Sean shook his head as he handed a tenner across. "Still can't get used to these prices. Cheers," he raised his glass to the others. Shaun did likewise. Bugs already had his to his lips and mumbled a salutation across the surface of his beer.

"He told me something else interesting, Mr Farrer," Sean went on.

"Oh," said Shaun, "what's that?"

"About this pub," said Sean, loud enough that the biker could hear. "He said it's been called Captain Swing's for at least a hundred years, but the reason it changed its name in the '80s was because of a murder. Someone who drank in here, he said."

The record came to an end, and in the silence before the next one started, the only sound was the thwack of the pool cue against the ball. Twinges ran up and down Sean's legs, but the adrenalin pumped harder.

"Anyone remember that? Shaun, you said you had your first pint in here in 1981, didn't you?"

Shaun's gaze dropped into his drink as the colour rose in his cheeks. He shook his head.

"That's funny," Sean went on, shifting his gaze to Bugs in time to see he and Farman break eye contact. "'Cos he also said there was something of a witch hunt. Surely you'd remember that?"

"Why," the biker cut in, speaking in a Belfast accent, "did Mr Farrer not tell you about the Witchfinder General?"

"No," Sean said, "he never got the chance. Like I say, he had another customer. Your friend . . ." He stared at the biker.

The Ulsterman laughed. "Then maybe you should look him up some time," he said, raising his glass in Sean's direction. "Anyways," he nodded towards the others, "cheers, gentlemen, I'll leave you to your history lesson."

Sean stared after him, trying not to let his agitation show. As he did, he felt a hand on his arm. He looked down to see the green eye resting there, on the hand of the girl who stared up at him through her black fringe, with her matching emerald pupils.

"Are you looking for me?" she said.

16

Crystal Days

December 1983

"Oh go on," said Debbie. "You in't been out for ages, Reenie. And it *is* New Year's Eve . . ."

Corrine stared at her reflection in Chelsea Girl's window. Her hair finally looked good again, though it was still much shorter than she would have liked.

"It's really cool," Debbie said, as if reading her thoughts. "That black really suit you."

Corrine touched the back, which had been cut into a short, layered bob. The front was spiked up, the sides razored short. Once the broken blonde streaks had been cut out, it had been safe to dye it again – and she'd had a proper job this time.

"Lizzy done it," she informed Debbie. "She's the top stylist at Oliver John's."

Corrine had a job at the salon on the weekends now. Just sweeping up and making the tea, but Lizzy had said that if she kept it up, she'd take her on as an apprentice when Corrine left school. It had been the social worker's idea. She was all right, that Sheila.

"It's brilliant," said Debbie.

Corrine looked at herself in the glass and smiled. "That is all right, in't it?" she allowed.

"Well," said Darren, who had his arm around Debbie, "if that in't worth celebrating, I don't know what is. Come on Corrine, we've missed you, you know."

Corrine felt herself blush. Since she'd been out of hospital and back in school, things had been going all right for once. They had put her in a much smaller class, where one nice teacher took all the lessons and let them talk about things that were bothering them. With the Old Bill breathing down her neck and Sheila threatening to take Corrine into care, her mum had backed off, stopped hitting her and let her keep the ten quid she earned at the hairdressers each weekend without making her go out and earn any more. So she had kept her newly coiffured head down, doing her best to forget the events of the past few months and avoiding socialising with her former classmates. Sheila said it would be better that way; it would stop other people from leading her into trouble.

But Corrine knew what was really behind her recent change in fortune. It was Noj's protection spell at work, the rituals they repeated together every Sunday night. Not that she could tell anybody about that. Not even Debbie.

"Where you now going?" she enquired.

"Meeting Jules down the Dodger's," said Darren. "What d'you reckon?"

"The Dodger's?" Corrine hesitated. Debbie and Darren were being so nice, surely it wouldn't hurt? So long as she stayed away from Sam . . . "Not Swing's?"

Debbie shook her head and smiled, as if reading her thoughts. "Not Swing's."

"All right then," Corrine decided. Smiling, she joined them, weaving their way through the crowded pavements, thick with shoppers touting bags of sales bargains and early evening revellers heading for the pubs. Above their heads, strings of coloured lights proclaimed the end of the festive season, shooting stars and sprigs of holly sparkling against the dark, midwinter sky. Paul Young singing lullabies of love for the common people from every shop doorway, the smell of hot chips and vinegar wafting over from the market stalls. It gave Corrine a sudden rush of cheer, the prospect of seeing out this bad old year in the company of her friends.

"So," she said to Debbie as they turned towards the pub doorway, wanting to be sure, "you meeting Alex and them later on, then?"

Debbie scowled. "No I in't," she said. "I told you, I in't going in Swing's . . ."

"In case *she's* in there," they said together.

✻ ✻ ✻

Alex looked up at the clock. Quarter past seven, it said.

"Anyone want another?" Shaun MacDonald, swilling the dregs of his bitter around his glass, looked round at the assembled table.

"Don't mind if I do," said Bugs, putting his own empty glass down with a belch.

"Al?" offered Shaun.

Alex looked down at his pint. He had drunk most of it in five minutes flat and it still hadn't given him any insights into what to do next. In his pocket was a ticket to a gig in Norwich, bought back in September, when they had first gone on sale. Right now, Bully and Kris would be at the station, waiting for the half-past train to come in, waiting for him to join them as they had planned.

But in his head was a girl with black hair, a girl who had

stolen him away from them with a kiss and more back in October. Her face filled his mind, a face he could not seem to put down on paper, no matter how hard he tried. Her image evaded his pencils and paints. But she had put her own markings on him.

Until the moment she had walked into this bar, Alex had been trying to accept the fact that his failure to feel genuinely aroused by women could mean only one thing, a sense that had been heightened by meeting Debbie's friend Julian and the look of recognition he was sure he had discerned in the younger boy's dark eyes.

But Samantha had turned that, and everything else, upside down. She had begun their first evening together by dropping into conversation how she had grown up in London surrounded by artists, contemporaries of her father's from his counter-culture days. She ended it just outside her house, lips and teeth all over his face, nails scoring lines down his back as she pushed him inside her, hot and fast, up against the old Tollgate wall. Alex's response had been instinctual, primal, a coupling of shock and lust that overrode everything else, including the memory of Debbie's ashen face as she watched him leave Swing's with the girl from school she so detested.

He had hardly been able to catch his thoughts since. This woman-child, so sophisticated in adult ways, so coolly able to surpass all his artistic endeavours, so increasingly wild in her carnal behaviour that his initial relief at finally proving he was normal after all had lately given way to a nagging doubt that he no longer knew what "normal" meant. The scars she made in his flesh every time she pulled him into an illicit embrace – down darkened alleyways, on the beach, even one time on the floor of her bedroom while her mother was making their tea downstairs – began to throb and itch as he remembered the other promise that he had made for tonight.

Marc Farman caught his eye. "Shouldn't you be heading?" he said.

Marc knew what time the train left, Alex had already told him about that plan. Marc had opined that it sounded better than hanging round here.

"I'll come with you," Marc offered. "Reckon I'll get a ticket off a tout, easy."

Alex looked at the minute hand moving round the clock, felt for the ticket in his pocket.

"Come on," said Marc.

* * *

Amanda cast her eyes around her packed front room, a plate of vol-au-vents in one hand and sausage rolls in the other. The clock on the mantelpiece said it was early days yet, but the party was showing every sign of success.

"I know I shouldn't," Mary Grimmer, one of the mothers from Sammy's school, plucked out another prawn and avocado pastry, "but these are delicious, Mands."

"Mum made them," Amanda replied, lowering her voice. "A bit of a Christmas miracle. Mind you, we've had a few of those this year . . ."

Her gaze travelled across the room to the bay window, where Edna, resplendent in pussy-bow and polka dots just like the prime minister, was engaged in an animated conversation with Wayne over the bowls of crisps and finger sandwiches.

It had been a combination of things that had gradually won her over. This house, for one, restored to what they imagined had been something of its former glory. The kitchen, both bathrooms and Sam's bedroom had all the modern fittings, but down here, in the lounge and adjacent dining room, they had kept the look traditional. Despite themselves, Edna and Eric had taken in the depth of the restoration, and the speed she and Wayne had achieved it, with respect. It had shown them there was a lot more to Amanda and Wayne's relationship than they had assumed.

The beams across the ceiling and the old fireplaces had been exposed and deep pile claret carpet ran luxuriantly underfoot. Oak dining furniture and crystal glasses gleamed from the dresser in the dining room; in the lounge were mushroom-brown suede sofas and walls hung with hunting prints depicting the nineteenth-century Norfolk landscape.

Assuming the role of master of foxhounds, Eric had assembled all the middle-aged men in the room around him in an admiring circle by the fireplace, where, foot up on the brass guard and a tumbler of whisky in his hand, he was spinning his repertoire of stories and blue jokes. By his side, Samantha joined in the laughter.

"I mean," Amanda went on, "look at that, for instance."

Sam's hair looked like someone had run an iron over it compared to the bird's nest they had got used to her wearing. She had fixed the front into a roll with a hairclip, to which she had attached a red tinsel bow, the rest hung down to her shoulders and flicked up at the ends. The black and red velvet dress she was wearing went over her knees and puffed up at the shoulders; she had teamed it with black tights and little pointy suede boots. And she'd reduced her pancake make-up to a mere smudge of shadow and red lipgloss.

"She almost looks human."

"Oh," Mary giggled, "you are awful, Mands. I think she look lovely in her new frock."

"She does," Amanda agreed. "That's the amazing thing. I never asked her to make an effort, just that she stay here to please her nana and granddad 'til they have to leave and then she can go off and meet lover boy. This is all off her own bat ..."

A frown crossed Amanda's face as she wondered if this was what Sam had spent her Christmas money from Malcolm on. There wasn't very much of it this year, no wonder she'd had to wait for the sales.

"Mind you," she added, dismissing her soon to be legally ex-husband from her mind, "she'll probably throw herself through a hedge backwards before she does go out."

Mary whinnied a laugh and then lowered her tone to a gossip's whisper. "She still seeing Alex Pendleton, then, your Sammy?"

Amanda nodded. "Best thing that ever happened to her, that boy. I mean, he hasn't done much to improve her appearance, but he has got her back into her painting again."

"I reckon it was that Corrine Woodrow," said Mary, "put them ideas in your Sammy's head. You see anything of her these days?"

"No," said Amanda, her eyes drifting back towards her mother and Wayne.

"Good job and all," Mary said. "She's a wrong 'un that girl. 'Bout time they put her in the special class, keep her away from the rest of them. 'Cos, you know her mum's a tart, don't you?"

Noodles the dog had had to be put down in the end. His ordeal had left him a nervous, incontinent wreck. Which wasn't something Amanda wanted to think about right now. She caught Wayne's eye, tilted her head towards the door.

"And God knows who the father is, probably one of them bikers what's always hanging about round there," Mary continued, getting into her stride. "Don't suppose she did have much chance of turning out all right, when you think about it. But you don't want your kids getting mixed up in it, do you?"

To her relief, Wayne's hand came down on Amanda's shoulder. "How's my girl?" he said. "Hello, Mary, you all right for drinks there? I'm just going to fetch some more bottles, we're running a bit low."

Amanda glanced down at her platters. "I'll give you a hand, darling, these could do with topping up too." She fixed Mary with her most dazzling smile. "Would you excuse us?"

* * *

It was warm and noisy in the pub, HAPPY NEW YEAR signs draped across the ceiling, tinsel and fairy lights hanging from the rafters and around framed prints of the Artful Dodger, Oliver Twist and Fagin. Only the Christmas tree was showing signs of fatigue, drooping under the weight of too much revelry, its needles in a pile on the carpet.

They managed to cram themselves round a little table near the jukebox, which Darren and Julian were busily scanning for decent singles, while for the moment Simple Minds' "Waterfront" crashed around their ears.

"So go on then," Corrine was urging Debbie, "what's happened?"

"You were right. That bloody Samantha Lamb," said Debbie, "has taken over everything. Every day she look more like me, she copy my hair, my clothes, my shoes ... I don't even know how she get hold of half of it. Like these," she stuck out her ankle to draw Corrine's attention to the boots she had saved up three months for. "They were the only ones in the shop, I got them up Norwich the last Saturday before we broke up. Monday morning I come to school and she's got on the exact same pair! How do she do it?"

Corrine shook her head. "She's a rich bitch, in't she?" she said. "Her folks give her whatever she want."

Debbie nodded. "She come in the art room every day and sit there, watching what I do, waiting 'til I've nearly finished – then she copy the whole idea." Debbie scowled, hating to admit what she was saying, but finding herself unable to stop. "Only she do it about a million times better, like she's got a camera taking pictures of whatever's in my head. So now old Witchell's putting my marks down 'cos he think I'm copying her!"

Debbie's eyes smouldered with outrage.

Corrine thought back to Sam in the art room, staring at Debbie's jacket and asking all them questions. Remembered the way she had made her say bad things about her friend, and how she couldn't seem to stop herself from doing it. Debbie was right. Sam did have a way of seeing into your mind.

"She's a fuckin' cow," she said, her own anger rising.

"But that in't even the worst of it," Debbie said. "Everyone else love her. I mean," she glanced up at Darren, still poring over the jukebox while Julian pressed the buttons, "not them two, thank God, but . . ."

Debbie reined herself in. If she told Corrine, would she blame herself? Or would she think Debbie was blaming her? Even if there was a grain of guilty truth to it, Debbie didn't want Corrine to feel any worse than she had that day in October. A shudder of emotion ran through her, like a blade twisting in her heart.

"What?" Corrine demanded. "Tell me, Debs. I can handle it."

Unwelcome tears stung the corners of Debbie's eyes.

"It's Alex, in't it?" Corrine pressed on. "She got him like she said she would."

Debbie raised a finger to dab at her eyeliner. "I only seen him once after that," she said, "and he didn't listen to a word I said. Now, every time I call for him, his mum say he's out, and it in't with his mates. Last time we seen Bully and Kris, they asked me if I knew what had happened to him, so maybe he don't go in Swing's with her either. But I can't face going in there now," her voice hardened. "She's got what she wanted, in't she?"

A tear dropped off the end of her lashes as she looked into Corrine's eyes. "It might sound mad, but it's like ..." She looked up to make sure Darren and Julian were still busy. She had never voiced this thought before and wasn't sure she wanted her boyfriend to hear it.

"No it won't," Corrine assured her. "I know exactly what she's like, remember?"

Debbie nodded. "Well it's like, how she's suddenly so brilliant at art and that, how she's got to be teacher's pet. It's like she's sucked up all Al's talent and now it's coming out of her instead." Debbie gave a snort of startled laughter at the ridiculousness of her own words. "Oh, I'm sorry, Reenie," she said, "that do sound mental, don't it?"

But Corrine's face was gravely serious.

"That in't mental," she said. "That's black magic."

She looked at Debbie, an idea forming in her head.

✱ ✱ ✱

"Byeee! Happy New Year!" Amanda and Samantha stood on the doorstep, waving Edna and Eric off. Eric sounded the horn as they pulled away, cigar clamped between his teeth. Edna blew them a kiss.

"Well," said Amanda, turning to face her daughter, "I'm proud of you, Sam, you were great tonight with your nana and granddad. And you look lovely, you really do. Did you go and have your hair done today?"

"M-hmm," Samantha nodded, twirling a strand of her shining black locks around her index finger. "New salon in the arcade," she informed her. "They were doing £5 specials so I thought I might as well."

"Don't suppose you're going to keep it like that, though, are you?"

"No," said Sam, her mouth twisting into a smile. "But it was worth it, wasn't it?"

"It really was," said Amanda, putting her arm around her daughter's shoulder and giving her a little squeeze. "Go on then, off you go and mess it all up again."

Samantha disentangled herself from the embrace with a little chuckle. "It proved something to me," she said, staring at her mother with undisguised disgust. "Just how easy it is to be as false as you." And with that, she bounded off up the stairs.

✳ ✳ ✳

Bully looked up at the clock for the tenth time in five minutes.

"Don't reckon he's coming," he said.

"In't like him to be late," Kris agreed, crumpling his empty beer can and tossing it in the bin. "But if we don't catch this train now ... Oh, hang about."

A figure appeared through the turnstiles, waving in their direction. He was wearing a long black coat the same as Al's, but he was shorter and thicker set, the black corduroy hat on his head barely containing a big ginger quiff of hair.

"Hold up!" Marc Farman called.

"Where's Al?" frowned Bully.

"In Swing's," Marc panted an explanation. "He said he don't really feel like going up Norwich tonight, so he sold me his ticket."

Bully and Kris exchanged glances.

"He have anyone else with him?" asked Bully.

"Shaun and Bugs," said Marc. "But he was looking at the clock the whole time . . ."

* * *

"Where you been hidin' yourself anyway, Al?" asked Shaun. "We in't seen you round for a while."

"I been working," Alex lied. "You know, on my course. They start laying it on thick in the second year."

"Oh," said Shaun, for whom working meant standing on a conveyor belt, slicing up dead turkeys, day in and day out. "That's hard, is it?"

Alex nodded, thinking of the times he had held the pencil up, measured so carefully with his thumb the proportions of her face. His eyes flicked up to the clock. Quarter to nine.

"You seen much of little Debs?" Shaun went on.

Alex shifted uncomfortably in his seat. Any minute now, he realised, Debbie could walk through that door. He didn't want to see that hurt, uncomprehending expression on her face. Not when he couldn't explain it to her any more than he could explain it to himself.

"Sorry, Shaun," he said, getting to his feet, "but I now got to be somewhere else."

Shaun didn't even have time to register his surprise before

his friend was out the door.

"What's up with him?" Bugs scowled at Alex's departing back.

* * *

"Oh, look," Shane Rowlands pointed a fat finger down the Victoria Arcade. "It's one of them weirdos!"

"Oh yeah." Neal Reeder swayed slightly as he tried to focus.

Rowlands turned to his other companion. "Look who it is, Smollet," he said.

Dale hadn't even put away the half of what his friends had sunk tonight and he was beginning to wonder what he saw in their company. His stomach flipped for a different reason as she snapped towards them into the Arcade.

Rowlands was studying Dale's face, while his own grew redder by the second. "You fuckin' fancy it, don't you?" he accused. "Go on then," he lunged towards Smollet, attempting to push him towards her. "Give it one, I dare you."

Dale stepped out of his way neatly, years of afterschool judo lessons combining with his comparative soberness to aid him. "Leave off, Shane," he said.

Samantha Lamb stopped in front of them, head cocked to one side, her eyes glittering.

"Yeah," said Reeder, stumbling to get out of Rowlands' trajectory and catching his balance on a doorframe. "Leave it out, I in't in the mood." He was starting to feel sick.

"Leave it out?" Rowlands was ready to blow. "I in't even started yet, you pair of queers. You," he stared at Samantha, "make me fucking sick." He wove in front of her, stabbing a finger at her face. "Posh fucking witch. Who d'you think you are?"

"Shane," Smollet's voice turned hard. "I said, leave off."

Rowlands turned to stare at him. His face was crimson, a vein pulsating on his forehead. "You're asking for it," he said, bunching his hand into a fist.

"Don't make me," Smollet felt icily cool inside, a lifetime's friendship falling away in the beat of a drunken heart. He could finally see how pathetic Rowlands really was.

Rowlands swung for him and Dale moved, like he was in slow motion, catching his arm and twisting it back, putting his right leg between his opponent's knees so that his legs buckled and he was sent sprawling down onto the concrete.

"Bloody hell," said Reeder, as the contents of his guts started to rise up his throat.

"Fuck," said Rowlands, tasting blood as a tooth dislodged where his chin had hit the floor. He looked up and saw stars dancing around the figure of Smollet.

Looking past him at Samantha disappearing out of the end of the arcade, walking towards the tall figure waiting for her there, without so much as a backwards glance.

Behind Smollet, Reeder sprayed the pavement several shades of brown.

17

The Yo-Yo Man

March 2003

"That's right," said Sean, staring down at the eye on her hand, feeling that strange, light-headed disconnection that had come to characterise each one of their meetings.

In the corner of his mind, a shape moved out from the shadows . . .

He dragged his eyes upwards, looked round at the others. "This is who I meant," he said, waiting to see if they would string out the feigning of ignorance any longer.

"Oh," said Bugs, lifting his pint and shaking his head. "Didn't realise. Thought you said a girl." He snorted with laughter as she slapped him across the arm.

"Pay no attention to this philistine," she said. "Would you like to talk to me? Maybe we should take a walk," her eyes narrowed, looking beyond him to the corner she had shared with the biker the night before, clocking him there and nodding a greeting. "It might be easier that way."

A shape taking on human form, raising both arms, pointing a weapon towards him . . .

Sean batted the image away, put his pint down on the counter. He didn't need any more of that, didn't want the side effects.

"Sure," he said, assuring himself that this slight figure could offer him no harm.

He followed her out the front door. "See you then, Mr Ward," Bugs called from behind him, to the chuckles of the others. Sean raised a hand in salute, didn't look back.

"I didn't catch your name," he said, as they stepped out onto the pavement.

"I didn't offer it," she said, smiling. "I have to say, though, you ought to be more careful. We're not completely thick down here, however we may sound to you."

Sean frowned. "I'm sorry," he began, "I didn't mean to—"

"In his time," she cut him off, "which was the days of the Civil War, the Witchfinder General's name was Matthew Hopkins."

Sean had a flash of Francesca standing outside the Greek restaurant, telling him about how women were tortured in the Tollhouse for witchcraft.

"However," she went on, "in our time, we knew him by a different name. We called him Detective Inspector Leonard Rivett."

Sean stared at her.

"That's why you're here, isn't it?' she said. "You've come about Corrine."

Sean felt his throat grow dry. He nodded.

"Then it is me you want to see," she said, and began to walk up the road.

Sean followed her, wondering exactly what he was doing. She walked swiftly, and he began to sweat keeping up, despite the sharp night air, the wind that was coming off the river, feeding into the chill that coursed up the metal within his bones.

She passed the bookshop and turned left into the row,

following it to its end and turning right into a little square where the remains of some ancient cloisters stood under a cluster of trees.

"Stop a minute," said Sean.

There was something about the trees, the streetlights shining through their bare branches. It was just like he was back in Meanwhile Gardens . . .

"What is it?" she asked.

Sean shook his head, trying to rid himself of the déjà vu.

"That old war wound I told you about," he said through gritted teeth. "I can't keep up with you."

"But we're here," she said, taking a key from her pocket and nodding towards the two-storey house at the end of the terrace. "If you'd care to come in. It's just that I'd rather not discuss these things out on the street, walls . . ."

"Have eyes and ears around here," Sean finished the sentence for her.

"Quite." She nodded, turning the key in the lock.

Sean hesitated on the doorstep, waiting for her to go on ahead, turn on the lights, suddenly unsure whether there'd be a reception committee of Swing's drinkers waiting to lynch him, or even if Francesca would be sitting there, joining in the laughter, ready to take him down the Tollhouse dungeons and clap him in leg irons . . .

Leg irons. The thought made him laugh, despite himself – he already had iron legs. He found himself looking down an ordinary hallway, cream walls and beige carpet, neat row of coat hooks along the wall, and through a door into what at first appeared to be a dentist's surgery. He took a tentative step through and realised the reclining chairs and surgical equipment were those of a tattoo studio; the far wall was covered in photographs of the work. Celtic knots and interlaces; tribal totems; whorls and swirls; flowers and peacock feathers; the horror-book imagery of the teenage dispossessed.

"So this is what you do," he thought aloud, his eyes catching the mohicaned head of Bully for the second time that day in a photo on the wall.

"Pays the mortgage," his hostess said, her eyes flicking from the montage to Sean and back again. "But come through to the kitchen. We'll be more comfortable in there."

Sean was further surprised by the comparative homeliness of this room too; the pine table and chairs, aspidistra in a pot by the French doors, red ceramic tea pot and stout, matching mugs – not really what he had been expecting.

"Like some tea?" she said, noticing his gaze.

"Love some," said Sean.

"Take a seat," she said, gesturing, picking a kettle up off its stand and taking it over to the sink. Sean's eyes roamed around the room as she turned on the tap. On the windowsill in front of her were a couple of spider plants. The sink and the draining board stainless steel, the work surfaces white Formica. A four-ring electric oven and a white fridge, white tiling on each wall apart from the dividing one, which was painted pale blue, and hung with a framed watercolour of a seascape. There was an animal's basket the other side of the French doors, two bowls next to it. A cat, judging from the ginger hairs on the red lining. Everything was neat and tidy but it didn't look as though an awful lot of money had been spent here. Except perhaps on the painting. His eyes were drawn back to it.

"English breakfast?" his hostess enquired.

"Please," said Sean, turning his head to face her.

"Thought so," she said. Under the strip lights that ran across the ceiling, Sean could see her more clearly, but would still be hard pressed to gauge her age accurately.

The kettle clicked off and she filled the pot, moving across to the fridge to retrieve the milk and placing it down on the table in front of Sean. She took off her leopardskin coat, putting it over the back of a chair, only after she had brought the pot, two cups and a sugar bowl to the table.

Everything else she was wearing was black – jeans and a long-sleeved ethnic blouse with embroidery on the front. Thin leather straps around her neck hung with amulets. Rings on every finger, including a giant green eye; metal bangles around her wrists. Tendrils of partially concealed tattoos snaked down her arms and around her neck.

"So," she said, raising the pot and starting to pour. "If you're inclined to tell me your name, then I might just tell you mine."

"Sean Ward," he said.

"Sean Ward," she said, nodding. "A strong name."

This close, he could see that her pupils really were the colour of emeralds, it was not an illusion created by coloured contact lenses. He could finally discern crow's feet under the kohl she wore around her eyes, fine lines between her nose and lips. Perhaps she actually could be as old as Corrine Woodrow.

"And you are?" he asked.

She smiled, dimples forming in her cheeks. "My mother wasn't much of a churchgoer," she said. "She never had me christened. But the name on my birth certificate is John Brendan Kenyon."

Sean smiled, marvelling at his loss of discernment. Of course, that was it; there had always been something about her voice that didn't quite ring true.

"Though my schoolfriends decided, by some form of collective unconscious, that she had got that wrong. They called me Noj – my name backwards – and it stuck. They thought that I couldn't really be a boy, I was so little like any of them," she raised one pencilled eyebrow, "so I became a girl."

She passed him a teacup. "I like the name," she went on, "so that's what you can call me."

Sean wondered if that was why he hadn't seen her in the old police files, because he was looking for a girl and not a boy. But he didn't think so. He was sure she was not among any of the mugshots he had seen.

"And you were at school with Corrine?" he asked.

She cocked her head to one side. "First," she said, "you tell me why you want to know."

Sean stirred his tea, keeping his eyes locked on hers. "That old war wound, yeah?" he said. "The reason I walk funny. That was done to me by a fifteen-year-old boy with a zip gun that, thankfully, he was too stupid to aim straight. He was a dealer, just a corner boy, you know what one of them is?"

"Oh yes," said Noj. "I could have been described myself that way, many years ago."

"Right," said Sean, "I thought I was trying to help the kid. I convinced myself that I'd got his trust, talked him into giving up someone higher up the chain. The bastard I was really after, who put all the naughty little boys in my neighbourhood out to work. He set up a meet for me," he shook his head. "Set-up being the operative words."

"He shot you?" said Noj.

Sean nodded. "There was a load of old guff written about it afterwards, embarrassing shit about me being some kind of hero. Huh. A mug is what I was; trying to help some disadvantaged kid get off the streets, when all along that was the only place he really wanted to be. So then, when they finally patched me back together, I was no good to the Met any more, had to take work as a private eye. That's what brings me here. There's a QC up in London thinks she might have enough evidence to get Corrine a review hearing. So she's hired me to see what else I can dig up."

Noj's eyes widened. "Really?" she said. "So there is a chance . . . ?"

"She's a clever lawyer," said Sean. "Don't mean she'll get anywhere. You saw how well my attempts to gain the confidence of Corrine's known associates just went."

Noj shook her head, put her hands out flat on the table in front of her.

"Don't worry about that," she said. "You wouldn't have got much off of them anyway. I mean, they were all around at the time, they all knew who she was – but they didn't have anything to do with it. They just got persecuted afterwards, like everybody else who was a little bit different. They think you're Old Bill and they wouldn't help the police with their enquiries if their lives depended on it."

"So I gather," said Sean, raising his cup. "So now, you tell me – where do you fit in?"

"I was there," said Noj. "I saw everything," she smiled, raising her eyebrow again. "But unlike everyone else you're chasing after, nobody saw me."

The tea was good, just as strong as Sean liked it, something not many people got right.

"All right then," he said, "so let's start at the beginning."

"Very well," said Noj, clasping her hands together. "Me and Corrine did indeed go to the same school, but we didn't exactly make friends in the classroom. We just kept bumping into each other, nights and weekends, round the same public toilets on the seafront."

She paused, watching that one sink in.

"You were on the game?" said Sean. "How old were you?"

She nodded. "Fourteen, fifteen. That's how we bonded. I did most of my trade there, Corrine preferred to take hers under the pier and come back to the lavs to clean up after. Different strokes," she raised her little finger to the corner of her mouth, brushed an imaginary speck away.

"Corrine hated it," she went on. "Her mum turned her out when she was twelve, made her do a load of dirty bikers. Three of them, she told me, and though she was a bit prone to exaggeration at times, I believed her. Can you imagine," she closed her eyes, squeezed her fingers closer together, "that for your first time?"

"No," Sean shook his head. "Thank Christ, I can't."

"Oh, don't thank him, please," said Noj, her eyes snapping open. "Anyway," she wiggled her fingers as if to dismiss the Almighty from any further discussion, "that woman was a monster. Corrine eventually made a compromise with her, that she wouldn't have to do it at home if she brought back enough money each week. The summer was OK, she worked in a guesthouse. But as soon as the season ended, well . . ."

Sean took another sip of his tea. It was details like this that had made him believe his job was worth doing, before that night in Meanwhile Gardens . . .

"It was different for me," said Noj. "I don't know if you'll be able to understand this . . ." A wry smile twisted her lips. "But I rather enjoyed myself with those fools I tricked. They were a means to an end."

Her stare became more intense. "It wasn't just the money I

wanted," she said, "though of course that did come in handy. It was the power. In a place like this, for a person like me, you need some kind of insurance policy, and that's where I got mine. It wasn't just the sad old men who hung around the toilets who were interested in my pretty young arse, you see. There were a lot more who were very respectable, very prominent upstanding members of our little seaside community. I made sure that every time they thought they were fucking me, I was fucking them right back . . ."

Noj wasn't looking at Sean now, she was looking through him, revisiting scenes from a past that Sean didn't even want to start imagining. But she also seemed to be on the verge of wandering away from the point.

"So," he said, trying to steer her back, "you felt sorry for her, then? For Corrine?"

Noj shot him a look of disapproval. "Yes," she said. "She was so defenceless. I tried to show her how to look after herself."

"By dyeing her hair black?" Sean suggested. "That come from you, did it?"

Noj blinked wearily. "No, it didn't. There was a bunch of them at Ernemouth High, as well you know. I was not one of them. You wouldn't have even noticed me in those days, which is just the way I wanted it."

"Then what?" Sean dropped his gaze to the eye tattooed on Noj's hand. "Black magic?"

Noj pursed her lips, hardened her stare. "You're starting to annoy me now," she said. "I'm starting to think I may be wrong about you. That you might be just the same as Rivett and all the rest of your kind."

"Maybe I'm not," said Sean, wondering if all of this wasn't just the ego trip of some death junkie, trying to weave herself

– or himself – into the story. Despite the dramatic flourishes, Noj really hadn't told him much he didn't already know. "You know what they used to call us, up in London? The Beast."

She laughed, a semi-shriek, then put her hand up to her mouth to stop herself.

"That's good," she said, "naming you after him. Although," her expression changed, her smile falling away, "he does play his part in this sad story, I'm afraid."

"What," said Sean, "are you talking about?"

"The misunderstanding that arose," she said. "The misconceived notion, spread by the press and a thousand gossips, that Corrine was involved in black magic, comes from the policeman that arrested her. Gray, his name was," she fixed him with her green stare. "He'd caught her once before, you see, with some pervert under the pier. And at the time she had a book with her, which bore the name of Aleister Crowley, or, as he liked to refer to himself, The Great Beast. You know who I'm talking about?"

Sean nodded. There was a shop that sold T-shirts of him on Portobello Road, a grumpy-looking, old bald guy, with pentagrams drawn around his head.

"Good," Noj carried on. "Well, Gray took that to mean something that it didn't. The ironic thing was I don't believe Gray was a bad man. But because he had colleagues who he'd told about this book, and because of how Corrine and her friends dressed themselves, two-and-two made six-six-six . . ."

"But I've seen the crime-scene photos," Sean interrupted. "There was a pentagram drawn on the floor, in the victim's blood. You're not trying to tell me Rivett made that up?"

Noj drew herself up, like a cobra about to strike. "You have no idea what that man is capable of," she said. "How he can invert anything to suit his own purposes."

It was Sean's turn to laugh now. "Oh dear," he said, putting his mug down, "I'm sorry, but you're going to have to come up with something better than that if you want me to believe a word you say. All you've offered me so far is tangential stuff that could have come straight out of the papers."

Noj looked down at her hands, spread her fingers out like a fan across the tabletop.

"Don't mock me, Sean Ward," she said quietly. "You are very alone in this town, remember. You need all the friends you can get."

"Well then," said Sean, equally softly, "you tell me something I can use."

Noj closed her eyes. "I will do my best to help you," she said. "Your concern for wayward teenage boys has touched my heart, truly. But you have to remember; I live here. I don't know if I can cash in all my insurance policies for you yet."

Her eyes opened, rested on the watercolour on the far wall. They had lost their earlier spark and so had she. At last she seemed to look her age.

"You know that Rivett's retired, don't you?" said Sean.

She shook her head. "No," she said. "Sharks never stop. If they did, it would kill them. I've set some bait for him though. You just see if he doesn't bite."

"What do you mean?" said Sean, rubbing his temples.

Noj shrugged. "Why don't you drop by again tomorrow, after you've made a few more enquiries? You might believe me by then." She waved her hand, a dismissive gesture. "And now, you can see yourself out."

He left her, still staring at the picture on her wall. The

moment he stepped into the square, his mobile started up. It was Francesca. "Hello," she said, "where are you?"

Sean smiled, thankful for someone relatively sane to talk to. "Not far from your office, if that's where you are."

"Hanging around Captain Swing's, are you?" she guessed. "Dig anything up there?"

"I'm not sure," said Sean.

"Well," she said. "I've found something and I think it's pretty good. Wanna come up and see me?" she affected a Mae West drawl.

"I'll be right there."

18

Sex (The Black Angel)

"Gentlemen," said Rivett, "I got a special little job I'd like you to do for me."

Alone out of the corkboard cubicles that divided the incident room up into work stations, Rivett had his own sealed office, with plexiglass windows on all sides so he could see out, soundproofed on the inside so no one else could lug in. Above his big mahogany desk, with its overflowing in-trays, was a picture of Mrs Rivett and their two young daughters, neither of which appeared to have taken after her. Big, chunky girls they were, with little eyes and flushed red cheeks, slightly older than Gray's kids, but still only junior-school age. Their mother was a slight, mousy wisp by comparison.

"If I may have the fullness of your attention for a moment," said Rivett, his eyes travelling around the assembly of night-shift officers, pausing for a moment to twinkle on his favoured detective sergeants, Jason Blackburn and Andrew Kidd. "As we are all aware," he said, "keeping perverts off our streets is an onerous task. But one that I know that you," he turned his gaze on Gray, "are particularly keen to respond to. Because of the diligence of officers of your calibre, I know my own precious little Charlotte and Thomasina can sleep safely in their beds at night."

Gray glanced down at his shoes. When he looked back up, Rivett was still studying him.

"What's also come to my attention during the course of your duties," he moved around to his desk, reached out a photograph, "is that you might have come across this woman."

He held up the mugshot. Even caught in the flash of a police arrest shot, she radiated insolent beauty.

"Janine Bernice Woodrow," said Rivett. "Or Gina, as she like to be known. Moved down here from Norwich about a year ago now, intent on making a name for herself. Quite a looker, in't she?"

"Until she open her mouth," said Gray, recalling their last encounter.

"Quite so, detective," Rivett nodded. "Now, I been having a word with the Harbour Master about a certain vessel making regular trips here from Holland. You know what them sailors are like, prone to making all kinds of bad company when they stop off in a port for a while. We got one of them under obs," he tossed Gina Woodrow's mugshot down on the table, lifted up a file from the top of his in-tray and took out another. "A certain Nicholas Knobel." A thin, angular face with high cheekbones and extremely pale eyes stared back at them. "Who is only gonna win the prize," Rivett went on, "of being the dirtiest bastard aboard the good ship *Sealander* when you apprehend him tonight."

"Oh?" Gray scratched his head. "What for?"

"Smack," said Rivett. "This here is the source of our latest epidemic in recreational suicide. And our friend Gina is his bag lady, the contact point for them bikers what have been doshing it all about. Fortunately for us, she couldn't keep her foul mouth shut about that. A little bird tell me," Rivett consulted his wristwatch, "she's got a date with him tonight, when he go on shore leave, which is round about now. By the time he make his way up to our favourite Market Row tavern, you lot'll be coming through the door to nick the pair of them, and bring 'em home to me. They will be carrying, I assure you."

He reached in his pocket. "I've signed you out a van," he said, tossing the keys across to Gray. "Pub backs on to a car park, so you won't have to drag her far."

✳ ✳ ✳

Gray got into the driver's seat, Blackburn and Kidd riding shotgun beside him, another couple of younger lads in the back.

"This is a laugh," said Kidd, "five of us to take down a tart and a Dutchman. Len must think we're a right bunch of poofs."

"You in't met Gina then?" said Gray, putting his keys in the ignition.

Kidd rubbed his crotch. "No, I in't had that pleasure yet. Or should I say, she in't."

"Mmmm," Blackburn rubbed his palm up and down his truncheon and they traded dirty sniggers. Gray steered out of the car park, trying his best to ignore their innuendo.

"That'll be because of the bikers," Gray said. "She's in with them, she'll have plenty of back-up, won't she? You'll most probably be needing that," he glanced sideways at Blackburn, still fondling his cosh, and accelerated down the road.

"Wee-hee!" Blackburn affected a good ol' boy accent.

"Looks like we gotta gunfight at the OK Corral on our hands, d'you hear that, boys?" He glanced at the youngsters behind them. Gray turned left and then left again onto George Street.

"Wooo-weee!" shouted another comedian from the back. "Let's go git them injuns!"

Gray pulled into the pub car park, the van's headlight illuminating a row of customised Triumphs and Nortons.

"I'll go in the front," he said, "you lot can bring up the rear. Like usual."

Gray entered the door nearest to the Market Row end of the pub, stooping as he did so. At the time this had been built, none of the patrons had been much over five feet tall.

His back filling up the doorframe, he took in the dimly lit room. The ceiling had low, black beams running across it up to the half-timbered, copper-topped bar; beyond that were partitions of wooden alcoves. A jolly roger was draped above the optics, and between the two rows, a mirror with the Confederate flag etched across it reflected the face of a whiskery barman raising a glass and pouring a measure of bourbon. Two men leant across the counter, their backs towards Gray, wearing black leather jackets with patched denims over the top of them, covered in the flags and regalia of their outlaw clans – skulls, wings, dominoes, dice, rearing cobras and naked women. All covered in a fine layer of dirt, the proof that they were no newcomers to the scene. Both had open-face motorcycle helmets at their feet.

The alcoves to his left and right took up much of the rest of the space and he had to walk forwards into the room to see who was seated inside them, which he did slowly, keeping his head low, a hand across his brow. The first was empty. The second contained a collection of lads from the local art college, Gray could tell from their long, '50s-style overcoats and quiffed hairdos, the packets of rolling tobacco on the table in front of them. In the midst of an earnest conversation about last night's John Peel show, none of the four young men even looked up as he passed.

From the room beyond, a pool ball ricocheted into a pocket and someone cheered. One of the bikers at the bar looked up, caught Gray's reflection in the mirror and started to turn his head, as "Radar Love" by Golden Earring came thumping out of the jukebox.

She was seated in the most concealed part of the room, the last alcove nearest the wall. He saw the Dutch sailor first, his pinched face instantly recognisable from the mug shot. He was bent forwards, his arms hidden beneath the table. As Gray grew closer, a black head came into view, the shiny, luxuriant tresses snaking across leather-clad shoulders. He looked down and saw her draw her left arm up beside her, stow something between her seat and the wall. Then she turned her head, a smile dying on her lips.

"What you got there then, love?" Gray said, positioning his body so that neither of them could easily get past, and flashing up his warrant card in the palm of his hand.

"Who do you think you're talking to?" her black eyes sparked incredulous.

"What is this?" the Dutchman's head snapped up.

Gray heard a whoosh at the side of his head and ducked instinctively. Two bodies barrelled into him, knocking him so that he had to reach out his hands and grab the side of the partition to avoid being pitched into Gina Woodrow's lap. In the split second that it happened, he saw her push the packet out from beside her and kick it backwards under her seat. She had the deft movements of a snake.

"Police," shouted Kidd from behind him. "Stay exactly where you are."

Then there was a mighty crash, as the biker whose arm Kidd had twisted behind his back seconds before he'd tried to brain Gray with his motorbike helmet, toppled into the table of art students, sending glasses and ashtrays flying. The air became thick with shouting.

Gray hauled himself upright as the sailor stood up, knocking his barstool over, and launched himself away. He didn't have time to think. As Knobel tried to veer past him, Gray threw his entire weight down on him, pitching them both onto the floor at the same moment a barstool and several glasses went flying over their heads and smashed against the wall, sending splinters of wood, glass and foaming beer down on them.

The Dutchman opened his mouth but no sound came out; Gray had knocked all the wind out of him. He wilted beneath the detective and, satisfied he could offer no further resistance, Gray shifted himself upright, swivelling his head to see what had become of Gina Woodrow. But all he could make out was a mess of legs.

Kidd had a biker pinned down over the table, his knee in his back, yanking his arms backwards to cuff him while the art students staggered out of their alcove, wiping beer from their clothes and grinding broken glass into the carpet. Blackburn had another one in an armlock, but this one wasn't going down easy, he was spinning around in a circle, taking Blackburn with him, knocking into one of the younger PCs who tried to come to his aid and pitching him over a table. Whoops, hollers and curses rent through the air, building to the crunching crescendo from the jukebox.

Bloody hell, thought Gray, *it really is like a Wild West saloon*. He got to his feet, another glass whizzing past his ear, and saw her, in the midst of the students, weaving her way towards the door. He took one more look at the prostrate Dutchman and made after her. On the threshold of the exit, he caught hold of her arm and swung her back round.

She used the impetus of the motion to land a punch with her free arm, boxing his left ear so hard he almost let go of her.

"You don't know who you're dealing with!" she said, and spat into his eyes.

Gray tightened his grip, dragging her back into the room.

"That in't me who want to see you, girl," he said. "It's the boss requested a special audience. You know, DCI Rivett."

Her expression of outrage relayed her disbelief at this statement and her mouth opened to protest. But then, as if drawn by magnets, her eyes rolled past Gray's head towards the shape that had filled the open doorway.

"Oh dear, Gina," said Rivett, "you have been a naughty girl."

As the DCI stepped forwards into the room, all the noises seemed to stop. Tongues were stilled; the song on the jukebox gurgled to a conclusion and there was a final tinkling of breaking glass before silence descended. Rivett looked down at the Dutchman and shot Gray an approving glance.

"Good work, detective. I knew you were the right man for this job."

Then he turned to Kidd, who had by now got cuffs on his own assailant.

"What's that, then?" he said, eyeballing the biker like he was staring at a reptile in the zoo. The biker returned the compliment with his own venomous gaze, spitting on the carpet that separated them. "Ah, don't tell me," Rivett smiled. "That's Rat, in't it? Known to your old Ma as Raymond Runton."

"He was trying to obstruct an officer from carrying out his duties," said Kidd, "with a motorbike helmet." He toed the offending article so that it rolled across the floor.

"Tsk, tsk," Rivett shook his head, then turned back towards Gina, who had gone completely still in Gray's grasp. "Where is it?" he said.

She stared back at him with blazing eyes.

"Where's what?" she said.

"If you'll allow me," Gray ducked underneath the alcove, found a plastic bag wrapped around a package stuck between the partition where she had kicked it.

"I think you mean this," he said, passing it to the DCI.

Gina's face twisted into an incredulous frown. "Never saw that before in my whole life," she said. "You just planted it. You all saw him!" she turned to scream at the room.

"All right," Rivett addressed the young PCs, "take down the names and addresses of everybody present, will you, lads?" He slapped his hand down on Gina Woodrow's shoulder. "And as for you and your gentlemen friends, I think it's time we moved this party down to the office. We can all get more cosy there."

✳ ✳ ✳

"What the fuck was all that in aid of?" Gina demanded, once they were in the interview room. She was rubbing her right shoulder. Underneath the leather, the imprints of Rivett's fingers would soon be showing through her white skin like a purple bouquet.

"Your little Dutch boy," said Rivett, "has caused me a spot of bother, as if you din't notice. Two dead junkies in the park, found by a young mother out walking her pram last Wednesday morning. Turned bright fucking blue they had, poor cow'll probably never get over the sight of it. And then another one," he leant across the table, "Friday night, who had the temerity to do himself in right in the middle of the Victoria Arcade. That in't the sort of image the Lord Mayor of Ernemouth want to project, now, is it?"

Gina stared back at him but said nothing. The tape machine had not been turned on, after all, and there was no one else here. The door had been locked from the inside.

"You see, Gina," said Rivett, "what your toerag friends do in the privacy of their own council homes is no concern of mine. They want to kill themselves with this shit, that's fine – so long as they do it out of my sight. But they cross a line, like these sorry bastards have just done, and I'm afraid I find myself duty-bound to investigate, don't I? And, as you should know by now, Gina, it don't take me long to suss anything out. Thought you'd been back here long enough to start pulling the wool over, did you? Go freelance?" Rivett got to his feet, started to walk around the table. "A bit on the side that I wouldn't hear about. In *my* town . . ."

Gina stood up, knocking her own chair over, backed away slowly across the room.

"Trouble is," he said, mirroring her steps, his cigar breath in her face, "that gear your clog-wearing friend's now touting – it's a little bit too good, too pure for the Ernemouth palette. Them stupid skagheads didn't mean to kill themselves. They just didn't realise they were taking three times as much as they normally get."

Gina felt the coldness of the wall behind her. She did her best not to look scared as the DCI loomed over her, but her pupils were dilating as her heartbeat quickened, Rivett's huge hands splayed flat against the wall, one on each side of her head.

"So, if you think you're gonna walk away from this one," he said, "I'm gonna need something special, very special indeed. Turn around, Gina."

* * *

Gray stood in the car park in the first grey light of dawn, gingerly touching his ear. It had come up like a cauliflower; he'd need to sleep with a packet of frozen peas on it now.

He took a last drag and then dropped his cigarette, toeing it out on the concrete, the events of the night before replaying in his mind as he walked to his black Vauxhall Astra. Knobel began squealing almost as soon as they had him in the interview room, naming Raymond Runton as his connection. The biker, also held in custody for attempted assault on a police officer, vehemently denied it. He claimed he had merely been coming to the rescue of what he believed to be a damsel in distress.

Meanwhile, the contents of the Dutchman's package had gone off to the lab for analysis.

Rivett, Gray couldn't help but notice, had taken on the task of grilling Gina himself. He hadn't seen him since they had clocked off their shift.

Getting to his car, he squinted up at the gradually lightening sky, the rooftops a gloomy vista rendered in pale grey, wondering if Gina was sent down, where it'd leave her kid. He hadn't been able to shake Corrine from his mind.

"Poor little mawther," he said to himself, turning the key in the ignition. Some people might say she'd be better off in care, but Gray would not be one of them.

He had looked up the book she had been reading. Mr Farrer had been most surprised that Gray should consult him about such a rare and esoteric tome. When he said he'd seen it in the possession of a fifteen-year-old schoolgirl, it was the first time Gray had ever witnessed the little old bookseller rendered speechless.

* * *

Gina bit hard into the leather belt Rivett had strapped across her mouth. It stopped her from screaming as her vision went black and her legs buckled beneath her, the huge hands of Rivett's on each side of her arse the only thing still keeping her upright.

It took a few seconds for her vision to clear, for her to realise he was saying something.

". . . the sort of performance we're after."

He pulled out of her, letting her topple forwards. Gina steadied herself with her hands against the wall, inching her way upright as the spasms rebounded through her body. Rivett watched her, taking a handkerchief from his pocket and wiping off the condom with it so he didn't have to touch where she'd been, zipped up his flies. She pulled up her black leather knickers, and slowly unbuckled his belt from around her mouth, handed it back to him, slick with her saliva.

Folding the handkerchief over, he rubbed the spit off before threading it back through the waistband of his trousers.

"I'll let you know the venue," he said, "when it's all arranged."

Gina ran her fingers through her hair, pushing it out of her eyes and her mouth.

"The fuck you on about now?" she said.

"Don't you ever listen to a word I say?" said Rivett.

"How can I, when you're fucking my brains out?" Gina pouted. "Big boy." She said it with all the scorn she could muster.

Rivett chuckled. "Well, I can't promise it'll be as good as that, obviously," he said. "Seeing as it in't gonna be me playing the leading man. But we both know what a good actress you are, so you'll just have to close your eyes and think of Leonard when whatever spotty young dick sinks it in you. I reckon we'll keep the strap, though. I like the idea of you wearing a scold's bridle. Might be a good lesson in there for you, and all."

Gina swallowed. It suddenly sunk in exactly what it was he was saying.

Blue movies. He wanted her in a blue movie.

It was one thing to fuck the big ape for favours; their brutal couplings had been the perfect mix of business and pleasure that had served her purposes very well since she'd returned to Ernemouth.

But this . . .

"Ready for your close up?" Rivett reached forward and stuffed his dirty handkerchief, condom and all, into the top pocket of her leather jacket.

19

The Wheel

March 2003

Francesca and Sean sat in the empty newsroom, facing the picture editor's monitor screen, staring five years back in time at an image of five smiling men. The occasion, the retirement of Ernemouth's Detective Chief Inspector Leonard Rivett after thirty years' loyal service to the town. Congratulating him on his achievement, the Lord Mayor, Mr Ernest Coleman, the Chief of Police for Norfolk, Sir Richard Meadows, the Head of the Board of Tourism and Commerce, Mr Peter Swift and the then Editor of the *Ernemouth Mercury*, Mr Sidney Hayles. With the exception of Mr Swift, who looked as polished and thrusting as any member of Tony Blair's cabinet, these were the faces of old men, with thread veins and protruding eyebrows.

"From the dawn of the *Mercury*'s digital archive," said Francesca. "After I spoke with the social worker, I thought I'd do a bit of digging around to see what I could find that could back up her story. Take a look at those faces."

"All the local dignitaries," Sean said, waiting to see how long it would take for her to tell him that Rivett was bent too. "What you would expect, ain't it?"

Francesca turned back to the screen. "I've found that it's always the same story," she said, "whether it's a national scandal or something tucked away in a little town like this. You'll always have the eternal triangle of business, protection and press. Good old Sid Hayles," she went into her Pat impersonation, tapping at her predecessor's image with the end of her pen, "was right in Len Rivett's pocket. There's glowing reports of every move he ever made, going back decades. Makes me wonder if we can trust a word of what our back issues say."

"I've just spent the day with Len Rivett," said Sean. "I got the impression he was eager to help. They dug out all the old files for me, found me some names and addresses ..." He studied her profile as he spoke. "Even took me out to lunch. Very friendly, he was. So how come you don't like him?"

Francesca kept her eyes on the screen. "You haven't heard what Sheila said."

"Well?" Sean prompted.

"Well," Francesca repeated, "the most interesting part of it is what she didn't get to say. At the time, that is."

She swivelled round in her chair to face him. "Sheila was Corrine's caseworker from when she arrived here, at the age of fourteen, to the time she was arrested. Corrine had been under social service supervision since she was at junior school in Cotessey, just over the other side of Norwich, where she was brought up." Francesca's eyes grew more intense. "If you could call it that."

Noj's voice in Sean's mind: *Her mum turned her out when she was twelve, made her do a load of dirty bikers ...*"

"Sheila had files and files of information about her background and her medical history and she was supposed to testify for the defence when it all came to trial. Only, the day before it happened, some young copper turned up on her doorstep and told her she was no longer needed in court.

"Sheila didn't believe him, for some reason," her eyes slipped away from Sean's to the floor, "so she turned up anyway. Only to be told by Corrine's barrister that she had agreed to plead guilty, no contest, and her testimony was no longer needed. Testimony," she looked back up at Sean, "that she believes would have proved Corrine's innocence."

"Which was?" said Sean.

"Did you know, or were you ever told, that Corrine suffers from catatonic schizophrenia?"

"Course," said Sean. "That was in her files, the doctor at the secure unit went through it with me. Told me about her medication, all the cognitive behavioural therapy, the art . . ."

He stopped, mid-sentence. In his mind's eye he was back in the ward, looking at the picture Corrine had painted, the sea-scape. Then he was in Noj's kitchen, staring at the very same picture on her wall.

"But," Francesca was saying, "did he tell you how it affects her when she has an attack?"

"No," said Sean, "but I have had some experience of schizo-phrenics before."

"Ah, but," Francesca's eyes shone in the reflected light of the monitor, "the kind of schizophrenia Corrine has doesn't make her act violently. It's completely the opposite, in fact. At times of severe stress, she seizes up, literally goes catatonic. She can't move or do anything, and if someone doesn't snap her out of it, she could die of exhaustion. Sheila saw her go into this state on several occasions, all of which were when she was being confronted by something she found terrifying. So it's perfectly possible that she witnessed the crime but was physically unable to do a thing about it, allowing the real perpetrator, the owner of that DNA you're searching for, to contaminate her with bloodstains. Sheila said that the policeman who found her knew this, because she had been with him at the station when she went into one of her trances before."

"Paul Gray," said Sean.

"The same." Francesca nodded. "Did you . . ."

"Wait," said Sean, "before we get onto him. If this Sheila is so certain about this, why didn't she speak up about it before?"

Francesca leaned back in her seat. "She did," she said, picking up her pen again and tapping back at the screen. "She told Sid Hayles about it, hoping that the *Mercury* could launch some kind of investigative crusade. The next thing she knew she was under investigation from County Hall, suspended from her duties under breach of confidentiality rules. Ruined her career, stopped her from gaining employment anywhere else where her talents would have been appreciated. And that's not to mention the slights and the whispers, the rumours spread by women like my dear personal assistant . . ."

Sean looked back at the photograph, at the faces of old men, the blotches and lines of long comradeship, the age spots of stories interwoven, histories created together.

"The very respectable, very prominent upstanding members of our little seaside community . . ."

"Sheila's evidence, on its own, might not have made any difference to your employer's first petition," Francesca went on. "The Home Secretary, acting with the advice of leading specialists, including Corrine's current doctor, Robert Radcliffe, turned her down on the grounds that there was insufficient new evidence and to proceed would not be in the public interest. But, as you also know, the use of DNA technology was still in its infancy then, and the National Database would not be set up until 1995. They might not be able to rule the same way this time."

Francesca gave the screen one more venomous glance and then clicked the picture away, dumped it in the trash and emptied it before shutting the computer down.

"In which case," she said, getting to her feet, "I think Sheila's files could now form a very strong back-up for you to take back to Ms Mathers. And, as an act of extreme good faith in our abilities," she walked over to her desk, lifted up her briefcase and snapped it open, "Sheila has given us both copies."

Sean watched her take out a thick Manila folder and hold it out to him. He stayed in his seat, shot her a question instead.

"This is personal for you, isn't it?" he said.

Her pupils widened for a second, a tiny pulse. She put the file down on her desk.

"Yes," she said, "of course it's personal."

Her eyes razored into Sean's, and for a second he thought she was going to burst into tears. Then she pushed her hair out of her eyes, put her hands on her hips. "Look, I know this isn't the same magnitude as taking a stand against the most powerful men on the planet," she said quietly, "but it is the same principal. Something went wrong here and we have the chance to put it right. Maybe our only chance."

Sean stared at her, wondering again what had happened to her. Had she been fired from a national newspaper for going against her editor's line, or discovering something that was never supposed to go public? Was she waiting here now, licking her wounds, to come back with something no one could ignore? And was he a cog in the wheel of that plan?

"You don't have to tell me what a dirty place Fleet Street is," he said. "So why are you so desperate to get back there?"

A slow smile spread across Francesca's face and she gave the smallest of laughs.

"The same reason, I suppose, that you're still working as a detective," she said.

Sean raised his hands. "All right," he said, "*mea culpa*." He found his own mouth twitching into a smile, a chuckle welling in his throat. He couldn't help it. He liked her.

He got up then, walked across the carpet and took the folder. He only realised afterwards that it hadn't caused him any pain to do so.

"So, partner," she said, putting on that Mae West voice again, "have you eaten yet?"

"Not since lunch," Sean realised. "And that wasn't actually very appetising."

Francesca picked up her phone. "Well," she said, glancing down at her watch, "it's getting late, but I reckon Keri could still sling us a few leftovers. Whaddaya say?"

Sean nodded. "I'd say the contents of Keri's bins are better than the rest of the crap around here. If he's willing to turn them out for us, I'm in."

✳ ✳ ✳

Len Rivett got back into his car, feeling a twinge in his kneecap as he did so. Bloody arthritis playing him up again, it was a bastard of a job growing old. He started his engine, raised his hand in salute to the security guard as he drove back out onto the seafront. He had to go all the way back down again, but he decided to go and pay Nelson a visit first. Several different scenarios were spooling out in his mind and he'd often found that a drive out to the edge of the harbour was good for clearing out the wrong notions and divining the best course to take. A little natter with Norfolk's proudest son, a little smoke at the edge of the world, would reveal to him what to do for the best.

He put his foot down, pedal to the metal, and accelerated down the long, empty road.

* * *

"So," said Francesca, dipping a piece of torn-off pitta into a bowl of kleftiko, "what did you find out about Paul Gray?"

Sean looked across the restaurant to where Keri was deploying his film star smile to charm the last of his night's patrons out of their seats and into their coats. He had put them on a table on the ground floor this time, tucked away in a corner at the back, piling their table up with food and wine almost as quickly as they had taken their coats off.

He saw in his mind the tearsheet Francesca had given him in her previous folder, another freeze-frame from the past. Rivett and Gray on the steps of the station, announcing that a suspect was in custody. Rivett's face a suitably grim mask for the cameras, Gray turning his away, so that all you could see was the side of his face, an angular man with high cheekbones, a cauliflower ear, thick, black hair slicked off a widow's peak.

Ask what happened to him, she had written on a Post-it note attached to the page.

"What prompted you to ask about him in the first place?" he said.

"Mmm," she said, swallowing her mouthful. "Just because, it was Gray who found her, I wondered what he had to say about how she was behaving. In light of today's revelations," she stuck her fork into a piece of lamb, "it could be really important. If Corrine was in some kind of catatonic trance, it backs up Sheila's story."

"Perhaps," Sean acknowledged.

"Did Rivett tell you anything about him?" Francesca asked.

"Just that he was a good detective," Sean said. "Sound, salt of the earth and all that. Nothing untoward. He even gave me his phone number, so's I could set up a meet."

"Oh?" said Francesca, raising her eyebrows, as if she had not expected it to be this easy.

"Yeah," said Sean, "first thing tomorrow morning, I'll see what I can find out for myself. In the meantime, there is something else that don't seem to fit that maybe you can take a look at for me."

He had been mulling it over since his meeting in the police station, whether to ask Francesca's help or not, whether he could trust her with it. Sheila's file seemed to prove that he could. Or at least, how good she was at the investigative side of her work.

"Something I did know before I came here," he said, "something my employer did think could be important is that your current Detective Chief Inspector of Police, Dale Smollet, was at school with Corrine Woodrow," he leaned forward as he said it, keeping his voice low, even though they were the last customers in the room.

Francesca looked up, startled. "He was?" she said.

Sean nodded. "Not just in the same school and the same year, but the same class as well."

"What, and he didn't say anything?"

"No," said Sean, "and neither did Len. In fact, if I was the suspicious sort, I'd say that Len deliberately tried to lead me astray about it. Just before we went in to meet the DCI, he strongly implied that Smollet was too young ever to have known Corrine. And then, when I met the man, he waved me off without even mentioning it. Now if that was me," Sean recalled the words Smollet had used to greet him, "I would have got that out in the open straight away. I wouldn't want anyone to think I had something to hide."

"Jesus," said Francesca.

"Yeah," said Sean. "The thing is, the pair of them made out like they can hardly stand the sight of each other, so I reckon they've got a bit of a double act going on. We can probably guess which one is the monkey, but you can never be too sure that anything's what it seems around here, can you?"

Francesca put down her cutlery, wiped her mouth with the napkin.

"You're learning Ernemouth Rules fast," she said.

✳ ✳ ✳

Rivett stood at Nelson's feet, looking up at the Admiral. The wind whipped around him, shifting the sand up from the dunes, catching the waves up into swells that roared and crashed against the harbour wall. He took a last drag at his cigar and pitched it away, an orange arc spitting tails of embers, disappearing into the dark.

Rivett nodded, satisfied. "Right you are, Admiral," he said, tipping the brim of his hat.

He turned to walk back to the car, tapping numbers into his mobile as he did so. By the time he had reached the steps to the promenade, he could hear the other end ring.

"Hello?" a woman's voice answered.

"Sandra," he said, "Len Rivett here. Mind if I have a word with your husband?"

"Oh, hello, Len," she said, surprised. "Course, I'll just get him for you."

He heard the receiver click on the table top in the hallway, heard her calling: "Paul . . ."

Nelson looked the other way, his gaze fixed to the horizon.

20

Shaved Women

March 1984

Corrine stood by the school gate, leaning against the wall. She could see her reflection in the window of the Ford Cortina parked in front of her and, at last, she liked what she saw. Her hair was perfect – down to her shoulders at the back, an expertly scissored flat top, the front just tilting into a quiff and razored at the sides. All of it a gleaming, inky black.

The clothes she now had formed a subversion of school uniform that ticked all the right style boxes – a white shirt untucked over a black mini skirt and thick tights, skinny black tie, long black cardigan and, on top of that, the icing on Corrine's personal cake, a three-quarter-length herringbone overcoat and a pair of leather winklepicker boots with a big silver buckle across the ankle. Lizzy, the head stylist, had given them to her over the course of the winter. Said she was welcome, that they had never quite fitted her properly. Deserved them, for all the work she had put in.

Lizzy said Corrine was shaping up to be one of her best trainees.

In the glass of the car window, Corrine saw Sam walking through the gate behind her, saw her eyes narrow with what looked like envy as they ran over Corrine's barnet, her coat and then down to her boots. Corrine smiled to herself and turned around to enjoy the expressions that passed rapidly across her former friend's face.

"Hi, Sam," she said.

"All right?" Samantha's mouth twitched momentarily upwards but the look in her eyes was pure ice. She sped up her pace, hurrying past. But couldn't help but cast another look back over her shoulder, just to make sure she was seeing things correctly.

"What's up with her?" Julian appeared beside Corrine.

"Dunno," she returned his grin. "Don't reckon I'm good enough for her no more."

"Well," Julian considered, raising his voice in the hope that Sam could still hear, "she's a silly cow anyway, in't she?"

Corrine felt a glow inside. She had accomplished the mission Noj had sent her on. She was sure of it.

* * *

Alex held the pencil up at arm's length, measured carefully the space with his thumb.

Samantha sat in front of him, on her bed, her head turned sideways, looking out of the window. "You seen Corrine lately?" she asked.

"No," said Alex, making a mark on the paper.

"Well, it's amazing what a few months in special class can do for you," she said, plucking at her duvet. "I wonder if they give them pocket money in there."

Alex frowned. "What d'you mean, pocket money?"

"I saw her today," Sam said, "wearing a coat and a pair of boots that never came from Tracey Fashions," she smirked as she always did when mentioning Ernemouth's cut-price teenage boutique. "I was just wondering how she managed to afford it, seeing as how she always used to have to freeload off me. Perhaps," she flicked a glance over in his direction, "Debbie's been helping her out. In her usual, big-hearted way . . ."

Alex didn't like the way this conversation was going. "She most probably nicked 'em," he said. "You know that's what she's like. Why you so interested, anyway? Thought you didn't want anything to do with her no more?"

Alex had been told the story of Nana's dog. He had never liked Corrine much to begin with, but that had sealed it for him. If Debbie still wanted to hang around with a dog torturer, she was on her own.

Although, the thought of Debbie was still troubling him.

Sam pushed her elbows forward so that her cleavage deepened, watched his eyes immediately travel down, his attention steered back to where she wanted it.

"Because, for once," she said, "she looked quite cool. She's had her hair done properly, and you can't nick a haircut. How'd she afford it, that's all I'm wondering. Unless . . ." She lifted herself off the bed, stalked towards him. Alex felt the air grow heavy, felt his mind start to twist into the shapes he was failing to put upon the paper. He couldn't seem to separate what his body wanted from what his mind was trying to tell him.

She put her hand over his, brushed the sketchpad off his lap and squeezed the pencil out of his hand, sat down on his knee and looked deep into his eyes.

"Is she on the game?" she whispered, licking his ear lobe.

"Sam," Alex protested. "Don't. What if your mum . . ."

"Shhhh," she breathed hot into his ear, starting to nibble the lobe with her sharp little teeth. "Do you think she gets paid for doing things like this?" She lifted his hand, put it over her right breast and held it there fast, so he could feel, even through the thickness of her school uniform, how hard her nipple was. "Mmmm?"

Alex felt a sick yearning, desire coupled with revulsion at what she was saying. He didn't want to equate the sordid goings on at the Woodrow house with what he had with Sam.

"No," he had a moment of clarity before lust fogged his brain completely, his mum repeating something Mrs Carver had told him. "She's got a Saturday job in a hairdressers up town. Oliver John's, is it called?"

As soon as he said it, Sam took her mouth and his hand away, slipped deftly off his knee. "I think you're right," she whispered, "I can hear my mum coming."

Before Alex could blink, she was sitting back on the bed, gazing demurely out of the window. He picked up his pencil with a shaking hand, put his sketchbook back down over the bulge in his trousers, just as the rapping came at the door.

"Cooeee!" called Amanda. "Tea's ready."

* * *

Corrine got into the salon early on Saturday, and, as she passed a cup of coffee to Suzy on the reception desk, glanced down at the appointments book.

There it was, in black and white.

Saturday 3 March

11 a.m. Samantha Lamb – Lizzy.

Touching the amulet Noj had given her, which she wore on a leather lace around her neck, Corrine allowed herself a smile.

* * *

It was ten o'clock and all was quiet in the Carver household. Debbie's dad, Bryn, who was on nights, was fast asleep in their bedroom. Downstairs, Maureen was in the kitchen baking, Ian Masters on Radio Norfolk keeping her company, drifts of conversation muffled behind the closed door.

Debbie padded out onto the landing, turned into her bedroom and sat down on the bed to put on her Robot boots. Glancing up through the window, she saw a flicker in Alex's room, his hand drawing back the curtains. He stood there for a moment, in pyjama bottoms and a black T-shirt, yawning, ruffling a hand across his dishevelled hair. Then he turned away, disappearing from view.

Debbie felt a little surge of anger deep inside her. So, at last he was in. It was an hour before she was due to meet Darren. Maybe it was time to pay him a visit, see what kind of zombie Samantha Lamb had turned him into.

* * *

"Alex?" Mrs Pendleton called up the stairs, "you decent, love?"

From the top of the stairs came the sound of a door opening, the thud of a bassline suddenly loudening. "Yeah, Mum," he replied. "Be down in a minute."

"Debbie's now here to see you." She winked at Debbie. "Go on up," she encouraged. "See if you can get him out of that pit."

Debbie didn't need to be told twice. She bounded up the stairs, rapped on the door and pushed it open. Heard the record Alex had given her when he came back from his summer holidays, before any of this had begun. The song about the girl in the party dress, bombed on tranquillisers, seeking comfort in the illusions of tarot cards and crystals.

Alex stood in the middle of the room, ill at ease, right hand clasped over his left bicep, leaning sideways like he was trying to hide something.

"Debs," he said, his face flushed. "I weren't expecting you."

"Al?" her hazel eyes bored into his. She stepped sideways, so she could see what was behind him. "That is still you, in't it?"

There was an easel set up in the middle of the room, the canvas on it facing her direction. A portrait of Samantha stared back at her. Uncommonly for Alex, it wasn't a very good likeness. But he had captured the gleam in her blue-green eyes, the way the top lip was curled over her crooked tooth and the expression of superiority.

Debbie drew her eyes away from that cynical gaze and around the rest of the bedroom where she had once spent so much of her time. Across the walls of posters, more drawings and paintings of Samantha had been pinned up. Over The Cramps, over The Ramones, even on top of The Sex Pistols at West Runton Pavilion. Tacked up with pins and masking tape, face after face after face looked down at her, mockery and mischief etched on to each one.

"Jesus," she whispered. "Reenie was right. It *is* black magic."

"What you talking about?" said Alex, straightening himself up, his expression changing from embarrassment to annoyance. He hadn't wanted Debbie to see any of this.

"I can't believe she's done this to you," Debbie stared at him incredulously.

"Done what?" he snapped.

"This!" Debbie spread her arms wide. "I mean, I know *how* she did it, I just don't know why you let her. I thought you had a brain, Alex!"

Alex felt his heart thudding in his chest, in time to the drum machine on the record. Her words were as unwelcome as

Debbie herself and her intrusion into his secret world.

"I din't ask you in, Debbie," he said, his face reddening, "and I din't ask for your opinion, neither. I think that'd be best if you go."

"And what's that on your arm?" Debbie had caught sight of red welts under the sleeve of his T-shirt as he moved.

"Nothing," his face flushed crimson as he pulled the sleeve back down.

"Bloody hell, Al. I can see why you din't want me coming round no more," said Debbie. "But I think there's something you ought to know before she make any more of a fool out of you."

"What?" Alex's eyes narrowed, finding Samantha's words on the subject of Debbie coming straight out of his mouth. "That you're jealous?"

"Jealous?" Debbie barked a laugh. "What you talking about, jealous?"

"You don't like it, do you," Alex went on, "that Sam come from London and she know more about art and music than you do?" He started to walk towards her. "If you hate her so much, how come you have to copy everything she wear?"

"Al!" Debbie's voice rose several octaves. "Have you got any idea what Samantha Lamb looked like five minutes before she met you? She had a blonde wedge and pink legwarmers! A spoilt little posh bitch," Corrine's words ran through her mind. "That's all she is."

He snorted. "Don't talk bollocks . . ." he began, but Debbie stuck a finger in his chest.

"She's a liar, Al, it's me she's jealous of, not the other way round. Don't you remember how you met her? She used Corrine to help her go after you. Corrine told her who you were and where you went drinking, she even did her hair for her that night. If you don't believe me, you can ask Mum, she saw her when she come round mine in a right state about it all."

Alex felt a shard of ice temper the rage that was rising in him. *Corrine; hairdressing – exactly the same subjects Sam was banging on about yesterday. What was really going on between these girls?*

"And now," Debbie's voice rose in volume, "now she's gonna stop you from getting into St Martin's, in't she? She's sending you mad, trying to draw the perfect picture of her. You'll never do it, and d'you know why? The person you think she is don't really exist!"

For a second, she thought he was going to hit her. Rage flared in his pupils and his hand clenched into a fist.

"*No!*" With a visceral vocal howl and a crescendo of guitar, the record came to an end. The crackling of the run-off groove filled the air around them.

Alex's face crumpled into a grimace, his eyes sinking to the floor. "Get out, Debbie," he said. "I don't want to hear no more."

Tears stinging behind her eyelids, Debbie ran back down the stairs, almost colliding with Mrs Pendleton coming out of the kitchen with two cups of tea.

"Debbie!" Alex's mother looked shocked.

"S-sorry, Mrs P," Debbie gulped and reached for the door handle, yanked it open and fled back to the sanctuary of her own house. Mrs Pendleton stared after her, her eyes becoming hard. She put the teas down on the telephone table in the hallway, wiped her hands on her hips and turned around.

"Alexander!" she shouted up the stairs.

✳ ✳ ✳

When Samantha swept into Oliver John's, Corrine made sure she was out of sight, in the stockroom. From the mirror on the back wall, she could see out into the salon, but no one could see in. She had offered to unpack a new load of dyes, and place them on the shelves according to the system of colour co-ordination. Corrine estimated it would take her about an hour. The whole while, she could keep watch.

It was funny the way Sam's eyes kept darting around the room, even when she was putting on that friendly front with Lizzy. She was looking for her; Corrine knew it; wondering if she had come to the right place after all.

All in good time, Corrine thought to herself. *All in good time.*

✳ ✳ ✳

"Mum!" Debbie croaked, throwing the kitchen door open.

"Debbie?" Maureen turned her head from where she was kneading dough in a Pyrex bowl. "Whatever's the matter?" she asked.

"It's Al," Debbie said. "We just had a row."

Maureen crumbled the mixture off her fingers, stepped forwards to put them on her daughter's shoulders. "What about, love?" she said, pushing her gently down into a chair.

"Mum," Debbie willed herself to calm down, "he's been seeing this girl in my class, this horrible girl called Samantha Lamb . . . She got Corrine in a load of trouble and now she's doing it to Al. Remember that day when Reenie came round here in a right old state after she in't been in school all week?"

Maureen nodded. That afternoon was etched on her memory too.

"Well, Samantha done something to her, messed up her hair, and something else she wouldn't even tell me. But part of it was that she got Corrine to take her in Swing's so she could meet Al. She had it all planned out. She was in there with him when me and Darren got there, had him wrapped round her little finger." Debbie knew she was ranting, but she couldn't stop the words from tumbling out. "And he in't been the same since."

Maureen stared at her daughter. "Listen," she said, trying to frame her words without sounding patronising. "I know it's hard, but all boys go through stages like these. Alex is growing up now, becoming a man, he's bound to get himself a girlfriend some day."

"I know," said Debbie, nodding angrily. "But not *her*."

"And if he's going to make mistakes," Maureen thought of the conversations she'd been having with Philomina next door recently, "he's got to make them himself and learn from them. You can't tell him, love. You'll only bring him closer to her if you do."

Debbie bit her lip. Something told her that on this point, her mother was right.

"Now then," said Maureen, "let's put the kettle on, eh?"

"OK," Debbie demurred. On the radio, Ian Masters was introducing his regular Saturday morning guest, Old Barney, a farmer who dispensed homespun wisdom in the Norfolk dialect. The pair of them burbled away as Debbie watched her mother brew a pot, soothed by this connection to the Saturday mornings that had come before.

"Do ya keep a traaashin'?" said Old Barney from the radio.

* * *

Corrine waited until Lizzy was holding up the hand mirror, allowing Sam to view her new haircut from all angles. Then she picked up the broom and walked into the salon, watching

Sam's face reflected, seeing the expression of satisfaction fall away as their eyes met through the looking glass.

"Happy?" Lizzy was asking her.

"Great, thanks," Sam recovered her composure swiftly. But not so quickly as Corrine had begun sweeping up her hair.

"Hi, Corrine," Sam said in her sweetest voice, "I didn't know you worked here."

Corrine smiled back. "Learn something new every day, don't you?" she replied, getting on with her task, carefully catching every last strand.

Sam's smile faded. Lizzy lifted the apron from around her neck, brushed away some more trimmings onto Corrine's pile.

"Well done, Corrine," the stylist winked at her. "Bringing me another satisfied customer. You two friends from school?"

"That's right," said Samantha, getting to her feet, brushing yet more hair from her lap onto the floor. If she thought she was making Corrine's job harder, she couldn't have been more wrong. "*Special* friends," she added, twisting the word for emphasis.

Corrine saw the hatred in her eyes but did as Noj had taught her. Made herself glass, reflected it straight back from whence it had come. Finished piling Sam's hair into her dustpan with slow, methodical care. "See you then," she said, lifting it all up.

"Yeah," Sam sneered down at her. "See you around."

Corrine found it very hard to stop herself from laughing as she took her bounty away. Emptied the hair, not into the dustbin, but into the little wooden box Noj had given her.

"Now I've got you," she whispered to herself. "You *witch*."

Part Three

* * *

THE HUNT

21

Echo Beach

March 2003

There were no nightmares this time. Sean woke at six-thirty feeling like a switch had been flicked in his mind. During his sleep, his subconscious seemed to have worked out the obvious course of action. He settled down to work straight away, making calls, checking his emails, firing out others, collating information and ringing the courier service his employer used to despatch Sheila Alcott's files to Mathers' chambers. He even managed a plate of Full English, his appetite returned with a vengeance.

He called Rivett on his mobile as he stepped outside.

"Top of the morning to you, Mr Ward," Rivett's voice rang in his ear. "What can I do you for today?"

"Morning, Len," said Sean. "I was wondering, do you think you can get your hands on some swab kits for me?"

"I reckon," Rivett sounded intrigued, which was what Sean had been hoping. "Mind if I ask what you want them for?"

"All Corrine's KAs you gave me yesterday," Sean walked towards his car. "The bikers and the drinkers from Swing's. I was wondering whether, as a sign of good faith and their own innocence, they might like to volunteer a sample, just so we can rule them out of any further enquiries."

"I like your thinking, boy," said Rivett. "How many d'you need?"

"Six should do it," Sean said, though at the moment, he was only interested in two. "D'you reckon DCI Smollet will be OK with that, or should I have a word with him first?"

"Don't you worry about him," again, Rivett responded as expected. "I'll take care of it."

"Thanks, Len," Sean unlocked the car door and slid inside. "I'll see you in a couple of hours. If I'm running any later, I'll let you know."

"I can make a start on it for you, if you want," Rivett sounded hopeful. "I do miss the thrill of getting shiftless toerags out of bed in the mornings."

"All right then," said Sean. "How about starting with Messrs Woodhouse, Hall and Prim?" He couldn't help but smile at the real surnames of men who preferred to call themselves Whiz, Psycho and Scum.

"Their check-ups are long overdue," Rivett concurred. "Consider it done. See you back at the office?"

"Yeah. Cheers, Len. See you then." Sean cut the call, happy. He didn't expect any of them to be a match, but it would keep the old sweat occupied, and more importantly, feeling as though he was in charge of things, for the morning. Sean intended to make good use of this time, starting with his visit to Paul Gray.

Under scudding clouds, he drove back down towards the station, turning right when he got to the roundabout, across the top of the market and down into Nelson Road Central. Past the long walls of the cemetery, where, according to one press report he'd read, Corrine had once sat up a tree, trying to conjure up the Devil.

The streets turned residential after this. Sandringham Avenue was in an area known as Newtown, built in the '30s, neat rows of mock-Tudor cottages under bare trees.

Gray had the front door open before Sean was halfway up the garden path. He was as tall as a man had to be to get in the force in his day, still lean and with a face that wasn't easily forgotten; high cheekbones and a hooked nose, startling, pale blue eyes under black brows. His hair would have been that colour once, now it was grey, cut short and neat, brushed off a high widow's peak.

"You must be Mr Ward," he said, offering a long, cool hand to shake. "Paul Gray."

"Thanks for seeing me, sir," said Sean. "I hope not to take up too much of your time."

"D'you want to come in?" Gray's gaze was penetrating and his handshake was brief.

"Well, I was wondering," said Sean, "if we could go for a drive instead."

"Oh?" Gray frowned. "Where to?"

"I'd like to see the murder site," said Sean. "I know it's not far from here, and I have looked for it on the map. Only, I'd rather go there with someone who knows the territory. I thought we could talk on the way."

Gray stood in silence for a second, assessing both Sean and his words. He looked like a hawk, Sean thought, a man who was good at keeping a still surface. It was a trait that Sean had often noted in men of his father's generation. Not so frequently of his own.

"Len in't run you out there, yet, then?" Gray said.

Sean shook his head. "He's been too busy digging up old files for me."

"I see," said Gray. "Well, all right then. Let me just get my coat."

* * *

"That's a pretty bleak spot," said Gray. "As you'd most probably expect."

They had stopped in a pub car park, the other side of a bridge that marked the end of Newtown, a few roads north of Gray's address. The Iron Duke was the last hostelry in Ernemouth, on the end of Marine Parade. Behind it was a middle school that backed onto the racecourse. In front of it, only the beach and the sea.

"We'll have to walk from here," Gray undid his seatbelt, "but that in't far. Be a bit bracing, mind you."

Sean got out of the car, the wind raw in his face. Above their heads, a flaking portrait of the Duke of Wellington creaked on its hinges. On the horizon, the wind farm, rows of giant turbines, their blades turning rapidly against the wind.

"Used to do a lot of stake-outs in this pub," Gray did up the top button of his black overcoat. "Thieves bringing in stolen goods and hiding them out here. Between the beach," he swept his arm in an arc that took in a hundred and eighty degrees of the landscape, "the field behind the school and the racetrack, there's plenty of opportunity. There's a holiday park beyond that and I in't joking, that was always filled with villains, too." He shook his head. "Talk about a busman's holiday."

Gray led the way from the car park and down the steps from the sea wall out onto the dunes, Sean falling into step beside him, wishing he had a thicker coat, bowing his head against the wind. The sand was soft underfoot and he soon felt out of breath.

"What made you come out here that day?" asked Sean.

Gray's brow furrowed, but his eyes stayed locked to the horizon.

"I'd been out here not long before," Gray recalled, "on the May Day bank holiday weekend. I'd been at the school the Saturday night; George Clifton, the old headmaster, needed some assistance. School was always getting done over. George had an alarm that went straight to the station, he ended up out here most weekends.

"Anyway," Gray reached the top of a dune, "this time, he'd found a family camping out on his field." He turned to Sean with a wry smile. "Not the kind that were inclined to move when he asked 'em nicely. So I dropped by, introduced 'em to one of our dogs. Said I'd let him off the leash if they didn't get out of it. They soon changed their minds.

"So after we seen them off," he went on, "I got back to the car and another call was going out, local resident reporting a party on the dunes. I was the nearest to it and I had the dog, so I took it. You could already see bonfire smoke rising over that way," he pointed northeast and Sean could make out a flat, grey concrete roof in the middle of a gulley. "Found a whole bunch of them weirdos down there, having a party."

He stopped again, on the top of another dune, letting Sean catch up. Lost in his memories, he hadn't seemed to notice his companion was struggling. But now a look of concern softened his eyes. "You all right, boy?" he asked.

"Yeah," Sean nodded, "don't mind me, I've got gammy legs, but I'll be OK. Please, go on with your story."

"You sure? Well," Gray nodded, "Corrine Woodrow was one of 'em. So, when Len told me one of them lot had gone missing, that's the first place I thought of, reckoned that was their hideout." He stopped, a look of pain passing over his features. "I was right, and all."

"It can't be easy . . ." Sean began.

But Gray had resumed walking. "Look," he pointed ahead, "here we are."

Sean followed him down another dune. The old sea defence was sunk between two humps, sand nearly piled up to the slit where the soldiers of the '40s would have set up their machine gun. The concrete was pockmarked, covered in yellow lichen, ragwort sprouting from the cracks and crevices.

"We go in this way," Gray ducked under a doorway.

It was dark inside, took a few moments for their eyes to accustomise to the gloom, while the lamentations of the wind shrilled in their ears.

"You'd come across Corrine before, hadn't you?" Sean asked.

"A few times," Gray said. "She didn't exactly come from a good home. Her mother was what you might call notorious."

"Yeah," said Sean, "so I've heard. But there was one time in particular . . ."

Gray lifted his index finger to silence him.

"Hold you hard," he said, "just a second."

He crouched down. "Don't move no further," he said. "Ha' you got a torch with you?"

Sean fumbled in his bag. His hands seemed to have turned into two blocks of ice during their short walk here.

"Hang on," he said, fishing it out. "Here," he passed it down.

"Look at this." Gray switched the flashlight on, ran it across the floor.

Someone had been here before them. Swept all of the sand off the concrete floor and then, right in the middle of it, they had drawn some kind of diagram.

"My godfathers," said Gray.

A white pentagram, that glistened as the torch beam ran over it.

Sean stooped down for a better look, resting his hands on his knees. As he did, a musky scent filled his nostrils. Of lilac, lavender and cloves.

"Funny," said Gray, touching it with the tip of his finger. "That look like," he lifted up his finger to his nose, small grains falling as he did so, "salt."

He took a cautious lick. "Yeah," he said, spitting it out. "That is salt." He put his hand down again, swirling the line with his finger. "They've drawn it in salt."

He looked at Sean. "This has been done recently. Another day or so and the wind would have blown sand in over it. And what's this?" he leaned forwards. "Wax," he said, poking at a congealed substance in the middle of the diagram. "Candles."

Gray stood up, running the beam of the torch across the walls. Stopped when it picked out a dark, pear-shaped object suspended from under the look-out slit.

Without a word, both men walked forwards, picking their footsteps between the lines of the pentagram. Gray reached it first, lifted it up in the palm of his hand.

"Well, I'll be . . ." he said.

It was an effigy, a little doll, of a man wearing a black coat and a black trilby with a feather in the side. Hung there on a length of string, tied around an old rusty nail and fashioned into a noose around its neck. A brace of coloured pins stuck into it.

For a long, drawn-out minute, Sean and Gray stared at each other, the wailing wind making such an eerie soundtrack that each one felt the hairs prickling up along the back of their necks. Then Gray let go of the doll.

"Black magic?" said Sean, thinking of Noj.

Gray whistled. "Or someone's seriously taking the piss."

His cool surface was shattered. The look on his face was one of pure shock.

"The book," Sean pressed the advantage. "Corrine had a book with her when you caught her that time, with the pervert under the pier. A book of black magic."

"So I been told," said Gray, still staring at the effigy of his former boss. "Only . . ."

He stopped himself, turned his face back to Sean's, his eyes hardening again.

"Who you been talking to?" he said. "Who else know why you're here?"

Noj had not been lying. The book she had told Sean about had not been mentioned in any of the old case files, not even Sheila Allcott's report that he'd been over with a fine tooth-comb the night before.

"No one," he said. "You're my first interview. Len Rivett, DCI Smollet and an old guy called Alf Brown in Records are the only other people I've spoken to so far."

Gray's eyes narrowed, a frown creasing his forehead. He looked as if he was on the verge of saying something but then thought better of it, shaking his head, turning instead to continue running the torch around the pillbox.

"Well," he said, his eyes following the beam of light, "at least we in't got another dead body in here. Just some bloody sick bastard . . ."

He switched it off, handed it back to Sean. "You want to show Len what we found in here," he said, referring to Rivett as if he were the officer in charge again. "But if you don't mind, I've seen enough."

It took Sean a while to snap off some shots of the scene, then fumble on the plastic gloves, bag up the effigy, a sample of the salt and the candle wax. By the time he stepped out onto the beach, Gray was halfway back to The Iron Duke, a stick figure of a man in a long black coat striding rapidly across the dunes.

Sean found him waiting by the steps up the sea wall, the rims around his eyes redder than they had been before, although that could have been the wind.

"Sorry," Gray said. "That was unprofessional."

"It's all right," said Sean. "It's not what I was expecting to find there either."

"No," Gray shook his head. "No," he repeated.

"Well," said Sean, putting his hand on the railings. "I'd better let them know at the station, they might want to get some forensics. You never know, there could be a match here for the person I'm looking for. Let me run you back first, though."

"Actually," Gray put his hand on top of Sean's arm, "I can see myself home, if you don't mind. I'd rather be on my own for a while."

"Sure," said Sean. "It must have been a shock . . ."

"Yeah," Gray nodded rapidly, lifting his hand and looking embarrassed. "You could say that. But listen," he looked at Sean earnestly. "I'm sure you want to ask me some more questions and that's fine. Only do us a favour and ring me on my mobile."

"OK," Sean nodded, taking his own out. "Let me put the number into mine."

"It's just the wife," said Gray. "I don't want her to have to think about all that again . . ." He glanced back in the direction of the pillbox.

He looked shell-shocked. Sean wondered how much of it was what they had just found and how much of it bad memories resurfacing. It didn't do to make snap judgements, but Sean had felt more comfortable around Gray than anyone else here so far.

He shook the older man's hand, pressing his card into it as he did, which Gray registered with a brief nod. Then he waited by the side of the car until Gray had disappeared over the bridge, thinking of fatherless children, the circumstances that connected his nemesis in Meanwhile Gardens to Corrine Woodrow and finally, to himself. The reason he tended to look up to men like Gray, like Chief Superintendant Charlie Higgins.

He pressed familiar digits on his phone.

"Charlie," he said as his old boss answered. "Just one favour, for old time's sake . . ."

22

Complications

March 1984

Julian was flicking through the "S" rack in Woolsey & Woolsey for the 12-inch remix of "Numbers" by Soft Cell, when he felt someone come up behind him.

"Interesting," she spoke softly, "that you like *them* so much."

Julian turned around, blinked, taking a second to recognise the person standing there. Samantha Lamb had changed her appearance yet again; now she had Corrine's hairstyle, the one she had been staring at so hard after school the other day. Only, Julian saw, she'd had to go that little bit further in her attempts to stand out.

"If you ask me," Samantha went on, tapping a fingernail on Marc Almond's face, "he's a poof." Her mouth twitched upwards into a smile that didn't meet her eyes.

"But no one did ask you, did they?" said Julian, smiling back at her.

Her expression didn't waver. "Are you a poof, Julian?" she asked. "Only you do look like one. And I've never seen you out with a girl. But maybe," she twirled a strand of her newly dyed hair around her finger, "they just don't like you."

Julian stepped backwards, frowning. "What is wrong with you?" he asked.

Samantha chuckled. "What's wrong with you, more like." She winked and turned away, sweeping out of the shop.

* * *

Amanda jumped to her feet as she heard the front door go. She'd been waiting for her daughter to return for hours, minutes stretched as finely as her nerves – especially since her doctor had told her she must give up smoking when he'd given her the news that she had been meaning to broach with Sam for the past week. Four cigarette butts she had guiltily thrown in the dustbin, one for each hour. The place reeked of air freshener, the synthetic notes of pine not quite concealing the JPS fumes that loitered beneath.

Wayne said he would back her up, that they should present a united front and tell Sam together. But Amanda could foresee the likely outcome of that. Trying to consider her daughter's feelings, she had given Sam the money for a haircut as a treat, an attempt to soften her up that she knew would only be condemned as another act of "falseness" and bribery. There was simply not going to be any easy way of doing this.

"Hello, Sam," she said, and stopped in her tracks. The top of Samantha's hair stuck up like a bog brush, but the sides were shaved to the skin.

"What on earth have you done?" Amanda gasped.

"Like it?" Samantha's eyes flashed and she did a little pirouette.

"No, I don't," Amanda replied. "Are you deliberately trying to get expelled from school?"

"Oh," Samantha's mouth dropped open in an expression of

mock-innocence, "now why on earth would I want to do a thing like that?"

Amanda's jaw clenched with the effort of self-control. "I need to talk to you, Sam," she managed to say. "Come in the front room a minute."

Samantha stuck her nose up in the air. "Sorry," she said, "but I'm meeting Alex and I'm late. I only came back to pick something up. You can tell me later, it can't be that important." She made to move past her mother.

"No," Amanda caught hold of Samantha's arm. "It's very important that we talk now."

Samantha's face turned bright red and she pushed her away with such force that she sent Amanda reeling backwards. "I've already told you," she hissed. "I'm late for Alex, I don't have time for this."

Amanda put her hand out to catch hold of the doorframe, trying to regain her balance from the sudden seasick lurch the push had given her. "Samantha!" she yelled. "You come in here now, or . . ."

"Or what?" Samantha's glittering eyes ran up and down her mother with undisguised loathing. "What is it, are you jealous or something?" she said. "That I've got a boyfriend who's a hundred times more intelligent and better looking than yours? A boyfriend," her mouth curled upwards, "who's actually *older* than me? What a novelty that is, eh?"

Amanda heard the slap before she realised what she was doing. She looked down at her tingling palm and then across at Samantha, crouching down in the corner with her hand to the side of her face, looking up at her in outrage, tears forming in the corners of her eyes. It seemed as though she was watching her in slow motion, from the end of an extraordinarily long tunnel.

"You bitch," Samantha's voice was an incredulous whisper. She scrabbled to her feet, putting her hand on the door handle. "You'll pay for this!"

She pulled the door open and was out of it, slamming it behind her before Amanda could gather her senses, before the red mist had cleared from her eyes.

* * *

Alex slumped across the bench at the top of the town square, watching a constant stream of people come and go. Glancing over his shoulder for the umpteenth time, he saw the hand of the clock in the shop behind him had only moved forwards a minute, even though it felt like ten. He pushed his hands further down into his pockets, dug his chin deeper into his collar. He was cold from sitting out here so long, and starting to feel foolish. There had been plenty of time for Debbie's words to revolve around his head, like the music of a carousel.

"She used Corrine to help her go after you. Corrine told her who you were and where you went drinking, she even did her hair for her that night.

"Have you got any idea what Samantha Lamb looked like five minutes before she met you? She had a blonde wedge and pink legwarmers!"

Not to mention the earful his mother had given him, wanting to know what he had done to upset Debbie. The hardness that came into her eyes when she asked him what he was intending on doing with himself today, as if she couldn't guess . . .

"She's sending you mad, trying to draw the perfect picture of her. You'll never do it, and d'you know why? The person you think she is don't really exist!"

Alex launched himself up off the bench. He couldn't stay

here any more, it had been half an hour and he couldn't toler-
ate the row going on in his head. Turning abruptly on his heel,
he barrelled straight into someone going the other way.

"Ooof!" the impact knocked the wind out of Alex's chest.
Looking up, he realised with shock that he'd walked straight
into Julian.

"Sorry, mate," he put his hand out to touch the other boy's
shoulder.

"S'all right," startled by the impact, Julian's first action had
been to make sure his record was still in one piece. "Nothing
broken," he said, his eyes travelling upwards from his bag to
Alex's worried frown. Then all the friendliness drained out of
Julian's face.

"Not with Samantha today?" he asked.

Alex cringed inside. "No," he said, looking over his shoulder, in case this would be the exact moment she chose to make
her appearance, "I mean, I . . ."

"I saw her when I was buying this," Julian swung his
bag, "Soft Cell record. She called me a poof." He raised his
eyebrows challengingly.

"No," Alex felt the colour pouring into his face. "She din't,
did she? I don't know why she said that, shit, I hope you don't
think that's what I think, Julian . . ."

Julian raised a palm to stop Alex's burbling. "I always
thought you were all right," he said. "But she in't. I don't know
what you're doing with her. That girl's mental."

He shook his head and strode away down the centre of the
marketplace. Alex stared after him, his mouth hanging open.
Then he turned around, eyes rapidly scanning for a girl who
still wasn't there. The clock now read four-thirty.

He hurried away towards the bus stop.

* * *

Rivett pulled the car up round the back, out of the bright lights, under the dark stairwells of fire escapes, laundry hatches and service doors, the rows of industrial-sized bins. So different from the elegant façade, that offered a smiling, vanilla-painted face towards the tourists, the service end of the Albert Hotel resembled a dark fortress, where slitty, frosted windows exuded the minimum of light and air vents belched hot blasts of second-hand oxygen into an atmosphere already heady with the aroma of rotting four-star meals.

Gina peered up at it through the windscreen the way a condemned man might take in his first view of the scaffold. Things had not been going well for her since she returned from the cop shop. She had found a sentinel waiting for her on her doorstep, a grizzled man in his early forties who went by the name of Wolf. Wolf was an unpleasant enough character to be around at the best of times, a man with flat grey eyes and a cluster of hairy moles sprouting up from his rubbled countenance that lent him an appearance more warthog than lupine. He was older than the rest of them and very suspicious.

Wolf made it clear that her card was marked. He followed her into her hallway, put a hand between her legs and forced her up against the wall, his fingers knowing exactly what to do to push the breath out of her, render her silent with fear.

"You turned Rat stupid with this, didn't you, bitch?" he hissed, his facial hair like wire wool rubbing against her face, the smell of stale sweat, engine oil and decades' worth of patchouli curdling in her nostrils. Dead fish eyes boring into her, letting her know there would be no reasoning, no compromises with him.

"Well, I in't so stupid. Things are gonna change round here . . . now *I'm* in charge."

Gina stifled the scream welling up in her throat, a strangled, bird-like gasp escaping instead. When he finally released his grip, her legs buckled and she slid down the wall, while he went upstairs and helped himself to her and Rat's entire stash.

"I get word of any other business going on in our patch while Rat's away," were his parting words, "I'll cut that treacherous cunt right out." A smile snaked across his lips, a dull gleam coming into his cadaverous eyes. "Give me something to look forward to."

A smile that was still dancing in front of Gina's eyes as she watched a fire door open.

"Off you go, Gina," said Rivett. "Your public awaits."

"Len," she said, putting her hand on his lap. "I know who's taking over, I know where you can find him. He's got everything," as hard as she tried, she couldn't keep the tone of her voice from rising, "that belongs to us."

Rivett lolled back on his headrest, an amused expression on his face.

"Go on, my little Venus flytrap," he said.

"I'll tell you," he saw himself reflected back in her black eyes as she spoke, her fingertips kneading into his flesh, "if you take me away from this."

"Awww," he crooned. "And where should we go to, my sweet? Somewhere where no one can find you?" He put his hand on top of hers and lifted it firmly up and off him, dropping it back on her lap. "Still expecting me to sort out all your problems after all we've just been through? Two-timing me with a Dutchman? Really, Gina," his expression hardened along with his voice, "it's time you were a big girl."

He leant across and undid her seatbelt. "Now," he pointed, "don't keep the man waiting." Gina saw a figure standing there, silhouetted against the light.

"I keep telling you, it was Rat's idea, not mine," she said. "Now you've got him banged up, do you really think his mates are going to share anything with you?"

"And do you really think," Rivett's voice was a whisper, his eyes dark, glittering, fathomless. "That I'll let them? *In my town* . . ."

Gina's mouth fell open, but there were no words left to say.

"Right," Rivett nodded, putting on his genial voice again. "You just concentrate on paying off your debt and let me worry about everything else."

With a loud click, the passenger door opened. Gina's head spun round and took in a tall, thin man with sandy hair and a pointed face, a moustache on his upper lip, a gold belcher around his neck above a pastel Argyle sweater.

"She's all yours, Eric," said Rivett, turning his key in the ignition.

"Much obliged, Len," the other man said, hauling Gina out of her seat.

"Have fun." Rivett chuckled as the door slammed. "Don't do anything I wouldn't."

* * *

Wayne turned the car north onto Marine Parade, slouching towards Edna's. He'd spent nearly four hours looking for Samantha, and having exhausted all the pubs in town, then the ones along the front, the 'musies and the skating rink, he was just about out of ideas.

He pulled in just before he reached the Hoyles'. This had

been his idea, and the main reason he'd insisted on coming out was to stop Amanda from bringing her parents into it. She had been in such a state when he got home that she'd actually been considering it, convinced that one of her dad's policemen friends could find Sam and bring her home.

Wayne had managed to make her see how bad an idea this was. He'd been sure that his CB buddies could help him track the miscreant down. But, normally so full of opinions and advice, tonight they had all gone strangely quiet.

He decided to give it one more go. Anything to put off talking to Edna.

"Breaker break, this is the Deuce," he said into his mic. "Do I have any takers?"

The unit crackled white noise. Wayne cursed under his breath.

"Deuce to Bald Eagle, do you copy?" he tried again.

Bald Eagle was a minicab driver. His real name was Reg Styles, but when he went on the air, he started to believe he really was an American trucker out there in the night. Wayne knew he was out working, Saturday being the cabbie's busiest night of the week. Most of the others were only talking from their bedrooms.

The road ahead of Wayne looked empty. He tilted his rear-view mirror so he could see the length of it behind him too. *One more time*, he told himself.

"Bald Eagle, this is the Deuce. You got your ears on, good buddy?"

"Ten-four, Deuce, the Eagle has landed," with a hiss of feedback, the taxi driver's voice finally came through. "In't you found her yet?"

"Negatory," said Wayne. "What's your twenty, Eagle?"

"Just dropped a fare at Garveston, got wiped out there for a while. Coming back over the bridge now. There's a lot of kids about tonight, but I in't seen one that look like yours."

"Well," said Wayne, "can you keep eyeballin' for me?"

"I'm getting another bleed out here," the Eagle's voice was lost in a violent spurt of feedback. "Catch you on the flip-flop, good buddy."

"Ten-ten," said Wayne, thinking, *Yeah, right. Just like everyone else round here, you ain't interested unless there's something in it for you.*

He replaced his mic on its handset, crawled a little further down the road until he was two doors away from Edna's. He could see a light on beyond the front-room curtains, but thankfully, no sign of Eric's car in the drive. *The lesser of two evils*, he thought, steeling himself to face his future mother-in-law.

Despite all recent family rapprochements, there was something in Edna's manner that put Wayne's teeth on edge. That sense of hysteria bubbling under those chintzy dresses and that helmet of hair was much too close to the surface. Amanda had never fully revealed to him the root of the animosity between her parents, her daughter and herself, it was a secret locked so deep inside her he knew it might be a matter of decades before she ever confided in him, if at all. But it only took a few moments in their company for him to make a good guess.

Wayne undid his seatbelt, taking a last look in the rear-view mirror.

Saw a pair of legs walking along the road towards him.

Wayne slid down in his seat, tilting the mirror as he did so, double-checking that his eyes were not deceiving him. No, it was Samantha, with different hair again, but that strange, blank expression on her face that Wayne had seen come over her many times before. When she wasn't scheming, screaming or pretending to come on to him. Amanda was right. In the end, she would always go running back to Nana.

But not if he got her first.

He opened the car door. For a second, she stared straight past him, the noise not even registering. Until he caught her arm.

"What?" she looked down at his hand, as if witnessing alien phenomena. Then her brain clicked back in and she sprang to life. "Get off me!" she shouted.

But Wayne's arms were strong from long hours of manual work. "No," he said, "you're not running back to Nana this time. You're coming home with me."

Keeping one hand firmly clamped to her arm, he tipped his driver's seat forward and pushed her into the back, paying no attention to her squeals and kicks of outrage.

"You've got your mother worried sick," he said, starting the engine, pulling away from the kerb. "I hope you're pleased with yourself."

"She is sick," Samantha spat, back to her usual insouciant self. "But that's got nothing to do with me."

Wayne couldn't stop himself. He knew Amanda wanted to tell her daughter their news herself, but at this moment, all he could think of was getting back at the little bitch for the continual aggravation she delighted in putting him through, to say something that might shut her cruel mouth up once and for all.

"She's not sick," he shouted, doing a wild U-turn across the road. "She's pregnant."

23

Playground Twist

March 2003

"Well, Mr Ward, I appear to have found your man for you."

Mrs Nora Linguard was a small, smart woman, with iron-grey hair scooped up into a bun, a pleated navy skirt and a cream jumper, with a string of pearls around her neck. The Welfare Assistant of Ernemouth High for the past thirty years regarded Sean through bottle thick, horn-rimmed spectacles, a smile dimpling her round cheeks.

They sat opposite each other, across a desk in her office. Two thick ledgers sat open in front of her. She handed the top one across.

"This is the Admissions Register," Mrs Linguard said, pointing to a name, written in blue ink, halfway down a page. "John Brendan Kenyon, date of birth 4.2.68, was admitted as a pupil here on the 8th of September 1981, transferred to us from Greenacres Secondary Modern. This was the year that the school went comprehensive."

Sean's eyes lingered on the page, the proof of Noj's existence in this time and this place.

"And," she flicked the pages forward to where she had

marked another entry with a Post-it note. "He left us on July 27th 1984. That's the good news."

"And what's the bad?" Sean drew his gaze up to level with hers.

"Well, if there had been a problem with this child, any special needs or social service intervention, I would have remembered his name, it would have brought a face to mind. Files are only retained for three years after a pupil has left the school, so his are long gone. Instead, I consulted this," she tapped the thick volume in front of her. "The School's Log Book, kept by the Head. This is where he records all the events of significance that occur over each term."

She looked at him meaningfully, her blue eyes like glass beads behind her lenses.

"And of course, as you know," she said, "June 1984 was a particularly eventful period in the history of the school. If your Mr Kenyon *was* mixed up in the Woodrow case, then I'm sure Mr Hill would have made a note of it. But I've searched the Log backwards from there up to the day he was admitted, and I can't find a single mention of the boy."

"Mr Hill was the headmaster in those days?" Sean asked.

"That's right." She nodded. "A war veteran, you know, fought at Dunkirk. He served the school for nearly as long as I have now, saw it all through from grammar to comprehensive and then," she grimaced, her gaze drifting through Sean, "during those terrible days. I know I won't see his like again."

"It must have been hard for you," said Sean, "having to deal with the fallout from that."

"Oh, it was," said Mrs Linguard. "We had them all around the gates for weeks, the papers, the television, the radio. Digging around for stories, trying to apportion blame. Stirring up the mob." She rolled her eyes. "You know how people talk. Especially when they've suddenly got an audience egging them on."

"I'm starting to get an idea," said Sean. "Some of the pupils were hounded out, I believe?"

"Yes," she nodded, "but your Mr Kenyon wasn't one of them." Her brow creased. "Look, I know it may not be sensible to rely on memory, but those events are fairly etched on my mind and I don't recall him having anything to do with it. To be perfectly honest with you, I simply don't recall this child at all."

"You'd never have even noticed me in those days," Noj's voice in Sean's mind. *"Which is just the way I wanted it."*

Sean motioned his head towards the Log Book. "Well," he said, "it has been nearly twenty years. Do you mind if I ask, what are your strongest memories of the time?"

Mrs Linguard paused, cupping her hands together under her chin. "The fateful form 5P," she said. "The first person who had to leave because of what that girl did wasn't any of her classmates. It was her teacher."

"Really?" said Sean. "I haven't heard this before."

"Philip Pearson," said Mrs Linguard, "was Corrine Woodrow's form teacher for a period, before she got moved into the special class. He was a chemistry don, a quite brilliant mind. And a strong disciplinarian, one of the best. But he also had a knack for bringing some of the worst pupils out of themselves, the ones that were more sinned against than sinning, so to speak. That's what he tried to do with the Woodrow girl. And that's what got him in trouble."

As she spoke, shadows passed across her features, deepening the lines on her forehead, tugging down the corners of her mouth. "He made the mistake of talking to someone from one of the papers. Someone he thought he could trust. He imagined he was going to be able to calm the situation down by explaining some of the background. But of course they just twisted his words out of context, you know how they do."

"Only too well," said Sean. "What was it, a local paper or a national, can you remember?" He hadn't seen any of this in Francesca's clippings.

"*The Times Educational Supplement*," Mrs Linguard said. "He wouldn't have spoken to a tabloid. But by the Monday, they'd all got hold of the story anyway and turned it upside down. Mr Pearson said something about the town that he probably shouldn't, that it was a deprived area with a higher than national average of children on the social services register. Which was true enough . . ."

She raised her eyebrows. "But when it gets translated into something like: *Incest Town a Breeding Ground for Murder says Corrine Woodrow's Teacher*, well – you can imagine how that went down. We had them baying for his blood at the school gates, had to call the police in to get him past them. Poor Mr Pearson was forced to hand in his resignation."

"Was this story in the local paper," Sean pressed, "the *Mercury*?"

"The *Mercury*," Mrs Linguard repeated with disdain, "comes out on a Friday, so they tried to capitalise by getting Mr Pearson to make a public apology for slandering the town. He declined, of course. So they made a big front-page splash about him being unrepentant, cold-blooded, arrogant and so on. It was a terrible paper in those days, run by a quite grubby little man. Now, what was his name? Hayles," she hit upon the correct moniker with some ferocity. "Sidney Hayles."

Not many flaws in this old girl's memory, then. "I don't suppose you know what happened to Mr Pearson?" Sean asked. "I'd like to talk to him, if I could."

"Well," Mrs Linguard hesitated, "he got another job all right, at the university in Norwich. But they didn't actually move, in the end – his wife had a business here and they managed to tough it out."

She paused again, her gaze losing focus as another emotion hit her. "It's terribly sad; she died quite recently, Mrs Pearson. She was only in her fifties. Cancer, you know. I haven't seen him since the funeral, but I don't think he would have moved since then. Let me just check . . ."

Sean nodded, looking back down at the Admission Register on the desk in front of him, the rows of names of the pupils who had left school at the same time as Noj. He saw it there in black and white: *Dale Smollet*.

"Here you are," Mrs Linguard jotted onto her pad and detached the page, handing Philip Pearson's number across.

"Thanks," said Sean, pointing to the entry on the Admission Register. "And what effect did all of this have on him, do you think?"

"Oh," Mrs Linguard's expression instantly brightened, "the Detective Chief Inspector. Well, that's what made him want to become a policeman in the first place. Because he was in with a bit of a bad crowd himself, at one point, he won't mind me telling you. Now he's one of our most successful old boys, comes back every year to give the prizes out on Sport's Day." She shook her head. "It just goes to show, doesn't it? How some children can go one way and others the complete opposite."

"It certainly does," said Sean.

* * *

Outside the school, Sean dialled Rivett's number, taking the calculated risk that Paul Gray wouldn't have called the old sweat first. He didn't want Rivett to know exactly what they'd just found in the pillbox.

"Two down," he answered on the second ring, "one scum-bag to go." As ever, Rivett sounded delighted with himself. Traffic noises whooshed in the background; he was outside, somewhere. "How's your morning been, so far?"

"Interesting," said Sean. "Someone's been back to the murder site."

"You what?" Rivett's voice suddenly rose in volume. "Sorry," he said, "a lorry now went past, I din't quite catch that. You say something about the murder site?"

"Someone's been there," repeated Sean. "Recently. Made a pentagram on the floor in what appears to be salt and burned a few candles. Looks like they've tried to recreate what they know about the original scene of crime."

There was a pause, only the sounds of a busy road from the other end. "Only, thankfully," Sean went on, "they haven't left us with a body this time."

"The sick bastards," Rivett's voice returned, a vehement echo of Gray's sentiments. Sean let out a breath. Rivett sounded genuinely aggrieved. So hopefully there wouldn't be any questions about the centrepiece of this little tableau, his effigy that was now on its way to London, along with the samples. Sean had felt it crucial, and his employer had agreed, that whatever DNA traces might be found on the doll be independently verified.

"I'll be right there," said Rivett. "Give me, what . . . twenty minutes? Oh, hold up, though. D'you think we should bring a SOCO?"

"Yeah," said Sean, thinking, *Could make life still more interesting*. "Yeah, we should. If the DCI can spare one."

"Better make it half an hour, then," said Rivett. "Seeing as I'm right over the other end of town." His voice crackled with agitation. "Maybe a bit longer, even. Blast!"

"Don't worry, Len, that's fine, it's not going anywhere. However long it takes."

The longer the better, he thought.

✳ ✳ ✳

Sean drove back along the seafront. The sun was trying to burn its way through the clouds, patches of golden light dancing on the waves. Like the illumination Sean sought that the second of his calculated risks would pay off, it glimmered, just out of reach.

Underneath the creaking pub sign, Directory Enquiries put him through to Hecate's House Tattoo Parlour. Sean hadn't noticed the name of Noj's emporium, since it hadn't advertised itself on the outside. Only that it was situated on Greyfriars Row – presumably, the ruined cloisters in the square outside it. There were a number of tattooists in Ernemouth, but only one such establishment there.

A man answered with a Belfast accent.

"Hecate's House, can I help you?"

Sean could picture him, standing across the bar at Swing's. "Is Noj there, please?" he asked, wondering if the Irishman would place his own accent so quickly.

"I'm afraid she's with a client right now. Could I ask you to call back in maybe . . ." Another voice came into earshot, cutting him short. Sean heard him place a hand over the receiver, so that the rest of the conversation was inaudible.

"Excuse me," the Irishman's voice came back, "can I ask who's calling, please?"

"Sean Ward," he said.

"One moment." The hand clamped over the receiver again, the reflex action of a suspicious mind. When he came back on, though, there was humour in his voice. "Just hold on one second there, Mr Ward. I'll pass you over."

There was a click, a bleep and then Noj picked up.

"I had a feeling it would be you," she said.

"Yeah," said Sean, "I got your message."

"Oh?" Noj sounded puzzled. "What message was that?"

"The one you left at the murder site," said Sean, clenching the fist of his free left hand involuntarily. "I'm on my own here at the moment, got about twenty minutes before Len Rivett joins me. You got a good likeness of him all right, but I'm not sure whether we should hurt his feelings so much. Especially when he's bringing a SOCO with him."

Sean found himself listening to another pregnant pause.

"A SOCO?" Noj finally said. "What's one of those?"

"A Scene of Crime Officer," said Sean. "He comes with a forensics kit, to take fingerprints and collect DNA samples."

"I *see*," Noj stretched the word out like an elastic band, like the invisible tightrope of trust between them that one was going to have to put their foot down upon first. "And you're suggesting that it might be safer to withhold something from him? A certain likeness that you currently have in your possession?"

"That's what I'm trying to ascertain," said Sean, "yes."

"Then I would have to agree with you," the tattooist conceded.

"Good," said Sean, relaxing his hand. "So that was the bait you mentioned?"

Noj chuckled. "You *are* a detective, then. Does this mean that you believe me now?"

"I'm starting to," said Sean. "But would you mind telling me what that was all in aid of?"

"I was clearing the way for you," Noj's voice was solemn. "Putting him on the back foot. He wasn't expecting it, was he?"

"No," Sean agreed. "He wasn't. But just to be completely clear, no one already has a sample of your DNA or fingerprints on a file anywhere?"

"No," said Noj. "As far as they're concerned, I never even existed."

"Good," said Sean. "Let's try and keep it that way. I'd better go."

"Are you still going to drop by this evening?" there was a trace of worry in Noj's voice.

"Yeah," said Sean. "But I'm not sure when. I'll call you back when this is over."

He opened the car door, the twinges in his legs not as strong as they had been earlier, but still telling him he needed to get on his feet. He stuck the phone to charge in the cigarette lighter while he leant against the side of the car, going over everything he did know as opposed to everything he thought he knew.

After five minutes, he retrieved his mobile, locked the car and began to walk. He wasn't sure he'd get a signal out there on the dunes, so he only went as far as the sea wall. His eyes locked on the distant wind farm. Francesca answered on the first ring.

"Did you make your meeting?" she asked him.

"I did," said Sean, "but I've only got a few minutes left before I'm back with Rivett. Just wanted to tell you, I've got an idea that you might want to pursue. There's a very interesting woman I've just been talking to at Ernemouth High, a Mrs Nora Linguard."

"Oh yes," Francesca said, "the Welfare Assistant?"

"That's right," said Sean, "the only person left on the staff who was there twenty years ago. She's got a good memory on her. Tells me that Smollet comes back every year to give the prizes out at Sports Day. One of their most successful old boys, she says. D'you think that could form the basis of one of those profiles, where you talk to an upstanding member of the community about what they're putting back into society?"

"I believe it could," Francesca sounded as if she liked the idea.

"Just a gentle interview, I'm thinking," Sean went on, "about his memories of his schooldays and why he's so keen to keep a link with the place. And then, just in the course of your research, perhaps you can look into his rapid rise up the career ladder and any relation that Rivett might have to that."

"I'm already working on that," she said. "I've got someone looking at any shared business interests they might have. An old colleague of mine in London," her voice turned a shade ironic, "who's good at these things."

"Good," said Sean, "that's exactly what we want to know."

"I'll get on with it then," said Francesca.

"Before you do," said Sean, "could you look me out something? It wasn't in those cuttings you gave me, but Mrs Linguard drew my attention to it. Would have been a front page in late June, 1984, about a teacher called Philip Pearson. Corrine's form teacher."

The third truncated conversational pause of the morning was followed by Francesca saying: "Ri-ight. That was remiss of me. But it shouldn't be too hard to track it down."

"I'm gonna be off radar for a couple of hours now," said Sean. "I'll catch up with you later. Good luck with your research. I'm sure you'll be able to get more out of the Detective Chief Inspector than I will."

"Oh, I will," of this she sounded sure, "you can count on it."

* * *

Sean made it back to the pillbox just in time to see a string of figures appear on the horizon. First Rivett, swearing as he skidded on the soft sand halfway down a dune. A younger man behind him, with a hefty bag slung over his shoulder, the SOCO. Then, coming up the rear, his jaw set in a firm line, DCI Dale Smollet.

Sean squinted as the sun made another sudden appearance between a gap in the clouds. "Make my day," he said.

24

Spellbound

March 1984

Darren put the needle down on the record. A crackle and then a glissando of strings soared into the room, a crashing piano playing a minor chord, a starry night painted around them in music of velvet-blue and silver. His favourite record, he had been playing the 7-inch over and over since it came out in January.

When he looked across at Debbie, lying across his single bed, staring out of the window, he could see that her mind was far away too. But the frown that was sunk into her features told him it was not in a very pleasant place.

"Are you all right, Debs?" he said, kneeling down beside her, putting his hand on hers. "You don't seem like yourself today. Is something up?"

Debbie turned her head to look at him. She had been looking out across the wall of the cemetery that ran opposite Darren's house, into the bare branches of the trees, but without really taking anything in. Her mind was full of the pictures on Al's wall, and a horrible feeling of guilt was snaking around her stomach.

"Sorry," she said, hauling a smile onto her lips. "I was miles away. What were you now saying?"

"I said," Darren raised her hand up to his lips and kissed her knuckles, "I'll just put this on one more time and then we'll go out and see what's happening. I in't made you sick of it, have I, playing it so often?" His blue eyes were so earnest, the scattering of freckles over the bridge of his nose showing through the day's foundation.

"Course not," Debbie swung herself up into a sitting position. "It's my favourite song as well. Play it as many times as you like."

"Great," said Darren, letting go of her fingers and getting to his feet. "I'll just spruce myself up, then." He walked across to the mirror, glancing out of the window as he did. What he saw stopped him in his tracks.

"Is that what you were staring at?" he turned back to Debbie, a puzzled expression on his face. "Someone's sitting up a tree out there."

* * *

From the Y-shaped hollow between the branches of the yew tree, Corrine could see the entire graveyard, and most importantly, the path that ran all the way down the middle of it, a grey ribbon under the orange glow of the streetlamps outside the cemetery wall. She was keeping lookout while Noj prepared the hole they needed to bury their working when the final words of the curse had been cast.

This was the best place, Noj had explained, as he had led her through the gap in the churchyard wall, the old yew tree the most potent protection against evil within it. More ancient than the Christian burial site around them, he had assured her, even the crumbling gothic angels and worn-away headstones that surrounded them. And tonight, at thirty-one minutes and seven seconds past the hour, the full moon would wax; the most auspicious time would be upon them.

He was digging away in the hollow base of the trunk while Corrine kept one eye out for intruders, and the other on the stopwatch he had given her. As essential to the working as not being disturbed, he had impressed upon her, was burying the box at the exact second of the first quarter.

"Noj," said Corrine, "that's now twenty-five past exactly."

"Excellent," came the voice from below her. "All is prepared. Toss me down the stopwatch in precisely three minutes."

* * *

"You know what?" said Darren, pressing his nose up against the window in an attempt to get a better look. "I reckon that's Corrine."

"No," said Debbie, getting up off the bed, "that can't be."

Darren's breath had fogged up the glass, so she wiped it away and peered into the night. The streetlight on the opposite side of the road cast a dim glow over the branches of a massive old yew tree. Sure enough, now that she was looking properly, Debbie could make out a figure up there.

"There is someone," she said, "but I can't see them all that clearly."

"Hold up," said Darren, "is this better?" he undid the latch, pulled up the sash window.

* * *

Noj had begun the incantation, speaking in words that Corrine couldn't understand. The hairs prickled on the back of her neck as he spoke, as if someone was breathing cold air down the collar of her coat. She kept her eyes fixed to the stopwatch. One minute and forty-five seconds to go.

* * *

Debbie leaned out onto the windowsill. The night was icily cold, not a cloud in the sky. Clear enough to make out a flash of white in the tree, the side of a head against the blackness that surrounded it.

"Oh, my God," she whispered. "You're right. That is her. What's she now doing?"

* * *

"Catch," said Corrine, dropping the watch into Noj's cupped hands. He retrieved it in one deft motion, then kneeling down under the tree, put it down on the grass in front of him, so the time was clearly in sight.

"Go back to London and leave us forever," Noj began the final part of the spell. "Go back to London and leave us forever." He raised the hammer above the black bundle that lay in front of him. "Go back to London and leave us forever."

"Woooooooo!" Darren yelled out of the window.

At that exact time Noj smashed the hammer down three times, onto the black candle within the cloth bindings, surrounded by the cuttings of Samantha's hair and the leaves from a blackberry bush, bound up with black string.

Corrine gave a start. "What was that?" she whispered, snapping her head around.

Noj, lost in the moment, heard nothing. What he felt was too powerful: a quicksilver rush running through his arms and down to his chest, expanding his heart and filling him with a sense of divine purpose. He dropped the hammer, lifted the bundle up to the moon and then dropped it into the hole he had prepared.

* * *

"Don't!" said Debbie, pulling the window down.

Corrine saw the movement out of the corner of her eye. Someone shutting a window across the street. Her heart hammered in her chest and her fingers slipped on the bark, grazing her knuckles as she pulled herself round for a better look.

Someone had been watching them!

"What?" said Darren, his face flushed. "I was only having a laugh."

* * *

His eyes glued to the hands of the watch, Noj smoothed the last of the soil over the top of the bundle. He felt like a thousand fireworks were detonating inside of him, the biggest surge of power he had ever experienced, as he entwined with Hecate at the exact second of the hour of the rising full moon.

Above his head, Corrine felt a stab of pure fear, as sharp as a dagger to the guts.

Someone had been watching them!

She didn't know what she was more afraid of. That the working had been disturbed, or that Noj would realise she had not kept a good enough watch, that she had let them both down right at the final, crucial moment.

Maybe, she thought wildly, *maybe he din't hear it. He in't said nothing. And if he don't know, then maybe it don't matter.*

She looked back towards the house. Whoever had closed the window had just whisked the curtains shut too.

"Corrine!" Noj's voice was an urgent whisper. She looked down, saw him standing there with his face turned upwards, a radiant smile across his countenance, reflecting back the luminescent glow of the moon. He didn't look like a boy any more, she realised. No one who didn't know him would believe he wasn't really a girl.

For a second, seeing him like that, she felt giddy with relief. *He din't notice. Thank God . . . No, thank the Goddess for that!*

Noj raised both arms up in exultation. "It begins!" he cried.

* * *

"Debs, look, I'm sorry!" Darren was stung by the expression of anger on his girlfriend's face. "I didn't mean anything by it. Debs, what's up?"

Just as quickly as her rage had flared her face crumpled and she fell forwards into his arms, tears spilling out of her eyes. "I'm sorry, Darren. It's not you, it's Alex . . ."

* * *

Corrine scrambled out of the tree, jumped the last few feet down and landed with a soft thud on the ground next to Noj.

"You did brilliantly, Corrine," he said, taking her hand and squeezing it. "Now, let's get out of here." He started to run down the path. Corrine went to follow him, but as she did, she felt herself hesitate, felt herself doing the one thing her friend had impressed on her she should never do, lest the spell be turned back on itself.

She looked round, over her shoulder, at the old yew tree.

* * *

Corrine was jolted awake by the sound of the door slamming. Her eyes opened on her narrow bedroom, still cast in darkness, but for the barley-sugar glow from the streetlamp that seeped under the gap beneath the curtains.

Two luminous spots on the hands of her Mickey Mouse

alarm clock told her it was 3:45 a.m. She'd only been back here a couple of hours herself, sneaking back unseen after a week and a half of bunking round Noj's. It wasn't that it was an odd hour for her mother to come home.

But, as she lay her head back down on her pillow, pulling her bedclothes closer around her, Corrine detected a sound she could not recall having ever heard before.

A low, snuffling noise, accompanying Gina's heavy footfalls up the stairs. Corrine sat back up, listening hard. It sounded like crying.

Could it have something to do with all those other things that weren't quite the same? There had been no lights on when she'd arrived, no motorbikes parked up in the front yard. Corrine didn't think she had ever returned to an empty house before, whether her mother was in or not – there were normally at least three of them to be found through the haze of pot smoke, lying around on the sofas, dismantling machinery on the front room carpet, listening to their loud, groaning metal at the maximum volume.

Psycho, Whiz and Scum . . . How she'd hated their stupid names, their acne-scarred faces, their straggling, bumfluff beards. Not that it was anything she could have put into words, but Corrine had instinctively known that they were the weak cards in this raggedy outlaw pack. They were here because they didn't stand a chance, any normal woman would shun them for being so crude, so they were forced instead to do the bidding of their elders. Ones like Rat, with his black, oily hair that ran like a snake down his back. His narrow, cruel eyes that always played over Corrine like a cat sizing up a rodent. His oil-stained fingers that were crueller still.

Rat was the one at the top. Rat was the one that was always here ...

Except that he wasn't here tonight.

Something's happened, Corrine realised. A tiny spark of hope flared inside her, and she pulled back her blankets, put one foot tentatively down on the carpet. On tiptoe, she stole across its nylon surface, opened her door a crack.

Gina had stopped on the top of the stairs, had her head down, a hand across her face. Her body was convulsing with the effort of trying to keep the tears in.

Frozen in the doorframe, Corrine watched her, conflicting emotions twisting her stomach into a knot. She should have been happy to see her mother like this, at last. All the times she had stood over Corrine while she was in a similar state of distress, dropping scornful words onto her that burned worse than salt on an open wound, burned deeper into Corrine's soul, convincing her that she was worthless, stupid, a sorry mistake that should have been flushed away in a condom and didn't deserve the right to happiness, the trouble her existence had caused.

All those times she had let Psycho, Wiz and Scum do what they wanted with her, sneering at her tears and saying she needed toughening up. And the times that Gina didn't know about, when Rat had put his hands around Corrine's neck and told her what would happen if she ever let on, pushing her head down towards the bulge in his jeans that concealed the blade of his hunting knife.

All the dirty men under the pier and the money she had stolen.

But Corrine had never seen her mother cry. Never seen her look vulnerable in any way. Never seen her look happy, either. And from her earliest memories, all she had ever wanted to do was make Gina smile. Make that face, that beautiful face that Corrine could find no trace of in her own plain features, light up with something like love.

Now that older, deeper motive, that emotion that had held her captive so long, rolled back over her. Without thinking, Corrine opened her mouth. "Mum," she said, opening the door fully and taking a step towards her. "What's wrong?"

Gina lifted her head. Her cheeks were black with mascara. She opened her mouth and shut it again, no sound came out. Opened her arms instead.

Corrine went haltingly towards her, wondering if she dared put her arms around that perfect figure, encased in black leather and fishnet tights, previously such an impenetrable fortress. Did so awkwardly at first, then, feeling Gina respond, squeezed tightly into her. Corrine smelt the miasmas of men clinging to her mother's flesh.

"It's all right, Mum," she said, feeling as if she were dreaming. "It's all right."

Gina began stroking Corrine's hair, softly, absently at first. But as their embrace grew tighter, more suffocating, her hands started to pull, started to clamp down on these new raven tresses her daughter was sporting, this pathetic imitation of her own, naturally thick black mane. She, Gina, who had never allowed herself to cry in twenty years, not since she was thirteen years old herself and her stepdad had come into her room, thinking he could help himself. Help himself to what, from that moment on, all others would have to pay for dearly, in money or in kind. A concept her thick, useless, ugly little daughter had never once got her head around, for all she'd tried to beat it into her. What had she been thinking of . . .

"Ow!" Tears sprang into Corrine's eyes as her head was

yanked back, one tiny moment of tenderness lost in the flash of Gina's opaque black eyes.

"What are you doing here anyway?" Gina demanded. "I thought you had better things to do with yourself these days."

"I . . . I just . . ." Corrine started, but found she hadn't any words to offer her mother.

"Things have changed," Gina hissed, her dirty, tear-streaked face transforming into a vixen's mask. "It's gonna cost if you want to come back here. As for that poncy social worker and all them teachers — they'll be doing me a favour if they take you off my hands. You can rot in an orphanage for all I care!" She gave a hysterical cackle.

"Oh shit," said Corrine, trying to wriggle free from her mother's grasp.

Gina slapped her hard across the face. "Oh shit is right!" she snarled. And then, another sea change rolled across her features, a crooked smile tugged up the corners of her mouth, the gleam in her eyes became more maniacal as she extended a finger nail to trace down the side of Corrine's face where the blood vessels were starting to engorge.

"But, hey," she said, staring at her daughter as if seeing something in her face for the first time, "you know, you've been making so much effort recently to look nicer. I don't think that should go unrewarded. Yes," Gina smiled. "I think I'll have just the job for you."

Corrine no longer knew what to say or do. The weight had come down on her mind again, she could feel her emotions shutting down, blanking everything out, so that her mother stood before her mouthing words Corrine could no longer hear.

Gina let her go, pushed her back towards her bedroom. "Get some beauty sleep," she said, "you're going to fucking need it."

25

No Doves Fly Here

March 2003

Dale Smollet stood on the threshold of the pillbox, nibbling one of his manicured thumbnails. It was the only sign of emotion he was giving off as he stared at the SOCO, Ben Armitage, working away inside.

Sean watched him, thinking of Paul Gray and what it would have been like for him when he made his discovery, on 18 June 1984. The crime scene photographs imprinted on his memory in black and white were starting to come into colour. The beach on a hot summer's day, the smell of the sea and suntan lotion, the cries of the gulls overhead – the scene of a thousand family holidays. Gray crossing from that world and into the concrete bunker for the first time, the tableau of ritual murder laid out in front of him – black hair, white skin and open red flesh. The initial disbelief of confronting something so unnatural and unexpected that would have rendered him unable to process what he was actually seeing for the first few seconds until the full horror of it truly sank in . . .

And something else.

Corrine Woodrow hunched in a corner, her knees drawn up to her chin, her arms folded around them, staring up at him with glassy, unfocused eyes. Sean had worked on this picture in his mind over and over, but the contents of it had started to alter now. The Corrine in his mental reconstruction, was she in shock over what she had committed, or convulsed with a psychological condition that rendered her incapable of defending either herself or her slaughtered school friend?

Gray had been thirty-three when he made the discovery, just a couple of years older than Sean was now. What had it done to him, walking in on this scene?

He looked across at Rivett, standing in the near distance, hunched against the wind on the top of a dune, keeping watch over the horizon to ward away any potential gawkers.

A thousand questions he wanted to ask the two of them, but none that he could voice right now. He turned his gaze back to the Detective Chief Inspector.

"You've never had anything like this happen before?" Sean asked.

Smollet frowned, turned his head slowly, as if it was an effort to disengage from what he had been observing. Maybe he, too, had been forming a picture in his mind.

Or was he reaching back into his own memory?

"I'm not sure what you mean," he said.

"Death trippers," said Sean. "You know. Sick individuals who like to come on pilgrimages to places like this, leave their own personal tributes. The more shocking the crime, the more likely it is to happen. I would have thought this place could be something of a magnet for them."

"Ah," said Smollet, nodding. "I get you. Well, it's not something I've ever heard about before. Len can tell you for sure, but I think I'm right in saying that the exact location of this was kept from the press at the time, to stop that sort of thing from happening. There's dozens of these pillboxes up the coast here, you know. Course, you can't stop kids from getting into them . . ."

"That's what I mean," said Sean. "The local kids. Surely there've got to have their legends? They get intrigued by nefarious activity, don't they? Don't you think this could just be some bored little scrote, messing about, doing a dare with his mates?"

"I don't think that's very likely." The SOCO emerged from the pillbox, pulling his mask away from his face. Armitage looked to be in his early thirties, but had the serious demeanour of someone older, a furrowed brow beneath his brown, curly hair and eyes that had the kind of squint acquired from staring down microscopes all day.

"From what I can see," he said, "it look a bit more purposeful than that."

Sean and Smollet exchanged glances. "How so?" said Smollet, folding his arms.

"First off," said Armitage, "you've got the candle wax. Someone sat in here for five or six hours, probably overnight, burning a load of them – and I don't think they're going to turn out to be ordinary candles."

"The smell," suggested Sean, remembering the fragrance that had hit his nostrils when he'd first leant over the congealed pool of wax. "Has that got something to do with it?"

"Well, that in't one of the posh scented variety like the wife gets in for the bathroom. These have had oils rubbed into them, that's where the smell of cloves and that come from. Then there's the different colours – silver, purple, blue, black and red. All of which suggest to me that they were prepared beforehand for some kind of ritual."

"What about the pentagram?" Sean asked. "Is it salt?"

"Saxa, most probably," said the SOCO. "Sort of table salt you'd find in any supermarket, any kitchen. The symbolism is probably the more important thing to consider. From what I know about these things, salt is used to protect against the devil – he in't supposed to be able to cross over the lines. The candles were burned in the exact centre of the pentagram, where whoever was performing the ritual would have been, to their mind, the most adequately protected. Which in't really the behaviour you associate with a load of drunken kids out for a lark. This is the work of an adept."

"So," said Smollet, his jaw tightening, "you mean we're looking for a witch?"

"A white witch," said Armitage, nodding. "Or a Wiccan, as they like to call themselves." He looked at Smollet with a smile that was not immediately returned. "I think you can safely forget the idea that whoever done this was trying to recreate the murder. It look to me like they were trying to cleanse the place instead."

"It's not black magic, then?" said Sean.

"The opposite," said the SOCO. "Like I say, I'm by no means an expert on the subject, but we do get a fair bit of this jiggery-pokery around here." He raised his eyebrows. "And if this was another bunch of would-be satanists there'd be blood, bones, feathers, most probably a load of threatening slogans painted all over the place. Not to mention a ton of empties and other recreational stimulants. No," he said, "whoever done this was very clean, very neat."

"I see," nodded Sean, understanding something more of what Noj had been trying to say to him last night, beginning to puzzle out what it was about the people of Ernemouth and their enigmatic ways. How the things they didn't say were often more important than the things that they did.

"Len!" Smollet called. "You can come down now."

Rivett turned his head, putting his mobile phone back into his coat pocket as he made his lumbering way back down towards them. Smollet watched him approach with narrowed eyes. Sean wondered what was riling him – whether the story the SOCO had relayed was not the one he had wanted to hear, or if he was just pissed off at being dragged out here in the first place.

"What gives then, guv?" asked Rivett.

"Ben was just saying," a tiny muscle twitched under Smollet's left eye, "that this looks like the work of a white witch."

"Ha!" Rivett exclaimed. "You're joking, in't you? Some sick little scrote, more like."

"Well," Armitage hefted his bag back over his shoulder, "the two things could be one and the same. But if you want the analysis back this evening, I'd best be off." He nodded at Sean. "I don't think there's much else I can really tell you at this stage."

"Course," Smollet made a show of looking at his wrist-watch. "I'd better get going myself. If there's anything else . . ."

"Yeah," Sean said. "Can I make an appointment to speak with you later?" he said. "When the results of the tests come back."

"Sure," said the DCI. "Six o'clock, you reckon, Ben?"

The SOCO nodded. "Should be OK," he said.

"Six o'clock, my office, then," the corners of Smollet's mouth drew upwards, more of a grimace than a smile. "In the meantime, maybe you can fill Len in on the rest of Ben's . . ."

he paused before delivering the last word in a withering tone, "*thesis*."

* * *

Paul Gray was still standing in the hallway, staring at the phone, when his wife Sandra came back through the front door.

"Paul?" she said, taking in the expression on his face, adding it to last night's late-night phone call from Len Rivett and feeling her heart jump in her chest.

"Sandra, love," he said, looking at her with hollow eyes. "I'm sorry . . . I wanted to keep you out of this."

He shook his head, bringing his hand up to pinch the bridge of his nose.

Sandra put her shopping bags down and stepped forwards. "What is it?" she said, putting her hand over his right bicep. "What's he now said to you?"

Gray looked at her. "What's who now said?"

Her reply shocked him with its vehemence. "That bastard Rivett," she said.

* * *

Rivett toed one of the lines of salt on the floor of the pillbox, a sneer on his lips.

"The devil, my arse," he said, barking out a laugh. "Fucking little scrotes. I reckon you're right. This is a waste of our time."

"Yeah," said Sean. "We'll see what the SOCO comes up with, but I think this is gonna turn out to be a coincidence. If I hadn't come out here, none of us would be any the wiser that some little Samantha has been using this pillbox for casting spells. I bet it's just some teenage girl with relationship problems."

Rivett frowned. "Samantha?" he said.

"Yeah," said Sean. "You remember *Bewitched* – that old sitcom about a housewife who was really a witch? She used to wriggle her nose." He mimicked the motion. "Her name was Samantha."

"Course," said Rivett, tipping his hat back off his brow. "I know who you mean." He laughed, shook his head. "Well, I don't suppose we'll get much further hanging around here, waiting for her to come back. Not in daylight, anyway."

"Yeah," said Sean, turning to walk back outside.

"Mind you," said Rivett, staying where he was, "it must have given poor old Gray a nasty turn, finding what you did in here."

"Yeah," said Sean, stopping on the threshold. "Yeah, I'm afraid it did. Must've brought back a lot of bad memories for him."

"I reckon," said Rivett, bringing his hat back down so that the brim shaded his eyes. "Tell you about it, did he?" He spat a piece of tobacco from his lips onto the ground, and finally came away from the pentagram, to join Sean in the doorway.

"No," said Sean. "In fact, I got the feeling that was the last thing he wanted to do."

Rivett nodded in the direction of The Iron Duke and started to walk. "Well," he said, "Gray's the strong silent type; but that weren't the sort of sight even a hardened old sweat like myself gets to see the like of too often."

Sean nodded. "What would you consider his state of mind to have been when you got here? Had he put Woodrow in handcuffs, read her her rights, or any of that?"

Rivett shook his head. "No," he said. "He'd took her out of there and called an ambulance. Reckoned she was in shock. I

242   Cathi Unsworth

said we'd get a doctor to look at her once we had her safely in custody. But it did concern me that he appeared more worried about her than what she'd gone and done."

"Maybe he was in shock too," suggested Sean.

"S'pose he could have been," Rivett looked like the thought had never occurred to him. "I don't suppose any of us really do know what we're capable of until we're tested, do we?"

"No," said Sean, "and I'm sure a man like Gray wouldn't have wanted a doctor looking him over, either."

"No, he din't," said Rivett. "Who would, in our game?" He shook his head. "You don't want to show your weakness, do you? Don't want anyone to see you're afraid."

* * *

The Grays sat on their sofa, Sandra's arms around her husband's shoulders, trying to rub away the tension as he finished telling her what he and the detective from London had found that morning. "That just brought it all back," Gray said, "in a way I weren't expecting."

"Rivett made you go down there, did he?" Sandra said, the edge returning to her voice.

"No, he din't, actually. It was that Ward's idea. Sort of threw me, the idea of going back there, but he's only doing his job, in't he? Thought I better do my best to help him out. He do come across like a decent bloke and all."

"So what did he need to talk to you about last night, then?" Sandra, withdrawing her hands, wasn't going to let this subject lie. "Len Rivett, I mean."

But Gray just put his head in his hands and said nothing.

Sandra stared at him for a long minute, while decades-old unanswered questions and suppressed emotions swirled back through her mind and her heart.

"Paul," she said, in a much softer voice. "There's something I in't never told you. About Edna, Edna Hoyle. You know I used to do her hair for her, every week."

Gray looked up at her from between his fingers.

"You used to think she were a right old battleaxe," Sandra went on, "but I come to realise that were all a front with her. She din't have a very happy life, and the reason she fussed about her hair the whole while was because it was like her armour, her way of facing the world. Oh, she had a nice house and a lot of money, but I don't think she had any love from that husband of hers. And in that last year she lost everything she held dear. First that was her little dog and then her grand-daughter . . ." Sandra's voice trailed off for a moment and she stared into space, shaking her head. "She was like a zombie by the last time I saw her. Which was the last day that anybody saw her."

Paul stared at his wife, the face he'd loved for all these years, a softness coming over her features as she spoke, pity in her eyes.

"Yeah," she said, "that's right. Edna come to have her hair done that day. Friday afternoon, three o'clock, same as usual. She wanted the whole works, even though it weren't that long since I'd last done her. I spent ages getting it all right, 'cos I knew what she'd been through. Thought I could make it better for her, somehow. She give me an enormous tip that day, ten quid, and told me she din't know what she would ever have done without me. She knew what she was doing, all right. Edna wanted to leave the world looking her best. And, d'you know . . ." Tears sprang into Sandra's eyes. "I in't never been able to spend that money, Paul. It's still in an old purse, up in one of my drawers upstairs. One of them big old ten quid notes what would have been more like fifty to us in them days."

Gray put his hand over hers and this time neither of them moved away. Both were lost in a reverie of the past, of Edna Hoyle's funeral and the shock that this matron of Ernemouth society could have taken her own life. Memories that shook something else loose, that had been long buried in the recesses of Gray's mind.

"Why din't you tell me?" he asked.

"You had enough on your plate, din't you?" she said. "But I'm telling you now. Secrets can kill, Paul, I seen it happen to Edna with my own eyes. And whatever Len Rivett think he's got on you, he won't have – if you can just tell me."

26

War Dance

March 1984

"Samantha Lamb," Mr Pearson's ice-blue eyes glanced up from the register.

"Here," came the muted reply.

She didn't look up as she answered him and, as the form teacher's gaze settled on his pupil's head, he understood why. He continued through the rest of his list, gauging as he went the atmosphere of this Monday morning, honing in on the two knots of tension that had been steadily growing within his domain since September.

Both Miss Carver and Miss Lamb appeared to have had tiring weekends, the dark shadows under their eyes not entirely the work of make-up alone. Dale Smollet sat back in his seat, staring at the ceiling, his chin squared and his mouth a tight line. Along with the improvements in Smollet's definition of what uniform rules actually meant, he was maintaining his distance from his former friends in the desks behind him. Complaints against Smollet had receded this term, his marks improving exponentially.

The same couldn't be said for Reeder and Rowlands, the former of whom was red in the face with the effort of containing his sniggers.

Closing the register, Mr Pearson stood up and walked around to the front of his desk. "Stand up please, Miss Lamb," he said.

"What?" Samantha looked around startled, as if another Miss Lamb would suddenly appear to take her place. Two dots of colour appeared in her cheeks.

"I mean you, Samantha," Mr Pearson nodded. "Stand up so I can see you."

With a grimace, Samantha got to her feet, keeping her head bowed.

"Head up!" Mr Pearson snapped. Involuntarily, Samantha obeyed.

The teacher let his critical gaze linger over her for a few seconds, while a low level of excitement grew within the room, the anticipation of a good telling-off.

"Could you come out the front please, Miss Lamb, and face the class."

Anger flared in her eyes, but she did as she was told, her face now bright crimson.

"Now then, Mr Rowlands," Mr Pearson directed his gaze to the fuzzy-headed Lurch lookalike grinning at the back of the class, "I'd like you to come out here too."

Rowlands pointed at his chest, feigning "what, me?" outrage.

"I need your help for a little demonstration," Mr Pearson said.

Realising it was not him who was in trouble for once, Rowlands got out of his seat, throwing a sarcastic glance back to Smollet as he swaggered down the aisle. Smollet parried the challenge with a hard stare, a flush travelling up his neck.

"Now, if you'd like to stand next to Miss Lamb," the teacher directed, "so we can all see you. That's right."

Satisfied, Mr Pearson turned to Samantha, lifting up the side of her hair that she had let flop down over her ears in a vain effort to conceal what lay beneath.

"What we have here," he said, "is what I would call a bit too much of a close shave. Now," he moved around the back of his pupils to stand beside the smirking suedehead, "Mr Rowlands here knows exactly what the limits of school rules are, don't you, Shane?"

"Yes, sir," said Rowlands, as if he were the model of decorum. He was enjoying this game as much as almost everyone else.

"Which is why he always makes sure to keep his hair," Mr Pearson rubbed his hand over the top of the boy's head, "neatly trimmed to half an inch. In't that right?"

"Sir." Not looking so pleased with himself now, Rowlands blushed, putting his own hand up to straighten out his perceived messing of his buzzcut. A murmur of laughter travelled round the room. Deborah Carver joined in with it. Dale Smollet did not.

"I'd like you to observe, Miss Lamb," said the teacher. "I don't want to see any part of your hair go any shorter than what Mr Rowlands has on his head," he raised his eyebrows, "no matter how inventive the rest of your latest style may be. Which means you'll have to stay here with me when the bell goes and you won't be coming back to school until you've reached the same level of decency as Rowlands here. Understood?"

As if on cue, a loud clanging commenced.

* * *

Edna put the phone down slowly, the conversation she had just had with her daughter still not quite sunk in. She had been getting on so much better with Amanda recently, had even begun to see the good side of Wayne, that he really was rather a mature and thoughtful young man, his initial sullen demeanour a mask for understandable shyness. But she was hardly prepared for this.

For a start, Amanda had begun the conversation in a tone she had taken to adopting that Edna hadn't yet got the hang of; one of matey confidence.

"Mum," she had said, "I've got some news. Are you sitting down?"

Edna backed into the chair by the telephone table. "What . . . ?" she began, her alarm registering down the phone line, which her daughter picked up with a chuckle.

"Good news, don't worry," she said. "Take a deep breath. You're going to be a grandma again!"

If Edna's hair hadn't been so carefully lacquered it might have stood on end. "Oh," she said. "Oh, I say."

So many emotions ran through her, so many images fought to escape from the back of her mind that Edna almost blanked herself out. "Are you sure?" she managed to utter.

Amanda trilled a laugh. "Yes, don't worry, I've waited until I was twelve weeks to tell you, but the doctor's happy and everything seems fine. I've even given up smoking, you'll be pleased to hear." Amanda crossed her fingers as she relayed this last piece of information.

"Well," Edna made a supreme effort to sound as any other new grandmother might in a similar situation, "congratulations," she said, groping around for a follow-up. "I suppose you've got Wayne decorating the nursery already?"

"Not quite yet," said Amanda, "but we're going to get some colour charts and wallpaper samples this week. I thought you might like to come and help me? Maybe we could go up to Norwich, have a look around Bonds? And a cream tea in Elm Hill while we're at it?"

Having been denied this opportunity the last time around, Edna recognised the olive branch when she saw it and grasped for it gratefully. "I'd love to."

"One more thing," Amanda said. "Would you be able to," she hesitated, "pave the way with Dad, do you think? So as it isn't such a shock for him?"

The question, and everything that went with it, hung in the air between them for a stretched-out minute.

"I'll do my best," said Edna. Her voice was faint on the line.

"Thanks, Mum," said Amanda.

For a long while after the call had ended the only sounds in the hall were the ticking of the grandmother clock and Edna's laboured breathing. When she at last stood up, she caught sight of her reflection in the mirror that hung over the telephone table.

It felt like she was seeing a ghost.

* * *

High up in the tower above the Leisure Beach, Eric Hoyle sat at his desk, a frown scoring lines across his forehead, blue tendrils of smoke rising up around him from an ashtray piled high with butts. Beneath him, the magic kingdom languished in darkness, the tourists still a month away, Easter coming late this year. Only the lights from the oil rigs twinkled in the distance, but he wasn't looking to them tonight. He took another sip of his malt, sour in his mouth with the aftertaste of tobacco and tar.

Across the desk, Len Rivett hunched forward in his seat, his eyes locked onto the TV screen. Bodies writhing on crumpled white sheets, filling the air with their moaning. The lanky young greaser at the foot of the bed, pumping away for all he was worth, was the prodigal son of the landlady of one of Ernemouth's most upmarket hotels, caught in the Back Room with enough speed and Red Leb on him to ensure a three-month stretch. His fear of his mother seemingly even greater than that of the law, he could hardly believe that this – along with future, unspecified favours to be called in at Rivett's request – would serve as his punishment instead.

In the foreground, the woman stared out from between the straps that held the ball-gag in place. Her flesh was white and plump in all the right places. Black leather binds criss-crossing soft flesh, trussing her into an unnaturally submissive position. Raised red welts across the globes of her arse, a cat-o-nine-tails hanging from the bedstead, limp from a pre-coital scourging.

Her black eyes were fixed on the camera with an unblinking gaze of hatred.

The last few seconds of Gina's screen debut dissolved into a grey rain of static. The machine gave its own mechanical groan, as if in appreciation of Eric's directorial masterpiece, and began to rewind.

Rivett leaned back in his seat. "Told you she was a natural," he said, turning to Eric with a grin.

Eric nodded. "Look on her face'd make a dead man come."

Rivett raised his own shot of whisky. "Here's to your Oscar," he said.

Eric murmured agreement, clinking glasses across the table.

Rivett took a hefty swig, enjoying the burn of it down the

back of his throat, while he contemplated his companion's demeanour. "You don't look too pleased about it," he said.

Eric's scowl deepened as he crushed his cigarette out. "You won't believe the grief I've got headed my way," he said.

"Try me," said Rivett, swirling the remains of the amber liquid round in his tumbler. "When you ever seen me shocked?"

Eric fixed him with a steady gaze. "It's Mandy," he said. There was a slight tremor in his fingers as he lit another cigarette. "She's only got herself up the duff."

"Ah," said Rivett.

"Yeah," said Eric, "and you seen what a fine job she done of bringing up the one she already got, in't you?" His fingers drummed on the tabletop. "Sammy's been suspended from school," he went on. "Some stupid haircut she gone and got herself, don't look much better than a slag these days. She used to be my little princess, that girl," he said. "But she's been running wild ever since Mandy let her go to the high school. She in't got a clue how to control her. What's it going to be like when she's got a screaming baby in the house and all?" Eric dragged hard on his cigarette, exhaling a cloud of smoke and malice. "And what am I supposed to do – sit back and let it happen all over again? Edna in't no help. All she can say is, 'Oooh, that's an innocent bay-bee,'" he mimicked his wife's voice cruelly. "Bloody women."

Rivett lit a cigar as he watched Eric reach for the bottle.

"The trouble with all the women in your life, Eric," he considered, "is down to how they look. You're a sucker for a pretty face, in't you?"

Eric glugged Scotch into his glass. "Am I?" he said.

"You should have done what I did," Rivett warmed to his

theme. "Pick a plain woman and you get a grateful wife. Now, my daughters in't got a whole lot going for 'em in the looks department neither, but they in't gonna cause me any grief. They're gonna make two good little housewives, just like their mum. But your Mandy, she was a looker, and look where that got you. Little Samantha's just the same. You want to make sure she don't go running off with some lanky, streak-of-piss student wanker," he nodded back towards the TV as the tape gave another gurgle and then ejected itself. "You better start looking out for some decent husband material."

Eric looked at him incredulously. "She in't even sixteen 'til next month," he said.

"Yeah," said Rivett, "and as you well know, they're never too young, are they?"

Eric held his tongue.

"Now, my sister-in-law's got a nice boy," the DCI went on. "Dale, his name is. Same age as your Sammy."

Eric's eyes narrowed as he rifled through the index folder of his mind for the reminder of that surname. "Smollet?" he said. "Ted's nephew? Worked out front with him last season, on the arrows?"

"That's the one," said Rivett.

"I'll tell you how nice he is," said Eric. "One night last July, half my staff suddenly go missing. Turns out, they're all up on the rollercoaster, getting a good look at your sister-in-law's boy – with his bare arse going up and down on some tart in the dunes."

Rivett chuckled affectionately. "Well, he were a bit of a boy, that's true," he said. "Which is why she sent him to me over the Christmas holidays, to have a bit of a chat and that. Turns out, he fancy joining the Force, making a man of himself. With the right guidance, he could go far. Next time there's a bit of a do on, I'll introduce you."

"You're joking, in't you?" said Eric.

"No I in't," said Rivett. "You know I only have your best intentions at heart, Eric. And a marriage between our families . . . Think what that could mean."

Eric opened his mouth and then shut it again.

"Right, well," Rivett continued cheerfully. "Now old Gina's got you your jollies like I knew she would, I gotta go clean up the rest of her mess." He winked as he headed for the door. "Got to catch me a mangy old Wolf – and you have put me right in the mood."

27

She Sells Sanctuary

March 2003

Sean and Rivett stood under the creaking pub sign, looking into the open boot of the older man's Rover, at an open cardboard box.

"Two for you," Rivett reached in and passed the sealed, labelled DNA swab kits over to Sean. "You still want me to look for the third?"

Sean nodded. "Yeah. Does our Mr Prim strike you as the sort of bloke who'd sit up all night burning candles in a pill-box?" he asked.

Rivett raised his eyebrows. "You ever been round a biker's house?" he asked.

"Can't say I've had that particular pleasure," said Sean.

"But you've seen your fair share of dope dealers' dives, though, in't you?"

Sean nodded.

"Then you've seen the amount of candles them prats get through. That's part of the mystical bollocks they all seem to believe in, that go along with their addled memories and poor personal hygiene." Rivett grimaced. "And according to Einstein back there, we're looking for someone clean and neat."

"Point taken," said Sean, with a smile.

"Still," said Rivett, his expression brightening. "That won't do no harm to bend his ear, though, will it? Oh, and here's them clean ones you wanted." He produced the remaining kits out of the same box.

"Thanks," said Sean.

"Right," said Rivett, slamming down the boot lid. "Happy hunting. See you back at the office."

Sean limped slowly back to the car, the effort of his reconnoitres across the dunes and the bitter wind having frozen the iron in his legs and rendered his fingers almost numb. Rivett, on the other hand, seemed keen to get away from the place. He exited the car park swiftly, honking his horn as he went.

Sean watched the Rover crest the top of the bridge and disappear from view. Then, casting around to make sure he was alone, he retraced their footsteps back to the sea wall. At the bottom of the steps he found what he was looking for.

The stub of Rivett's cigar went into the first of the plastic bags.

* * *

"Hello?"

Sean had stood on Sheila Alcott's doorstep for ten minutes, ringing the bell and then, deciding it must be broken, rapping the brass knocker against the front door. He stood back, looking up at the diamond-patterned windows, as he shouted out a greeting.

The windows returned a blank gaze.

Sean shook his head and walked around to the back of the building, checking his watch. Ten minutes past three, it read, the second hand still gliding steadily around the face. He was on time and he was expected.

"Hello?" he called again.

The dull cawing of rooks was the only reply.

The Alcott smallholding, optimistically named Greenfields Farm, comprised of a flint-clad farmhouse, clasped so deeply within the gnarled embrace of an old wisteria that it looked as if the plant was holding it upright, and a series of outbuildings clustered around a concreted yard. Behind lay acres of grazing, dotted with the distant, black-and-white bodies of Friesian cows.

The buildings were surrounded by a copse, the bare upper branches of the trees thick with the nests of the rook parliament. The sun had given up its earlier attempts to break through the clouds, which had darkened to the point of a rainburst as Sean drove up the Acle Straight. Now clouds hung like a shroud over the humps of the buildings, droplets running along the telephone wires overhead.

Sean's eyes travelled around the yard. One of the barn doors was open, revealing an ancient tractor in shades of rust and mud, and various other pieces of machinery that seemed to Sean like an assembly of medieval torture implements – spikes and scythes, great rolls of chains on giant spindles. His mind drifted back to the book he'd bought in Farrer's, the stories of the Swing mob.

A pair of green eyes peered out of the gloom. For a split second, Sean's heart jumped in his chest, before he realised what it was. Just a fat tabby cat, sitting on top of a hay bale. The creature opened its mouth, revealing sharp white teeth, and emitted a yowl. At the same time, a creaking noise and the crunching of feet made Sean jump, his head snapping around to see a short woman in a wax jacket, corduroys and Wellington boots, a headscarf barely containing her frizz of salt-and-pepper hair, come trundling into the yard, pushing a wheelbarrow.

"Oh!" she looked at Sean aghast, plonked the handlebars of her wheelbarrow down and scrabbled up her sleeve to find her watch. "Is that the time?"

Sean chuckled with relief. Sheila, with her lopsided head-gear and Mother's Union badge pinned to the front of her jacket, was a far cry from the sinister apparition of bloodthirsty nineteenth-century villagers his mind had conjured out of the gloomy farmyard.

"I was just down at the compost heap," she explained, picking up the handles again and manoeuvring the barrow into the open barn. "I'm so sorry to have kept you waiting. You must be Mr Ward?"

"That's right." Sean followed her in. The cat roused itself onto its legs, stretching and yawning, then jumped down from the bale and made a beeline for Sean, rubbing its big, flat head against his legs and purring like a steam train.

"Sheila Alcott." She took her right hand out of a thick, yellow leather glove and offered it to shake. "You *are* honoured," she glanced down at the cat. "She doesn't normally talk to strangers, do you, Minnie dear?"

Sean caught a trace of a Midlands accent as she spoke. She had been here a long time, but Sheila wasn't local.

"Come in," she ushered him out of the barn, closing the door behind them, "and I'll put kettle on. You look frozen."

"Yeah," Sean admitted as he followed her out. "Does it take very long to acclimatise?"

"Oh," said Sheila, opening the back door, "only about thirty years."

Sean had to duck to get through the doorway, but inside

the farmhouse was as full of colour as the outside was grey. In Sheila's kitchen, wildflowers spilled from red and blue glass vases, dried herbs hung from the beams that ran up the walls and along the ceiling and cheery faces in photographs smiled out at Sean from every shelf and windowsill.

"We might as well sit in here," said Sheila, turning the dial on an old gas boiler, which responded with a foreboding rumble. "It's the warmest room in the house."

Sean sat himself down at the pine kitchen table, watching Sheila put the kettle on and fetch down willow-patterned china from the Welsh dresser. The cat slunk its way into its basket, turned three times and sank down onto a patchwork blanket, from where it maintained surveillance on Sean through half-closed eyes.

"My husband's out doing home visits," Sheila brought a homemade fruitcake to the table, "he won't be back for few hours yet."

Sean followed her glance to the smiling face of the man in the dog collar in some of the photographs, then back to the ornate, interlaced cross she wore around her neck. They were obviously a couple whose faith sustained them.

Sean often wondered if he could have benefited from such conviction himself. But his vision of a just God had shattered when his dad had come back from Goose Green in a box. Even in the darkest hours of his hospitalisation, he had not groped to find Him since.

Sheila sat down opposite him. She picked up a teaspoon and lifted the lid of the pot.

"Stir up tea, stir up trouble." Her accent thickened as she spoke and she shot him a grin that was the opposite of pious.

"I've read the report you gave to Francesca Ryman," Sean

nodded. "And I have to say, it disturbs me that none of this got to come out at the original trial."

Sheila snapped down the lid on the teapot.

"If I have one thing to thank God for today," she said, "it's that after all this time, someone's finally investigating who isn't part of the bloody Ernemouth police force."

* * *

In the basement of The Ship Hotel, Damon Boone sat at a laptop, his fingers rattling across the keyboard as a series of windows opened on the screen.

"Won't be much longer now," he said, flicking his long, greasy fringe out of his eyes.

"All right, boy," Rivett, sitting next to him, gave a smile that was more of a grimace, his eyes travelling around the land-lady's son's room.

There was nothing but computers in here, in various shapes and sizes, humming away from the racks of shelves, their innards connected by spaghetti junctions of thick grey wires and banks of blinking lights. Some of them had scrolls of numbers rolling up and down their monitors, others showed sequences of graphic images, lines folding into themselves, taking the eyes on a kind of fairground ride of optical illusion. It made Rivett feel uncomfortable, this *Tomorrow's World* vision of the future come true – and what it had amounted to.

Bloody boffins ran everything now. From Einstein with the forensics to Q sitting here next to him, talking "three-way-encrypted passwords" and other such voodoo.

"Room four was the easiest one for me to set up," Damon said. "The pelmet on the top of the bay window hides four spycams that just about cover each angle. There's another one in the headboard and, of course, one in the light above the desk. Which is just as well," he pointed towards the screen. "Your bloke don't half move around a lot."

Rivett took in the series of images now being displayed in the windows on the screen. Each showed Sean Ward at work on his laptop in his hotel room from various angles, overhead and sideways. In some, he sat at the desk, in others he was lying across the bed, or leaning against the headboard with the computer across his lap. The most interesting one to Rivett so far showed him reading the case notes of a social worker.

"This is the magic one," Damon clicked onto the window that showed Sean sitting at the desk, so that it expanded to fill the screen. "Look, you can see him logging on."

Rivett peered at the grainy image.

"It's his fingers that are important," Damon leant in a little too close for Rivett's liking, tapping something else on his keyboard that made the image on the screen slow down.

"By watching this carefully a few times, I could see exactly what he inputs on the keyboard to access his files."

The look Rivett exchanged with his companion was one that prompted the younger man to stop trying to show him how clever he had been, and instead, cut to the chase.

"Which brings me to this," Damon rapidly clicked all the windows closed, opened up another file instead. A page of emails spread out across the screen before them.

"His inbox," said Damon, leaning back in his seat and swivelling his chair to the side, a slight churning in his stomach. "He deletes them as he goes along, but I managed to retrieve them. It's all yours."

Rivett's eyes scanned down the screen. The most recent email had come in not five minutes ago, from FRANCESCA

RYMAN entitled ORGAN GRINDER/MONKEY. It took him a beat to place the name as he clicked it open, and then rapidly dissemble the implications of Ward's correspondence with the *Ernemouth Mercury* editor.

Following the money, he read. *Got an expert looking into R&S's possible business dealings. If there's something there, he will find it. About to call press office to set up interview with S now.*

Rivett whistled through his teeth. These two were sharper than he thought. Which just went to prove the wisdom of always having a contingency plan.

"I always said you'd go far," he told Damon. "Mind if I borrow your phone, while you go make us a cup of tea? Take a nice, long time about it, won't you, boy?"

"Course." Damon virtually pushed the landline into Rivett's lap as he got to his feet.

Closing the door behind him, he heard Rivett say: "Hello, Pat?"

* * *

Out in the hall, a grandfather clock chimed five times. The fruitcake had been decimated over the past couple of hours, the remains of the third round of tea a mere dribble running out into Sheila's cup.

She put the pot down and rubbed her eyes, smudging pale blue shadow over one cheek as she did so. Tired now, from the effort of unloading all that had been bottled up for the past two decades.

"Shall I make another?" she asked.

Sean shook his head. "No, you're all right," he said, putting his hand down on the tape recorder. "I should be thinking about going, really, I've got another appointment at six. I'm sure we've covered everything. Oh," he stopped short of turning the machine off, "but there's just one more thing I wanted to ask you."

"Yes?" Resting her head in her right hand, Sheila gave a faint smile.

"How did Francesca find you?"

Sheila frowned. "Through her father, of course," she said.

"Her father?" it was Sean's turn to look puzzled.

"Philip," said Sheila. "Philip Pearson. You know, he used to be Corrine's form teacher."

Sean's eyes widened. "She never said."

Sheila bit her lip. "Oh," she said. "Then . . ."

"But now it makes sense," Sean cut her off. "Philip Pearson went to the nationals and told them some painful truths about Ernemouth, got hounded out of his job for his trouble. You tried the same with the local press and found yourself being shut down and slung out too. How old was Francesca when all this was going on – about ten, twelve?"

"Something like that . . ." Sheila hesitated, a frown creasing her forehead.

Sean pressed the stop button on the Dictaphone and forced a smile.

"No need to look worried, Mrs Alcott," he said. "I'm not . . ." he stopped himself short of saying "Len Rivett" and instead, changed tack. "I'm just trying to figure her out. Francesca's been very helpful to me, and I wondered if she had some ulterior motive. This job I have, you see, it gives me a suspicious mind. So, that's the reason she became a journalist . . ."

"She was doing very well at it," said Sheila, "until her mother got ill."

Sean spooled back to the morning's conversation with Nora

Linguard. *"It's terribly sad; she died quite recently, Mrs Pearson. She was only in her fifties. Cancer, you know . . ."*

"She came back to take care of her," said Sheila, "only I think it was Philip who needed her help the most. That's why she gave up her job in London and her marriage . . ."

Sheila's fingers flew up to her lips. "Sorry, I shouldn't have said that. It's too personal." Then a fierce expression came over her. "But that's the thing about Francesca," she said. "I wish I could ever have been as strong as she is. I thought it was fate when that Sid Hayles died and she ended up getting his job."

Her face softened again. "That's why she didn't tell you," Sheila patted Sean's hand. "She wouldn't have wanted you to think she was doing this for any other reason but to get to the truth. None of us ever expected that this would ever get looked into again, you see. We thought it would die with us."

"But," Sean stared into Sheila's eyes, "what is the truth, Mrs Alcott? You and Francesca have done a good job of convincing me that Corrine Woodrow is not the murderer and it seems we have evidence to back that up. But if she isn't, then who is?"

The fear came into Sheila's eyes again. She averted her gaze to the window where the grey gloom of the afternoon was darkening into night.

"That," she said, "is the one thing I can't tell you."

* * *

Rivett was still talking when Damon came back with the teas. He stood outside his room, straining for the sound of the back door closing, his mother's footfall on the stair. The churning in his stomach had worsened as the long minutes of the afternoon ticked on and he wrestled with what he had done.

The decades' long string of favours that Rivett had spun out of him for one stupid teenage transgression.

Up until yesterday, Damon had thought that the worst thing that could happen would be for Rivett to show his mother the videotape. But now, he felt with a sick certainty, he had gone and got himself embroiled in something much worse.

"That's right, Andy," he heard Rivett say through the door. "Same as last time, that mad old fen famer Alcott . . . No, I don't believe she has or ever will . . . Well, you know, all that rusty old machinery lying around out there. Accidents will happen . . ."

Only when he heard the receiver being slammed down with characteristic grace did he dare nudge the door open.

Rivett swivelled in his chair, smiling up at Damon. "Would you mind putting all this on one of them things for me?" he said. "Memory sticks, or whatever you call them."

"Sure," said Damon, putting the teas down on the desk in front of Rivett, fighting down the bile that was rising up his throat as he walked over to the filing cabinet.

Memory sticks, he thought bitterly. *That's all my life has been. One big dirt file in that bastard's memory, where nothing can be hacked and nothing can be deleted.*

The last time Damon had tried to break out of his control, Rivett had shown him what he called a souvenir, from that brief, happy evening he had spent in the Albert Hotel. A tyre iron, with something stuck to it. Black hair and matted blood. "Her crowning glory," he had said. "Remember? Pity she had to step out of line . . ."

So Damon did as he was told, copying the private detective's files across to a piece of plastic and metal, watching it disappear into the depths of Rivett's sheepskin coat.

"Ta very much, Damon," the older man got to his feet. "I'll be round the same time tomorrow." He made his way to the door and then stopped on the threshold, leaning against the frame. His dark eyes glittered as they ran up and down Damon's waxy countenance. "You better get some rest, boy, you're looking a bit green around the gills. Why don't you have a nice, afternoon kip? You're gonna need all your wits about you later, in't you?" He winked. "*Spying* tonight . . ."

Damon forced the corners of his mouth up into a smile, and prayed that his guts would hold, at least until Rivett had seen himself out. When he finally heard the back door slam, he dived back into the filing cabinet, to the bottom drawer this time.

The one where he kept the vodka.

28

Thorn of Crowns

March 1984

"Here he come," DS Andrew Kidd passed the binoculars across to Rivett. "Home to his mum, like a good little cub."

Rivett peered through the back window of the Transit van that Kidd and his partner, DS Jason Blackburn, were using to keep Wolf under obs. Posing as painters and decorators, with splattered overalls and ladders on the roof rack, an ashtray brimming with the dog-ends of roll-ups, tabloids open at page 3 and discarded food wrappers adding to their air of authenticity.

"The She-Wolf," added Blackburn, as the spluttering of their target's Norton engine brought a twitch to the net curtains in an upstairs window, a face appearing behind the glass. "Look more like Vera Duckworth, don't she?"

"But don't be deceived," said Kidd. "We reckon this is where he keep the stash."

Wolf cut his engine, kicked down the bike-stand and dismounted his iron steed. While he undid the strap of his open-face helmet, he surveyed the low-rise estate in front of him, his eyes travelling from left to right, pausing to acknowledge the blue-rinsed figure of his mother with a raised hand, and then looked around the car park.

The three men ducked as he glanced in their direction, then resumed their vigil as the biker leant down to take something out of the pannier on the side of his hog. A package, wrapped in a plastic shopping bag.

"In a whole week of watching him," said Kidd, "that's been the same every day. He don't make no other regular stops and he don't carry that package into anywhere else. That's either drugs or money in there."

Wolf took his helmet off and ran a hand through his unkempt mane of grey hair. He slowly turned his head, taking in another hundred and eighty degrees of his terrain before making his entrance into the stairwell at the side of the block.

"I see where he gets his looks from," said Rivett, as the lights came on along the first runway and Wolf reappeared, making his way to where his mother now stood on her doorstep, narrowed eyes darting furtively around in a mirror image of her offspring's sly demeanour. As he reached the door, she reached up to put a hand on his shoulder, plant a kiss on his whiskery cheek and then usher him inside.

"He go up there to kip," said Kidd. "Don't usually leave until late morning. And he don't come out carrying nothing visible. We reckon she make up all the wraps for him, so he can hide 'em in his leathers."

"A mother's love," said Rivett. "How touching."

"Yeah," said Kidd. "But if you were him, who would you rather trust? The She-Wolf or that bunch of mangy cubs he run with?"

"Good work," Rivett smiled approvingly at his apprentice. "You've earned yourself a warrant." He took the document from inside his jacket pocket.

"Should we go in now?" asked Kidd.

"There's no rush," said Rivett. "Let's enjoy ourselves. Let them get comfortable first."

* * *

While his deputies went to deliver their tidings to the She-Wolf's front door, Rivett took a stroll around the back of the building. There was only about a ten-foot drop down from the flat's windows, and he wondered if the Wolf would be bold enough to attempt this manner of escape.

The flats backed on to what was designed as a garden and kiddies' play park, back in the '60s when the estate went up, but had now mutated into a communal dump. A muddy scrub, pitted with discarded fridges, car bumpers and the skeletal remains of a burnt-out motor scooter. Not for the first time, Rivett marvelled at how these vermin could afford the appliances they discarded so thoughtlessly on their weekly cheques from the DHSS. Then the sound of a dog barking, rivalled in ferocity only by the accompanying yowls of a female voice, diverted his attention back to the first-floor flat.

As if on cue, a window opened. Wolf's shaggy face appeared at it and he took a few seconds to scope out his descent. Crouching behind the nearest fridge, Rivett watched the head go back in, to be shortly replaced by a leather-clad arse. Wolf began to shimmy his way out of the window, dangling by his fingertips and swinging there as he extended his full length down, leaving about a four-foot drop.

The noise from the She-Wolf's flat increased to include banging, crashing and smashing, and an outraged shout from what sounded like one of Rivett's deputies in distress. More lights pinged on in windows across the estate, illuminating the Wolf's descent. He dropped onto his feet and only wobbled momentarily as he landed. It looked like he'd had plenty of practice getting out of tight spots like this in the past.

Satisfied he was still in one piece, the biker turned towards his hog. But the din from the flat that had masked the sound of his departure had also prevented him from hearing the soft soles of Rivett's shoes creeping up on him. He only knew the DCI was there when he felt something cold at the back of his neck, and heard a sharp click.

"That was quite impressive," said Rivett. "Can't wait to see what you do for your next trick."

Thoughts blipped through the wired Wolf's brain simultaneously, chief amongst those being: *There's a gun in my neck* and *Pigs in't supposed to carry firearms.*

What came out of his mouth was just one strangulated: *"Whaaaat?"*

"I know," the voice hissed in his ear, "let's have a race, shall we? See what you're really made of, man to boy. Go on, get on your bike and piss off out of here. I'll chase you."

Wolf stumbled as he ran towards his bike, convinced he was about to get used for target practice. His fingers scrabbled for the keys in his jacket pocket and he dropped them, unwittingly kicking them forwards, underneath the wheels of his bike. By the time he had recovered them, flung his leg across the saddle and revved up the engine, the pig – or whatever he was – was behind the wheel of his black Rover, smiling at him.

The car's headlights came on as Wolf's iron steed flew out of the car park.

As he turned left down South Denes Road, away from town and down the side of the docks, where there were fewer lights and less traffic to negotiate, Wolf remembered what Rat had told him, from the other side of the cell bars.

"Don't touch Gina, she's protected. Just sell the gear and stay out of her way. Otherwise, he'll come for you too."

But Wolf had been sure Rat's brain had been turned to mush by the black-eyed bitch he'd been screwing. He didn't reckon any pig would give a toss if he put her in her place. As far as Wolf could see, she'd had it coming a long time. Women weren't supposed to run things. This was men's work.

He accelerated past the hulks of container ships that lined the quayside. The sky was turning a deepening blue, the inky stillness that descended just before dawn, and both Wolf and his pursuer were able to run through a succession of red lights without anybody getting in their way.

The pig didn't bother to put his siren on. Each time Wolf glimpsed back at him in his wing mirror, he had the same expression of amusement on his face, his elbow leaning casually over the side of his door, like he was out for a Sunday drive, the gun still in his hand. Again, the biker wondered whether he was actually genuine filth at all.

Warehouses flashed past as the road bent around to the left. They were at the mouth of the harbour now and, as Wolf negotiated the corner, he could see the burning rim of the sun begin to shimmer above the dark, flat line of the sea. Glancing back in his wing mirror, he saw the Rover begin to gain on him.

Wolf twisted his wrist hard against the accelerator. Adrenalin and fear coursed in his veins like a snakebite as the bike shot forward. By now, he was going as fast as the machine could take him, but the Rover's bumper was drawing dangerously close to his rear mudguard. Despite a lifetime's experience of never looking back, his grey eyes seemed pulled of their own accord to stare at the reflection of the man behind him, his grin widening on his face, revealing his teeth, as his more powerful engine nudged him effortlessly forward, the gun in his hand levelling with Wolf's petrol tank.

There was a shower of sparks as metal scraped metal with a sickening rattle and scree. The bike jerked under Wolf's legs, skidding sideways across the road in the direction of the harbour wall. Before he even had time to open his mouth to scream, he was pitching towards the concrete balustrade, free-falling into the air for a second that seemed to spiral out into a slow-motion eternity. Calmly and coolly, a detached spectator at his own suicide, Wolf's mind processed the fact he had been completely outmanoeuvred by a pig.

Then he slammed into the wall.

When he opened his eyes, he was looking through a red mist. He could hear a loud hammering inside his skull, but it took him a moment to realise it was the sound of his own heart, pumping out arterial blood from the leg that had twisted at such an angle it was a mercy he couldn't turn his head to see. Wolf felt as if he were hovering somewhere just over his body as he tried to focus on the face in front of him, to hear the sounds those moving lips were making.

He realised the pig was opening his jacket, rummaging through the pockets, taking out the score of wraps he had hidden there. But Wolf was fading too fast to resist. He didn't have time to feel outrage, anger, regret, nor even to register the depth of the pain he was in. The hammering noise seemed to merge in his head with the roar and hiss of the sea and he felt himself being lifted.

He comprehended one last sentence as it dropped from the killer pig's lips: "This is *my* town, boy."

And then he was falling again, falling down towards the sea, the icy deeps of eternity.

* * *

Gray rubbed sleep from his eyes as he got in the front of his unmarked car. The results of an all-night stake out at the Golden Sands Holiday Park sat slouched and silent in the back, radiating outrage that their plan had failed. Two teenage boys, the masterminds behind a string of recent opportunist burglaries, had been seen burying something in the dunes by the park's security guard. He'd found a bag of jewellery and trinkets and called the police – then he and Gray had sat up waiting for their return.

They were South Town estate kids from a notorious family, bred into thieving and petty crime. Gray could remember arresting their older brothers and their uncles before them. It wouldn't be long, he thought with a sigh, before they graduated to borstal and beyond.

Dawn was breaking as he pulled out onto the road, a big yellow sun rising like a fireball above the horizon. The wind, always strong along the unsheltered tip of the beach, brought foaming tips to the waves and filled his ears with its whistling moan.

Gray checked the road ahead, his eyes travelling in a southwards arc towards the statue of Nelson that guarded the entrance of the port.

Underneath the statue, he made out a shape. It looked like a man pushing something big and lumpy over the harbour wall.

* * *

The cells were close to full that morning; it had been a busy night. Kidd and Blackburn had come in just ahead of Gray, with a prisoner they were all calling The She-Wolf. Roy Mobbs booked in the teenage thieves that followed her with the manner of one who thought he'd seen it all, only to discover there were still fresh surprises out there in the world. Said that Kidd had tooth marks in his ankle.

Gray understood when he looked in on the She-Wolf – far from the Gina Woodrow type, there sat a little old grandma with a blue rinse and an even darker scowl on her face.

A couple of hours later, as he went back through the office on his way out, he caught a drift of conversation floating from the huddle around Rivett's office door – the DCI and his favourite deputies debriefing.

" . . . lost control of his bike as we went around the corner," he heard Rivett say. "Skidded clean across the road, hit the wall and splat," he punched his fist onto the palm of his hand, "threw him right over the harbour wall. By the time I'd got out of the car I reckon he'd sunk. Couldn't see him floating around, anyway. Most probably broke his neck with the impact. I've got the coastguard out fishing for him now, fuck knows if we'll ever find him though."

"Nah," opined Kidd, "I doubt it. Tide round there would have ripped him straight out to sea."

Blackburn gave a throaty chortle.

It wasn't until he was back in his bed, drifting off to sleep, that it came back to Gray what it was he had seen, the strange images in his mind suddenly making sense.

Rivett pushing a suspect over the harbour wall. Turning, as he finished, to salute the statue of Admiral Nelson.

29

The Killing Moon

March 2003

In the front seat of his car, Sean checked his messages. Mathers had received everything now, even the DNA sample that had been picked up at the train station just before Sean had driven to Sheila's. It was now at the lab, being analysed. Charlie Higgins had come back to him too. John Brendan Kenyon was not a name that showed up on the Police National Database, no chemical traces there of Noj to compare and contrast. Higgins' recorded voice held a trace of concern as he relayed the message. "Be careful with those farm boys, won't you?" he said before he signed off.

Sean eyed the dashboard clock. Time for one call before he had to move. As the numbers connected, he wondered where she would be. Sheila had told him, on the way out, that Francesca didn't live far from here. Shared a house with her father on the edge of Brydon Water, was always out walking her dogs along the old marsh wall.

But when she picked up, the sounds of the busy newsroom surrounded her.

"Just stepping outside," she said, "where I can hear you better. Have you had an interesting afternoon?"

"Very," said Sean. "How about you?"

"Well, I think I've been stalled," she said, "by a very determined press officer. Apparently the subject is much too busy to take an interview request at the moment. But don't worry, I put my time to good use anyway." The background noise receded and Sean pictured her coming out of the office and down the stairs, Pat's eyes narrowing as she passed by her desk.

"That old colleague of mine in London has had a result," Francesca went on, "on both the organ grinder and the monkey's assets. I'm getting the data from him tonight," there was a slight echo to her voice now, like she was standing in the stairwell, "and I've asked him to send it home, rather than here. Is it OK for you to meet me there later?"

"Yeah," said Sean, "I think that's a good idea. Only I'm still not quite sure what time later will be. I'm heading back to the station now and there's someone else I need to talk to after that."

"It doesn't matter," she said. "Just call me when you're free and I'll give you directions. It's kind of off the beaten track."

As she spoke, Sean felt a prickling down his neck, a sensation not caused by the cold, but by the certainty that someone was watching. He turned in his seat, looking back towards the house. Sheila's cat sat on the doorstep, illuminated by the porch light the social worker had left on for her husband, licking at one of its raised front paws and staring at him with eyes like twin orange moons, reflected in the car's rear lights.

"You still there?" Francesca said.

"Yeah," Sean turned back, shaking his head. "Yeah, I got you. I'll call you back as soon as I can. Take care, Francesca."

"I will," she said, a trace of amusement in her voice. "See you later, Sean."

* * *

Sean pulled out of Sheila's drive and up the narrow lane that led back to the main road. Just before he reached the junction, headlights momentarily dazzled him. A Land Rover, bouncing into the lane, veering over to one side as it saw him, across the grass verge. Sean steered hard right, his outer wheels mounting the side of the bank from out of which the hedge grew, brambles and hawthorn raking against his windows. The two vehicles managed to manoeuvre past each other, the other driver raising a hand in thanks as he passed. *Sheila's husband?* wondered Sean. But he didn't see the man's face.

* * *

Francesca reached the top of the stairs, level with the eyes of her secretary. Pat was talking to someone on the phone, her expression terse, her lips turned down at the corners. She didn't return Francesca's smile as the editor walked past, but continued to speak in a voice much softer than her usual brusque tone.

"That's right," Francesca heard her say. "Yeah, I most certainly will."

When she got back to her desk, the Call Waiting light was flashing on her phone.

* * *

Noj sat in darkness, illuminated only by the flickering light of a circle of candles. Black for binding, shape-shifting, repelling negativity and protection. Purple for the third eye, psychic ability, hidden knowledge and spiritual calm. Blue for wisdom, protection, opening blocked communication and spiritual inspiration.

She had anointed them all in her favourite oils. The air was fragrant with the scents of flowers and herbs.

Her hands rested on the crystal ball as she concentrated on the task ahead, visualising a face behind her closed eyelids. Strangely, after all this time, it took a while for the cranial contours Noj had thought she knew so well to form a perfect alignment in her mind. It was as if the subject was trying to shrink from sight.

But then, at once, it came.

Noj lifted her hands and opened her eyes, staring deep into the globe before her.

* * *

With a clatter, the cat shot back through the flap in the front door and ran into the kitchen, hackles up, hissing. Sheila looked up through the window, heard the sound of tyres crunching down the lane. Listened hard to the noise it made and looked down at the basket where the cat stood on tiptoe, hair standing out on end, teeth bared and emitting a low, yowling sound, eyes fixed in the direction of the door.

"We thought this might happen, didn't we, Minnie?" Sheila said. She put her cup down and walked through the kitchen to the laundry. Took the oiled and loaded twelve-bore down from its rack.

* * *

"Come," Smollet's voice rang out behind his office door.

Sean pushed it open, surprised to see the DCI sitting alone.

"The forensics not through yet?" he asked.

Smollet picked up the paperwork he had been studying, handed it across the desk.

"Ben's finished all right," he said, "only I din't think it was worthwhile him hanging round. Take a look for yourself, but there in't really all that much more to it than what he told us this morning – his so-called witch was so neat she din't leave us any fingerprints. Could be that witches don't have them, I s'pose."

Sean sank down in the seat opposite, his eyes scanning the report. It appeared just as Smollet had said.

"So all that drama turns out to have been a bit of a false lead," the DCI went on.

"You're not going to pursue it, then?" said Sean, looking up at him.

"You think I should?" Smollet raised his dark eyebrows a fraction.

Sean shook his head, maintained the line he had used with Rivett earlier. "Well, they haven't committed any crime, have they? Except perhaps, against taste and decency."

"My thoughts entirely," said Smollet.

The DCI's eyes across the table were as unyielding as a pair of mirror shades.

"So what else did you want to ask me about?" Smollet gave an encouraging smile.

"Well," said Sean, "there are a couple of things bothering me. If I was doing an official enquiry, I would have to say to you that Len Rivett is much too close to the original case. He's not so much helping me as steering me into the direction he wants me to take. I also get the feeling that although he might have formally retired, he still believes that he's in charge of this gaff."

Smollet's brows drew together. "No," he said, "that in't the case at all. As I . . ."

"And two," Sean didn't give him the chance to finish, "why you didn't think to tell me that you were in the same class as Corrine Woodrow at school. Maybe we do things differently where I was brought up, but if I was in your shoes, that would have been the first thing I would want to get out in the open.

Seeing as," he smiled, "you say you ain't got anything to hide?"

* * *

Francesca put the phone down, wondering what the best course of action was. Came to a decision as she left the office and called her father as she crossed the car park towards her bright red Micra.

"Dad," she said, "I'm going to be later than I thought. Could you do me a favour in the meantime? Ross is going to be faxing me some documents this evening, I'm not quite sure when, but if I'm not back by then, as soon as the machine comes on, could you check them for me? Yeah, they are. Very important. In fact, if you do get them before I'm back, would you ring this number," she reeled off the memorised digits, "and speak to a man called Sean Ward? Tell him what they say. I know, but it's for a reason. I do," she gave a short, ironic laugh. "And when it comes to business, yes, I do trust Ross as well. He owes me, remember? And, Dad, you have to trust me on this too. Tell Sean what the documents say, word for word. Yeah. Thanks. Love you, Dad. See you soon."

Francesca unlocked the car door, hesitating a moment before she got in.

No, she reassured herself, if Smollet had granted her an interview now, it was best to get down to it first. It was what Sean had wanted.

She slid into her seat, turned the key in the ignition and set off towards the sea front.

* * *

"What," said Smollet, "you mean that weren't in all them notes of yours? I would have thought your employer would have had you fully briefed on that before she sent you down here. Would have saved you a lot of unnecessary running around." He stretched his perfectly manicured hands out on the desk in front of him.

When Sean said nothing, he went on. "No, the reason I kept out of this so far was in case you thought there was some sort of conflict of interests. I din't want to prejudice the independence of your enquiry, did I? But seeing as you now asked me, I'll tell you. I was at school with Corrine Woodrow for about a year, when I was fifteen, sixteen. I spent about ten minutes of every morning in the same form room as her, she weren't in any of my other classes and I din't socialise with her out of school. She weren't the sort of girl you wanted to get involved with. And that's all there is to tell."

"Hardly," said Sean. "The phantom DNA from that pillbox could feasibly belong to any one of Corrine's schoolfriends. What would you say if I asked you for a swab?"

A small smile twitched at the corners of Smollet's mouth. "You don't half go about things a funny way," he said. "If that's what you want, you only had to ask."

Sean smiled back at Smollet. "So," he said, "when Len Rivett told me that you were only in your short trousers when it all happened, that was just a figure of speech, yeah? Maybe a local colloquialism I'm unfamiliar with?"

"Most probably," said Smollet and his smile grew broader, his perfect white teeth lending him a politician's glow. "He's always making out I'm younger than I am." He shook his head, his demeanour giving way to one of solicitude.

"Look," he said. "I do take on board what you said to me about him acting like he never retired. That's all part of it, and don't think that don't get to me sometimes, too. He had a hard time letting go of this job and that is fairly obvious he resent me being here instead of him. But, I honestly thought he'd be an asset to you. Nobody know the ins and outs of that case better than he do and there in't no one else in this town, myself included, who can sniff out what and where people are hiding quite like Len can. But," he opened his palms, "I don't want you to go thinking that I do no special favours for no one. If you're suspicious of him, I'll take him out of the picture. Starting tomorrow, I'll get a new man assigned to help you, I'll second you one of my best detectives. And," he looked down at his wristwatch, a chunky piece of platinum and gold, "for the next hour at least, I can answer your questions about any of my old classmates you want me to recall. I'm afraid I have got an appointment later, I'll have to be away by half-seven, but we can continue this tomorrow, anyhow. Is that all right with you?"

Sean raised his eyebrows. "Quite," he said, reaching for his Dictaphone.

* * *

Francesca pulled into the car park at the front of the portico entrance of the grey flint and cream stuccoed Victorian mansion. She got a sudden chill, looking up at it. How her father would hate to think of her entering this building, even if he knew what she was doing it for. Subconsciously she touched the emblem she wore around her neck, given to her by her cousin, Keri, which she had felt the urge to wear today. A blue eyeball, set in silver.

She took out her phone, dialled Sean's number. It went straight to voicemail, so she left him a message.

"The monkey kindly agreed to finally meet me this evening – I'm just about to do the interview now. Should be through by about half-seven, eight at the latest. I know you said you had someone else to see first, so just give me a call when you're free. You might also get a call from my dad, if he gets that information I told you about before I come home I asked him to ring you with it straight away. Hope that's all right. See you later."

She checked she had everything she needed in her briefcase and got out of the car. Hesitated again before the entrance of the place. The clouds had parted overhead, revealing the moon, fat and low in the sky above her.

"*Ola dika sou matia mou*," she whispered, touching the evil eye again. A line from a song of her childhood, that reminded her of Sean's sad brown eyes.

Then she went inside.

* * *

Noj jerked back from the crystal ball, her heart leaping into her mouth.

"No," she said. "No, I don't believe it."

She willed herself to be calm, to return the vision back from where it came. The globe became cloudy, the image of a sea-front villa fading into mist.

"Thank you," said Noj, bowing her head, putting her hands back around it and lifting it up with care, returning it to its place. Her heart hammering, she ran downstairs to the phone, punching out Sean's number from the card she had left beside it.

It went straight to voicemail.

"Sean," she screeched, "as soon as you get this, call me back on my mobile. You're in more danger than I realised. I'll try to find you in the meantime. But whatever you do, don't go anywhere with either of those two pigs."

She cut that call and hit speed dial. "Joe," she said. "Where is he and who is he with?"

Across the road from the Masonic Lodge, the Irishman replied: "In his ancestral mansion. The journalist has just arrived but there's no sign of your Mr Ward yet."

Noj tried to think straight. "OK," she said. "You stay with them. I'm going to find him."

"Right ye are," said Joe.

* * *

"I'm meeting DCI Smollet," Francesca gave the polished-looking little man on the reception desk her best smile. "My name's Francesca Ryman."

"Yes of course, madam," he bowed his head politely. "Allow me to show you the way."

Francesca's heels were loud on the tiled floor as she followed him down the wood-panelled hallway, lined with portraits of Victorian men with mutton-chop whiskers. The lights were a low glow and somewhere in the distance, a piano tinkled.

"Here we are, madam," the man opened a door and ushered her in.

Francesca's eyes took in another wood-panelled room, with floor-length red velvet curtains pulled across the window. In front of her, a table was set for dinner for two, with a bottle of wine opened in the middle, one glass half full of red.

But both seats were empty.

Frowning, Francesca turned around. "Are you sure . . ." she began.

But the door was closing on the polished little man and, as

it did, she could see the figure standing behind it, a tall, broad, shape in a sheepskin coat and a black trilby with a feather in the side of it.

"You know me, don't you, girl?" said Rivett.

30

A Liberal Education

"But I don't want to go back there! You don't know what it's like!"

Samantha sat on her bed, her hands bunched into fists, her face red not so much from crying, Amanda thought, but from the exertion of throwing a fit that had lasted so long.

She sat down on the bed beside her. Sam immediately turned her head away.

"Sam, listen to me," Amanda said, keeping her voice calm, while putting a firmer hand on her daughter's chin and propelling her head back round. "You are going to have to learn some day that life isn't fair and you can't always get what you want. If you make a mistake, you have to live with the consequences. Learn from them."

"What," Sam looked pointedly down at Amanda's stomach, "like you do?"

"Yes," Amanda smiled as sweetly as she could, "like I do. I know there are plenty of things you think you have every right to be angry with me about. You won't believe me now if I tell you I know how you feel, but trust me when I say that, a few months down the line, this will all seem like nothing. All you have to do is be brave. And I know you're not a coward, are you, Sam?"

Samantha stared at her mother hard, as if trying to puzzle out a trick question.

"No," Amanda answered for her, "you are a beautiful, intelligent, talented girl and I don't doubt you can get the best over anyone."

She raised her hand to stroke a strand of hair away from her daughter's eyes. Edna's hairdresser, Sandra, had done a pretty good job of reshaping the grown-out sides and spiky crown into a more sophisticated style.

"All you have to do is make it to the end of the school year," Amanda said, "without any more dramas. Then you can go to art college, or sixth-form college, to wherever it is that you want to go that your brain can take you. And that could be anywhere, Sam. It really could."

Samantha dropped her gaze, but she didn't pull away. Her fingers pummelled into her duvet, while she bit hard at her bottom lip. Finally she looked up. "You're right," she said, "I'm not a coward."

"Good." Amanda hoped her smile didn't betray too much relief. "That's what I want to hear." She gave her daughter's shoulder a squeeze, then stood up. "Right, I'm going to make spag bol for our tea, and then we'll go to the pictures. Your choice, Sam, whatever you want to see."

Both of these things were far more of a treat than was usually allowed on a Sunday night.

When Sam smiled back, for one brief second, Amanda was reminded of what she had looked like as a child – sweet, demure, innocent.

She didn't see the expression change as she shut the door behind her.

✳ ✳ ✳

"You coming to the party at the weekend?"

In the corridor by the fourth- and fifth-form cloakrooms, Marc Farman was putting his books back in his locker when he spotted Darren Moorcock and Julian Dean.

"What party's that, then?" said Darren, stopping to watch Marc do up his padlock. There was a sticker of a skull-and-crossbones placed above it.

"It's Bully's idea," said Marc. "A beach party. To celebrate May Day."

Darren frowned, something he'd once heard on the local news resurfacing. "Don't you have to get permission off the cops to have one of those, though?"

"Ah," said Marc, tapping the side of his nose, "it's in one of them old World War Two pillboxes, up on the North Denes, well out of sight. We scoped it out last Saturday. There ain't no houses around for miles out there. We'll just bring a boombox and build a bonfire – reckon it'll be a laugh."

Darren and Julian exchanged glances.

"Sounds great," said Darren, warming to the idea. "So, who else is going?"

"Bully, Kris, Lynn, Al, Bugs, Shaun," Marc counted them off on his fingers, "you know, all the usual firm. Bring whoever you want," he said, touching the side of his nose again and winking, "only spread the word discreetly. Know what I mean?"

None of them noticed the figure following behind them, on soft soles and with radar ears.

* * *

"Wahey!" The rocket launched itself from the top of the dune, veered a little to the left as it gained momentum, accelerating skywards. Bully fell backwards onto his arse with a delighted yell as it exploded in a fountain of blue and pink sparks. Spiked and gelled heads shot up below him from the loose circle they had formed around Marc's ghetto blaster, where a lazy, sleazy saxophone solo drifted into the evening air.

"Oy!" Kris looked up at his friend. "You're supposed to save them for when it gets dark!" he yelled. "'Til after we've built the bonfire!"

Bully laughed. "Just testing, in't I? Gotta make sure they still work," he called back, doing a silly dance on the top of the dune before sliding down the side of it.

Alex got to his feet and hopped across the sand to meet him, catching Bully's arm and pulling him around in a mock square dance. Debbie watched the pair of them flailing around with a smile of relief on her face.

The Sunday morning after their row he had turned up on her doorstep, clutching a black vinyl peace offering. They had shaken hands, made up, and taken the record up to her room to listen to. After a while, he told her that he wouldn't be seeing Samantha Lamb any more. It wasn't just what she had said, but a few other things had changed his mind. Debbie found out the rest on the Monday from Julian, after Samantha got suspended. Alex got rid of all the portraits from his wall. The next time Debbie went over, everything looked pretty much as it had before.

Though Samantha had finally been back at school that week, she'd kept a wide berth. She hadn't been in the art room, hadn't raised her head to even speak to anyone in class. Maybe she was embarrassed about the haircut her mum must have made her have, that made her look like Pat Benatar.

But most probably she was smarting from Al's rejection. Maureen had told Debbie that when Samantha wouldn't stop ringing him, Mrs Pendleton had taken her calls instead. She didn't disclose what had been said, but it seemed to have finally put an end to it.

Debbie wondered what would happen to Samantha's art now. The thought made her shiver involuntarily.

"What's up, you cold?" Darren, sitting next to her, put his arm around her. It had been hot and fine all day, and now the sun was just beginning its descent, thin strips of clouds gilded with the rays of its passing floating across the horizon, over the sea.

"No," said Debbie, smiling up at him. "Just thanking my lucky stars that a certain person is no longer with us."

Darren's blue eyes looked iridescent in the golden evening light.

"You can say that again," his gaze travelled from Debbie to Al and then back to his girlfriend. He was just as relieved to see the back of this relationship, which at one point seemed to him would end up ruining their own.

He leaned in to kiss her. Debbie closed her eyes, the sweetness of his breath and sensation of his lips on hers merging into the yearning tilt of the song, the distant sigh of the sea against the pebbles on the shore.

✳   ✳   ✳

Fishing around in the cooler box Marc had brought with him for a decently chilled bottle, Julian watched Alex and Bully dance into the pillbox and crash onto the old sofa they had put in there for the party. Corrine, sitting on the other end of it with Bugs, fell about laughing. Julian smiled as he watched, trying to shake off the absent presence that was also weighing on his mind.

Samantha had waited for him at the end of a corridor last Friday, stepped out and hissed in his ear: "I'm gonna make you pay for what you did, you sneaky little freak."

Julian had flipped his middle finger at her, told her to get lost. But the look on her face had actually scared him. And when he had gone to his locker at the end of the day, someone had written POOF across the door in black marker pen.

From inside the pillbox, Alex looked up into Julian's stare.

"'Scuse me a second," he disentangled himself from Bully, got to his feet and walked out into the sunlight towards Julian, hoping the right words would come that could make up for the embarrassing fool he had made of himself in the market square. "Julian," he said, dropping down beside him. "I owe you an apology. What I said the other day, it was stupid, I didn't mean it like it came out . . ."

Julian's smile widened into a grin. "Don't worry about it," once more the younger boy cut him off with the shake of his head. "I know what you meant. At least, I think I do."

That gleam of understanding was back in his eyes, Alex felt sure now, as he offered his hand to shake. "I'm quite into Soft Cell myself," he said.

* * *

Inside the pillbox, Corrine stared intently at the tattoo on Bully's arm: a silhouette of the profile of a man, coloured in black, but with his eyes left as colourless slits. A man who looked like an avenging angel, made from smoke and soot. Down the side, in what looked liked stencilled letters, was the word: VENGEANCE

Corrine got a funny feeling when she looked at it. "That's fucking brilliant," she said, her hand hovering over the surface.

"'S'all right, you can touch it. The scab come off weeks ago," said Bully.

Gingerly, she put her fingertips onto the inked skin. The feeling intensified. It was as if some long-forgotten dream was trying to push its way to the front of her mind. "Where do it come from?" she whispered.

"Funny you should ask," said Bully. "Kris!" he shouted. "Put the Army on!"

"Right you are," Kris nodded. From the pile of tapes around the ghetto blaster, he selected a cassette. Ejecting Julian's compilation, he loaded it and pressed play.

A tense pattern of notes sprung out, loose as an elastic band but still deadly precise. A bassline that seemed to call out to that feeling of expectation blooming inside Corrine, that propelled her to her feet.

The notes got louder, more urgent, the drums joining in, quickening the pace. Bully took hold of her hands, pulled her into a dance. Corrine had never danced with a man before but the music told her what to do, stomp her legs to the persistent beat, sand flying across the concrete floor of the pillbox from her twisting feet and Bully's boxing boots.

A man began to sing, simmering rage compressed into each syllable. His voice bounced along the surface of the song, like a pebble skimmed across the sea. Corrine couldn't make out exactly what he was saying, but as the verse built towards the chorus, she felt she knew his intentions clearly – he was enunciating something she had yearned for all her life. Freedom . . .

"*I believe in justice.*"

Bully threw his arms in the air, singing out the words.

"*I believe in vengeance.*"

Made his hands into fists, leaning towards her, a wild grin cracked across his face.

"*I believe in getting the bastard, getting the bastard, NOW!*"

Yeah, thought Corrine, *yeah*.

Retribution.

Faces flashed through her mind as she laughed and danced on. The faces of the dirty old men under the pier, the sad cavalcade of twisted souls whose only release from the shame, disgust and hurt inside them was to inflict it on others, to corrupt as they had been corrupted. Psycho, Scum and Whiz, laughing their dull, deadly laughs. Rat and his knife, the knife she had dreamt of turning back on him over and over, plunging it into him and seeing the red come out, the evil gushing forth from his guts, one sweet, visceral purge. Making him feel all the hurt he had inflicted on her, but worse, making him feel it forever, making him watch the life draining out of him, horror and sheer disbelief in his eyes.

Oh God, that dream, she had had it so many times. It almost felt as if she had actually looked down on her own bloody hands, with the knife clasped inside them.

And Gina – what would she do with Gina?

"*I believe in justice*," the chorus kicked in again.

Make her take all of them. All of them that had been forced on her.

"*I believe in vengeance.*"

With her watching, her laughing, her holding up Rat's head on a stick. A legion of townsfolk behind her, bearing torches and whooping with laughter, curses crackling on their lips like fire. Preparing the scaffold for Gina. A man made of smoke and soot rising up behind them all, bigger than the sky . . .

I believe in getting the bastard

Oh yeah, and one other.

Getting the bastard

Samantha Lamb. Yes, Samantha Lamb must die!

NOW!

Bully grabbed hold of her hand again, spun her round in a circle. Corrine saw passing through her mind's eye in rapid succession, like a carousel wheel spinning: *Knives. Blood. Black hair. White skin. Mouths open, screaming.*

Then they crashed down on the sofa. Bully's laugh shook the vision away.

Corrine looked through the door of the pillbox at her friends outside, their faces flushed with joy. Happiness poured through her veins like molten gold.

The sun was nearly set now, the sky painted crimson, the still sea the palest of blues.

"You gonna help me build this fire, then?" said Bully.

* * *

Up on the Iron Duke forecourt, Gray responded to the call-out. "I'm up North Denes now," he told the controller, "I'll go take a look. Let you know if I need back-up."

The dog started whining, straining on the leash.

"What's that, then?" said Gray, following the direction of the animal's snout. He raised his palm over his eyes and saw a plume of smoke drifting up into the dimming light, coming from the middle of the sand dunes. "That's where they are, is it boy?"

* * *

No one saw him coming. The music was too loud and they were all too intoxicated – by the beer, by the songs, by the sense of euphoria that had grown since they lit the fire. Out here in the primal, beautiful night, by the sea, at the edge of the world.

The first that Corrine knew of it was a dog pushing its snout into her palm as she was sat sideways on the sofa, looking into Bully's eyes while he talked about this band. When she looked up, that policeman was standing over her, the one from under the pier, the dog's lead in his hand.

"Corrine," he said, and though he was trying to look stern, there was a glimmer of amusement in his eyes. "Sorry, love, but the party's over. Time to put that fire out."

No one saw them, except for the person who had made the call of complaint from a seafront phonebox and now crouched in the darkness, watching the policeman bring events to a premature conclusion, making the gang kick sand over the fire and pick up all their empties. Then escorting them back across the dunes and up onto the sea wall, fun and games over for the night. Watched the deflated procession walking back along the promenade towards town.

The sound of soft laughter drifting in their wake, ringing around the walls of the pillbox.

Part Four

* * *

RUB ME OUT

31

Spiritwalker

March 2003

At the same time the fax machine pinged and whirred into life, Digby, the larger of the two black Labradors lying in front of the fire, began to whine in his sleep. Mr Pearson, who had been staring into the flames ever since he took his daughter's call, returned from the world of memory with a start.

He looked down at the dog. His front paws were moving, as if he was trying to give chase, and he gave out another strangled-sounding whine that provoked his brother, Lewie, to a response in kind.

"What you dreaming about, boys?" asked Mr Pearson, getting to his feet.

His eyes drew level with the picture on the mantelpiece. It showed him with darker, more luxuriant hair, his arm around a woman of about thirty, clouds of black curls snaked around her shoulders. Between them, a skinny young girl with her hair tied back in a red bandana, wearing a huge smile. Both females fixed the camera with arresting, turquoise eyes. Behind them lay an azure sea and craggy mountains rising into a clear blue sky.

"Sophia," not for the first time, he asked his favourite image of his wife, "what am I going to do with her?"

Sophia smiled back, sphinx-like. Digby, in contrast, rolled right over and lurched to his feet, shaking himself vigorously awake. He pushed his nose into Mr Pearson's hand, looked up at him with searching brown eyes.

"Let's take a look then, boy," his master said, padding out of the living room and across the hall into the crowded, book-clad room that Francesca called her office.

Pages of paper had begun to spew out of the fax machine.

* * *

"Leonard Rivett," said Francesca.

"The very same." He took a step forwards, doffing his hat with one hand, offering her the other. Francesca looked down at it, big and spotted with age, each finger encircled with a band of gold. *And the thumbs of a murderer*, she thought.

But she gave him her most charming smile as she placed her own slim palm in his. "Then I don't believe I need to introduce myself," she said.

"Indeed not, Miss Ryman," Rivett agreed. He did not apply any pressure, just the merest of touches, before he let her hand go. "I know you weren't expecting me, but I'm afraid DCI Smollet's been delayed, he ran into a spot of bother on his way out of the station." Rivett shook his head and raised his thick brows. "You know how it is in our line of work. So he asked me to go ahead and meet you."

He turned, indicating the table. "I'm sure he won't keep you waiting long, half an hour tops, he reckoned," he said. "In the meantime, I took the liberty of ordering myself a drink. Would you care to join me?"

"Thanks." Francesca nodded politely, sat herself down at the side of the table with the empty glass, taking in the label on the bottle of red as she did so. It flashed through her mind whether Rivett already knew what she liked drinking – and if so, how he had found that out. From the moment he'd stepped out from behind the door, she'd realised that his presence here was no accident.

"Good, good," he followed her gaze, lifted the bottle up.

"Only," she put her hand over her glass, "unfortunately, I came here in my car. I don't think I should risk it, do you? Especially not in front of a member of the constabulary," she smiled sweetly. "Could you order me a mineral water instead?"

"Of course." Rivett refilled his own glass, then leaned back in his seat, pressing a little button on the wall next to his right hand, summoning another dapper little man in a white jacket and black bow tie, who took her order with a bow and shut the door behind him.

"You know," said Rivett as the waiter departed, "that I'm no longer an official member of the constabulary, don't you? So," he leaned forward conspiratorially, nodding back towards the wine, "we don't have to play by the normal rules."

Looking at his pointed yellow teeth, Francesca fought down a feeling of revulsion that was stronger even than the first jolt of fear she had got from seeing him emerge.

"Is that why the DCI sent you?" she said.

* * *

As she came out of her front door, Noj wasn't sure which was the right direction to take. She stopped for a moment, her eyes travelling around the square. Her instincts told her that Sean was close. Maybe he had gone back to Swing's? Yes, that felt right.

As she hurried across the street, she heard the distant sound of dogs barking.

* * *

"I had an interesting chat with Mrs Linguard today," said Sean, "up at your old school. She told me you were in with a pretty bad crowd yourself at one point, and that you wouldn't mind admitting it."

Smollet gave a smile that was intended to look rueful. "She mean Shane Rowlands and Neal Reeder, the village idiots of Ernemouth High. She's right, they were bad lads – even the special class kids were scared of Rowlands. You could say he were the ringleader."

Smollet nodded to himself as his memory spooled back. "I s'pose I got swept along with it, you know, the folly of youth. But fortunately, I seen the error of my ways. I washed my hands of them at the start of the fifth year. Didn't have no more to do with them until I was in uniform," he started to smile again, "and they tried to rob a Post Office in the March of '89. First people I ever nicked, Rowlands and Reeder."

He was about to say something else, when a light flashing on his telephone caught Smollet's attention. He frowned. He had given orders that he was not to be disturbed.

"Excuse me one moment," he said, lifting the receiver.

* * *

Mr Pearson's eyes narrowed as he took in the information on the fax and his stomach hollowed. Old, bad memories suddenly crowded in.

"Oh, dear God," he said. "I hope this don't mean what I think it do. Not again . . ."

Digby, who had been standing in the doorway, staring at him while he was reading, gave a loud bark. In the next room, Lewie whined and rolled out of the basket.

* * *

Rivett chuckled. "Now that's a leading question," he said. He raised his glass, studied Francesca over the rim of it. "You think he wants me to soften you up before the interview, do you?"

Before she could reply, the waiter came back with Francesca's bottle of water. She watched him break the seal, then pour the bubbling liquid into her glass, trying to still the effervescence in her stomach, to think one question ahead. Telling herself she had dealt with his kind before, dirty old men in every newsroom she'd ever worked in. That he wasn't any different.

She kept the smile fixed on her face as the waiter bowed again and left them.

"Why?" she said. "What kind of interview did you think it was going to be?" She took a sip of water, parrying his stare, raising her own eyebrows in what she hoped looked like amusement. "I think your press officer must have got a bit over-excited. This is what we call in our trade a puff piece. I'm sure you know what that means, Mr Rivett. A profile of an upstanding member of the community, what they've gained from their time in Ernemouth and what they're giving back."

"Is that right?" Rivett put his hand inside his jacket, pulled out a box of slim cigars and a long, thin, gold lighter. "Mind if I . . . ?" he asked.

"Not at all," said Francesca.

"Thanks," he said, clicking the lighter into a flame. The end of the cigar crackled as it ignited, turning a glowing red. Rivett inhaled, blew out a plume of smoke.

"Go on," he said. "What's he giving back to this fine old town of ours, then?"

"Well," she said, "I know DCI Smollet is keen on maintaining links with his old school. I'm assuming his motivation is to set a good example to the pupils of Ernemouth High, that they could follow in his footsteps if they work hard enough."

"Very noble," said Rivett. "So what give you the idea for that?"

"You know," Francesca put on a serious face, leaned forwards into his smoke, "one of the things that bothers me the most about society today is the breakdown of the family. You would probably know more about this than I do," she looked at him earnestly, "but so many boys today are growing up without a father, or even a decent father figure. It's no wonder there's been such a rise in youth crime and anti-social behaviour. They don't have any positive male role models, do they?"

Rivett nodded. "Sad but true, Miss Ryman, sad but true. We have lived through godless times," he said, his countenance becoming grave, in a mirror of her own, "and now we reap what we have sown."

* * *

"Jason," said Smollet, still looking at Sean, "I thought I told you . . ."

Whoever was on the end of the line cut him off mid-sentence. Sean couldn't hear the caller, but as Smollet ducked his head, eyes sweeping down to the desktop, he guessed that this was unexpected news being relayed. Either that, or a prearranged decoy.

"You what?" said Smollet, frowning. "Slow down a minute, Jason, you in't making no sense." He looked back up at Sean for a second, mouthed the word "sorry".

"Who?" he said, sounding astonished. "What? *My* orders? I don't know nothing about it . . ."

His eyes shifted focus, so that he now appeared to be looking straight through Sean at the wall behind. That muscle beneath his eye began to flicker again.

"Enough, Jason," he snapped. "I'll be right down."

He replaced the receiver, staring down at it with a look of disbelief. Then, gathering himself swiftly together, he looked back up at Sean.

"I'm ever so sorry, Mr Ward," he said. "But I'm going to have to leave it here for now. Duty calls." He pushed his seat back, got to his feet. "We'll continue tomorrow morning," he looked down at his wristwatch. "Nine-thirty all right with you?"

Sean reached for his Dictaphone, put it back into his bag. "OK," he said. "Is . . ."

"Now I'm afraid I'm gonna have to ask you to leave," the tension emanating from the DCI was palpable as he walked round the desk and opened the door before Sean even had chance to stand up. "I got something urgent to attend to."

* * *

"So," said Francesca, not expecting this burst of Old Testament thinking that so closely resembled her own thoughts, noticing that Rivett's eyes had come to rest on the pendant around her neck as he spoke. "I think what DCI Smollet is doing at his old school sets a good example. I'm going to make it the first part of a series, a weekly thing."

"Oh yeah?" Rivett's eyes shifted back up to meet hers. "Who else you got lined up for it, then?"

"A community youth leader, a scout master, a stay-at-home dad," Francesca reeled off a list of the role models she thought would probably irritate Rivett the most. But then, as she took a breath to say the next thing that came to mind, a jolt of fear ran through her.

What if he already knew?

As she thought it, the smile returned to the old detective's face, and he leaned back in his chair. "A male teacher, I would have thought," he said. "There in't too many of them left, these days, are there? Or so I hear . . ."

* * *

"Thanks again, Mr Ward," Smollet hurried Sean towards the door of the station, holding it open for him. "Nine-thirty then."

"Nine-thirty," repeated Sean as the door swung shut behind him.

He stood for a moment on the top of the steps, watching Smollet hurry away across the foyer, nod to the copper on the front desk and then disappear through a door behind it. Then his mobile phone began to ring.

* * *

Francesca gave a start as someone rapped on the door, spilling some of the water out of her glass as her hand jerked upwards.

Rivett snapped his head round impatiently. "Yes?" he demanded.

The waiter stood in the doorway. "Sorry to disturb you again, sir," he said, "but you're wanted on the phone. He said to say it was about Eric. And that it was urgent."

* * *

"Hello?" said Sean. The number that flashed up was not one he recognised.

"Is that Sean Ward?" a man with a Norfolk accent, a hesitant delivery.

"That's right," said Sean, "who's calling?"

"Oh, well, you don't know me, but my daughter asked me to ring you. Francesca Ryman. I got some information for you she said would be important."

Philip Pearson, thought Sean. "What's that then?" he said, starting to walk down the steps, away from the station, back to his car.

"Well," the other man said, "if I'm reading this right, I think she's about to put herself in some serious trouble. Do you mind me asking who you are first?"

"Hold on one second," said Sean, picking up his pace, rummaging for his key in his pocket and pressing unlock. The lights flashed on his car. "I just want to get to a place where no one else can hear me," he explained. He opened the door, slid inside throwing his bag down on the passenger seat beside him, and glancing up into the rear-view mirror as he slammed the door shut again.

"Sorry about that, sir," he said. "I'm a private detective, working for a London QC."

"A detective?" Mr Pearson sounded puzzled.

"I've been sent here to work on a cold case," said Sean, "and your daughter's been giving me a hand with it."

"Don't tell me," Mr Pearson said, "that's something to do with Corrine Woodrow?"

His voice was drowned out by a cacophony of barking.

* * *

"I won't be long," said Rivett, standing up and crushing out his cigar in the ashtray. "Don't go anywhere."

As soon as the door shut behind him, Francesca saw again in her mind that terse expression on Pat's face as she'd passed her desk, heard that muttered comment of suppressed rage, before she forwarded the call from the police press office . . .

Replayed the caller's voice in her mind. She was sure of it now. The "press officer" she'd spoken to was actually Rivett.

Feeling panic welling in her chest, she pulled herself into her coat and grabbed hold of her bag. Then she realised – she could not simply leave by the door she'd come through. Rivett, or one of those dapper men, would see her, make some smooth excuse to keep her here. Her heart hammering in her chest, she pulled back the red velvet curtains.

✳ ✳ ✳

"Mr Pearson?" In the rear-view mirror, Sean saw movement in the station.

"Sorry about that," Francesca's father came back on the line. "Just had to shut the dogs in the other room. They've been giving me gyp all night. Right now, I don't know what the pair of you have been up to, but Frannie said I had to trust her on this, so I hope you know what you're doing. I got a load of faxes through from Frannie's ex-husband, Ross. He's been doing some kind of company search for her, and there's a name on here I don't much like the look of. Leonard Rivett," he said. "It say here that he and Dale Smollet are partners in Leisure Beach Industries Inc of Ernemouth . . ."

In the rear-view mirror, Sean saw Smollet remonstrating with another man, a uniform of about his own age. Smollet was red in the face, shouting and waving his arms.

" . . . and have been since the March of 1989. Do that mean anything to you?"

Sean watched Smollet open the station door and run down the steps. It took him a second to process everything that Mr

Pearson had just said to him and realise that the man was expecting an answer.

"Yes," he said, watching Smollet sweep straight past him, heading towards a silver Audi TT, its lights flashing with an electronic bleep as he keyed it open. "Yes, it explains a lot, Mr Pearson, thank you for telling me. Where is Francesca now, do you know?"

"She rung about half an hour ago," said Mr Pearson, "said she was going to be late back this evening. But she didn't say why. If you've put her in any danger ..."

"Maybe she's left me a message," said Sean, watching the Audi's headlights come on, Smollet reversing past him without registering him, manoeuvring out of the car park.

"Well, would you mind checking?" said Mr Pearson. "Only that in't just the dogs that have got the wind up 'em tonight."

"Course," said Sean, "I'll call you straight back soon as I have."

Smollet was pulling into the road as Sean got the first of his saved messages, the one from Noj, which he had to hold away from his ear, her voice was so loud.

"*Second message. Message recorded at eighteen-thirty,*" his phone informed him.

"*The monkey kindly agreed to finally meet me this evening,*" he heard Francesca say. "*I'm just about to do the interview now. Should be through by about half-seven, eight at the latest ...*"

Sean looked down at the dashboard clock.

Eighteen-thirty. When he himself had been interviewing Smollet. Here, in the station.

Which meant ... *The organ grinder?*

When Sean looked in his mirror again, the monkey was long gone.

32

Seven Seas

May 1984

"You two are at school together, aren't you? Mr Pearson's class?"

Smollet's mother stood between himself and Samantha, a glass of Asti Spumante in her hand. Samantha, who had been talking to her grandfather, turned her head, casting her eyes over Mrs Smollet with a quizzical expression.

"Oh," she said, flicking a glance towards Dale, "yes, that's right. Are you ... ?"

"Karen Smollet," the woman with the Alexis Carrington shoulder pads offered a hand encrusted with gold and diamonds. "Dale's mum. And you're Samantha, aren't you?"

Samantha's smile was incredulous. Dale felt the colour travelling up his neck. He couldn't believe his mother had just dragged him all the way across the crowded room just to embarrass him like this. He already felt stupid enough in the black tuxedo she had insisted that he wore for the occasion, the little dickey bow she'd tied around his neck.

"That's what a black-tie dinner means," she had said. "Remember that. It won't be your last."

He stared down at his Italian leather slip-on shoes, the only piece of clobber he was not ashamed to be wearing.

"Eric!" Karen blabbered on. "Happy birthday, darling!"

Eric leaned across to kiss her on the cheek. "Karen," he said, "looking glamorous as ever."

"Oh," said Karen, mock coquettish, "this old thing?"

She did a twirl, so that her red sequinned dress swished around her hips.

Dale closed his eyes, wishing the floor of the Lodge would open up and swallow him. Almost jumped out of his skin when he heard a soft voice beside him say: "God! I didn't realise your mother was as embarrassing as mine."

Opened them to see Samantha standing there, grinning at him mischievously.

He started to laugh and she winked.

"Which one is yours, then?" he replied, *sotto voce*.

"That shameless old bitch over there," Samantha motioned with her head towards a woman who could have been Karen's blonde twin, except for the fact that she was wearing a layered black chiffon creation that didn't completely hide the bump in her stomach. "With her toy boy, *Wayne*." She pronounced the name with disdain.

Dale took in the sight of an uncomfortable looking guy with curly brown hair, sideburns and an ill-fitting tuxedo that made his own look like the razor's edge of suave. Wayne appeared to have left style behind some time in the middle of the last decade.

"Let me guess," he said. "Underneath that jacket, he's got a tattoo of an anchor on his arm. Underneath where it says your mum's name."

Samantha's eyes widened and her mouth formed a perfect "O".

"How'd you know that?" she said.

"My uncle Ted," said Dale, motioning his own head backwards, "is just the same."

Samantha strained her neck, then put her hand over her mouth and giggled delightedly as she caught sight of the only other man in the room wearing flared trousers.

Dale didn't think he had ever seen her look more lovely. Her hair had grown out of that stupid style that Rowlands kept taunting him about. It was long and feathery, quite sophisticated. And the simple, long black dress she wore did everything for her figure – although he quickly moved his eyes back up when she had stopped laughing at Ted.

"Well," she said. "We've got more in common than I thought."

* * *

"I say," Edna leaned across to whisper in Amanda's ear, "who's that nice-looking boy talking to our Sammy?"

Amanda followed her mother's gaze. "I don't know," she said, "but he does look smart, doesn't he?"

"Much more like it," Edna agreed.

* * *

"You see," Rivett slipped alongside Eric, "what did I tell you? Make a handsome couple, don't they?"

"He scrub up all right, I s'pose," said Eric, grudgingly.

"He's going to go far, Eric," said Rivett, "right to the top. He's got all the qualities I need to make an outstanding policeman and a model member of society. And in the meantime, something to put a smile on your face, even before I do my speech. I've found you a lovely new ingénue for your next production."

"Yeah?" said Eric, not taking his eyes off Samantha. "She won't be as good as the last one."

"I don't see why not," said Rivett. "She's a chip off the old block. And," he leaned closer, whispered into Eric's ear, "she's only sweet fifteen."

* * *

"Corrine," Gina yelled up the stairs, "get down here now. And," she added as an afterthought, "make sure you look decent."

Corrine looked down at the collection of talismans she had spread across the surface of the pink plastic dressing table, given to her long ago by a grandmother she barely recalled. She had no idea how much of it was down to what Noj had taught her and how much of it was the absence of Rat, but in the weeks since she had been back here, Gina had not come into her room to steal, destroy or disturb any of the items from what she now thought of as her altar.

Corrine's eyes ran across the red and black crushed-velvet scarf that served as her altar cloth. Noj had bought her the candles and the highly patterned little Indian brass dishes in which they sat from the head shop in Norwich, impressing upon her the need to keep things tidy and in order for the spell to continue its work.

Two white candles, which she had first rubbed with sandalwood oil while saying the incantation, were burning between a brass bowl containing sea salt, dissolved in hot water. Beside each one, joss sticks smoked from lotus-shaped brass holders, filling the room with the scent of frankincense and myrrh.

Protected by the candles were her prize possessions, the books and the pack of tarot cards that her mentor had given her. *The Goetia* and *The Necronomicon*. The first one, the one that had saved her from Gina that night in the police station, was the one she treasured the most. Without Noj's guidance, she wouldn't have been able to pronounce it, let alone understand a word of it. But Corrine felt that this book in particular, radiated a protective power all of its own.

"Corrine!" Gina's voice got louder and there was an ominous banging from under the floor. "I said get down here, now!"

Corrine stared at her face in the mirror, imagining a white light all around her. Repeated the lines that she now knew off by heart. Said them three times and then bowed her head to the altar, stood up and went downstairs.

There was a man standing in the kitchen with her mother.

A man she didn't think she had ever seen before, but at the same time, seemed so familiar she did a double-take as he turned around to face her.

A tall, broad shape in a sheepskin coat and a black trilby with a feather in the side of it. Dark, almond-shaped eyes deep-set under black brows in a wide, weather-beaten face. A broad smile cracked across it, revealing pointed canine teeth. Corrine put a hand up to her own face as she looked at him, a question forming in her mind.

"This," said Gina, before Corrine could find her voice to ask it, "is your Uncle Len."

Corrine frowned. Her first thought dissolved into a lurch of fear. Was this, then, Rat's replacement?

"Hello, Corrine," said the man, offering her a huge paw of a hand. Gold rings flashed on his every finger.

Corrine took it gingerly and he gave her palm a little squeeze. The funny feeling came back as she looked back at him. The

"So?" she said. Her black eyes were out of focus.

"So you wasted my time," said Rivett. "Wasted my partner's time and all. Which all mean, it's not looking good for you again, Gina. And so soon . . ."

Gina exhaled a stream of smoke in his face. "D'you know what?" she said. "I really couldn't give a fuck." She opened her arms theatrically, stumbling as she did so, having to catch herself against the wall. "You want to fuck me? Fuck me. You want to beat me up? Beat me up. Whatever you like. It's nothing I in't took before. Just get it over with."

Rivett looked at her in disgust. "Where's the rest of your wares?" he said.

"I don't know what you're talking about," said Gina.

Rivett shook his head, left her in the hallway and went upstairs. Noticing lights glimmering in the front bedroom, he stepped inside.

"What the . . . ?" His eyes travelled around Corrine's pink plastic altar, the candles almost burnt out now, wax congealing over the side of the bowls and dripping onto the velvet scarf. He moved in closer, trying to puzzle out what he was seeing. Picked up the black book in the centre of the dressing table. *The Goetia*, he read, *The Lesser Key of Solomon the King, Clavicula Salomonis Regis*.

He looked around at the rest of the room. The single bed and the ill-fitting curtains, the cheap nylon carpet. The pictures of over-made-up pop stars taped onto the lurid '70s wallpaper. This was Corrine's room.

"I wouldn't touch that, if I was you." Gina stood in the doorway. "That's Corrine's black magic altar. *Woooo!*" She gave a scornful, drunken chuckle, then seemed to reconsider her words. "Still," she said, her eyebrows raising, "it seem to have worked for her all right tonight, don't it?"

Rivett put the book back down where he'd found it.

The candlelight flickered and then guttered out.

"So why din't your partner like Corrine then?" Gina taunted. "Thought you said he liked 'em young. Too ugly for him, was she?" She shook her head. "Don't surprise me, really."

"You're feeling brave now, Gina," said Rivett. "But that'll wear off when the skag do and you find you in't got nothing left to play with."

"Yeah," said Gina, "you're probably right. But while I still am feeling brave, and before you beat the shit out of me or whatever you intend to do next, I think you should know one thing."

"I in't really interested," said Rivett, walking towards her.

"You should be," said Gina, "it's about Corrine. The reason she don't look like much, in't got too much up there neither," she tapped her index finger against the side of her head. "It's sad really. It's 'cos she take after her father."

Rivett caught hold of her wrist.

"The amount of scumbags you've entertained in your time, why should that surprise me?" he said.

A mad light came back on in Gina's eyes as his grip tightened.

"Because she belong to the biggest scumbag of the lot of 'em," she said. "You."

33

My Kingdom

March 2003

Noj pushed open the front door of Swing's and walked into a wall of noise. Metallic guitars screeched against a barrage of drums, vocals a guttural roar over the top of it. Pushing her way past a couple of students, she leant across the bar, shouted at the landlord's back. "Marc!"

Laughing with a customer, he didn't seem to hear her. "Marc!" In frustration, her voice reached several decibels higher than the emo blare. Farman span around, his attention finally caught. "Marc," Noj leaned across the bar, "that policeman hasn't been in tonight, has he?"

"What?" said Marc. "Sean Ward? No, he ain't, I'm afraid. Why, what you after him for?"

"Something very important," said Noj, "I haven't time to explain. But if he does come in, get him to call me straight away – on my mobile, yeah? And don't let him leave."

* * *

"Hello again, Mr Pearson," said Sean. "Francesca did leave me a message. She's doing an interview, said she'd be finished about half an hour to an hour's time," he looked back down at the dashboard clock.

"Oh, right," Mr Pearson sounded doubtful. "So she should be home by eight, then."

"Sounds like it," said Sean, with a confidence he didn't feel.

"Yeah, well, I think I'd better go and let the dogs out before they tear the house down."

"All right, Mr Pearson. I'll let you know if I hear anything more from her," said Sean, hanging up. Immediately, his phone went off again.

"There you are at last!" Noj's voice shrilled in his ear.

"Noj," said Sean. "I only just got your message. I was going to come and meet you, but something's just come up, something important . . ."

"Nothing's more important than what I've got to tell you," said Noj.

"It is at the moment, I'm afraid." Sean's thumb hovered over the cut-off button.

"Rivett," said Noj, "is with your journalist friend right now. What do you think of that?"

"What?" Sean flicked his thumb back. "Where are they?"

"Where are *you*?" countered Noj.

"Outside the station," said Sean. "Don't fuck me about Noj, where are they?"

"Pick me up outside Swing's," she said. "I'll take you straight to them."

"I'll be right there," Sean cut the call and started the engine. As he drove out of the car park, he saw the officer who had been remonstrating with Smollet standing at the station door, looking down the road, an agitated expression on his face.

✳ ✳ ✳

Francesca's eyes rested on the window. It was at ground level, a sash opening. Providing it wasn't locked, it should be easy enough to step straight out of it. She reached up to the fastening, began to unscrew it. It worked easily enough. But when she tried to lift the window, the frame would hardly budge. "Shit!" she swore under her breath, the pane raised off the sill only a couple of inches. Her eyes travelled down the sides of the wooden frame; it looked like it had been painted shut.

This is useless, realised Francesca. *Think again.*

Using all her might, she pulled the window back down again, screwed the fastener back in place and swished the curtains shut. Sat back down at the table, her mind racing. *OK, what about the toilets? They'd have windows, wouldn't they?* At least he wouldn't follow her in there – well, not at first anyway. Or even better, just say she needed to go and then walk straight out of the front door while he was waiting for her. Yes, that was a good idea. Only, to make it look good, she'd need to leave her coat here. *Shit, that was a good coat.* But what did that matter? She could get another one.

She pulled it off, put it back around her chair, sat down and took another fretful gulp of water. She realised she could have taken the opportunity to call Sean, at least let him know where she was and who she was with. Realised that this was what she should have done all along. But there still might be time . . .

As she delved into her bag, the door opened again.

"Change of plan," said Rivett.

*   *   *

Sean pulled up opposite Swing's, where Noj stood in her leopardskin coat, a bag slung over her shoulders. She opened the car door, slid into the seat, looking up at Sean with flashing eyes. "They're at the Masonic Lodge. I've just checked, they're still in there. Do you know how to get there, or shall I show you?" she said.

"You navigate," said Sean. "If you can get me round the one-way system then I really will start to believe in magic."

"OK," said Noj, "take the next left."

Sean accelerated away, navigated the first corner, following Noj's instructions. "So maybe you can tell me what you know about Miss Ryman and how you know she's with Rivett right now."

"I've had someone keep an eye on him," said Noj, "since our last conversation. I knew things would start to move fast, so I wanted to know exactly where he was at all times. That's how I know she's with him. About her, I know very little . . ."

"Right," said Sean. "You said she was my journalist friend, though, so you do know something."

"I know what she does, I read the paper like anyone else and I've seen her face in it. She's pretty different from the last *Mercury* editor. She's pretty different all round, isn't she?" Noj studied Sean's profile for a second, then turned her attention back to the road.

"Have you been following me too?" asked Sean.

"No," said Noj. "I'm just putting two and two together. You needed all the help you could get here, it makes sense you'd ask someone at the local paper."

"OK," said Sean. "I'll buy it."

"Turn left again at the next junction," said Noj. "We're nearly there."

* * *

Francesca got to her feet. "Yeah, for me as well," she said. "I've just got a call, I . . ."

"DCI Smollet wants to meet you elsewhere," said Rivett. "Said I was to escort you, make sure you arrive safely."

He was smiling again, moving over to the table to lift his glass and drain it.

Francesca laughed, her nerves jangling out a harsh sound, while her brain tried to stay calm. "Why?" she said. "What's wrong with here?"

"That's to do with the story you want to write," said Rivett, putting the empty glass down, leaning forwards over the table so that he loomed above her. "He want you to have a bit more background information. Reckon you'll be able to write a more accurate profile that way."

"I see," said Francesca, swallowing one more mouthful of water to try and combat the dryness in her throat. "So, what, are we going to join him in action, then? Is he out on a case at the moment?"

"No," said Rivett, cocking his head to one side. "I s'pose you could say that's more to do with his personal life. His idea is show you some of his roots, where it is he's coming from. You know, so you can form a more rounded picture of him," Rivett indicated his head towards the door, "see where all that natural philanthropy stem from." His smile deepened, along with the lines down the side of his face.

Francesca got to her feet slowly.

"That's right, miss," Rivett encouraged her. "The sooner I get you to him, the sooner you can get rid of me. And that don't take a seasoned detective to realise that's what you really want, do it?"

* * *

"There it is," said Noj, "you can turn right here, straight into the car park."

Sean clocked Rivett's Rover as they drew in, felt a rush of relief.

"You're right," he said. "They're here. Let's go and get them."

Noj gave an embarrassed chuckle. "I don't think it's wise that I should go in with you," she said. "They don't take kindly to my sort here. They might not let you in."

"All right then, stay here," said Sean. "Keep an eye on his car for me, just in case he comes out some other way. I take it you already know which one's his?"

Noj nodded. "Good luck, Sean Ward," she said softly.

Sean got out of the car, was halfway to the front steps when he felt his mobile vibrate in his jacket pocket. He plucked it out, glanced down at the caller. Janice Mathers.

He stopped. "Ma'am," he said, "can this be quick?"

"OK," her voice was cool. "Can anyone hear you?"

Sean took a step backwards, keeping his eye on the door. "No," he said.

"I got the results back from those two samples Rivett got for you. One of them, name of Adrian Hall, is a direct match for the phantom DNA."

Sean took a sharp intake of breath. "Really?" he said. "He's one of the bikers that hung around with Corrine's mother, the ones he keeps trying to lead me to. Do you actually think it could be that simple?"

* * *

"It does seem a mite convenient, doesn't it?" Mathers said. "Still more interesting," she went on, "is what we got from the cigar butt you sent. An extremely close match to Corrine Woodrow's DNA."

"What?" Sean's mind rewound as he turned his head to look back at the car, to the exchange he'd had with Noj the night before.

Him saying: *"But I've seen the crime-scene photos. There was a pentagram drawn on the floor, in the victim's blood. You're not trying to tell me that Len Rivett made all that up?"*

Her saying: *"You have no idea what that man is capable of . . ."*

"Where are you now?" said Mathers in his ear.

"About to meet with Rivett," said Sean, "in what he calls his office. The Ernemouth Lodge."

"Be careful with him," said Mathers. "Don't reveal anything you now know. He's on his home turf and he could get dangerous. Just be friendly, act naïve – use your skills to buy some more time, Mr Ward, while I work out how best to proceed. I don't want you coming to any grief."

"You don't have to tell me that," Sean said, feeling a twinge in his knees, thinking how close Francesca had come.

"OK," said Mathers. "Call me back when you're free."

Sean cut the call, walked through the front door. A dapper little man on the front desk smiled brightly at him as he approached.

"I'm here to see Len Rivett," said Sean.

"I'm sorry," the receptionist said. "Mr Rivett left here, oh, about five minutes ago."

Sean shook his head. "You must be mistaken," he said. "His car's still parked out the front there."

"That's right," the man's smile never wavered as he reached down into his desk. "He left the keys with me for safekeeping." He held them out in front of Sean's face. "He often does," the receptionist went on, "when . . ." His expression turned into a frown as he looked past Sean. "Oh. What on earth is that?"

Noj was standing on the doorstep, waving a mobile phone around in her hand, a wild expression on her face.

"Nothing," said Sean. "I'll take care of it."

He turned and hurried outside.

"They're not here!" cried Noj.

"So I gather," said Sean. "What about your mate who was following them?"

"He just called. They left in her car, two or three minutes ago." Her eyes flashed with agitation. "They're headed down the seafront now, going that way," she pointed left, in the direction of the Britannic Pier. "Come on!"

✱ ✱ ✱

"How do you manage," said Rivett, as Francesca steered the Micra down the seafront, "in a poxy car like this? You in't got no leg room in here." He felt the twinge in his knees again, the arthritis kicking in when he least needed it.

Francesca stared at the road ahead. "I could have followed your car," she said. "I wouldn't have run off."

Rivett chuckled. "Is that right?" he said. "That in't quite the impression I got. And I can't afford to take no chances where the guvnor's concerned, can I? Anyway, that in't that much further, thank God."

"Would you mind giving me some idea of where it is that we're going?" Annoyance was beginning to get the better of Francesca's nerves.

"To the garden of earthly delights," said Rivett. "Where the fun never stop and the sun never set." The dark towers of the deserted Leisure Beach lay just ahead. "You can start indicating now," said Rivett.

34

Eve Black, Eve White

June 1984

"Can you see what she's now doing?" Debbie spoke under her breath, tilting her head towards the other end of the corridor where, like the rest of the O-Level Art students, Samantha was hanging the highlights of her coursework for the final part of the examination, the end-of-year display.

Darren was standing at the top of a ladder, putting his favourite painting in place. It showed a long, blue wash of sky meeting sea, four figures in black with their backs turned, gazing out at the horizon where a flock of gulls were taking flight. Old Witchell had been pretty impressed by it, said it was in the best traditions of East Anglian watercolour painting. Didn't realise Darren had copied it from the front cover of his favourite LP. Well, his second favourite now. Darren had practically worn the grooves off the new Bunnymen album in the space of the last month.

He turned his head, leaned forwards to get a better look. Samantha was kneeling on the floor, her portfolio open in front of her. Leaning forward, her hair fell in front of her face, shielding hers from prying eyes.

"Don't look like she's doing anything," he said. "She in't put a single thing up yet."

He started to lower himself down the rungs. Debbie's eyes were full of trouble. "I don't like it," she whispered. "I reckon she's waiting for us to finish."

Darren jumped down beside her. "Yeah, then what's she gonna do?" he asked. "We already got into art college, she can't do nothing to stop us now."

"I don't know," said Debbie, "I've just got a bad feeling."

* * *

Debbie started to feel sick later that afternoon, on the way home, in the Norfolk Kitchens tearooms near Darren's house. One sip of tea made her feel nauseous, so she pushed her cup back across the tabletop, tried to concentrate instead on the conversation.

In less than a month, school would be over. Julian was going to do A-Levels at the Sixth Form College. Darren had been accepted for the BTEC Graphics course at Ernemouth Art College, Debbie herself for General Art and Design. Alex had got into St Martin's after all, and Corrine had her apprenticeship at the hairdressers sorted out, thanks to the new YTS scheme.

But right now, all Darren could talk about was music, the York Rock Festival at the end of the summer. They were going to save up their money from their summer jobs for it, go on their first adventure. The Bunnymen, The Sisters and Spear of Destiny were playing, all their favourite bands.

Corrine was playing a game with Julian while they talked. She had a packet of sugar in her fist that she kept emptying into Julian's cup when he wasn't looking. He meanwhile, was flicking bits of foam off the top of his coffee at the back of her head. Both pretended not to notice what the other one was doing, but this would only last so long.

Debbie's cup felt cold now and the very thought of the tea made her stomach heave. She started to get up from her seat just as Julian slammed his cup down, shouting: "Oy, you tart, what you done to my coffee?"

"Urgh!" Corrine screeched, putting her hand up to the back of her head. "What you done to my hair?" A fistful of sugar flew across the table into Julian's face.

Debbie shot out of her seat before he could retaliate and made it to the toilets just in time. It felt like a mule was kicking her in the guts. Or like she had been poisoned.

✳ ✳ ✳

Mr Pearson put his red pen down, the pile of marking finally done. He yawned as he got to his feet, stretched his arms. The clock on the wall said five-thirty and he allowed himself a smile of satisfaction as he put the books into the bottom drawer of his desk.

He walked up the corridor, thinking about the weekend. He'd pick his daughter up from the station now, go straight to his wife's restaurant on the sea front, their favourite way to spend Friday night. Frannie's commute meant she had longer hours than most schoolgirls of her age, but she seemed to be thriving at the prep school in Norwich she'd started last September. Mr Pearson was glad about that. It might make him a hypocrite, but he had not wanted his daughter to attend the school he taught at. He wouldn't have wanted her to be bullied. Wouldn't have wanted her to have to come up against a girl like . . .

He stopped in his tracks as he turned the corner past the library. Samantha Lamb was standing just a few feet away, reaching up with a black marker pen and drawing something onto the display of fifth formers' art. So involved was she in her task that she didn't even register her form teacher's presence until he was standing right behind her.

"What d'you think you're doing?" said Mr Pearson.

* * *

Corrine banged hard on Debbie's front door with the one hand that wasn't supporting her friend. "Mrs Carver!" she bellowed.

Beside her, Debbie swayed, trying to force down another wave of nausea.

"You'll be OK," Corrine tried to reassure her. "You're home now."

* * *

"I understand entirely, Mr Hill," said Amanda. "And it's me who should be sorry. I stupidly thought she might learn something of value, going to my old school."

The headmaster stood on her threshold, seeing for a second the erstwhile Amanda Hoyle with her Crystal Tips hair and platform heels, the bright smile suddenly extinguished, sometime around her fifteenth birthday.

"I wouldn't be too hard on yourself," he said. "I'm sure this is just a phase."

Amanda saw the sympathy in Mr Hill's watery grey eyes, an expression of understanding that she had never expected to find there. It was as if the old man had looked right into her soul and she had to catch hold of the doorframe to stop herself from wobbling.

"Well," she whispered, "thank you for bringing her home, at least."

Mr Hill put his hat back on. "Good evening, Amanda," he said.

Amanda closed the door, catching her breath and shutting her eyes for a second as she gathered her strength. When she opened them again, she could only see red.

"Samantha!" she screamed. She ran up the stairs to the top of the house, the music emanating from her daughter's bedroom getting louder and louder, pushed hard against the door.

Sam had obviously been expecting this, had wedged herself on the other side, as it opened an inch before slamming shut again with a violence that made the record player jump, the needle screeching across the vinyl.

Amanda banged her fist against the door. "Let me in!" she bellowed.

"No!" screamed Samantha. "I don't want to talk to you! I don't want to hear anything you've got to say!"

"I thought you said you weren't a coward, Sam," Amanda yelled back. "So what are you doing, hiding in there? Same as what you were doing at school, isn't it? Sneaking around, ruining things behind people's backs?"

Amanda felt a superhuman strength pulse through her, and this time, when she put her whole weight against the door, it flew open, catapulting Sam across the room. Amanda strode across the threshold, turned off the record player and stood above her daughter. "Now you listen to me," she said.

"Get away from me!" screamed Sam, wriggling away across the floor. "Don't touch me!"

"You spiteful little coward," Amanda's eyes glittered, her voice dropping to an icy whisper. "I don't know why I ever bothered with you."

"Nor do I," Sam spat back. "I know you never wanted

me, you made that obvious from the start. You never wanted me and you never loved me. Is that why you made a point of taking me away from everyone who ever did – first Dad, and now Nana and Granddad? Why didn't you let me stay with them, eh? Why couldn't you leave me where I was happy? Why do you want to make me suffer so much?" her voice began to crack, tears of self-pity flooding into her eyes.

"Make you suffer?" said Amanda. "You don't know the meaning of suffering, Sam, you never have. I was protecting you, more fool me."

"What?" Sam gulped indignantly. "Protecting me from the father who loved me? Protecting me from the house I grew up in and all my friends, to bring me here? To this bloody dump, to watch you and your stupid, embarrassing Wayne drooling all over each other, day in, day out? To watch that," she pointed to Amanda's stomach, hysteria crackling through her words, "that *thing* inside you that's going to take my place, grow up and be loved like I never was?"

Sam jumped to her feet, picking her schoolbag up off the floor. "If that's what you call protection, Mother, then I'd rather be out on the street. I'm going back to Dad. I don't care what you say, he loves me and you don't. He'll take care of me; *protect* me like you never will! I hate it here and I hate you!"

Amanda felt something snap inside her as she moved to block Sam's path, to dig her nails into her daughter's arm so hard she could see the pain of her rage reflected back in Sam's expanding pupils.

"If I had left you with him," she said, surprised to hear her own voice sounding so calm, "you would have ended up babysitting an alcoholic while you watched that house, that school and everything else being taken away from you, bit by bit. Malcolm's bankrupt, Sam. I wanted to protect you from that too, but there you have it, that's the truth for you. Go back there and you go back to nothing. Find out the hard way if you have to, but you'll see."

Disbelief danced in Sam's eyes. "You'll say anything, won't you, Mother?" she hissed, struggling to shake off Amanda's grip. "Absolutely anything to make yourself look good and everyone else look as if they're in the wrong."

"And what is more," Amanda went on, knowing she couldn't stop now, knowing she was headed for the crash barrier at the end of the line and even that was not going to prevent her from ploughing on, over the cliff. "I couldn't leave you with your beloved Nana and Granddad either. Not now that you've got to the age he likes. It's not safe any more. She wouldn't have done anything to protect you from him and I've seen the way he's started to look at you, it was exactly the same with me."

Sam stopped struggling. She stared at Amanda hard, her mouth dropping open. "What are you saying?" she breathed.

"All that effort I've gone to on your behalf, none of it was worth it. I thought you were an innocent baby," she shook her head. "But the apple never falls very far from the tree . . ."

"What are you saying?" Shock struck across Sam's white face. Amanda let go of her arm. The lump in her throat prevented her from speaking.

"Mother!" hysteria rose in Sam's voice. "What are you saying? Tell me!"

But Amanda could only fall back on her daughter's bed, shaking her head, tears streaming down her face.

"No," Sam croaked, looking down on Amanda who had begun to shudder violently.

"No!" she screamed, running out of the room and down the

stairs, leaving Amanda cramping up on her bed, the pain in her stomach kicking in. She heard banging and crashing below her like a dervish had been let loose, turning out draws and shattering glass, cries becoming a keening, high-pitched wail. Then, with a shocking finality, the front door slammed behind her.

* * *

Corrine watched Debbie's house from over the road, saw the doctor talking to Maureen on the doorstep. To Corrine's relief, Mrs Carver was smiling as she turned back to go into the house. It meant it couldn't have been anything really bad, or Debbie would have gone off in an ambulance. Probably just a tummy bug, Corrine thought, as she drew back the curtain and slumped down on her bed. She picked up her schoolbag and upended it, spilling the contents over the counterpane.

Frowned as her fingers raked through the books, the pencils and rubbers. Picked the bag up again, as if by some miracle, a fat, leather-bound tome could have stayed hidden inside it. Panic welling inside her, she checked the altar, under the bed, went through all her drawers until the floor was awash with clothing and underwear. Tore back through the bag again, tears of frustration pricking the back of her eyelids.

It wasn't there. She had definitely had it with her when she went to school this morning. She never left it anywhere that Gina might find it.

But it hadn't been a normal day. She hadn't been in class all afternoon; she'd been putting her display up on the wall instead, must have left her bag unattended for a while as she went back and forth to the art room.

And now, *The Goetia* was gone. Corrine fell back on the bed. A face appeared in her mind, with a mocking smile and a wonky front tooth. Sam had said goodbye to her today, the first time she had spoken to her since that day at the salon, smiling like she knew something Corrine didn't. Hitching her bag over her shoulder and winking, giving a little, mocking wave.

An ice-cold fear flooded through Corinne.

* * *

Wayne woke with a start, his mouth dry, his neck cricked from sleeping at an unaccustomed angle. It took him a moment to get his bearings, realise what the alien smell and dim lighting, the electronic beeping sounds that surrounded him meant. Then it all came back to him in a rush – finding the house in disarray, the kitchen turned over as if they'd been burgled. Amanda's cries from upstairs leading him to Samantha's bed, where she lay, sobbing her heart out, clutching her stomach, blood pooling around her, seeping into the duvet. Knowing already that it was too late even before they got to A&E. Their baby girl was gone.

Amanda was sleeping now, in the bed next to the chair that he had fallen asleep in, an expression of serene peace on her face that he'd never once seen while she was awake. She'd had to be heavily sedated.

"It's all my fault," was all she would say, over and over again.

He had been so panicked, so concerned with her health that he hadn't given a second thought to anything else. But now, in the sepulchral light of the hospital room, at the lonely hour of 4 a.m., one face came into his mind, with a jolt like an electric shock.

Samantha. Where was she?

* * *

Corrine swept the hair up off the floor like she was moving through a dream. She hadn't been able to sleep all night. She'd rung Noj, but his mum had answered, informing her flatly that John was out and she didn't know when he'd be back. So she had trailed up the seafront, spent hours circling around the lavatories opposite the pier. Knowing in her heart that she wouldn't find him. Trudged back home before she was due to start work, splashing water on her face, trying to make herself look respectable, while down below, loud music blared and male voices hollered. Her mother, entertaining again.

The night in the graveyard kept coming back to Corrine. *Never look back, don't ever look back.*

She had broken the spell. Or worse. She had made it turn back on itself. Yes, that must be it, she thought as she swept. All the signs were there. Debbie being taken suddenly ill yesterday, that was the start of it. Then the book vanishing . . . Or being stolen . . . Taken from her bag . . .

Corrine lifted the dustpan and her eyes along with it. Nearly dropped the thing back on the floor as she looked through the window.

Sam was standing outside. She didn't look her normal neatly ordered self – quite the opposite, in fact. Her face was smeared with dirt, her hair a tangled mess and there was a big graze across one of her knees, like she'd taken some kind of tumble. But the worst thing, the most shocking thing that Corrine couldn't pull her eyes away from, was the smile of demented triumph on Sam's face as she held up a big black book.

35

What Difference Does It Make?

March 2003

From where she sat on the sofa in her lounge, Sandra Gray saw the light finally go off in her husband's shed at the bottom of the garden. All afternoon he had been in there, the place where he kept all his old police things, saying that he needed to dig something out for the private detective before he could tell her anything more.

Sandra had tried her best to distract herself with the TV, with preparing the meal that was now in the oven, with pretending that everything was as normal. But she hadn't seen her husband in this way for nigh-on twenty years. Paul had fallen apart once before, because of this case. She didn't know what she would do if he got that way again.

The porch light blinked on, illuminating his passage back up the garden path. Paul's face looked stern and resolute. He was carrying a book in his hands.

* * *

"The Leisure Beach?" said Francesca.

"That's right," said Rivett. "Pull in just here, the guard'll wave you through."

A frown crossed her face and she glanced down at the dash-board clock as she slowed the car down to make the turn. It was coming up to ten past seven. The panic that had gripped her earlier began to subside as her mind began to focus.

Those documents Ross was sending her must have come through the fax. Dad would probably have them in his hands right now, be speaking to Sean, telling him about the business links between Rivett and Smollet she'd asked her ex-husband to look into. Did they have something to do with the old fun-fair? What other possible reason could Rivett have for bring-ing her here?

There was a security booth by the entrance and sure enough, when the shaven-headed young man inside caught sight of Rivett, he smiled and pressed the switch that brought the bar-rier up, waving them through into the car park.

"Seem a bit strange to you, do it?" said Rivett. "Coming here?"

Francesca turned off the engine, keeping her expression deadpan while her mind shifted gears. Maybe the former DCI did not know quite so much about her as she assumed.

"Are you making fun of me, Mr Rivett?" she said, fixing him with a stern gaze. "If DCI Smollet really didn't want to do an interview, he only had to say. There's no need to go to this much effort to try and put me off."

Rivett chuckled softly, shook his head. "No, girl, you got me all wrong," he said. "That might not look that way to you now, but this place is a vital part of his history. You could say that this is where it all began."

He undid his seatbelt, opened the car door and hefted him-self out. Vicious pains jabbed at his kneecaps as he rose to his feet and for a second he had to steady himself on the side of the car so as not to let his discomfort show. *Bastard old body*, Rivett cursed inwardly. *Don't you let me down now*.

Francesca stepped out of the car, looking back towards the security guard, who had settled down into his chair and the sports pages of a tabloid. She locked the car, put the keys in her jacket pocket, where she could get to them quickly.

"This way," said Rivett, putting his hand on her elbow and steering her towards the turnstiles. Francesca did her best not to wince at his touch, kept her fingers curled around the keys. Beyond the one spotlight that illuminated the car park, rose the skeletal outline of the log flume, the curves and dips of the old wooden rollercoaster and the silent spheres of the stilled big wheel and the rock-a-plane. It suddenly made perfect sense to Francesca that these two men could be joined by this place of smoke and mirrors, this land of delusion and deception, lying silent and sinister without the coins of the tourists to work its fancy lights and cheap thrills.

At the door of the turnstile, Rivett rapidly keyed numbers into a pad and turned the handle. Stopped on the threshold and said: "I hear you done a pretty good job keeping the old *Mercury* afloat."

"Did you?" Pat's face flashed through Francesca's mind. "From who?"

Rivett ignored the question. "I used to know Sid Hayles, way back when. He were a good friend of mine, as it goes. There were none of these, what d'you call them, *profiles*, all this social concern in his day. Now I know, times do change, as you already pointed out. But I reckon what your paper needs is a little sense of historical perspective." He pushed the door open, made a sweeping gesture with his arm. "After you," he said.

* * *

Sean put his arm around Noj's shoulder, propelled her away from the steps of the Lodge, where he could see the man behind the desk reaching for the phone.

"Where do you think they're going?" he asked, heading the pair of them back to his car.

Noj hurried round to the passenger side. "To DCI Smollet's house, " she said, yanking the door open, sliding in and slamming it shut. "We should hurry."

Sean put his key back in the ignition, then paused. "You seem very sure of yourself," he said. "Why do you think they're going there?"

Noj stared at him with incredulous eyes. But it seemed she was lost for an answer. Her mouth opened and closed as she bounced up and down on the seat, but no noise came out.

"Go on," said Sean.

* * *

Gray sat down on the sofa, next to his wife.

"My old log book," he said, "from 1984. You in't supposed to keep them. But this is the only insurance I've got for you if something now happen to me."

Sandra felt a rush of panic, scanned her husband's face for traces of impending breakdown. But his eyes were sharp and focused.

He put his hand down over hers. "Sandra," he said, "what you got to understand about Len Rivett is that he's got this way about him, like he already knows what's in your mind and you're just doing yourself a favour unburdening yourself to him." He shook his head, smiling ironically. "He's almost like a priest."

"What is it, love, what did you tell him?" Sandra's hand balled into a fist.

Gray looked her straight in the eye. "The summer of 1973," he said, "you might remember. There was this new bloke taking football with the cubs. Ron next door asked me about him. Bloke said he was a qualified PE teacher but Ron had a funny feeling about him, wanted to know if I could do any kind of check. So I done a bit of digging and sure enough, the bloke had been a teacher – until he got the sack and done five years for child molesting, somewhere over Coventry way."

Sandra closed her eyes. Gray squeezed her hand tighter.

"Now, what I should have done," he said, "was just told the scout leader and had him removed. But that didn't sit right with me. He'd still be lurking about, wouldn't he, and until I had proof he were up to his old tricks again, there weren't much more I could do about it. Meanwhile, children were in danger. So I decided to take matters into my own hands. I nearly bloody killed him, love."

Sandra's eyes opened, glittering with tears.

"Len covered it all up for me," said Gray. "After I told him why I done it, of course."

Sandra saw her husband's knuckles whiten around the book he was clutching.

"Got the whole lot out of me," Gray went on. "About the home, my foster father and all. I mean, it weren't something I'd ever admitted to anyone before, except you." He paused. "He never mentioned it again, or even alluded to it. Until Corrine Woodrow."

"And then last night," Sandra deduced.

Gray nodded. "But this," he slapped the cover of his log

book, "has got a few facts about my side of the investigation he won't want coming to light."

"But I thought you weren't in on the official investigation?" she said.

"I weren't," nodded Gray. "This is what I found out for myself."

* * *

"This place," said Rivett, opening his arms as the door to the inner sanctum shut behind them, "used to belong to a man called Eric Hoyle. A great man."

"Another good friend of yours?" said Francesca, trying to place where she had heard the name before. An image of her parents flashed into her mind. Huddled over the kitchen table together, talking in whispers.

"That's right," said Rivett, catching hold of her elbow again and steering her towards a row of sideshows, all locked and boarded up now, but their garish hoardings still in place. "And this one," he pointed towards the letters that proclaimed *Magic Darts*, "was where it all began for the young Dale Smollet. His Uncle Ted run the concession, still do, in fact, despite the fact he's pushing seventy. They do say the carnival get in your blood, you never want to leave it, no matter how old you get. Retirement in't an option. Don't suppose men like Ted can afford it to be."

Francesca eyed the plastic depiction of a dartboard and arrows, surrounded by stars, her mind conjuring back the photograph she had shown to Sean in the newsroom, those old men with all their secrets.

"Men like you, too, Mr Rivett," she said. "I don't get the feeling you ever really retired."

"I can see why you became a journalist," said Rivett. "What I don't understand, though, is why you come here in the first place. You had a good job in London, I hear, on one of them daily papers. What would a bright, and if you don't mind me saying, attractive woman like you want to jack that in for, come and work in a sleepy old town like this?"

"I like a challenge," said Francesca, smiling. "Like yourself, I should imagine. Was Dale Smollet your challenge, Mr Rivett? Did you help him on his way from the funfair to detective chief inspector?"

Rivett shifted back and forth between his toes and his heels, hoping that this would keep the circulation flowing, the pain at bay.

"I see the potential in everyone, Miss Ryman," he said. "That's why I make such a good detective. In many ways, our jobs are similar, in't they? We gather up all the knowledge of how everything work round here and then, that's up to us to project an orderly, respectable image of the town. If we don't, that's bad for business. And we can't have that, can we?"

The smile faded from Francesca's lips.

* * *

"Smollet," Noj eventually spluttered, "and Rivett are in this together. They always have been."

"In what together?" said Sean. Earlier events replayed themselves in his mind. The phone call Smollet had taken in his office, his rapid, flustered exit – it did fit into the time-frame of Francesca's supposed interview. And if Rivett had been there to intercept her, it was perfectly possible they were rendezvousing now.

"Setting up Corrine!" Noj wailed. "She was the scapegoat!

And if you don't get after them now, not only is your friend going to be the next one, but the person you're really after is going to get away."

"The person I'm really after?" Sean looked at the strange creature beside him, whom he had known for mere hours. Thought about the matching DNA, sure in his bones that it wouldn't belong to this biker, that Rivett was pulling some other sleight of hand with him. Making another scapegoat. But to believe that was to trust that Noj wasn't just some vindictive fantasist looking to settle a twenty-year-old grudge, that she really could lead him to the culprit's door. However unlikely it seemed.

"OK," he reached into his jacket pocket for the other clean swab kit, "just to prove we're on the level, I want you to do one thing for me. It will take one second, then we can go."

*   *   *

"That's getting a bit chilly out here, in't it?" said Rivett. "Let's go and wait for him in the office. He said he'd call us there when he's on his way."

He stopped by the door to the tower, keyed in some more numbers and opened it up. Striplights illuminated a red-carpeted lobby, a metallic wall with a lift set into it.

"To the penthouse suite," said Rivett, " . . . where all the secrets are kept."

36

The Sky's Gone Out

June 1984

"Corrine? Is anything the matter?"

Lizzy's voice filtered through Corrine's synapses some moments after the head stylist had spoken. She turned around slowly, not wanting the book to slip out of her sight.

"Is it all right to go outside a minute?" she said, putting her hand up over her brow. "I just come over a bit funny, like I'm gonna faint or something."

Lizzy frowned, following Corrine's gaze to the figure standing outside. Samantha shifted, turned away, as if she knew she was being observed, but not before Lizzy recognised her as the girl who she had styled to look like Corrine earlier in the spring. Something strange had been going on between those two then – and if she wasn't mistaken, still was.

Lizzy was very fond of Corrine, but she didn't like being lied to. "Two minutes," she said. "And make sure your friend is gone by then."

Corrine went bright red, almost falling over her broom to get out of the room fast enough. Outside, on the other side of the road, Samantha started to walk away.

"Sam, stop!" Corrine yelled, loud enough for everyone in

the salon to hear her, launching herself across the road.

Samantha wheeled round, her eyes dancing with malice as she held out the book.

"Give that back, Sam," said Corrine, tears of frustration welling up in her eyes. "You in't got no right to it, that in't even mine."

Samantha ducked away from her, turning in a circle around her. "Why?" she said. "What's so special about it?"

"It's rare, that's why," Corrine made an unsuccessful lunge. "There's only a few of them in the whole world."

Samantha skipped out of Corrine's reach. "It doesn't look much to me," she said. "Bet you can't even understand it."

"I do all right," Corrine balled her hands up into fists. "That belong to a master magician and if he find out you've got it, that'll be the worse for you."

"A master magician?" Samantha burst out laughing. "That's a good one, Corrine."

Corrine's punch fell through thin air. "Give it back, I said!" she wailed.

"I might do," said Samantha. "But only if you help me first." She looked over Corrine's shoulder to where Lizzy was coming through the salon door.

"Corrine!" the head stylist yelled. "That's enough. Get back in here now!"

"Just a minute," Corrine yelled back. She didn't take her eyes off Sam. "What d'you mean, help you?" she said.

"I said now!" Lizzy started walking across the road towards them.

"That old pillbox where you had the party," said Sam. "The one that the police found out about. Yes, I saw you, Corrine," she smiled at the gobsmacked expression this revelation provoked. "I don't need a crystal ball to keep my eye on you, *sister*. Meet me there when you've finished here tonight. Then I might give it back to you."

Lizzy's hand came down on Corrine's shoulder, but she was looking at Samantha. The girl looked shocking, like she'd been sleeping rough.

"Get out of here," Lizzy snapped, "and stop bothering my staff."

"But Lizzy, she . . ."

"And you," she propelled Corrine back towards the salon. "Get back to work right now and keep your mouth shut for the rest of the day. Otherwise we might have to rethink your employment here."

The words stung Corrine harder than a slap around the face.

✳ ✳ ✳

At six-thirty, after Corrine had swept up the last tendril of hair and cleaned the last coffee cup in complete silence, Lizzy's head came around the kitchen door.

"Corrine," she said, in gentler tones than she'd used earlier, "what was all that about?"

Corrine gave her a hard stare. Up until today, she had idolised Lizzy. But the way she had spoken to her, in front of Sam of all people, had made her wonder if the stylist just wasn't like all the rest of the adults that had let her down over the years.

Lizzy, in her turn, was shocked by the hostility of Corrine's glare. "Corrine," she tried again. "Don't you understand that I can't have you fighting right outside the salon window?"

"Samantha Lamb nicked that book out of my bag yesterday," she said. "I was tryin' to get it back off her. An' you stopped me."

"Well, if you had told me that—" Lizzy began.

"You wouldn't have cared," Corrine cut her off abruptly. "Like everyone else. You're only nice to me when you want something." She pulled her overall over her head and hung it up on a peg, picking up her bag and slinging it over her shoulder.

"Corrine," Lizzy tried again, feeling like she was floundering in deep water.

"Can I go now?" the girl's dark eyes bored into her mentor.

Lizzy took a step backwards. "Can't I try and help you?" she offered.

"Don't bother," said Corrine. "I'll sort it out myself, like always." With that she pushed past her boss and left the salon for the last time.

✶ ✶ ✶

"How many times do I have to tell you," Noj's mother's voice crackled in Corrine's ear, "he in't here and I don't know where he is. Or when he'll be back."

Corrine heard a man's voice in the background. *Noj's dad,* she thought, *back off the rigs. No wonder he in't around.* Mr Kenyon took the receiver from his wife.

"If you see the little poof, you can keep him," he said and put the phone down.

Corrine stepped out of the callbox. Without Noj, she simply didn't know what to do.

She looked up at the clock at the top of the market square. Quarter to seven, it said. Hunger pains stabbed at her stomach, and she found herself walking in the direction of the fish and chips stall. She didn't have a clue what she was going to say or do when she saw Sam. But, she told herself, she didn't have to do any of it on an empty stomach.

She was just pouring vinegar into her cone, when she heard a voice beside her. "All right, Corrine?"

"Darren!" she spun round, a spark of hope igniting at the sound of his voice.

"Just finished work?" he asked, taking a cone of chips for himself.

"Yeah," said Corrine. "What you now up to?"

"Not a lot," he said, taking the vinegar from her. "Debbie's still in bed."

"Debbie!" Corrine's mouth fell open. She had all but forgotten her friend's plight.

"Don't worry," said Darren, "she's all right. Just in't really in any state to come out at the moment. I now brought her the music papers, to cheer her up."

"Oh," said Corrine, passing him the salt. "That's all right then. So," she said, popping the first chip into her mouth, "you in't meeting up with Jules then?"

"Nah," said Darren. "He's gone up Norwich with Alex." He raised his eyebrows, put the salt back down on the counter. "Early night for me, I reckon."

"Darren, d'you reckon you could help me out?" Though chewing with her mouth open, Corrine's expression was solemn. "Fuckin' Sam Lamb's dropped me right in the shit again."

✳ ✳ ✳

As they headed towards the seafront, Corrine did her best to explain. "I reckon she's lost me my job," she concluded.

"Nah." Darren shook his head. "She like you, don't she, your boss? She wouldn't let you go over one mistake like that."

"She really shouted at me," Corrine protested. "In front of everyone."

"Well, that most probably din't look all that good from her point of view, did it?" said Darren. "Not if all her customers could see you having a barney. She din't know what was really going on, did she?"

A sudden stroke of guilt clawed at Corrine as she recalled her last exchange with Lizzy. "No," she said, "'S'pose not. Shit, Darren, I really lost my temper. I shouldn't have done it, should I?"

"Don't worry about it," said Darren. "That'll all look different in the morning. You say sorry and I bet she will too."

"Fuckin' Sammy Lamb," Corrine crumpled her empty chip cone, wishing it was Samantha's neck instead. "Why can't she just leave me alone?"

Darren shrugged. "I wish I knew what her problem is," he said. "But look, Reenie, you don't have to say nothing to her. You just wait outside and let me get the book back for you. She won't be expecting that, will she?"

"Oh, thanks, Darren," Corrine put her arm through his as they came out onto Marine Parade and turned left towards the North Denes. "I'll make it up to you."

"You don't have to," said Darren. He smiled, nodding to himself. "That'll be good to get one back on the silly cow, all the hassle she put Debs through."

* * *

The tourists had come up off the beach now for their teas, the few remaining stragglers taking down their windbreaks and packing up their picnic things. A mother and two toddlers still paddled on the shoreline in the distance, the sea glimmering like diamonds.

"That look beautiful tonight, don't it?" said Darren.

"Yeah," said Corrine, looking at the two little children and feeling a pang, knowing that she had never paddled in the sea with her mum, wondering if she would ever have a daughter of her own to share this novel experience with.

"Are you going to have kids?" she heard herself asking. "You and Debbie, I mean?"

Darren hadn't really considered this possibility. "I s'pose so," he said. "One day."

"D'you think you'll move away, like what Alex is?" The possibility dawned on Corrine for the first time, and with it a new sense of fear, of everything she had known slipping away, everybody moving away, leaving her here on her own.

"Well," Darren seemed to sense what was going on in her head, "I'd like to go to art college in London if I could. But that's years away."

"I s'pose," said Corrine doubtfully.

"Well, you don't have to stay here, do you?" he said. "Not if you don't want to. Think about it. You qualify as a hairdresser and you could go anywhere too."

It was another idea that hadn't occurred to her. A smile replaced her frown. "Yeah," she said. "You're right. I could, couldn't I? God, Darren, I am going to say sorry to Lizzy first thing tomorrow. I'm really glad I bumped into you. You're a lifesaver."

They were drawing level with Sam's nan's house now. Corrine shuddered, remembering the night of the little dog, feeling the windows of the villa like glassy eyes upon her.

"Let's walk across the dunes," she suggested, jumping down off the sea wall, out of sight.

"Hold up!" Darren levered himself down more carefully, not wanting to get sand all over himself. They were very nearly at the pillbox now. "Here, Corrine," he said, catching up with her. A mischievous smile played over his lips. "Something I meant to ask you."

"Oh yeah?" Corrine turned her head to look at him. "What?"

Darren laughed, a blush coming into his cheeks. "Debs'll kill me," he said.

"What?" said Corrine, not knowing whether to smile back or not, wondering if he was going to start taking the piss now.

"Well," he said, "if you don't mind me asking – what were you doing up a tree in the graveyard that night?"

Corrine stopped still in her tracks, on top of the dune in front of the pillbox. Remembered the voice coming out of the window across the road from the graveyard, just at the moment Noj had begun to cast the spell. Saw in her head Debbie pulling him away, pushing the window down. The hairs stood up on the back of her neck.

"No," she said, her pupils widening.

"Sorry," said Darren, "I knew I shouldn't have asked." He patted her on the shoulder, clearly embarrassed. "Look," he said. "Forget I asked. Now you stay here and I'll go get the book back for you. Now I've got something to make up to you."

"No," Corrine repeated, the vision she had had in the pillbox coming back to her – *red, black, white. Blood, hair, skin. The flash of a blade, slicing through flesh ... Like the blade of grass Sam had used on her, the black magic she had summoned to blend their blood together, calling her sister, entwining their destinies forever ...* In a sudden flash of premonition, Corrine realised what everything meant. The spell *had* rebounded on her, she and the person who had broken the silence around the incantation. She knew what was going to happen if Darren went inside the pillbox . . .

She tried to move to stop him, but it was like her limbs had frozen as the appalling destiny was revealed to her.

"Don't go in there," she croaked. "It's all right, really, Darren. I'll get it back another way. Let's just go."

"Don't be daft," said Darren. "That's no bother. She can't hurt me, can she?"

She put her hand out, grabbed his sleeve. "Please, Darren. Don't go!"

But Darren just laughed, shook her fingers away. "It's all right Corrine, honest."

"But . . ."

Corrine stood there powerless, caught in the rays of the evening sun, as Darren walked on, down the side of the dune, spraying up sand as his momentum increased by the steepness of the slope. Watching him go . . .

✳ ✳ ✳

"*Aieeeeeeeeeeee!*" the piercing scream brought her back to her senses.

Corrine ran down the dune, fear powering her footsteps, ran down the dune and into the dim shade of the pillbox, where her legs moved faster than her eyes and she found she couldn't stop, found herself tripping over his legs and falling with a tremendous thud over the top of Darren.

"Oh my God!" she screamed, heels of her hands skidding over concrete and sand, fear abnegating pain. Darren didn't move as she landed across him. Trying to right herself, she found her right hand had come into contact with something hot, wet and sticky. Something coming out of the back of Darren's head.

"Oh my God!" she started to lash out with her legs, desperate to untangle herself.

"*Aieeeeeeeeeeee!*" the scream came from behind her now. The sound of it was terrifying enough to propel Corrine up and away, send her scuttling into a corner.

Silhouetted against the sunlight streaming through the entrance to the pillbox, Samantha stood, her legs apart, her arms swaying slightly from the huge chunk of concrete she was holding above her head. Her eyes flashed as she took in the scenario unfolding in front of her.

"Sam!" Corrine's voice came out like a strangled wail. "Sam, you've fuckin' killed him!"

"Him?" Samantha looked down at Darren and then back at Corrine, her face twitching madly. She dropped the concrete.

"Corrine? What ... ?" She stood over the splayed body, regarding the contours of arms and legs with a quizzical expression. "Darren?" she said, kneeling down beside him.

She touched the back of his head and brought her fingers up to her lips.

"Darren," she repeated, looking back up at Corrine with a smile of such radiance it seemed to Corrine that she was glowing, a perverse angel of death. "But that's perfect, Corrine. That'll hurt her even more than if it had been you."

"H-hurt h-h-her?" Corrine stammered.

"Your precious Debbie, of course. She ruined everything for me – and now I've ruined everything for her!" Samantha shrieked with laughter and reached forward, rolled Darren over onto his back with such ease he might have been a rag doll.

Corrine could see his face now, the expression of shock caught in his wide blue eyes. His arms flopped sideways helplessly, so pale and skinny and unyielding. She crawled further towards the wall, screaming inside but unable to make any sound come out of her.

Sam knelt beside him, cocking her head at different angles. She started to rummage in her pocket, drawing out a packet of John Player Specials and a lighter she had stolen from home. She took out a cigarette, lit up and inhaled deeply. Her hands didn't shake, Corrine realised, as she began to shudder uncontrollably herself.

Sam lifted one of Darren's arms, took the cigarette from her mouth and touched his skin with it.

"Don't!" Corrine croaked. She tried to shut her eyes but they wouldn't obey her. Tried to put her hands over her eyes instead, but they slid back down her face, leaving smears of his blood in their wake.

Sam tried again, putting the end of the cigarette a little further up his arm. She frowned, took another puff and repeated the gesture. Kept repeating it, over and over, until she broke the cigarette in half.

"For fuck's sake," she said. Corrine saw a string of saliva drool out of Sam's mouth. "I'll start again," she said, in a tone half-pitched between boredom and rage.

This time, she put the end of the cigarette down on Darren's forehead.

Corrine opened her mouth again, but it was useless. She could say nothing, hear nothing but her own blood pounding through her veins. But she could still smell all right, and the stench of scorched flesh that entered her nostrils sent another shaking fit coursing through her body.

Sam dotted the cigarette all over Darren's face. "Not so pretty now, are you?" she said, throwing the butt down. "Not that you ever were all that much." She looked over at Corrine. "But still, I can do better than that."

Corrine must have shut her eyes for a second without realising it. For the next thing she realised there was something silvery in Sam's hands. A kitchen knife. She raised it up and plunged it down into the centre of Darren's stomach. There was a sickening crunch as the blade went in, an even worse sound as she drew it out. "Oh yes," Sam said, looking up at Corrine with a hideous smile of desire. "That's better. This is for Debbie!" She raised the blade again.

Corrine stopped shaking as rapidly as she had begun. She felt the familiar sensation of numbness overtaking her, as Sam lifted the blade.

"Debbie Carver," Sam said, her voice getting lower, more guttural. "Debbie Carver, Carver, Carver, carve her up!" She thrust the blade up and down, up and down, the tearing and sucking sounds of rendered flesh filling the old pillbox with a nightmare cacophony. Again and again and again she stabbed, rocking and gulping, her own body twitching now, her thighs bucking up and down. She didn't stop until she was hoarse and breathless, foam flecking the sides of her mouth.

Then she lifted her hands one by one, clenching and unclenching her fingers, moving the knife from one hand to another, staring transfixed at the patterns of blood. Finally, she looked up.

Corrine, pushed up against the wall, stared back at her, mouth open and eyes wide, blood smeared all over her face. Staring between Samantha's thighs, to where Darren now resembled the contents of a butcher's board, although the expression on his face remained curiously unchanged.

Samantha stood up, weaving unsteadily from side to side.

She looked at the knife in her hand, frowned, and threw it over at Corrine. It hit the wall and clattered down beside her. Then Samantha took the cigarettes and the lighter back out of her pocket and dropped them where she stood. She walked backwards, stumbling as she went, until she was at the entrance of the pillbox.

Outside, she blinked in the sunlight, looked down at herself, at her hands, at her legs.

Then she began to run.

* * *

Edna was in her kitchen, working dough in a Pyrex bowl. She needed to have something to do with her hands, some familiar ritual to comfort and divert her from the terrible thoughts that were circling through her mind.

From the phone call from Wayne that had come early this morning, telling her of the granddaughter that she would now never get to see, never get to hold in her arms. Of the other that was roaming somewhere out in the streets, somewhere where even Eric's best police contacts had not been able to find her. From the atonement with Amanda that she would now never get the chance to make. To all the pain and suffering her weakness, her stubborn refusal to see what was right in front of her, had caused her daughter, her granddaughters and herself.

And the empty dog basket in the corner of the room.

A middle-aged woman forcing herself to stand upright in her kitchen, the highlights in her rigidly styled hair catching the golden light of the slowly setting sun, her hands kneading and kneading away at the dough, worries working through her fingers, her fingers that already ached to the point where she wanted to scream.

The banging on the back door almost made her jump out of her skin.

Sammy's face pressed against the glass, filthy with dirt and something else, something of a darker hue. Her eyes two enormous saucers filled with an absolute void of expression. For a second, Edna thought she was seeing a creature from a nightmare – a troll, a boggit or a witch, with a raggedy mane of upstanding hair. For a second, something deep within her told her not to let the thing over her threshold, to pick up a crucifix and send it far away. Then a more powerful emotion took hold of her, an emotion stronger than fear and stronger than reason. A grandmother's love.

Edna ran towards Sammy, turned the key in the lock and pushed down on the handle, stepping backwards as the door opened and her granddaughter fell into her arms, sobbing and saying over and over: "*Nana, Nana, Nana.*"

* * *

Edna got Sammy bathed and into bed before she rang Eric. She sponged and scrubbed her granddaughter clean as new, washing away all the dirt and everything else down the plughole, wrapping her in her biggest, fluffiest pink towel, and singing to her the songs of her childhood as she dried her hair at her dressing table.

Sammy was meek and compliant, slipping into one of Edna's nighties and snuggling down in her bed, in the room that Edna had kept in pristine order for her. Almost as soon as her head hit the pillow, Sammy's eyelids drooped and her breathing slowed into a slumber.

Edna crept back down to the kitchen with Sammy's clothes over her arm, loaded up the washing machine and set it to boil wash. Stared through the glass for some time at the cycle spinning around.

When she eventually picked up the phone to call Eric, she found that she didn't know quite what to say. "Sammy's here," she started with, "she's safely asleep upstairs."

"Thank God," said Eric, drawing out a long breath. "Do you know where she's been? What she's been up to?"

"No," said Edna. "But I think she's had some kind of a shock. She's acting very strangely."

"Do she know," said Eric, "about Mandy?"

"I don't think so," Edna's fingers worried up and down the telephone cord. "I didn't like to say, she seemed so . . ." But she couldn't find the right word to express what she was thinking.

"No, you're probably right," Eric spared her the anguish of articulation. "Best to let her sleep. I'll tell Len to call off the dogs. Maybe we can get it out of her in the morning."

"Are you coming home?" Edna's voice wobbled as she said it.

On the other end of the line, Eric put down the glass of Scotch that was halfway to his lips. On the other side of the windows, the tourists whirled and flew through the neon-lit wonderland, whooping with fear and delight as they traversed the wooden hills and the painted jets, the spinning, glittering wheels. On the desk in front of him, Amanda held the infant Samantha, a radiant smile on her face.

"I'll see you in ten minutes," he said.

37

The Price

March 2003

Standing by the front doors of Ernemouth nick, Jason Blackburn watched the squad car come to a halt in front of the steps. His mouth was completely dry. Since Smollet had left him to deal with all this alone, he had tried calling Rivett several times. But the old sweat had left his mobile switched to voicemail and, without his guidance, Blackburn felt as if he had entered a parallel universe. A world where everything he was used to just got turned upside down and none of the usual rules applied.

Blackburn had experienced much in the way of strangeness during his long career in the force. But nothing to top the sight that met his eyes now. Arthur Bowles, the Deputy Chief Constable of Norwich Police, escorting his old comrade, DS Andrew Kidd up the steps towards him. Bowles looked straight ahead, his face a stern mask. Kidd, dressed entirely in black with a woolly hat pulled down over his eyes like some kind of terrorist, looked down at the ground, his wrists handcuffed in front of him, blood congealing around deep scratch marks on his cheeks.

* * *

Francesca felt a flicker of fear return as the lift doors closed behind them. There was barely room for the pair of them in there, and it was difficult to hide her discomfort. She tried to disguise it with humour. "He liked to live like a king did he, your mate Eric?" she said. "A red carpet, a private lift to his office?" The image of her parents flashed back to the forefront of her mind.

"As befitted his status," said Rivett.

"And what were you to him?" she asked. "Some kind of courtier?"

The door opened on a circular room, windows all around it. Rivett stepped out first, turned on the lights.

"Every king need 'em," he said. "You need brains to maintain power. The one thing that money can't buy."

As she followed Rivett into the room, it came back to Francesca what she had overheard her Dad saying about Eric Hoyle. *"With that for a grandfather,"* he had said, *"I s'pose it's no wonder there's something wrong with the girl."* It was one of his pupils he was telling her mother about. But he had stopped when he realised she was standing by the door, listening to what he was saying.

"Take a seat, Miss Ryman," said Rivett.

There was a big film producer's desk in the middle of the room, with a leather chair behind it, facing in the direction of the sea. Another similar but smaller one opposite. As she trod across the white, shagpile carpet towards it, Francesca noted that the desk was bare of any ornament, save a big, round, smoked-glass ashtray, a matching table lighter and an old-fashioned black telephone with a ring-shaped dial. Rivett plonked himself down in the larger of the chairs, reached in his pocket for his cigars.

"They've kept it the way it was, then," said Francesca, watching him light up. "Whoever owns it now."

Rivett exhaled smoke. "That's right," he said. "They have. Not much longer to wait now," he consulted his gold wristwatch. "I reckon he'll call any minute. Sure I can't get you a drink? They keep a well-stocked bar up here, so I'm told."

"Whose courtier are you now, Mr Rivett?" asked Francesca.

Rivett looked down at the phone and back across at her. "The new boss," he said, "has got a lot in common with the old boss. As you can see, appearances mattered to Eric. Mattered too much, in the end."

Rivett put his cigar down in the ashtray, tendrils of smoke curling up Francesca's nose as he took a small key from his trouser pocket and unlocked the drawer in front of him. Took from it a thick A4 envelope and dropped it down on the desk between them.

"I got to hand it to you, you are good, Miss Ryman. You in't got none of the usual little twitches that give the weaker minded away." He raised his eyebrows suggestively as he pushed the envelope towards her. "That's what you're after, in't it?"

* * *

No sooner had he opened the back door to let the dogs out than Mr Pearson's phone began to ring again. He turned on his heel, rushed back to the hallway to answer it, the dogs brushing past his legs as they ran in the other direction, out into the night.

"Frannie?" he said, lifting the receiver.

"Philip?" came a voice with a Midlands ring, familiar from somewhere in his past.

"Philip, it's Sheila Alcott, are you all right, dear?"

"Sheila?" Mr Pearson put his hand up to his temples, closing his eyes. In a beat, a picture formed in his mind and he realised who he was talking to. "Oh, Sheila, I got you. Sorry about that, I must be having what they now call a senior moment."

"Well, I did wonder," said Sheila. "After what's just happened to me, I thought I'd better check to see if you were OK."

"Why?" Mr Pearson felt his knees weaken again. "What's going on?"

* * *

"Where is DCI Smollet?" demanded the DCC. "I gave specific orders I would speak to him and no one else."

Blackburn dragged his gaze away from Kidd, who was still staring at the floor.

"He got called away, sir," Blackburn said. "Urgent business. Told me I had to hold the fort. Said he would be out of contact for the rest of the night. That's all I know, sir."

Bowles pushed Kidd forwards.

"Put this man in the cells," he said. "He's already under caution. No one is to speak to him until I return. And by no one," the DCC's flint-sharp eyes bored into Blackburn, "I most specifically mean you."

* * *

"I caught a man trying to break into my property," said Sheila. "But it's all right, I was prepared for him, ever since your daughter came to see me yesterday and then that detective from London turned up, I thought something like this would happen."

"My daughter?" Mr Pearson's voice sounded faint, even to himself. "A detective? Sean Ward, d'you mean?"

"Yes, that's right, dear, nice young man, I thought. Not like our local force at all. And that's who it was, trying to come after me," she said, her voice hardening. "One of them. The very same one that turned up on my doorstep all those years ago to tell me I wasn't needed in court, would you believe? Did he get a shock when he found himself staring down the barrel of my son's shotgun. And I'm afraid Minnie went for him too. I wasn't able to stop her, not when I was holding a loaded weapon . . ."

From outside the back door, a ferocious cacophony of barking erupted.

"Oh my God, the dogs!" said Mr Pearson. "I'm sorry, Sheila, I'm going to have to call you back."

* * *

Francesca stared at Rivett's grinning visage.

"Go on," he said. "Take a look."

Her fingers felt too big and too clumsy as she slid them underneath the flap of the envelope and pulled out a sheaf of documents. The one on top had the name of a firm of Ernemouth solicitors on the letterhead. Her eyes ran down the typewritten page.

THE LAST WILL AND TESTAMENT OF ERIC
ARTHUR HOYLE

I, ERIC ARTHUR HOYLE being of sound mind
and memory do undertake on this day
29.3.1989 to make the following

instruction. Upon my death, the business premises and trading interests of ERNEMOUTH LEISURE INDUSTRIES INC should be split equally between LEONARD HORATIO RIVETT and DALE ARMSTRONG SMOLLET, with the provision that neither party attempt to wind down, sell off or in any way discontinue the trading of the business.

"Save you a bit of bother, don't it?" said Rivett. "The old boss," he put a fat finger down on Eric's name, "and the new boss," he moved it over to Smollet's. "I in't finished telling you about Dale, but there's only really one thing left to say. I can only do business with someone after I've found their Achilles' heel. I knew what Eric's was, I know what his is, and," he smiled his most carnivorous smile, "I know what yours is and all."

Rivett leaned back in his chair. "Your dad's Philip Pearson, in't he? Good old Phil, who gave this town the worst name that's ever had. I see where you get them instincts of yours from."

Horror seeped through Francesca's bones as she stared at him, trying to work out how he could possibly have known.

"Pat," was the best she could do.

Rivett shook his head. "Nope. That was actually Paul Bowman who helped me out with that little detail. The other person you inherited from Sid that had a cast-iron contract you couldn't get rid of. And there you was, thinking he was just the clapped-out, Viagra-popping old pisshead he appear to be."

Francesca's throat tightened. Rivett was right. Her aging Lothario of an ad manager was the last person she would ever have suspected of having such guile. Rivett's smile deepened. "Yes, Miss Ryman, Bowman done a bit of digging for me this afternoon and you'd be surprised what he's capable of. When you worked for that paper up in London, you were married to the business editor – Ross, in't it? But they say you left the job for family reasons. Well, what family could that be, then? That lanky frame of yours, that streak of Bubble you've got running through you ..." Rivett nodded. "Philp Pearson's wife died not six months after you got here. The second Greek tragedy of his life."

"Bastard!" Rage enlarged Francesca's pupils.

Rivett tapped his finger back down on Eric's will.

"That's your motive," he said calmly. "Eric's too. Family is at the heart of all this tragedy, Miss Ryman. You've come this far. Don't you want to know how it finally all connects?"

* * *

Outside in the night, Mr Pearson heard a car reverse on the gravel of his drive and then career away at high speed. By the time he had run round to the front of the house, he could only make out the taillights disappearing in the direction of Brydon Bridge. The dogs' feet skittered on the loose stones as they ran back towards him, tails thrashing. Digby had something in his mouth that he pushed into his master's hand.

"What's this, boy?" Mr Pearson felt something limp and soggy. "My godfathers," he said.

* * *

"That's very commendable research," Francesca said, summoning from deep within what her mother used to call her Gorgon stare. "But aren't you forgetting one thing? Sean

Ward. He knows all about this too."

"Oh yeah. He's a good boy, that Ward," said Rivett, his expression softening. "I could have made use of a brave soldier like him, if we'd met in another time." He shook his head regretfully. "But that in't his town, is it, and anyway, I should think he'll be off by now. He's got what he come here for."

Francesca did a double take. "What are you talking about?" she said.

"That DNA sample he was after," said Rivett. "I was able to help him out with that, lead him to the person he need. You were both on the right track, you see, you just didn't have the missing element. See this?"

Rivett took something else out of the desk and handed it across to her. An old, fading photograph of a woman wearing a psychedelic kaftan, her blonde hair tumbling out of a matching headscarf, holding in her arms the tiny bundle of a newborn child.

"Eric's family," said Rivett. "His daughter Amanda and her little girl Samantha. That baby is the reason why all of this happened, the reason Smollet's about to come here now to try and stop you from breaking in and finding out the rest of it. Only, I don't reckon he's going to get here on time. Ward's probably had that DNA verified right now, while you were busy ransacking this office. No, that in't looking good for poor old Dale right now. Just like you, he din't know what he was really getting into."

Rivett reached inside his jacket pocket and withdrew a pair of white magician's gloves.

"Still," he said, putting them on, "tomorrow's headlines should be a scoop. Shame you won't be around to write them."

Francesca watched, as if in slow motion, as his gloved right hand went back inside his pocket and drew out a small, flat handgun.

"Sorry," he said, aiming it towards her, "but I reckon we've just about run out of time."

The phone on the desk began to ring.

"This'll be the DCI for you," Rivett said. "And then that'll all be over."

38

Premature Burial

June 1984

Monday 18 June dawned warm, the sun rising through a clear blue sky by the time Gray arrived at the station at 6 a.m. He felt sweat under his arms as he closed the car door and locked it, and made his way indoors to the canteen.

He loaded his tray with eggs, bacon and a strong cup of tea, needing more fuel to get going on these early mornings. Gray had always preferred nights, but staff levels were strained just now by the fact that half of them were up north, policing the miners' strike. A fresh busload had shipped out yesterday, relishing all that overtime pay.

Gray grimaced as he sipped his tea. Unlike most everyone else they knew, he and Sandra never voted for Margaret Thatcher.

"Penny for 'em," came a voice behind him.

"Len?" Gray looked round.

The DCI winked. "Thought I'd find you here," he said. "Come to my office when you've finished? Something I could use your expertise on."

Gray raised his eyebrows. "All right," he said.

"Good boy," Rivett squeezed his shoulder and moved off.

Gray sat for a few moments more, feeling the imprint of the DCI's fingers. He took another sip of his tea and looked down at his half-eaten breakfast. Though he tried not to think of it, a blip of memory flashed through his mind and suddenly the eggs and bacon looked a whole lot less appetising. He picked up his tray, disposed of the half-eaten meal, and jogged downstairs to Rivett's office.

The DCI did not get up from his desk, just motioned for Gray to sit.

"You know all about them weirdos, don't you, Paul?" he said, offering a school photograph in a brown cardboard frame across the table.

Gray took in the smiling, freckled face of a teenage boy, blue eyes peering through a corrugated black fringe. He was wearing a black V-neck sweater, white shirt and skinny black tie, a badge on his chest that read *Echo and the Bunnymen*.

"Darren Moorcock," said Rivett, "lives at 89 Northgate Street, pupil at Ernemouth High. Didn't come home on Saturday night, but his parents didn't realise 'til the morning. He normally let himself in after they've gone to bed, they trust him that way." Rivett raised his eyebrows. "Only, when he din't come back last night either, they started to get worried that he weren't just being some randy stop-out. They went round all the places he normally hang out and couldn't find him, rang round all his friends, and no one's seen him since he called on his girlfriend Saturday afternoon. Deborah Carver, her name is, she live up South Town, only she's been in bed sick all weekend, so he couldn't have been having it away there."

Rivett saw a flicker cross Gray's features as he said this, then the detective looked down, swallowing, studying the photo.

"Course, we'll be waiting to see if he turns up for school,"

Rivett went on. "But in the meantime, I wondered if you had any bright ideas."

There was something familiar about the boy, Gray thought, although not from any of his usual late-night reconnoitres. His mind travelled back to the party he'd broken up on May Day, the pillbox on the North Denes with the old sofa inside it. Darren Moorcock looked like he belonged to that gang, even if he couldn't directly place his face. Corrine Woodrow had definitely been amongst them and this struck Gray as strange – Rivett had taken a sudden interest in her only a couple of weeks ago. Those seizures she suffered from and the rumours he'd heard about black magic; the Aleister Crowley book he seemed to know all about – from the Duty Sergeant Roy Mobbs, Gray could only deduce.

He looked back up at his boss. Rivett sat in his seat, a smile playing on his lips, an intensity in his eyes that caused the knot in Gray's stomach to grow tighter.

"There is somewhere," he said, "I reckon they use as their hide-out." He stood up, the urge to get away from Rivett stronger than his conviction that this was where the boy would be. "I'll go take a look, shall I?"

* * *

Rivett waited five minutes, then picked up the phone, dialled the familiar number.

"Get home all right?" he asked the voice on the other end of the line.

"Len," Eric sounded sore, hung over. Rivett knew he hated being roused early, given the amount of whisky he would no doubt have sunk the night before. But Eric deserved every-thing that was now coming his way – for what Rivett was about to do, there was going to have to be one long, carefully executed game of payback.

"You know what time it is?" said Eric, and Rivett could just picture his crumpled face against Edna's freshly laundered pillows.

"Time you told me what you got sorted out yesterday," said Rivett. "I already got my men moving, we in't got a lot of room for manoeuvre, you want this to go off straight."

Eric groaned and there was a shuffling of sheets. "Sammy's back in London," he said, no doubt mindful of Edna rousing next to him. "We got her in a clinic where they'll take care of her proper. One benefit of Malcolm being a degenerate alcoholic, I s'pose. He know all about them sort of places."

Rivett picked up a pencil, twirling it between his index and middle fingers. "Good," he said, "now you've got that all sorted out, I reckon you ought to be on your way up Edith Cavell's," he referred to the hospital where Amanda was recuperating from her miscarriage. "Make sure you're seen to be looking after *all* your family at a time like this. That's been hard for Sammy to deal with, of course," the pencil snapped in Rivett's hand, "but I expect that's a whole lot worse for Mandy, now, in't it?"

* * *

Gray parked up at the Iron Duke, slung his jacket over his shoulders as he set off down the steps and across the North Denes. The horizon shimmered in front of him. He noticed trails of footprints in the soft sand of the dunes sloping down towards the pillbox, heard a faint humming in the distance, sounded like one of them 50cc scooters, vaguely aware that, as he neared the old fortification, the sound was getting louder.

Gray blinked as he entered the pillbox, his pupils rapidly dilating to adjust from the bright sunshine to the gloom within. The sound was really loud now, but that was not the first thing that hit him. It was the smell, the unmistakable iron-and-bowels stench of death – death which seemed at that moment to hover in front of him, taking a tangible form, a black cloud, rippling and undulating in front of his eyes. For one second, Gray thought that he had walked into another dimension, that he was part of some surreal animation.

He took a step nearer and the cloud rose and rushed straight at him. All of a sudden he knew what they were – flies, airborne legions of them, tiny insect bullets hitting his face, his mouth, his nose, his eyes. He staggered backwards, choking, trying not to lose his balance, still thinking at the back of his mind that he mustn't mess up a crime scene – before instinct overcame training and the contents of his stomach roiled and rose straight up his throat. Gray staggered back out and hurled his guts out, kicking sand back over the mess he had made and then staggering dizzily, scratching his hands against the rough concrete exterior of the pillbox as he righted himself.

He took a handkerchief out of his jacket pocket, wiped his mouth and then his sweating forehead. Took long deep breaths, telling himself it was all right. "Easy now," he told himself, going back in. "Easy."

That was when he saw her. Pressed up against the wall with blood on her face, her mouth open and her eyes all glazed. Like she'd been freeze-framed in the middle of a scream.

Gray put his own hands up to the sides of his head, his mind racing. Had there been some sort of massacre? Lying on the floor in front of him, where the flies had been, were the remains of one of them. Whether it was Darren Moorcock or not, he couldn't tell – just that it once had a load of dark hair and white skin but now most of it was red.

He stepped around the body, fighting down the pounding noise in his ears that he knew was his own heart, knelt down in front of Corrine. She looked straight through him. Though her face was smeared with blood, he couldn't see any sign of actual injuries. Trying to remember what the social worker had done that time before, he put a hand down on her shoulder, shook her gently, spoke calmly and clearly. "Corrine, wake up. It's all right, Corrine, they've gone."

He saw her eyelids flicker and then she exhaled a great breath, falling forwards like a rag doll into his arms.

* * *

When Rivett arrived at the Iron Duke with a van load of constables and the head of forensics, Alf Brown, at his side, he was annoyed to see an ambulance was already parked up there. "Get the whole area sealed off," he barked at his men as they descended the steps from the sea wall. "Tourists'll be out in a few hours and I don't want them getting a whiff of it."

As the constables fanned out around him, Rivett honed in on Gray, who was helping a paramedic lift Corrine Woodrow onto a stretcher.

"Hold you hard," he said, his eyes skimming over her bloodied face, turning towards Gray. "Din't you say you got a body in there, officer?"

Gray's eyes flashed with a ferocity Rivett had seldom witnessed before. "Yes, sir," the detective sergeant said, "but I'm more concerned with the living right now."

Rivett's eyes darted across at the paramedic, then back at Gray. "You both stay where you are," he told them. "No one's going anywhere until I seen this myself."

He came back out of the pillbox, a handkerchief over his mouth. He coughed, spat on the ground and then looked at Gray. "In't you read her her rights yet?" he said.

"Sir?" Gray looked from Rivett to Corrine and back again. "This girl's just been seriously traumatised, I want to get her to hospital, not read her her rights. Can't you see . . ."

Rivett's face darkened. "Din't *you* see what she done in there, Detective Sergeant? She's a bloody murderer! Alf," he called over to his forensics man, "get in there now, get it all down. And take a bloody deep breath before you do it. You," he turned to the paramedic, "give her any treatment she requires here and now. She in't going to the hospital, she's coming straight down the station with me."

Gray opened his mouth to protest, but Rivett raised his hand, a look of sheer malevolence in his eyes. For the second time that morning, Gray saw a bundle falling over the harbour wall and the words he was going to say got stuck in his throat.

✳ ✳ ✳

"What's this, Corrine?"

The man sitting opposite her tapped a big, blunt forefinger down on the black leather-bound book that lay on the table between them.

Corrine squirmed uncomfortably on the metal chair, her wrists aching from the handcuffs that kept her arms behind her back. The room swam in front of her.

"Don't know," she managed to mumble.

"Yes, you do, Corrine," said the man. There was something familiar about his voice, something familiar about the big, bear-like shape of him. But Corrine couldn't think where from. Her memory seemed to have short-fused. All she could recall was Darren, walking down a sand dune in front of her, saying something she couldn't hear, as if she was watching a film with the sound turned down.

"Your mum told me," the man went on, "that this is your special magic book."

Corrine frowned, the shadow of a memory tapping at the corner of her mind.

"In fact, your mum showed me the altar, where she say you cast your spells from."

The man's voice was soothing and Corrine closed her eyes, drifting away back to the reel of Darren that was playing through her mind. Where she was, how long she had been there and why things had turned out this way were not thoughts she had got to yet.

Abruptly, a jagged flash of red, black and white scored through her mind. *The yew tree in the graveyard. Noj standing beneath her, his arms outstretched.* She jolted back to wakefulness.

"Ring some bells, do it, Corrine? Bells and spells? Is that what you done it for?" the voice persisted.

Corrine remembered something. "I only wanted her to go away," she said. Her voice was a fragile whisper.

"What was that?" the man leaned forwards, his face coming closer to hers, closer into focus. There was something familiar about his eyes . . .

"I din't mean for no one to get hurt," said Corrine. "The spell rebounded, see . . ."

As she said it, it all came back to her. Darren walking down the sand dune, into the pillbox. The unholy scream that rent the air as she came running after him, too late. Falling over his dead body, falling into all that blood and seeing Sam standing there with that concrete in her hand ...

"I'm sorry!" Corrine screamed and pitched forwards, sobs wracking through her body, the chair scraping across the floor. "I'm sorry!"

Rivett turned off the tape recorder.

"That'll do," he said.

* * *

Back in his office, Alf Brown was waiting with the photographs. Rivett studied the mess that had been made of Darren Moorcock in more detail than he had allowed himself at the crime scene. His eyes travelled across a pentagram rendered in blood.

"Time to call the press," he decided aloud. "Where's the arresting officer?"

* * *

Gray was down in the overcrowded interview rooms, talking to one of the drinkers picked up in the lunchtime raid Rivett had ordered on Swing's. Harvey Bunton was speaking in a slow, deliberate drawl, maintaining he couldn't rightly say for sure he knew anyone or anything Gray was talking about. Gray was struggling to pay attention to his charade, trying to blink back the shimmering black cloud of flies that kept appearing at the corner of his mind.

"Paul," Roy Mobbs' voice behind him. "The boss want you upstairs now."

* * *

Standing by Rivett on the steps of the station, Gray turned his head away from the cameras, from the questions led by

Rivett's pet journalist, Sid Hayles from the *Mercury*. Coming up from the interview rooms, he had forgotten how bright the day was.

"I can confirm that I have been talking to a suspect," Rivett was saying. "You can let your readers know they'll sleep soundly in their beds tonight, the miscreant has been taken in hand and has just made a full confession. We just need to speak to a few more of her associates before we release the full details."

Gray swallowed, trying to take it all in.

"Did you say *her* associates?" Hayles' eyes goggled.

Rivett smiled grimly. "Need an ear test, Sid? That'll be all for now, gentlemen . . ."

Across the road from the huddle of reporters, Gray saw Sheila Alcott stepping out of a beaten-up Citroën 2CV, pushing her hair off her pinched, white face. For a second, their eyes met, then Rivett's hand was on Gray's shoulder, propelling him back inside.

"You heard that all right, then, Paul?" Rivett leant in close, so no one else could hear him. "I got her full confession on tape. Now I want you to get back down there and find out who else out of these jokers fancies themselves as a fucking wizard."

The black cloud moved in Gray's peripheral vision. "What are you trying to do?" he said, rubbing his brow, trying to brush the apparition away.

"Bikers and bloody weirdos," said Rivett, "I don't want them in my town."

* * *

Maureen Carver paused on the landing, trying to fight back the tears that were swimming in her eyes. She could not believe what she had just heard on the evening news, could not countenance the fact that the smiling, softly spoken young man she had last seen only two days ago would never walk through their front door again. Doubling the shock of the news of Darren's murder was the fact that the newscaster had announced that a suspect was being held in custody, believed to be a schoolmate.

Believed to be a girl.

Maureen's mind rewound past events. Debbie bringing Corrine home and how much that had troubled her, the persistent fear that no good could come of this over-dependent friendship for her daughter. The strange afternoon when Corrine had come round after disappearing for a week, the conversation they had that worried Debbie so much. The falling-out with Alex next door and Debbie's angry ranting about this new girl at school, this Samantha Lamb and what she had done to them all.

Maureen choked back a sob, buried her head in her hands for a second, trying to gather up every last ounce of strength she possessed.

She pushed open Debbie's door gently. Her daughter finally stopped being sick yesterday, but was so exhausted by lack of sleep that Maureen had let her stop home from school today. She had already worked so hard, anyway, to finish her O-Levels and get into art school . . .

Debbie lay in her bed, hair fanned out around the pillow, one hand raised up to her mouth, a finger on her lips as if she had fallen asleep with a question on her mind. Spread across the sheets were the opened pages of the music papers Darren had brought with him on Saturday. Maureen shut her eyes, prayed to God for the courage to wake her daughter from this blissful idyll into a world that would never, ever be the same again.

"Mum?" Debbie's eyes blinked open and a smile spread across her face for a moment, before the look in Maureen's eyes gave her pause to wonder. "Mum, what's wrong?"

* * *

Maureen didn't know how many hours had passed, only that it was dark now and Debbie had cried herself out, lying in her mother's arms, passed into the merciful haven of sleep.

Across the road, Maureen heard the sound of running feet. Then a metallic clink, followed by the smash of breaking glass, and the feet running off again, up the road. There was a sudden whooshing noise and the room became illuminated; then a piercing scream from the house across the road.

* * *

The flames had destroyed the downstairs and were licking up the front of the house by the time that Gray got there. Hundreds of people were out of their houses and standing around the spectacle, men with walking sticks and women with babies in their arms, their faces in the flickering light lit up with expressions of strange and cruel delight.

"Burn her!" he heard someone yell.

Smoke belched from the top of the building, where firemen now stood on ladders, aimed arcs of water into the conflagration, sparks and ash falling through the air, the sky lit up with reds, oranges and purples. For a second, Gray's sore eyes rested on the plume rising into the sky, merging in his mind with the swarm he had witnessed earlier.

"Whore!" a woman screamed beside him, making Gray

jump, bringing his eyes back to a black figure silhouetted against the flames. Rivett walked up the garden path towards him, Gina lying across his arms, coughing into her fist.

Rivett staring into the crowd, shouting, "Get back from here! Go on, all of you!" The hiss of the water hitting the flames. Pieces of debris sailing through the air around him. Rivett's face red and his eyes as dark and unfathomable as the North Sea.

Gray stared at his boss and found he could no longer think any more.

* * *

They watched the dawn from the car park of the Iron Duke, Rivett and Gray in Gray's car, Rivett at the wheel. Sipping whisky from the DCI's hipflask at the end of twenty-four hours neither would ever wish to live through again.

"Said you were a Barnardo's boy, din't you, Paul?" said Rivett.

Gray stared at the rim of the orange orb, glimmering over the blue horizon.

"That's why it get to you," Rivett passed him the silver flask.

Gray took it and swallowed, the liquid burning the back of his throat.

Rivett watched him, continued: "You know, I admire you for that. You come from nothing but you pulled yourself up by the bootstraps. Had the guts and determination to make a man of yourself, become a proper detective. Don't think I don't appreciate it."

Gray turned his head towards his boss. His pupils were red-rimmed, but they had lost the wild incoherence Rivett had seen come over his DS as they stood outside Gina's burning house. Gina had nothing but smoke inhalation and the unwelcome news of what her daughter had been up to to deal with. Which was enough, for now.

"You're a good bloke, Paul," said Rivett, "and a good policeman. The two things in't always mutually exclusive, are they? That's why I want you take a few weeks' leave – on full pay, of course. Take the wife on holiday, somewhere nice and quiet. Relax, get away from here and don't think about work for a while. 'Cos I don't want to have to lose you, Paul." He rested his hand for a moment on Gray's shoulder. "I really wouldn't want that."

Gray's lip trembled and he closed his eyes, to stop the tears from coming.

Rivett put his key in the ignition. "Come on," he said, "let's get you home."

39

Resurrection Joe

March 2003

Smollet looked at her, the woman he had been married to for all these years. She stared back at him with eyes that appeared green in the glow of the bedside lamp, but in direct sunlight, turned the same colour blue as the sea.

"Please, love," he said. "We've got to go."

He glanced at the clock at the bedside. If it hadn't been for Jason Blackburn's panicked call, he would have been meeting Len Rivett at the Leisure Beach by now. In the time he'd had since he fled his work, he could have been half an hour on the road. There was a noise in his head like the whirring of a trap being sprung.

His wife dropped her gaze to the counterpane, began to pick at imaginary threads. As she moved, her carefully styled fringe fell forwards, and for a brief instant, the old white ridge of a scar could be discerned across her temples.

"I told you, I don't want to," she said, in a voice little louder than a whisper.

Smollet knelt down beside her, took hold of the hand that was worrying itself.

"It's only for a couple of days," he said. "I've booked your favourite hotel. I've packed your bags for you. The car's ready downstairs. All you need to do is put some clothes on. Please, darling. Do it for me?"

Her nails dug into his fingers and she looked back at him, a strange expression there. "I don't understand," she said. "Why do you want to get rid of me, Dale?"

She bit her bottom lip with a perfectly white and straight set of front teeth.

"I don't, darling," he said. "I'm just making sure you're safe, like I always have."

He reached her hand to his mouth and kissed her knuckles, closing his eyes, wondering if he should use sedatives to keep the promise he had made to her grandfather when he asked for her hand in marriage, the promise he intended to keep for the rest of his days. Even though the old man hadn't wanted it, had had to be persuaded, and not by him either. By the only one he ever took advice from.

"Uncle Len was here today," she said. "Has that got something to do with it?"

Smollet opened his eyes. "What?" he said. "When was that?"

"This morning," she said. "He came in for a cup of tea." She bit down on her bottom lip harder. "Uncle Len never liked me," she said. "It's him, isn't it? He wants you to get rid of me." Her eyes welled with tears.

* * *

"What's in there?" said Sandra.

"The interviews I done with the headmaster of Ernemouth High and Corrine Woodrow's form teacher," Gray opened the book at a well-thumbed page. "Another one who got hounded out over this. The thing is, they in't all about her. The biggest troublemaker in that year, in both of their opinions, weren't Corrine or any of them weirdos. It was another girl, one what the headmaster had only just that minute had to expel."

"Who was she?" Sandra's voice was a whisper.

"That's just it," said Gray. "She was Eric Hoyle's granddaughter."

Sandra's hand came up to her throat. "Edna," she said.

Gray nodded, flicked forwards a couple of pages.

"Another interview here, with Lizzy Hurrell, who run Oliver John's hairdressers and took Corrine on as an apprentice. She told me Corrine and Samantha Lamb had a fight outside her salon on the Saturday morning."

Sandra shook her head, her eyes hardening. "She knew, Paul. Edna knew."

"Something else Ward told me," said Gray. "Len had Alf Brown helping him go through all the old files yesterday. Alf Brown retired five years ago – but he's the one who done all the forensics on the Woodrow case. And there was one thing that always bothered me about what they said about the crime scene. Up until today, I put it down to the shock of what I saw, that I din't take it in or remember it properly. But I never saw no pentagram in blood around Darren Moorcock's body." He snapped the logbook shut.

"Ring him," Sandra's voice was urgent. "Ring Ward before Rivett get him too."

* * *

Smollet went into the en suite in the spare bedroom, stared at his face. His skin looked grey and he could see lines by the corners of his eyes that hadn't been there a couple of days before. His teenage infatuation might have burned itself out over the many years of his marriage, but until the dawn of Monday morning, he had still cherished the idea that he had done the honourable thing. That matrimony hadn't just been an enterprise engineered to benefit his uncle – to benefit himself.

Smollet had been told that Samantha's teenage breakdown had been precipitated by a row with her mother that had led to Amanda's miscarriage, the culmination of months of bad blood between the pair. That was why she had had to go back to London to have treatment in a private clinic and then been returned to the custody of her father, Malcolm. When Smollet's training took him to Hendon, Rivett had helped instigate the resumption of the tentative courtship that had only just begun before she was forced to go away. After two years' engagement, Smollet married Samantha in Chelsea Town Hall, brought her back to Ernemouth with him when he passed out as a newly qualified PC. Told everyone she was a girl he had met in London. They said it would be better that way.

Smollet's love had still burned brightly then, even though there were few traces left of the girl he had known at school. He understood that the sterilization, the dentistry and the other surgery had been necessary, for her own good, and it had certainly rendered Smollet's beloved the perfect policeman's wife. Her childlike frailty made him love her even more, so that the promise he had made to Eric had not been entirely down to Rivett's ulterior motives, the rewards he was promised he would reap from their union – and had, in due course, received.

Samantha never alluded to the time when they had first

met, and Smollet didn't expect her to – from his understanding of the medical facts, she'd had to blank a lot out of her mind in order to recover. She sometimes recalled her earlier childhood, often forgetting that her nana was no longer with them, although she never mentioned Eric. Only Rivett seemed to make her uncomfortable, as if there was still something lurking in the corner of her mind that she half-remembered about him.

She had never reconciled with her mother. Amanda now lived somewhere in Hertfordshire, still married to her toy boy Wayne and, from what Smollet had gathered, taking on a constant stream of foster children as some form of penance. Eric had died in 1989, succumbing to a second heart attack not long after the wedding. He left half of everything he owned to Smollet, so long as he continued to act as Samantha's custodian.

Smollet had risen rapidly to take command of Rivett's old station. The long hours, his dedication to the gym and his carefully cultivated standing in the community had been compensation enough for the holes at the heart of his home life, holes that gradually widened over the years. As his wife drifted further away from him and into the shell of herself, Smollet's good looks continued to attract the kind of similarly frustrated, middle-aged women who appreciated string-free assignations and were compelled by the bonds of their own marriages to remain discreet.

He had accepted that his lot was not a bad one, until Sean Ward rolled into town.

Smollet opened the cupboard door, banishing his ruffled image. He'd already packed her normal medication, but the doctor had given him an emergency supply of something stronger, in case she ever became violent. He'd seen some flares of temper over the years, but nothing that had ever made him think it would be necessary to use it.

But, as he picked up the packet of Rohypnol, he felt unknown territory opening up before him. Sean Ward had deduced correctly that from the moment he had first contacted Rivett, things had reverted to exactly as they were before he retired: Rivett giving the orders, telling Smollet to be as gracious as possible to the PI while letting Uncle Len take care of the real business his way. Suggesting that he might like to take Samantha out of town for a while, that if she caught wind of anything about Ward's enquiry, it might rekindle unwanted memories of a very unpleasant time for all concerned.

As usual, Smollet had deferred to Rivett's wisdom, making arrangements to take Samantha to a trusted retreat after work this evening where he could leave her in safety to be properly looked after, while biting back the nagging doubts that popped into his mind with every fresh turn of events. All the strangeness up at the old pillbox had brought back a lot of memories Smollet thought he had buried years ago. Of the days when he was at school with Darren Moorcock and Corrine Woodrow, of that brief time when Samantha had been one of them weirdos herself.

But, until Blackburn's call, Smollet had assured himself that there could be no repercussions from the twenty-year-old case, that, as usual, his uncle had everything in hand. Perhaps, he admitted to himself, as his eyes ran down the label on the bottle, he hadn't wanted to think anything else was possible.

He had rung Rivett to ask him if he knew anything about what DS Kidd had been doing up at Alcott's farm. Rivett had denied any knowledge of it and, for the first time, Smollet realised he was lying. He knew how far back Kidd went with

Rivett, knew the part he had played in the original Woodrow investigation. These last two nights, Smollet had sat up late, reading the old case files himself, along with the reams of Ward's notes, trying to see between the lines of history, to divine if there was anything that had been hidden from view back then that Rivett had not revealed to him since.

But before he was able to articulate any of this, Rivett had told him that they needed to meet before he left, up in what they both still referred to as Eric's office.

"Why?" Smollet had been dumbfounded. "I thought we sorted all the business stuff up there last night? You know, so's I could get off early? Which was your idea anyway . . ."

"Dale," Rivett's voice took on the jocular tone he liked to use just before interrogating a suspect, "you know I'm taking special care of your interests, like I always have. But something's been brought to my attention that could be a problem for you if we don't sort it out now. There's been a journalist sniffing around. She might have stumbled on something that could harm you. I can't go into it on the phone, I shouldn't have to explain why. But you want everything to keep being all right for you and Samantha, don't you?"

"For me and Samantha?" Smollet still didn't quite compute what he was hearing.

"That's right," said Rivett, "your lovely wife. That's her I'm thinking about and you should too. I'll see you in half an hour, Dale. Give me a ring when you're on your way."

Then the phone had clicked off. Smollet left the station in a daze, ordering Blackburn to deal with the mess his best friend had made for the DCC of Norwich, while he drove home way above the speed limit, unable to dampen the fuse of fear that last comment from Rivett had lit in his head.

In all his thirty-six years, Smollet might never have managed to decode how his uncle's mind worked, but he could read enough of the signs to know when the old man was setting something – or someone – up. He came home to find Samantha in the deepest torpor he had seen in months. And now she was telling him Rivett had already paid a visit here this morning . . .

When Smollet came back into the bedroom, his wife was still sitting in her silk nightie and dressing gown. But she was holding something he had never seen before. A big, old, black, leather-bound book.

"Look," she said, "what Uncle Len gave me. He said he was returning it, like I'd lent it to him or something. But Dale," her eyes were fearful. "I don't like it. It reminds me of something . . . Something bad . . ."

* * *

Gray put the phone down. "I'm meeting him now," he told Sandra. "At DCI Smollet's house."

"Do you think—?" Sandra began, but her husband cut her off with a kiss, pressing the logbook into her hand.

"Take good care of it, love," he said. "I've got to go."

* * *

Rivett picked up the receiver. The voice on the other end was not one he had been expecting and for a second he struggled to comprehend what he was hearing. Something about Kidd knowing he'd be at this number. Something about the selfsame Kidd getting arrested for B&E at Alcott's farm, the old biddy holding him up with a twelve-bore while her husband rang Norwich police. It was Blackburn doing the blabbering and, as this registered, Rivett thought he must be playing some kind of spectacularly unfunny practical joke, of a type he excelled at.

"And if that weren't bad enough," Blackburn went on, "DC Snell went down Pearson's place, to take care of him like you told me, and he's now in casualty with half his arse ripped off. You never said the old boy had dogs."

"Dogs?" repeated Rivett, and as he said the word, he thought he could hear the sound of barking. He got to his feet, putting the gun back down on the desk. "You're fucking me about, in't you?" he said, loosening his collar, looking straight through Francesca, his face flushing a vivid red. "Tell me you're fucking me about."

"I wish I was, sir," Blackburn's voice was a pathetic whine. "But that DCC from Norwich left here ten minutes ago and I reckon he's headed your way."

"What?" Rivett's face turned from crimson to chalk white. "And where's Smollet been through all this?"

"I don't know," Blackburn said. "He run out of here 'bout half an hour ago, screaming his head off that I shouldn't talk to you about it, then left me to deal with all this shit . . ."

Rivett dropped the phone. The sounds in his ears were getting steadily louder, a pack of hounds he could hear now, yammering and howling, baying for blood. Pain shot up from his legs and into his chest, down from his arms and towards his heart, so strong he felt it throwing him upwards, throwing him backwards, Eric's old chair tipping over beneath him. Then he was falling, falling, towards the dark water, images racing through his mind.

Eric's granddaughter, her hair fanned out around her on the pillow, telling him she had seen a murder, the boy who had been reported missing that morning. The words dropping out of her with an actress's precision, a story so complete no innocent could have possibly made it up. Eric holding her hand and telling her that she was a good girl, she looking up at him expectantly. Him looking down at the girl's hand in Eric's, at her broken nails, her skinned knuckles.

Edna in the kitchen, kneading dough.

Paul Gray nodding as he looked at the picture of the boy. Paul Gray going to work. Alf Brown going to work afterwards, moving slowly through the foul air of the pillbox, stoic and unmoved, a good soldier who never questioned orders.

Corrine Woodrow crying in the cells. Corrine Woodrow with no cuts and grazes on her knuckles, her black-painted nails unbroken. Darren Moorcock's dried blood smeared all over her face.

Fires in the night in the South Town terraces, cries of vengeance on the lips of the people, smoke billowing into the night air. Riots at the gates of Ernemouth High, a tall, thin man being ushered away under a blanket into the back of a police van, while a mob of mothers screamed for his blood.

The weight of Edna's coffin on his shoulder, the sombre dirge of the church organ as they processed up the aisle.

Eric, lying on a hospital bed, wired up to all them machines. Leaning in close to give him the last rites, whispering the words of benediction: "A marriage between our families, Eric, that's what we said. Now that's all set in stone ..." – fanning his best friend's brow with the solicitor's documents, with Eric's Last Will and Testament – "your part is done." Fingers closing around the oxygen tube, pinching it shut, seeing the realisation bloom in Eric's eyes just before they clouded over.

And Gina, Gina running towards the river in Norwich, down a narrow alleyway, GET INTO ARCHEOLOGY – GIVE

SNOWY ONE daubed across the wall in white paint. Gina stumbling and falling, her red lips framing curses, her black eyes flashing up at him, stone cold with hate to the last.

Fading into Corrine, waiting by his car, dancing with herself.

Rivett felt an iron fist clench around his heart, felt the hounds' hot breath on his cheek as his head hit the floor.

❊ ❊ ❊

"Here," Smollet offered the glass across to his wife. "Drink this. It'll make you feel better."

But she shook her head.

"Don't want to," she said, sounding like a child. Or a petulant teenager.

"Please, darling," Smollet pleaded, looking sideways at the clock again, thinking how much longer they had got, feeling as if everything was slipping away from him, wondering why he had never comprehended before what Rivett and Eric Hoyle were really capable of.

He put the glass down on the bedside table, reached to take the book out of her hands.

"What is it?" he asked.

"It belongs to a master magician," she whispered, and her eyes rolled away.

Smollet could take no more. If he couldn't get the drugs down her throat, he would have to use another method. With a deft flick of his palm, she slumped forwards across the bed, the book falling from her arms and sliding onto the floor.

❊ ❊ ❊

The rain started suddenly as they passed the Britannic Pier, sheeting down hard on the windscreen. Noj looked up in time to see a fork of lightning cracking across the horizon, a jagged line in the sky momentarily illuminating the turbines that towered above the North Denes. She felt a quickening in her blood, a sense of time coming full circle.

"Here," she said, pointing across the windscreen towards a '6os-built faux Scandinavian villa looking out to sea.

Lights were blazing at every window and Sean could see the same car Smollet had left the station in still standing in the driveway. As he pulled in, the front door opened and Smollet stepped out, carrying a woman in his arms.

Smollet's head snapped around as Sean braked, blocking off the exit to the drive. The DCI's face registered surprise as Sean opened the car door and got out, an expression momentarily lit against the slanting rain by a second set of headlights, Gray's car pulling up behind Sean's. The woman in his arms didn't move.

"DCI Smollet," Sean moved swiftly across the driveway. "I need to finish my interview with you now."

"What's all this?" Smollet tried to bluff it out. Saw the retired DS Gray coming up behind Sean. "Get out of my way, can't you see my wife's ill?" he said. "I've got to get her to hospital."

Sean moved in closer to study the woman. Her eyes were closed, her face tranquil. She didn't look ill, just sleeping.

"That's her, in't it?" said Paul Gray from behind him. "That's who you've been protecting, all this time."

Smollet's jaw slackened. "What?" he said.

"Who is she?" asked Sean, no longer sure what was going on.

"She used to be called Samantha Lamb," said Gray. "Her granddad owned this house, the Leisure Beach and half of the rest of Ernemouth. Died a widower in '89, estranged from his daughter, left half his fortune to his best mate – Len Rivett."

Francesca's face flashed into Sean's mind. "Leisure Beach Industries Inc of Ernemouth, you mean?" he asked. "The other half owned by DCI Smollet, here?"

"Sound about right," said Gray. "And if I in't completely lost my marbles," he nodded towards the sleeping woman, "she'll be the one with your missing DNA."

"No," said Smollet, taking a step backwards. "No, get away from us."

"The missing DNA," said Sean. "Rivett already provided me with the match." He looked Smollet dead in the eye. "From a sample he took this morning."

The DCI looked down at his wife and then up again at Sean, an expression of horror on his face. "No," he said, "he can't have done. He couldn't have . . ."

"He did," said Sean. "I'm looking forward to hearing his explanation for it almost as much as hearing how come his own DNA is so similar to Corrine Woodrow's."

"My godfathers," he heard Gray say. "Gina."

Sean glanced around, wondering if any of the cars parked on the road belonged to Francesca. "Where is he, anyhow?" he said. "Where's Rivett?"

But Smollet had started to sway. Gray stepped forwards, catching hold of him. "Steady," he said. "I think you need a brandy."

He looked down at the slender woman lying compliant in Smollet's arms, a raindrop sliding off her eyelashes. Wondered how it was that she could look so peaceful.

"Let's go inside," he said, propelling the pair of them back through the front door.

Sean looked round. No one had answered his question

about Rivett, but he clearly wasn't here. He glanced back at his car. Noj wasn't there either, her door was wide open.

"I'll catch up with you in one second," he said to Gray, his hand closing over the swab kit full of Noj's DNA, still nestling safe in his pocket.

On the passenger seat of his car he found another little effigy, like the one he'd retrieved from the pillbox. A doll-Rivett lying with his feet in the air, a pin piercing his heart.

* * *

Noj was running, running in the rain, the book safely in her bag, racing through the back streets, choking back sobs.

The moment they had pulled into the driveway she had seen it in her mind's eye, lying on the white shagpile carpet of the bedroom floor. While everyone – including Gray, the copper come back from the past – had crowded around Smollet and his sleeping beauty, she had seized her chance to slip inside the open front door, moving rapidly up the stairs, locating her target as if the book itself were guiding her along. None of them had seen her come out again, none of them had seen her go. She was as sure of that as she had been of the vision in the crystal ball that had led her to Samantha Lamb. Even so, she could hardly believe she had finally got it back again, finally retrieved it from a source more powerful than her conceited teenage self would ever have given credit for. Although Corrine always had.

As she ran, Noj cried for Corrine, who, so anxious for knowledge, so hungry for power, she had abandoned on that crucial night to study with the master she would now finally return the book to. The master who had made her what she was today – but at what price? Had she only been there for

Corrine, then none of this would ever have happened . . .

But time had come full circle now and she could feel the transformation, the same as it had come to her in the graveyard on the night she had placed the curse on Samantha. The streetlights blurred into the tears that ran down her cheeks, this lesson was the hardest one to learn of all.

When she arrived at Mr Farrer's door, Noj put her hand up to her face. Felt a prickling of stubble, there beneath her skin.

* * *

Francesca knelt beside him, but Rivett didn't see her. He was on the edge of the harbour wall, looking up at the statue of Nelson. Only, it wasn't the Admiral there. It was Sean Ward staring down at him with his dark brown eyes, a grin upon his face.

"*Justass!*" he called out. "*See you on the other side!*"

Then Rivett fell backwards, let the water take him.

40

Ocean Rain

June 2004

Janice Mathers followed Dr Radcliffe down the long grey-green corridor, their footsteps echoing through the unadorned walls and the rows of windowless doors, under fluorescent light and air heavy with antiseptic.

After they passed through the security gate, splashes of colour started to appear along the walls, the artwork of inmates proudly displayed. The sound of voices could be discerned and shapes moved behind the frosted, reinforced glass of the classrooms. Dr Radcliffe didn't pause until they had reached the dormitory rooms that were allowed, within certain hours, to keep their doors open. All except for one, the last door on the left.

Here, the doctor came to a halt, and turned to face the barrister.

His eyes had lost the flinty hostility she had grown to associate with him on her previous visits here. Now they were soft, with a slight sparkle to them, an emotion mirrored in his voice as he started to speak. "I feel I owe you an apology, Miss Mathers," he said.

The QC shook her head. "You always did what you thought

was best for her," she said. "Which was more kindness than most people in her life have ever shown her. You kept her safe," she smiled sadly, "in here."

Dr Radcliffe nodded curtly, put the key into the lock of the door. "Her insistence," he felt duty-bound to add, "not mine." He turned the handle gently.

Corrine didn't raise her head. She was sitting on the bed, a watercolour spread out in front of her that had recently been taken down from the wall. It was a picture she had painted continuously since she'd first arrived in Dr Radcliffe's care, a replica of the one he had shown to Sean Ward fifteen months ago, that Mathers' defence team had in turn exhibited to the Court of Appeals. There, they had managed to convince a jury that Corrine hadn't, as her psychiatrist had always maintained, been duplicating this image in an attempt to access the innocent child she had left behind long ago on Ernemouth beach, but as a way of trying to assuage her guilt over Darren Moorcock – for leading him into the lair where his murderer waited.

Her former form teacher, Philip Pearson BSc, testified that it was the same depiction as one of the paintings he had caught the sixteen-year-old Samantha Lamb defacing on the school wall, the day before Moorcock was killed by those same hands that had covered the original with obscenities in black marker pen. Although, like Dr Radcliffe, he had no idea where Moorcock's idea had originated, also assuming it had been sketched from life along the local beaches.

Janice Mathers had been able to tell them all where it was from. The cover of Darren Moorcock's favourite – or maybe second favourite, he had never had the time to really decide – LP. Some of the jury had been moved to weep at the irony of its title: *Heaven up Here*.

This time, when all the evidence had been presented before the court, including the testimonies of Pearson, Sheila Alcott and Paul Gray, the real tragedies at the heart of this case had finally been allowed to emerge. Darren Moorcock as a person who had lived and breathed and dreamed of his future, rather than a sensational element in a lurid farce. Corrine Woodrow as a girl whose unfortunate circumstances, including her unsuspected blood ties to the man who had been allowed to take charge of the original investigation, had been spun into the deadliest propaganda, effectively robbing her of the rest of her life too.

The only point that the QC had not been able to fully prove was that the pentagram drawn around the corpse in the victim's blood had been added to help frame Corrine as a devil-worshipping murderess after the body was found. Former DS Gray reiterated on oath that he could not remember seeing it when he made the discovery. His former colleague Alf Brown was equally adamant that he had – and his original crime-scene photographs appeared as unequivocal evidence. But by then, Brown was the only member of the original murder squad who was left in a position to testify.

DS Andrew Kidd and DS Jason Blackburn had both been dismissed, pending their own trials for misconduct brought by the Independent Police Complaints Commission. Rivett was in the ground and Smollet, unable to come to terms with events, had resigned on medical grounds.

Mathers had some sympathy for Smollet, unaware that he had also been set up by Rivett, to shield his best friend's murderous progeny for the past two decades with the myopia of his love. But then, the QC had never thought that Smollet was really all that bright.

She had always known that it would take an outsider to see through the complex web woven by those two terrible old men in that small town so long ago, to see what had been hiding under everybody's noses all along. Sean Ward had brought it down strand by strand, revealing both the arrogance and ignorance of Leonard Rivett in the process.

From what they had managed to piece together, Rivett's last act had been an attempt to murder Francesca Ryman and frame his protégé for it. The gun he had aimed at her was Smollet's police issue, removed from the safe in his office without the DCI's knowledge. Documents linking Smollet's marriage to Samantha and the business assets he acquired through it had been left on the desk of the Leisure Beach office, along with a tell-tale photograph of Samantha and her mother. Rivett had intended to make the scene look as if Smollet had stumbled into a break-in that would have given the *Ernemouth Mercury* editor the evidence she needed to tie up the business interests between the Hoyle and Rivett families, while pointing Ward towards the identity of the person with the phantom DNA.

It hadn't take Mathers long to ascertain that the identity of the DNA match Rivett provided for Ward was a fake: the biker, Adrian Hall, had gone under a lorry ten years ago, another of Rivett's dark little jokes. Perhaps he had intended to reveal Samantha Smollet's identity after her husband had been safely arrested, claiming it as part of a strategy to draw him out – while getting rid of Ryman with the same stone. But Ryman and Ward had no idea how Rivett had been one step ahead of them when they started down this trail.

The premises of The Ship Hotel, where Ward has been staying, were searched for clues and the landlady's son was found to be a computer expert. Damon Boone had admitted that he let Rivett use his computers and had taught him some elementary programmes, but maintained that he had no idea to what end the man he considered to be an old family friend was using them for. After due consideration, and with a lack of any other evidence, he had been let off without any charges.

Rivett's belief that he was both indestructible and impenetrable had been his downfall. His doctor had warned him of a heart murmur, told him to give up the booze and the cigars and all the rich food. But even in death there was still something of a last laugh in it for him. He had evaded both capture and public scrutiny. Still, Ryman was writing up as much of the truth as anyone could discern, for the record at least.

Samantha Smollet would not have to stand trial either. Once a fresh test had matched her to the phantom DNA, she had been admitted to a high-security hospital – long before the appeal took place and the public had a new face to focus their outrage on. Not for her the hysteria of the mob. Where she was, not even the front pages of the tabloids could reach. She had swapped places with Corrine one last time.

"I'll leave you two alone," said Dr Radcliffe. "Knock on the door when you need me."

Mathers nodded her thanks, stepped inside the room and waited for him to close the door. Corrine turned her head slowly. As the QC walked towards her, her gaze fell to the paper stretched across the covers of the narrow single bed.

It was blue, so blue. The long stretch of the sea, the seagulls taking off from the shoreline, the four figures standing there, hunched against the wind. She had lost count of how many times she had stared into this picture, willing with all her might that the figure on the second from the right, the one he had modelled his hair on, would somehow turn around and that she would see Darren's smiling face again. But, unlike Corrine, she did not believe in magic. When, many years before, she had changed her own name, she had chosen the surname Mathers as a dark joke, a way of proving, once and for all, that there was nothing to the superstition and folklore that had brought down this disaster on them in the first place.

That book, the one that everyone had mentioned at the original trial, but that no one could actually produce, that book that had sent Corrine and Darren down to the pillbox and their damnation, had been written by Aleister Crowley and Samuel Liddell MacGregor Mathers. But Crowley was the only one anybody mentioned. Everyone always forgot about Mathers.

She put her hand down gently on Corrine's shoulder, looking through the painting now, another image replacing it. *At last*, she thought, *I can leave him there, in peace.*

Darren Moorcock, her one and only love, still young and beautiful on the shore of memory, his eyes an iridescent blue, captured in the last golden rays of the sun.

"Reenie," she said, "it's safe now. We can go."

Acknowledgements

For those interested in finding out more about Captain Swing, the book recommended by Mr Farrer, *Unquiet Country: Voices of the Rural Poor 1820–1880* by Robert Lee (Windgather Press) was a major inspiration for this book. Mr Farrer would also recommend *Captain Swing* by Eric J. Hobsbawm and George Rude (Pheonix).

My most profound thanks to Caroline Montgomery for every piece of advice and support during the making of this book and those previous, none of this would have been possible without you. Likewise to John Williams for all your wisdom, patience and insight, Pete Ayrton for being The Unsinkable Lord of Misrule and Doreen Montgomery for always being awesome.

This book owes a large one to Dr Theodore Koulouris, for invaluable help on all that is Greek to me, Ruth Bayer for consulting her crystal ball and The Lone Ranter for embodying the spirit of Captain Swing. Special thanks also to Mum and Dad, Lynn and Kriss Knights, and Paul Willetts for the Remembrance of Things Past.

Champagne for my dear friends, Pete Woodhead, Joe McNally, Ann Scanlon, Emma and Paul Murphy, Lynn Taylor, Richard Newson, Benedict Newbery, David Knight,

Martyn Waites, Cath Meekin, Danny Meekin, Frances Meekin, Danny Snee, Eva Snee, Meg Davis, Ross MacFarlane, Phoebe Harkins, Chris 'I can't walk' Simmons, Jay Clifton and Vanessa Lawrence, Billy Chainsaw, Damjana and Predrag Finci, Lydia Lunch, Max Décharne and Katja Klier, Mark Pilkington, Mike Jay and Louise Burton, Fen Oswin, Stephen Prince, Roger K. Burton, James Hollands and Dr Paddy, Ken and Rachel Hollings, Raphael Abraham, Jake Arnott, David Peace, Stewart Home, Marc Glendening, David Fogarty and All The Good Sohemians. Cheers to my fellow drinkers in a certain pub not unlike Captain Swing's: Hel, Luke and Adam Cox, Sal Pittman, Andi Sapey, Marc Fireman and Shaun Connon. Glasses charged for the assistance and support of Anna-Marie Fitzgerald, Rebecca Gray and Niamh Murray at Serpent's Tail, Guy Sangster Adams at *Plectrum: The Cultural Pick*, Andrew Stevens at *3AM*, Suzy and Ian Lowey-Prince at *Nude* (RIP), Katie Allen at *Fat Quarter*, Dave Collins at *Planet Mondo*, Jane Bradley at *For Books' Sake*, Danny Bowman at *Pulp Press*, Alan Kelly in Psychoville, and all at The Bishopsgate Institute and Housman's Bookshop. Salutations to François and Benjamin Guerif, Karine Lalechere, Jeanne Guyon, Hind Boutaljante, Estelle Durand, Claire Duvivier, Thomas Bauduret and Ced Fabre.

Special Reserve for my dearest Mr M, Michael Meekin – you will always be the guv'nor.

The music of Bauhaus, Crass, The Cravats, Echo & The Bunnymen, Joolz, Killing Joke, The Mob, New Model Army, Poison Girls, Public Image Ltd, Theatre of Hate, Shock Headed Peters, Siouxsie and the Banshees, Sisters of Mercy, Southern/Death/Cult and Spear of Destiny – who made the worst of times into the best of times.

And in loving memory of Carol Clerk, Charlie Gillett and Paul 'Hofner' Nesbitt – Heaven Born and Ever Bright . . .

Stanza from 'Some Man's Business' reproduced by kind permission of Benedict Newbery.

Lyrics from *Vengeance* by New Model Army reproduced by kind permission of Justin Sullivan.

© Fen Oswin

Cathi Unsworth began a career in journalism at nineteen and has since worked for many music, arts, film, and alternative lifestyle journals. She has been called "the Queen of Noir" in the United Kingdom and is the author of four novels, including *The Singer* and *Bad Penny Blues*, and the editor of the award-winning crime compendium *London Noir*. She lives in London, England.